THE OTHER REBECCA

THE OTHER REBECCA

Maureen Freely

BLOOMSBURY

First published in Great Britain 1996

This paperback edition published 1997

Copyright © 1996 by Maureen Freely

The moral right of the author
has been asserted

Bloomsbury Publishing Plc, 38 Soho Square,
London W1V 5DF

A CIP catalogue record for this book
is available from the British Library

ISBN 0 7475 3166 8

10 9 8 7 6 5 4 3 2

Typeset by Hewer Text Composition Services, Edinburgh
Printed in Great Britain by Clays Ltd, St Ives plc

Art lets you get away with murder

Pablo Picasso
as quoted, or perhaps misquoted, by another artist

I
Lost Souls

Chapter One

There was a gate where there hadn't been one before. I think that was what made me forget my resolution. I got out of the car and gave the gate a push, just to make sure it was locked, but to my surprise it yielded, and so, without pausing to think, I swung it open, got back into the car and drove into the village I had once assumed would be my home for ever.

I parked between the two cottages. How many years had it been? Six going on seven. Someone had mowed the communal lawn, but our old flowerbeds were strangled with nettles. The rose bushes had intertwined with the ivy to cover the walls, choke the windows and wrap around the mesh that covered the thatch. The tennis court was no longer – the concrete had buckled, the fencing had disappeared, the poles teetered at precarious angles over what appeared to be the remains of a bonfire.

It was only with difficulty that I was able to fight my way through the long grass to the walled garden. Here the gate was padlocked, but to no avail, because it had rusted off its hinges. Inside I found more nettles, and the raspberry bushes threatening to smother the grape arbour, but rising above the weeds and the thorns were my magnolia trees in full blossom. I couldn't resist the idea of taking a branch or two home with me. There would be no need to tell anyone where they came from. While I was choosing my trophies, I noticed a ladder propped up against the northern wall, and, again, I'm not quite sure what prompted me to take it as an invitation. There was a baby bird learning how to fly in the upper branches. Its desperate chirps disappeared, then merged with a chorus of other baby birds. My first thought must have been to find the nest, but when I had, it seemed like the most natural thing in the world to climb to the top of the ladder and look over.

3

I knew what to expect, but it was still a shock. There before me was the field of daffodils, the orchard, still pink with blossoms, and the bluebell wood leading up to the charred remains of the manor garden's outer wall. But beyond it, nothing – or rather, just another slope of trees, tall grass and daffodils spilling past their prime over the crest of the hill into the marsh in the distant horizon.

It was like looking at a picture with the centre ripped out. Where was the proof that the house had ever existed? I felt afraid, as if there were someone else in the walled garden, watching me, and so I hurried back down the ladder, took my branches and retreated, went home and put the whole thing behind me. That was four days ago – Wednesday, to be precise. Then last night, in a dream, I returned to Beckfield again.

This time the manor was back where it belonged, rising tall and grey over its implausible emerald lawn. It was early evening as I walked down the drive. There, at the top of the steps, were the bronze lions, unsinged and intact. I paused in front of them to watch the last glints of sunlight fade from their eyes.

I surveyed the windows. They were dark except for the one looking into the little sitting alcove. Here I saw a man I did not know – a weekend guest, he had to be – doing the crossword in front of a tame but glowing fire. The mantelpiece was as usual cluttered with engraved invitations. The tables and chairs were still covered in their old paisleys, and there, next to them, was the stool I had once, to the embarrassment of all present, said resembled the lid of a sewing basket. Standing on the sideboard was a silver drinks tray that held six tumblers, a bottle of vodka, a glass jug of tomato juice and – proudly, emphatically – no ice. Looking beyond into the unlit entryway – and even as I use that word, I remember that they had another, better word for it – I could just make out the dark outline of the grand piano, and sitting on it, but in this inconstant half-light seeming to float in midair, the contours of Bea's peacock feathers rising out of their slim ceramic vase.

And there, I noticed, as I moved to look through the little window to the left of the doorway, was that other table where she kept her guest book and her African basket for outgoing post, except that this

4

evening it was filled with those strange black and white dolls she used to knit whenever she felt her nerves unravelling. Had anyone ever dared mention to her how undemocratic they looked, how very much like black and white minstrels? Someone must have done, because, as I remembered now, during those last months, she had switched, with a telling refusal to explain or apologise, to knitting black cats and white mice.

I turned my back on the window and continued walking along the wall past the offices. These were too dark for inspection. All I could see through the Venetian blinds was the occasional green or red glowing electronic button. I paused at the folly to watch a purple mist creep up the hill, and when it had overtaken most of the garden, I used my memory to keep to the path leading into the courtyard, where I found the magnolia trees draped in fairy lights, and beyond them, in the bright, tiled kitchen, the housekeeper and the caterer standing over the Aga, the butler Bea hired for dinner parties inspecting a crate of wine.

I knew they couldn't see me but I felt awkward standing there envying their inaudible gossip, their offstage excitement, their pleasure in their unnecessary uniforms, and so I continued my journey around the edges of the house. The round table in the dining room was, I counted, set for twelve, with three crystal glasses standing at the head of each place. The only light in the room came from the candles inside the transparent pyramid that stood at the table's centre. This highlighted the gold-lettered spines of the books while at the same time obscuring the shelves that housed them; emphasised the gilt frames on the walls at the expense of the dour ancestors in the portraits. A collar here, a pair of beady eyes there – that was all that I could see, but it was a different story, I now saw, in the sitting room next door. There, over the mantelpiece and another fire, was the painting that had brought about my downfall – or my reinstatement, as some would say – the painting of the young girl on her way to a ball, wearing the black gown with the ribboned sash.

Except that this evening the gown was white. And there, just a few feet away from the French doors, striking that odd rocking-horse

5

pose that people fall into when they are trying to give the impression of being uplifted by great art – there, with her forefinger poised on her raised chin, was an intently gazing Bea. Standing next to her was the crossword man from the alcove. I recognised him now. He was the art historian whose third wife was Bea's oldest childhood friend, and he had just noticed a detail in the painting, somewhere in the lower left-hand corner, that he was now telling Bea he found perplexing and exciting. What a good thing she had thought to have it cleaned, he proclaimed to her in his – to me, somewhat muffled – Etonian trumpet. 'It could well turn out to be an unsigned work by G himself, instead of just a study by one of G's students.'

'Hmm,' said Bea. Then her eyes darted to the door. Enter the butler, with two glasses of champagne on a tray. 'Oh, thank you so much, Frith. You *are* kind. Yes, that will do very nicely.'

The butler retreated and closed the door behind him. Bea and the art historian took their first sips of champagne. Bea told the art historian how pleased she was to see him again. The art historian told Bea how sweet it was of her to have invited him. Bea apologised for the invitation having been 'at such short notice'. The cuckoo clock behind the photograph of Queen Mary on the side table struck seven, and two cars rolled into the courtyard.

Out of the first stepped two of Bea's long-necked, aquiline-featured nieces – the one who used to be an obituarist, and the one who used to belong to a repertory company somewhere in the Midlands. Out of the second car stepped a flashily dressed blonde woman whom I recognised as the Merry Widow. Audible groans from the nieces as she approached them. 'Oh no, not *that* again,' said one, and the other hissed, 'Just pray she hasn't brought her friend!'

But she had. Out of the darkness came lumbering a large man in a kilt. He didn't see me as I walked past him. He looked drunk, and sounded ungracious as the Merry Widow presented him to the nieces. 'You've met before, I'm sure,' said the Merry Widow, in a loud voice clearly intended to compensate.

'Yes, of course we have,' said the obituarist brightly. 'It was at Giles's sixtieth birthday party.'

I left them to it and moved on in the direction of the cottages.

I skirted the tennis court – as usual, it was lit but empty – and was heading straight across the lawn towards the cottage that had once been my home when suddenly I stopped, as if in response to a shouted warning. Looking over my shoulder into the brightly lit sitting room of the other cottage, I thought I saw the reason why, because there, panting at the window, was Jasper the dog, and at his side, brushing her short ginger hair with those slow, exaggerated strokes of hers, strokes that would have been excessive even if her hair had reached to her waist – there, staring vacantly through me, was Danny.

Now she seemed to see me. Her lips curled. She sucked in her breath as if to prepare for speech, but then she let it go again, shrugged her shoulders and moved away from the window and out of my view. An old hatred passed through me. But why? I asked myself. What did she matter? When had she ever mattered?

I moved on to the cottage that had been our first marital home. I looked into the long room, and the scene I saw was familiar or so I first thought, down to the last detail. But I paid no attention to the books, the pictures, the carpets or even the toys, because there, sitting on the sofa in the far left-hand corner, were the children. They were dressed in their pyjamas, robes and slippers, their hair wet and recently combed and parted. Their eyes were on the television, which I could not see. At the other end of the room, sitting at the head of the dining table, his head bent over an open book, was Max.

He looked the way he used to look, the way he would still look, I suppose, if I hadn't tried to save him. By this I mean to say that there was a spring to his gestures that made him look younger, or at least more hopeful. His hair was longer and fairer than it is now. He was dressed in a dark-blue shirt I did not recognise, and an unusually baggy pair of black trousers. He kept looking towards the low-beamed door that led to the back of the house, but because I was looking at him, I saw the startled smile that brightened his face before I saw the cause, before I realised that the scene predated and so could never include me – that the family I saw inside, the family I had been so convinced was my family, did not want or even need me; it was complete unto itself.

7

The woman who had entered the room, for whom Max now rose with such pleasure, for whom the children now abandoned their television programme with eager cries, was Rebecca.

As she wrapped her arms around them, she looked over her shoulder, locked eyes with me and gave me a triumphant smile.

That was where the dream ended, but it reminds me of the curse that caused it, and so brings me to the beginning of the story I now have decided the time has come to tell. I don't know what will become of me once I've told it. Some would say that it was not mine to tell. But there's nothing worse than living inside someone else's story. Let them talk you out of believing your own story, and you might as well bury yourself alive. Here's how I found out: I fell in love with a man, only to find myself in a book written by another woman.

Chapter Two

I had a few minutes of impartiality. I return to them often, because I need to remember how he looked before I knew who he was. We met in Deia, seven years ago this July. I was there courtesy of a Mrs Van Hopper, who had taken me on as a sort of upmarket lady's companion. She had a house on the point overlooking the *cala*, and a small circle of devoted friends, but her sights were on the infamous Irish novelist who had once been only the second best the village had to offer, but who had moved into first place since the death of Robert Graves four years earlier. Or rather, her sights were on the man's large, powerful, but not particularly brilliant family; the novelist himself was now confined to his bed.

On the eve of what promised to be his last birthday, while she was sitting in the café waiting for me to finish her shopping, Mrs Van Hopper happened to overhear two of the novelist's sons discussing a staffing crisis. Their father's night nurse had failed to turn up the previous evening. Rumour had it that she had left for the mainland. Although the day nurse had stood in for her, she would need to be relieved by the end of her present shift. The local agencies had failed to come up with a stand-in. The agency in London was not going to be able to get anyone down to Mallorca for at least two days. To complicate matters, a dozen house guests had just arrived, with twice that number expected for the birthday celebrations the following evening. Hoping to be included, Mrs Van Hopper offered to lend me to the novelist's family. They took her up on it without bothering to return the favour with the invitation she coveted.

This put her into a foul mood, but there was no going back on it. A foot in the door, she told me, was better than nothing at all. It was not the first time she had used me to advance herself socially, but in the past it had been my small literary reputation

9

she had presented as her calling card. As much as I resented the fairy tale she had woven around it ('She was destitute, poor thing! She lost everything after the tragedy, everything! If it hadn't been for me, she would be waiting tables in Kansas City!'), I could not afford to talk back. And anyway, as I was the first to remind myself, I was as curious about the Forbidden Villa as she was. I set out that evening without too much complaint.

The novelist's wiry and deeply bronzed wife was busy in the kitchen when I arrived. She took me straight up to the sickroom. 'It's so so kind of you to have come,' she said distractedly. 'You have no idea how very grateful we all are. Everything's gone wrong at once. You'll find the supplies and the instructions in the desk. We've just turned him over, so he's good for a few hours, I would say.' With that, she had returned to her house guests on the terrace.

There were no instructions in the desk – just charts, illegible notes and a collection of pills and syringes. But it didn't seem urgent to ask for help as the patient appeared to be sleeping. I settled down in the chair next to the bed. At first I was, I'll admit it, curious to look at the face, or rather at the changes that had occurred in it since he had last exposed it to a camera – his once rugged countenance now relaxed into a childish frown, his famously accusing eyes opening to unfocused confusion whenever a passing car startled him out of his light sleep.

From time to time he remained awake long enough to notice me. Once, when I made the mistake of trying to fix his covers, he grabbed my arm and wouldn't let go. I had to prise his fingers loose, only to have him grab my hand, and then my other hand, my other forearm – but none of this threw me. I had dealt with it before. I knew what happened to old men when their minds began to go. The erasure of this man's intelligence did not seem unusually tragic. I admired his writing, but I had never been a disciple. He set his sights too high, just as in those days I set mine too low. Human error, that was what I looked for then – the way the mighty tripped and revealed themselves unworthy of Mount Olympus. This great man had long since fallen. He could no longer be caught out. I was more interested in his family's frenetic efforts to rest on his laurels.

This, in any event, was how I saw the dinner party that was playing itself out on the terrace below.

My view was restricted by the grape arbour that covered the inner half of the terrace. This meant that I could hear only the people I couldn't see. But sometimes conversation can be a distraction, can keep the unfeeling witness from seeing the obvious. In this case, it was that the dozen or so guests at the far end of the terrace belonged to two incompatible groups. One consisted of my charge's sons and their beautiful but (I knew from previous observation) braindead acolytes. The other was made up of visitors. You could tell from their pallor and the slight awkwardness with which they wore their summer clothes that they hadn't been on the island long. You could tell from their vague, beaming smiles that they were chuffed to have been invited. Yet the nervous way they picked at the nuts and olives, and the deep, dark looks they bestowed from time to time upon their wineglasses, suggested that they were far more important at home, or at work, than they were here, and not quite certain what to do when they weren't the centre of attention.

The only time they lost their self-consciousness was when someone asked a direct question, the kind of question that requires five or ten minutes to answer fully. The important person would lean back, take in a breath and then hold forth, punctuating his long sentences with his forefinger and smiling at his own neat ironies. The listener would nod repeatedly, his eyes never wandering. Sometimes he would ask another question, then nod his way through another long response. Sometimes the speaker would graciously cede the stage by asking the listener a question, at which point one or the other would gesture at an empty stretch of terrace wall, where they would retire to continue their discussion.

These were the men. Only one of the women – a pretty but anxious-looking creature with a fixed pout and a blue straw hat – seemed able to address them as peers. The other women were clearly wives, almost all in their eager-to-please early fifties, and better at circulating. But even they had trouble keeping conversations going when they tried crossing over to the other camp. The novelist's sons and their hangers-on killed their every attempt at an opening with monosyllabic answers and repellently brilliant smiles. They were passing around a joint in the usual, unnecessarily surreptitious fashion. Occasionally, they would glance in the direction of the village, the conical hill half a mile away that seemed to merge, in this light, with the steep terraces of olive trees and citrus groves behind it. I imagined they were looking for a missing guest.

In due course he appeared, just as the setting sun was slipping from the windows of the village, just as the terraces began to darken and the cliffs above them turned from pink and gold back into grey. He was tall and lean with unruly light-brown hair. I guessed from his slow gait that he was keen to delay his arrival for as long as possible. He was smoking a cigarette. A few hundred yards away from the villa, he sat down on a boulder at the side of the road to finish it. He sucked in on it so hard it looked as if he were trying to inhale the view.

The sea remained where it was, a thousand feet or more below, but fortitude came suddenly and before the end of the cigarette. He threw it in the road, stamped it out and proceeded briskly towards the villa.

Big embraces with the hostess, who was fussing with the barbecue. Lots of 'lovely's and 'marvellous'es floated through the failing light, and 'how long's – how long was he staying? How long had it been since their last meeting? How long had Himself been 'this bad'? A shrug of the shoulders in answer to this last question, followed by an explanation I couldn't hear. As hostess and guest glanced up at the window, I had my first good look at his face. It was long, with fine features given substance by a strong chin. The large eyes hinted at thoughtfulness and kindness; the hand that brushed the hair back spoke of a lifetime of being indulged; the mouth, despite the half-smile, of a day survived on nerves, of desperation barely suppressed.

I had seen this man before.

No, more than that. I *knew* him. It was the surprise of recognition, I think, that made me forget who I was and where I was and what I was meant to be doing. Now, when he moved onto the terrace to greet the other guests, I was no longer content with the challenge of the restricted view. The stage had become too interesting, my questions too urgent, the unheard conversations withheld too many clues. Both groups, I noticed, converged on him. He was the long-awaited missing link. They waited their turn for a chance to speak. Now it was a very important visitor, now it was a local hanger-on, now it was the sulky woman in the blue straw hat. She took him by the arm and chided him in a way that I ought to have seen was proprietorial. He responded with annoyance, and looked over her hand to greet the novelist's eldest son, who passed him the joint. He took a few drags from it and then tried to pass it back – overhand, not underhand as the others had been doing. The son said something like, 'No, I have more, you have the rest of this one, you look like you need it.'

At this point, our new arrival noticed the hostess struggling with a plate of barbecued chicken. He rushed across the terrace and under the grape arbour. 'Here,' he said in a loud and, even to my untrained ears, confidently upper-class English voice. 'Let me take that for you.'

'Not until you've put that thing out,' the hostess replied. 'Goodness, Max, you ought to know better! Under the circumstances, particularly! Do what you like elsewhere, but I'm not having anyone smoking tobacco *here*.'

'This is not tobacco,' he said. 'It's marijuana.'

'Then I'm even more appalled. When *will* you grow up? Honestly! Bringing contraband to a party!'

'It's not illegal, Lydia. Surely even you know that? People smoke it in the cafés.'

'They do not!'

'They do. The only reason you haven't noticed is that you don't know the smell.'

'Yes, I can, young man. It smells bad. Put it out.'

'Find me an ashtray, then.'

'I don't have any ashtrays,' she said petulantly. 'Throw it over the wall.'

'I'm not going to throw it over the *wall*, Lydia. What a menace you are! I'm surprised you haven't burned the whole place down.

13

I'll give it to someone else, how about that? I'll make sure you don't see anything compromising.'

'That shouldn't be difficult,' said the hostess. 'Lots of hypocrites to choose from here! I'll be in the kitchen when you're ready.'

'This won't take long.'

The conversation ended. I waited for him to appear again at the far end of the terrace. When he did not, I moved to the window on the other side of the bed and leaned out, and as I did so, my patient took advantage of my inattention and clamped his hand around my thigh.

Once again, I prised his fingers loose. No sooner had I succeeded than he grabbed hold of my arm. Then he grabbed my thigh again with his free hand. When I shouted at him to let me go, he let out a Hammer horror howl, and then let go of my thigh to lunge for my arm. He tried to haul me onto the bed. I threw my weight in the opposite direction, with the result that we both rolled to the floor.

I landed on my side. He hit the floor head first, and then went limp. My legs were pinned underneath his torso. After I had freed myself, I tried first to pull him back up on the bed, and then, when that proved impossible, to sit him up – but no sooner had I done that than he keeled over on his head again. Fearing that he was dead or dying, I rushed down to the kitchen to get help.

Here, under the harsh fluorescent light, I found the hostess cutting up red peppers. 'So you think he's dead, do you?' she said. 'Weren't you able to get a pulse?'

'I didn't look for one.'

'Why not?'

'Because I don't know how,' I said. 'I'm not a nurse.'

'You're not a nurse? Then what the hell are you doing with my husband?'

'I'm not quite sure.'

'And what is that supposed to mean?'

'That I was sent over here by Mrs Van Hopper without having been given very much information, and then sent upstairs without much more, and then left stranded there. Since you ask.'

14

'If you're complaining about my not having fed you, you're being childish and unreasonable. No one else here has eaten yet either. This is *Spain*, my dear. People eat *late*.'

'I'm not talking about food. I'm talking about your possibly dead husband. I apologise if my timing is wrong. If you prefer, I'll just go back upstairs and try to settle him into a spare casket.'

I heard a snort of laughter behind me. I turned around. It was Max.

'Oh!' he said. 'Goodness.' It was as if he recognised me. 'I never . . .' His voice trailed off. 'Yes,' he said, trying to look stern. He cleared his throat. 'Yes, where were we?'

'Oh, *you're* a big help,' the hostess said to him.

He paused, then gave us both a long, affable and puzzlingly inappropriate smile – a ploy he still uses, I've noticed, with restless underlings when they challenge his authority. In a soft, measured voice, he said, 'I suggest we all go upstairs.'

He led the way. Arriving at the old man's side, he kneeled down and took his pulse. 'Well,' he said, 'he's not dead. Dead drunk, maybe, but not dead.'

'He can't be drunk,' Lydia protested. 'He hasn't—'

She stopped when Max lifted the ruffle to reveal a dozen or so empty wine and vodka bottles and an unopened carton of Camel cigarettes.

'Oh!' said Lydia. 'Oh, dear!'

'It doesn't really matter what he does to himself at this stage, so stop fretting,' Max said. 'Grab hold of his feet.' He turned to me. 'And you take the right arm. That's it,' he said, as we hauled the poet back onto the bed. 'Now all we have to do is get someone up here who knows what he's like. And let Not the Night Nurse here go home.'

'I also think you ought to apologise to her,' Max told Lydia as I lamely gathered up my things.

'Oh, stop being such a bore!' she said.

I followed them down the stairs. Two of the sons were waiting in the kitchen. 'What's wrong?' one of them asked, to which Lydia replied, '*Pas devant la bonne,*' to which Max said, 'Come, come now,

15

let's not get our knickers in a twist, the days are gone when you could reasonably expect a nurse not to know French.'

'But she's not a nurse, and she's American,' Lydia protested.

I took advantage of their turned heads and slipped out of the house.

The road was dark. I made my way towards the point haltingly, picking out the hard shoulder with my torch. I was just rounding the first bend when Max drew up alongside me in a white Panda. 'Get in. I'll drive you home.'

'Is this your car?' I asked after I had told him where to go.

'Why are you so sure it isn't?' he asked.

'I saw you arrive on foot.'

'If you know it's not my car, why are you asking?'

'You could have been returning from a walk,' I said. '*If* you were a house guest.'

'Which I'm not.'

'So this is another house guest's car.'

He said, 'Presumably.'

'But you're not sure.'

'No.'

'And you didn't stop to ask.'

'I hadn't the time,' he said. He took a drag from his cigarette. 'I promise to thank the owner when I get back.'

We had arrived at the double hairpin bend that led down to the point. Max negotiated it without hesitation or caution. 'He's attacked people before, you know,' he told me. 'That's why the real night nurse left. He probably needs locking up. I can see why Lydia is reluctant to take that step, but she can't keep sacrificing innocent virgins to him. She really can't. It's just not on. I'm going to tell her. In fact, I'm going to tell her tonight.'

'But not until you've thanked her house guest for the Panda.'

'No. Not until I've made myself known as a thief.'

The road was dark, but he drove as if from memory. He pulled to a sharp stop outside the cliffside stone house people called Schlomo's Tower. 'Come in for a drink,' he said.

'Is this where you're staying?'

16

'No, but I know where the key is, and I'll bet there's some wine in there, and if you'll join me, I'll promise to ring Schlomo as soon as I get back to London and confess.'

He was right. There was a bottle of Franja Roja under the sink. He brought it outside with two glasses, a corkscrew, an ashtray and a candle. 'That's more like it,' he said as he lit it with his butane lighter. Taking a drag from his cigarette, he added, 'I can't bear parties.'

He stretched himself out on the terrace wall, seemingly oblivious to the five-hundred-foot drop.

'So tell me. You're not a relation, by some ghastly chance? If you are, now's the time to tell me.'

'I'm not sure what you mean,' I said.

'No one's ever remarked on the resemblance before?' He gave me a long, curious look. 'No one? Look into my eyes again. Straight into my eyes, like you did before. No, I'm sorry. It's gone. It must have been the light. Sometimes I read too much into things. Never mind. Let's talk about something more interesting. What are you doing in Deia?'

'What would you say if you had to guess?'

'I'd guess that you're here . . . to finish off a book of exquisite short stories. Each one a gem intended to stand on its own, but also to reflect and refract the brilliance of the others.'

'How did you know?'

'That they were exquisite?'

'No. That I had written short stories.'

'Well, it was just a case of narrowing things down. You had to have some sort of pretext, I knew that much. You could have been a musician, I suppose. But you didn't have the Look.'

'My clothes are too conventional, you mean?'

'Well, just slightly. Not that the Look is anything to aspire to.'

'And?'

'And you could have been an artist, but you didn't have the Gaze. There was also the matter of your sharp tongue, which suggested to me that your poison was the pen. And as for short stories – well, you wouldn't be a lady's companion or whatever you are if you had lots of novels under your belt, and you don't have that anointed look first novelists have before publication. Neither do you have the tragic look they have just afterwards. And you're young and American, and Americans who want to be taken seriously tend to concentrate on the short story, and when they aspire to greater things they are prone to make their short stories "interconnect".'

'And I can tell that's a word you dislike.'

'Yes, but not as much as I hate "commit" when used as an intransitive verb when discussing the inertia of a bachelor who's trying to put off marriage. So,' he said, without missing a beat, 'you've been slaving away on your short stories when Mrs Van Invalid or whatever her name is gives you the time—'

'No, I'm through with my short stories. I'm on to my first novel.'

'Even better. You've been struggling with the opening pages of your first novel whenever the old hag gives you five minutes of peace, and you've been here a month or two, and you've made friends with . . .'

Here he rattled off names of a number of people I knew by reputation only. No, I told him, I didn't know Aline. She wasn't here because she had a show in Copenhagen. So far she had sold five paintings. Her nephew, who claimed to be a sea captain, was staying in her house. I didn't know Kelsey either, although I did know that she had just returned from Guatemala, nor her partner Bert, who talked too much about Wittgenstein. She had a house guest named Joe, who was meant to have been staying at the McAllisters', except that it was being occupied without their permission at the moment by Aline's husband's discarded Spanish girlfriend. Max was amused by my ability to retain gossip about people I hadn't met. Encouraged, I began to embroider in my usual way. Then, reckless with my unexpected success, I made my first mistake.

'And what have you heard on the Deia jungle telegraph about me?' he asked. He gave me that strange smile, the one that now tells me he's upset.

I said that I had heard nothing.

'Nothing?' he echoed. Again, his expression didn't fit. He looked

18

right into my eyes, too long for comfort. I looked straight back. Exactly what I saw then I do not know, but it felt familiar, and it hurt.

'I'll tell you what I do know,' I said, 'although I can't tell you how I know, just that I'm always right about these things. It's that we have something in common.'

'How interesting,' he said, but he didn't mean it. He glanced at his watch, stood up, stretched, and then, looking at the sky, not me, said, 'It's about time I got back.'

Chapter Three

M rs Van Hopper's house stood on the edge of a steep incline that slid into a cliff. The view was like an overblown postcard, too beautiful to believe and too far away to touch. But that next morning, I remember, the air was so clear that for once the horizon looked close enough to trace with your finger. The dark-blue sea was smooth but you could see how it registered the course of every passing breeze. The cliffs along the two clawlike promontories that enclosed the *cala* looked newly chiselled. You could count the silvery leaves on the olive trees, the lemons nestling in the scattered citrus droves. You could taste the thyme.

'Good Lord, another beautiful day,' was my employer's response as I wheeled her out on the terrace for her breakfast. 'I'm not sure how much longer I can bear it. It's too hard on the eyes. Makes you feel like it's your job to be happy. Which I definitely am not this morning.'

She didn't know how to take my account of the previous evening. On the one hand, she was furious at the skilful way they had managed to snub her while still availing themselves of her services, and therefore delighted to hear they had been put in their place by someone else. On the other hand, she could not but conclude that the Forbidden Villa would be closed to her for ever on account of my poor performance as a nurse. Normally, she would have chastised me for my ineptness ('When you look after the elderly, my dear, you have to put up with such things') but that left the puzzle of my deliverance. If a house guest – in other words, a member of the inner sanctum – had seen fit to rescue me, something must have been very wrong.

'Who do you think he is?' she asked her friend Marco when he arrived towards lunchtime. By now she had decided to turn the story into an intrigue, starring me as spy.

'He sounds like a relation, if you ask me,' said Marco importantly. He pretended to be thinking as he set up the chessboard. Like all the old-timers here, he felt obliged to appear in the know about the goings-on at the Forbidden Villa. He proposed a number of names that meant nothing to me.

'I just don't know,' I said. 'He never introduced himself. His manner was quite abrupt.'

They quizzed me on his appearance. This yielded more suggestions, more dead ends.

'You're hopeless, my dear,' Mrs Van Hopper said. 'There you were, right in the centre of it all, and you noticed nothing. No wonder writing comes so hard to you. Don't tell me you were reading, or, God forbid, knitting?'

'Aha, oho,' said Marco. 'Mademoiselle LeFarge.'

I did not join them in their laughter.

'You're beginning to annoy me,' Mrs Van Hopper now said. 'I don't like you peering over my shoulder unless you have a useful suggestion, and judging from our last chess game, I can't imagine that you have. Why don't you run along and do whatever it is you do when you're off duty.'

'Do you have a lover?' Marco asked.

'If she has, she's certainly done a brilliant cover-up,' said Mrs Van Hopper. 'Run along now! Be back at five.'

During the two months I had been in Deia, I had written eight first chapters and thrown away seven of them. Now that I had one I could live with, I was gathering up my nerve for a second chapter. I had thought to spend the afternoon sketching and gathering my thoughts, but the sun grew too hot, the cicadas too loud, the smell of thyme too much like dust. I convinced myself I wasn't ready yet. So I gathered up my things and walked down the steep, winding path to the *cala*.

Although it was neither a Sunday nor a holiday, the little restaurant was packed. Only one chair remained, at the end of a long table occupied by acquaintances of Mrs Van Hopper. One of the men – a Macedonian playwright – waved at me to join the group. I sat down, somewhat tentatively, but already he had forgotten me and returned to a discussion with the young woman sitting opposite him. I recognised her as the one from the previous evening, the one with the blue hat. She was looking the worse for wear today: her slightly popping eyes were bloodshot, and she was catching her breath as if she had only just stopped crying. The Macedonian playwright seemed to be trying to distract her from her distress with a general topic. It was, I recall, on the subject of love declarations. Anyone who came out and said 'I love you' was by definition a liar. It was, he said, like Nixon saying, 'I am not a crook.' I remember trying to look intrigued by this conversation because no one else at the table acknowledged my presence.

The other people at the table all had that blend of uniformity and uniqueness that people so often mistake for social poise. Bronzed, relaxed, smiling broadly as if in memory of the world's best joke, they wore their odd, colourful clothes carelessly and their distinctions like necklaces. Although I had talked to very few of them, I knew their labels: the beautiful young woman between the playwright and the tearful blue hat was the daughter of a German poet; she lived in Paris with her young son. The Latin American painter sitting opposite – the child's father – spent the summers with her and the winters with his real family in New York. His wife, a literary agent, was also at the table, along with her new lover, a young Australian who had been living in Deia for three or four years and, until now, supporting himself as a carpenter. Sitting at my end of the table was an American psychoanalyst who had retired on a pittance after a scandal and bought a big villa here after his war-profiteer father left him a few million; a Canadian writer who had settled in Paris after the war and squandered his fortune on a string of expensive wives; a journalist from London and his wife, who was from Senegal; a Portuguese Buddhist; a shoe designer from Madrid; an Italian film director; and a man who was said to be a member of the Spanish cabinet. The conversation flowed from French into Spanish into English into Italian and back into French; when the waiter passed by, the younger members of the group would break into Mallorquin.

I didn't dare move. With the usual paranoia of the insignificant,

I had convinced myself that if I did they would suddenly notice me and ask me why I was there. It was only with the greatest willpower that I managed to eat my salad: I was sure they could hear the lettuce crunching. I was afraid to eat the olives because I wasn't sure what to do with the pits. As I gathered my things and crept off to settle my bill, I gave myself a lecture. I was not being ostracised. It was all in my head. After all, wasn't that the film star Michael Douglas standing with his son on that outcropping of rocks? He had arrived several minutes earlier by motorboat. My table wasn't paying any more attention to him than it was to me.

The lecture didn't work. The only space I could find on the beach was just beneath the restaurant. There were, I was convinced, too many eyes on me for me to follow the custom and sunbathe topless, but as I lay there overcovered, I began to imagine that my audience was mocking me for my lack of nerve. I had been meaning to get some thinking done before I took my swim, or, failing that, at least some reading, but I could not concentrate, could not bear the groundless doubts that crowded my brain, and so I made my way over the seaweed-covered stones to the dock and slipped into the water.

It was a third of a mile out to the point. Beyond were a series of protected pools and hidden coves known as the Naked and the Dead. It was here, crouching on one of the tiny bars of sand, that I found Max.

'Oh, good,' he said, looking up with a pleased smile. 'It's Not the Night Nurse.'

'I hope I didn't get you into too much trouble,' I said.

'Of course you did, but you mustn't apologise. As my hostess told me only this morning, I've always had a nose for it.'

'I should have stayed,' I said. 'Either that or been more assertive.'

'Assertive. Hmm. I assume you mean you ought not to have let Lydia treat you like a doormat. Not to worry. Lydia treats all of us like doormats, and she still treats me like a twenty-year-old doormat. Gregory was my tutor, you see. Come out of the water. You could use some sun.'

I found myself a natural chair in the rocks.

'I'm going back there for the party tonight, and then I hope that will be it,' he continued after I had made myself comfortable. 'I can't take another day of it. It was bad enough when he was a healthy man, but now . . . well, you saw for yourself what she's turned him into. Although I'm beginning to wonder if it isn't the curse of – the price you pay for being too well known.' He picked up a handful of stones. 'He never admitted it, but he must be very disappointed in his children. Do you have children?'

'No,' I said.

'Married?'

'He died.'

'I'm sorry. I oughtn't to have asked.'

'He slit his wrists,' I offered. 'He was a writer, too. He had the opposite problem. He was afraid of being forgotten.'

I almost went on, but then I stopped myself, shocked at my own words. In the six months since it had happened, I hadn't talked about it with anybody who didn't already know the details. 'I'm sorry,' I said. 'That sounded callous.'

'How do you mean?' my companion asked.

'That flip remark about his problem.'

'I don't think you meant it as a flip remark. In any event,' he added, his voice suddenly hoarse, 'that's not how I took it.'

I opened my mouth to change the subject, but I couldn't. 'I'm pretty sure he didn't mean to die,' I now found myself saying. 'He had done it before. But this time, the thing was we weren't living together any more. I had moved in with a friend. He had been playing games, you know what I mean, I'm sure, upping the ante to get me back, so I didn't take the warning signs seriously.' I paused, then added, for no reason at all, 'His name was Sasha.'

'Had you been together long?'

'Too long,' I said. 'You see, he was my stepbrother.'

'Ah.' His tan was not deep enough to conceal the fact that he was blushing. It was almost as if he was too embarrassed to ask me to stop. And so I left it hanging. There was a long silence. I wondered what had possessed me to reduce my ragged tragedy into an anecdote.

I watched him grimace at the rocks. 'Why exactly are you telling me this?'

'I'm not quite sure.'

'I suppose you want me to tell you that I understand?'

'No,' I said, 'not really. If I don't understand, then why should you?'

He winced, as if I had slapped him. There was another long silence. Then, suddenly, he managed to recompose himself. 'I think we should change the subject,' he said. He pointed at a pile of tiny shells. 'Those are for my children.'

'How many do you have?' I asked.

He looked at me sharply and, after a pause, said, 'Two, a girl and a boy.'

'And where are they now?'

'With their aunt in Italy, which is a shame, because I think they'd be happier here.'

'Then why aren't they?'

'Because my aunt had other ideas. She's a bit like Lydia, only much, much nicer. She decided I needed some time on my own, although I suspect what she really wanted was to get me out of the way so that she could have them to herself. And then there was this profile I had to do – of Gregory – although God only knows what I'm going to say now. I'd rather not think about it today. The deadline's not until the day after tomorrow.'

'Do you work for a newspaper?' I asked.

He gave me another sharp look. 'Yes,' he said. 'Well, in a manner of speaking.'

'What does it mean to work for a newspaper in a manner of speaking?' I asked.

He looked at me quizzically and then broke into a smile, a smile so happy, so appreciative that I still return to the memory whenever I need to remind myself that his face is – or was once – capable of registering pleasure. 'You honestly don't know, do you?' he said.

'Honestly don't know what?'

Laughing, he grabbed my hand and squeezed it. Then, letting it go, but still beaming, he said, 'I'm sorry. It's just that it's been a

25

very long time. To return to your question, I work for a newspaper part of the week. I do their book page.'

'And the rest of the week?'

'I stay at home and write. And try to steal time alone with my children. Speaking of whom, I notice you're wearing a money belt. Would you mind if I asked you to carry my shells?'

I said I would take as many as I could.

'That's lovely,' he said. 'You won't mind, will you, if I swim on ahead? I like going fast, or rather, I have never been able to swim slowly. I'll wait for you in the restaurant. I'll order us up a couple of coffees.'

This time, when I walked into the restaurant and over to the small table where Max was waiting for me, I did have an audience. The same in-group that had ignored me at lunchtime was now taking turns to study us with surreptitious glances. By now he had told me he was a poet who also wrote novels and biographies; I gathered from the interest he was provoking that he was a well-known poet. I didn't read poetry any more. Or biographies. Or novels written by English men. As I didn't wish to advertise these facts, I didn't ask him for his name.

And so, in trying to save face, I failed to save him from Mrs Van Hopper.

It was in the café in town, after supper, that same night. He came in with a group of people I recognised from the Forbidden Villa. When he caught sight of me, he interrupted the man who had been talking to him, made his apologies, and came over to our table.

Mrs Van Hopper's face turned purple with excitement when he asked to join us. 'Oh, do, do, do,' she said. 'Please. Our pleasure.'

'Allow me to introduce myself,' said Max, but before he could continue, Mrs Van Hopper interrupted him.

'We've met before,' she said. 'But years ago, you probably won't remember. A lunch party, at our mutual friends the Oswalds'. On their yacht. In that darling bay next to that hotel of your father's. Rebecca was quite uncomfortable, as I recall. She was eight months pregnant.'

Max stared at the table in front of him and said nothing.

'I suppose you don't see the Oswalds any more,' Mrs Van Hopper persisted. 'Not after that dreadful book. And quite right, too, if you ask me. We were all appalled, I assure you, and no one so much so as yours truly. Such disloyalty! I hope you don't think it impertinent, but we can't understand why you didn't sue.'

'I have no interest in what you think,' said Max as he rose to his feet abruptly. 'And I find your remarks vulgar and very rude.' Turning to me, he said, 'I'm sorry, but I'm going to have to leave. I hope you'll forgive me.'

With that, he was off. 'Well, well, well,' chuckled Mrs Van Hopper as her eyes followed him into the bar. 'Who would have imagined? I suppose you're going to tell me that this is your mystery house guest. Now, honestly! You can't tell me you don't know what he is.'

'I know *what* he is. He's a poet. He told me.'

'Yes, dear, but he's not just any poet. He's Mad Max, you silly girl.'

Mad Max. He was Mad Max. As the full horror of this news registered, I felt my face grow hot. How could I have failed to work that out? How well I had blinded myself! How badly I had repaid him for his kindness!

Misunderstanding my paralysis, Mrs Van Hopper continued. 'You must have heard the story. Even in Kansas City, the name Max Midwinter must ring bells. Not, by any stretch of the imagination, for his own slim volumes, but as God's gift to feminism. As the man who turned his lovely wife from a minor literary light into an international martyr by inducing her to take her own life.'

From my place at the table, I could see Max's back as he stood, alone, stiff and unprotected, at the bar. Now I turned my chair so that I wouldn't have to face him if he turned around. I didn't want to have to face him ever again. I wanted to run, run and run, far away from Mrs Van Hopper, the Forbidden Villa and all my mistakes.

'Actually,' I said, in as steady a voice as I could manage, 'actually, it wasn't suicide. If my memory serves me, she drowned.'

27

Chapter Four

*I*n my wrong-headed way, I had been right. I *had* seen this man before. But I hadn't paid attention to him. He was not the star that evening. The star was Rebecca.

I was still a student at the time. It was 1972, the year Sasha and I had spent in London. We had come up to Oxford for the weekend to visit a classmate who was a Rhodes scholar. He had taken us to a poetry marathon at the Oxford Union. The pretext was to raise money for a disaster fund – I forget which. The challenge, as far as the participants were concerned, seemed to be to get to the end of your poem without being jeered down by the spectators.

The quality of the poetry was more or less what you would expect from a privileged, overeducated group of twenty-year-olds. Predictable irony, conventional surrealism, crude radical politics dressed up in foreign four-syllable words. Derivative anger from the women; desperate but, because unsuccessful, endearing macho posturing from the men. Their looks were far more impressive than their words. Despite their torn jeans, leather jackets and wild hair, they reminded me of angels. Despite their beautiful voices, they were brought down one after the other by their hecklers. These were far wittier and more original than the performers. Until they found their match in Rebecca.

At first it looked as if they weren't going to give her a chance to say a word. The jeering and foot stomping began before she even reached the podium, but she seemed to welcome it, or rather, she responded to it as though she were walking down a catwalk to applause. She was wearing a long red knit dress, a black suede hip belt, black suede boots and a black suede handbag with a fringe at the bottom. Her hair in those days was longer and curlier than in her best-known photograph, but she had drawn it away from her face for this occasion with a thick tartan ribbon.

Her face was softer then, the famous cheekbones still concealed by the last of her puppy fat. She had not yet acquired her haunted inward gaze; her eyes were happy, open, interested. She appeared to have no sense of self at that moment, giving her full attention to the taunts coming from the audience. When she propped her elbows on the podium, it was with the expectant smile of someone who hopes to be amused. The worse the insults became, the more responsive her eyes, the more appreciative her silent laughter. It was as if she were sitting in a seminar, listening to a brilliant wit make some very naughty remarks at the expense of Virginia Woolf.

How long this went on, I cannot say. Ten minutes, maybe even fifteen. Until the hecklers were running out of originality. Then, with the same detached confidence – as if she were sitting on a bus, lost in thought – she began to rummage through her handbag, eventually retrieving a lighter and a packet of Lucky Strikes. She lit up, looked up towards a far corner of the ceiling while she took a long drag, and then screwed up her face, as if considering a nagging mathematical paradox. When the crowd fell silent, she looked up sharply. She turned to us as artlessly as if we were not an audience at all, but a friend sitting on the other side of a restaurant table, and said, in a loud, clear but confiding Texas twang:

'The understanding open wide like an eye towards truth in God, towards light, is confronted by that act of its own that blotted out God and so put blackness in the place of light. Against these acts of its own the lost spirit dashes itself like a caged bear and is in prison, violently instresses them and burns, stares into them and is the deeper darkened.'

She took another drag from her cigarette, wrinkled her forehead again, and said, 'Everything that is threatened by time secretes falsehood in order not to die, and in proportion to the danger it is in of dying. That is why there is not any love of truth without unconditional acceptance of death. But it takes so long to become young, doesn't it? Courage faces fear and thereby conquers it, but where does that leave me? I don't need to tell any of you furious little swots that my words are not my own but come to you through me courtesy of Hopkins, Weil, Picasso and Martin Luther King. I am suffering from the modern disease. I have lost the capacity to think for myself.' She paused for effect and then she said, in a mock heroic whisper that carried better than any shout, 'I have been smothered by the best minds of my generation.'

It was the early version of her inversion of Allen Ginsberg. She delivered it as if she were making it up on the spot, even the infamous Women's Catalogue of Unfeminine Graffiti. Every line was more outrageous than the one before, but no matter how funny she was, no matter how wicked her litany of trivia became, she never lost her seriousness of purpose. She never courted the audience – she didn't have to, she has us as willing captives. She dared to go to the centre of things while the rest of us dithered on the periphery – what took our breath away that night was not just her nerve, but her sense of direction.

I knew – we all knew – that we were watching the real thing. The real thing ahead of her time: a woman who could fly out of the cage, and who would continue to do so, no matter what the cost. She spoke to our generation as Sylvia Plath had to the generation before – over her shoulder, saying, 'Follow me.' Still I felt proud, almost responsible, when her name started appearing in the highbrow places. My copy of *Vices and Follies* was dog-eared long before it became a collector's item. My dream, when I set out to become a writer, was that one day I would write something the calibre of *The Toy of Man* or *The Rich Are Like Women*. When I read *Shoestrings* for the first time, I was so impressed, and so depressed by the gulf between my talent and hers, that I almost gave up writing for good. Or perhaps I should put it differently, because there was an affinity between her writing and mine, or at least I saw one – and still do. Rebecca is the writer I could have become if I had taken myself seriously.

So I was a founder member of the cult. That's what makes it all so odd. What people forget is that she wasn't a household name in those days, at least not in America. Even in London, she was still known mainly for being the only woman poet in the group known as the Hertford Five. All I knew about her life was what I read in her author's notes. Born into a family that ran a roadhouse somewhere between Austin and San Antonio, put herself through college and graduated from the University of Texas by the age of nineteen, fetched up in Oxford knowing no one but armed with an Irish passport, got herself coached for the exam, and after the second try got in to do a second degree. Married to the poet and novelist Max Midwinter, with whom she had two children, and well known in London as a literary critic. It was *The Marriage Hearse* that turned her into a Cause, and that didn't come out until after her death. Like everyone else, I read this book as disguised autobiography. And so I believed that, like the heroine, who was also Irish-American, and the only woman in a group of experimental Oxford poets, and also published by her husband's uncle, and so sensitive as to be almost skinless, she had been driven to the edge by her husband and his powerful family.

In the book, of course, the heroine rallies. But for me as for most readers, its strangely abrupt but still hopeful ending made Rebecca's own death seem even more tragic. We wanted to know what had happened between the time she finished the book and the time she died. Most particularly, we wanted to know what had happened during her last week on the Caribbean island of St John the Baptist. We were outraged to read, in Max's preface to the first volume of her journals, that he had lost the penultimate notebook and destroyed the last for the sake of the children. We were not satisfied with the statements released by her husband's family, not inclined to believe them either. We were ready to believe the Oswald exposé before it was even written. And when we bought it, we took one look at the now famous photograph of the then oh-so-happy literary god and goddess on their marriage day, one look at this slender, patrician aesthete guiding his bedazzled new wife down the church steps, and thought, No doubt about it, this man is guilty.

The lack of any up-to-date photograph only served to fuel our fantasy. He was, after all, the perfect illustration of our fears. We couldn't blame Rebecca for succumbing to him or for wanting to become part of his family. We admired her for daring to be herself amid all their pomp and circumstance, for daring to live out the highest form of romance, as we had redefined it, were all in our different ways attempting. And her death gave us the perfect excuse not to try so hard to do the same, or to stop trying altogether. We could look at Rebecca and say, See? The marriage of true and equal minds is not possible. There is no such thing as equality. The marriage of the minds is a con. Lay yourself open to a man and he'll destroy you the way Max destroyed Rebecca.

Now I had met, and failed to recognise, the object of my hatred. No, it was worse than that. I had met the enemy without the armour of prejudice, and everything I had seen of him said to me that he was a good man.

And if that was so . . .

I spent the next two days in hiding in Mrs Van Hopper's villa. I did not dare go down to the *cala*. I got Marco to do the shopping by claiming to have pulled a tendon in my knee. During the long, hot hours between breakfast and lunch, lunch and dinner, I pretended to be working: I sat with my pen and my pad at the marble table under the grape arbour at the far corner of Mrs Van Hopper's garden, but I didn't even try to put down the thoughts in my head. Instead I went back over – and over and over – my three meetings with Max, first looking for the clues I had missed, and then trying to figure out why it was that I had failed to make the connection.

It was, I decided, because there *was* no connection between Max and the husband in *The Marriage Hearse*. The only points of similarity were of circumstance. The man and the character had similar backgrounds, families, interests, habits. But I could not imagine Max being consumed by jealousy, nor wanting to destroy anyone, let alone a wife. And if there was anyone who was an expert on that kind of marriage, it was I.

I added up the points against my new and already lost friend. He drove too fast. He drank, he smoked. He appropriated other people's belongings when he needed them, was not predisposed to explanations or apologies, did not follow any rules except his own. But his own rules were honourable. He had stood up for me, looked after me, treated me like a human being. Since I couldn't see what

32

he could possibly gain from it, I could only assume he treated other unimportant people as equals, too. He could not be a snob in that case. He could not, like the husband in *The Marriage Hearse*, be so obsessed with questions of hierarchy that he couldn't see himself as thriving unless his wife was wasting away. It followed from there that Rebecca had drawn her villain from her imagination and not from her life – except for the external details that would convince everyone that she was writing about her husband. It followed that Rebecca had deliberately fooled her audience as an act of revenge. It followed that she had set out to destroy him, instead of the other way around.

How could she have done such a thing? Our idol, how could she?

And Max! Poor Max!

I knew what it was like to be blamed for things you hadn't done, or rather, I had had a small taste one day the previous winter of the reception Max probably got every time he walked into a room.

My first and, I hope, only encounter with pure hatred was at Sasha's cremation. It was in the eyes of each member of his family, our family, as they took turns to see me sitting at the back of the chapel. They wouldn't have looked at me that way if they had known what I had been through. But to subject them to the full story would have been worse than spitting on the coffin.

Especially since . . . especially since . . . Now, as I sat in the accusing shade of Mrs Van Hopper's arbour, I gave up that last protecting lie and admitted it to myself: I had failed him. I had failed to give him what he needed, I had failed to give him even what I had promised. I had failed to look after him, I had failed to see the signs. The army of ifs came back, the thousands upon thousands of things I could have done to save him. It wasn't good enough to say you can't save people, that the best you can do is help them save themselves. Anyone who spouted that kind of pap had never had a death. There was no evading the accusing finger, no consolation, no edifying lesson to retrieve from the ashes.

I had learned nothing – nothing! – from Sasha's death. After all, how long had it taken me to find another tyrant? Now, only six months later, I had Mrs Van Hopper as my foil, Mrs Van Hopper to make me look good by being bad. And while she gave me exactly what I needed, she was paying my way around the world! For the foreseeable future, I would never have to stay in any one place long enough for my sympathisers to find out who I really was.

A stronger woman – a normal woman – would not have put up with Mrs Van Hopper, nor, for that matter, would she have let matters get out of hand the way I had done that first night at the Forbidden Villa. And even if she had read the signals wrong the way I had done, this stronger, normal woman would have had the presence of mind to find out who this man was who had stood up for her, and taken the small measures to save him from Mrs Van Hopper's virulent curiosity.

That's what I told myself, but at the same time, I could not tame my own. The more I tried to think honourably, the more questions crowded into my fevered mind – about Max, about Rebecca. What had gone wrong between them, and when and why? What had gone wrong in her head? And why, when she went wrong in her head, had she still been able to write the book we all thought of as her masterpiece?

If I had thought of that book as her masterpiece, what did that say about me?

The same thing, I decided, as it said about anyone who called a new book a masterpiece: that I was inclined to admire works that dignified my prejudices. I had used – we all had used – Max as a scapegoat. That was the shameful conclusion my soul-searching brought me – but, typically, I did not have the courage to come out and say this when I found myself presented as Exhibit A at a dinner party I went to with Mrs Van Hopper in the Clot two nights later.

What was Max like? the hostess asked me after my employer had served her piece of juicy gossip.

A perfectly normal person, I replied. He was a bit prickly perhaps. 'But who wouldn't be with the public so prejudiced against him?'

'Is that what he told you? That the public has misjudged him?'

'No, he didn't,' I said. 'That's the conclusion I've drawn myself.

If anything, he gives too little thought to what other people think. He doesn't protect himself. He lays himself open to criticism.'

'Such as?'

'Well, for example, you should have heard the things Lydia said to him.'

'Oh, it's "Lydia" now, is it?' Mrs Van Hopper said. 'Goodness, how have the meek risen!'

Everyone laughed. I could feel myself flushing.

'As for not caring what people say,' Mrs Van Hopper continued, 'he certainly cared about what *I* said.'

'That's because you mentioned Rebecca.'

'Nonsense, my girl! It's because I dared to suggest there was a part of his life that was not the private property of the old-boy network. They're all alike, these public-school types. They think they own the world. More precisely, they think they can get away with murder.'

This served as a lead-in to a more general discussion about the effect he must have had on Rebecca, and wild surmises on the struggle of wills that had culminated in his victory and, it followed, her suicide. It was a conversation that I would have joined in eagerly only a few days earlier, but now it angered me to hear them blame Max without bothering to base their suspicions on the known facts, and then complain about the other facts he was unjustifiably concealing. What sloppy reasoning! I thought but did not say. What hypocrisy! I was glad when Mrs Van Hopper sent me up to the café for cigarettes.

As I climbed the hill past other candle-lit dinner parties discussing other scandals in other languages, I decided I would apologise to him. If I ever saw him again. If he was still here. He had never said how long he was intending to stay in Deia. For the first time it occurred to me that he might be back in England already. I could see no reason why this possibility should make the slightest difference to me – after all, wouldn't it make life easier if he had left, if there was no longer anyone to worry about bumping into or embarrassing? Yet the thought that he might have left made me gasp out loud, made me feel as if I had walked through a door into a room without a

35

floor. It was only after I had decided that I would write a letter of apology (to what address? was my first panicked thought) care of his publisher that my pulse slowed down.

As I made the final climb to the café, I began to compose the letter. I was into my third imaginary draft when I reached the bar – and there he was, sitting with a large group at the table in the corner. He had a deeper tan than when I last had seen him. He looked relaxed, carefree, even happy. At any rate, he appeared to be enjoying whatever the woman sitting next to him was saying.

It ought not to have mattered that he was talking to a woman, but it did. I felt old because she looked younger than I. Ugly because she was pretty. Fat and clumsy because she was thin, badly dressed because her clothes became her. Every time she smiled, every time she made Max smile, I felt older, fatter, clumsier. As I stood at the bar waiting to catch the bartender's attention, I fought a war with myself. Here was my chance to apologise in person, to prove to myself that I was not the coward I had so far shown myself to be. Here was my chance also to thank him for his kindness. Or: here was another chance for me to make a fool of myself. He was talking to a woman, a woman he appeared to like. Would he want me to barge in and remind him of an episode that was probably nothing to him, nothing but a typical annoyance, the type of annoyance he had to endure twenty times a day? He had probably forgotten all about it by now. By apologising, I might do nothing but embarrass and annoy him again. The best way to repay his kindness might be to leave him alone with this woman.

I bought Mrs Van Hopper her cigarettes. I was on my way out when I heard Max call out my name.

He was right behind me. He had an anxious smile I could not account for. 'Did you get my message?' he asked.

'What message?'

'The one I left for you at the post office.'

'I haven't been to the post office in days,' I said.

'Oh, well, then. That explains it.'

'I'm glad I've found you,' I said, 'because I wanted to apologise.'

'Oh, there's no need for that. I'm only sorry you felt responsible.

Also sorry that you have to work for her. She's horrible. You're a saint. I would have killed her by now. Let me buy you a drink.'

I explained why I couldn't stay.

'Let me drive you,' Max said. 'Then perhaps you can make your excuses and I can drive you back up again.'

First I said no. Then, pressed, I agreed.

'Whose car is it this time?' I asked as he unlocked the door to a Citroën with French plates.

'Don't even ask,' he said. He was about to turn the key in the ignition when he stopped, turned to me and said, 'Actually, if you don't mind, what I'd really like to do is take you out to eat. Outside town.'

'What about your friends?'

'They're not my friends,' he said darkly. 'You have no idea how happy I was to see you. Now direct me to your dinner party.'

We drove down the narrow lane in silence. When he pulled to a stop outside the designated house, he turned around and stared at me. 'Go on then,' he said. He sounded so unfriendly that I almost asked him if he had changed his mind about supper. 'I'll be at the fork in the road if I have to move for someone,' he added.

He was still there when I returned. He coasted down to the fork in the road without turning on the engine. There he stopped and turned to stare at me again. Without warning, he pulled me towards him and gave me a hungry and desperate kiss. 'I was afraid I'd never see you again,' he kept saying in a strangled whisper. 'I was afraid you were avoiding me. I was about to go looking for you. I was sure you weren't coming back.' Then it was over, as abruptly as it had begun.

We drove back into town. Just before we reached the café, he stopped the car, apparently to make way for a group of young Spaniards. But we had stopped at a distance, as if he did not wish the party to see him. We waited until the road was empty again. Then he broke the uncomfortable silence by saying, in a loud, seemingly casual voice, 'I can't tell you the whole story right now, but I'm going to have to pretend I haven't seen someone. I'll keep my eye on the road. You keep me posted.'

And so it began, in the same spirit as it would continue.

Chapter Five

We went to a restaurant in the hills outside Soller. Although he drank too much – we went through a bottle before we even got to the main course – he remained tense. He kept looking at me as if I were an apparition that might disappear at any moment. From time to time he would put his hand on my hand, as if to reassure himself that he hadn't invented it. It had been a long time since anyone had cared whether my hand was real or not. His concern elated me, and his solicitous questions put me off my guard. What a novelty it was to say, 'I'd like red wine,' and then have it in front of me faster than if I had waved a wand; to say, 'Would you mind if we moved to another table? I'm getting height fright,' and find myself instantly with a choice of four other tables. To have him ask for permission before lighting up his after-dinner cigarette, to have him encourage me to finish his crème caramel after I had finished mine . . . The other day I asked him, hadn't he been in agony? He can't drink red wine without inviting a migraine, he has no patience for people with minor phobias, he thinks eating off other people's plates is vulgar, and is not in the habit of asking anyone permission for anything. He gave it more thought than usual and then said no, he hadn't been in agony – 'as strange as that may seem'.

We did not go back to his hotel after supper. We went back to Mrs Van Hopper's – I through the front door and Max (despite the fact that my employer's car was nowhere to be seen) through my bedroom window. This did not strike me as odd, for I thought I knew why he needed privacy. I kept him hidden in my room all night and for the better part of the next day.

Mrs Van Hopper woke up feeling ill and full of self-pity. She had never been considerate of my feelings, so I didn't feel guilty about the fun Max and I had at her expense. She was in the habit of exaggerating her health problems, but she must have been very ill indeed not to notice my barely suppressed smirk, my monosyllabic replies to her questions, the eagerness with which I kept rushing back to my room. I now wonder if it was my inattention that broke the normal rhythm of our conversations, because by late afternoon she had abandoned her usual half-joking abuse and had decided to confide in me. She began telling me about her father, whom she had met only once . . . her mother, who had abandoned her to an aunt who had abandoned her . . . her husband, a good-for-nothing who had died in a car crash . . . her daughter, a disappointment . . . her son, a disgrace . . . her only love affair (with a Presbyterian minister) that didn't last long enough and ended badly. Another day I might have been moved. We might have made friends or at least become allies. But I could hardly sit still. All I could think, as I sat there simulating attention, was how much Max could hear and what he made of it. Did her admissions of weakness make her sound even more vulgar, I wondered? I suppose it was love that did this to me. As he himself is so fond of saying, love means slumming inside someone else's head.

Already, I was throwing my own thoughts away. But perhaps I can be forgiven. I had been alone too long, chilled by the dead too long. I had forgotten what it was like to touch another body, what it was to be caressed. I had a man in my bed, a man who wrapped his legs around me, who pulled my hair away from my face, who kneaded my neck and shoulders and the small of my back, who talked to me, who made me laugh while guessing, always better than I could have done, what I needed next. His clothes remained where he had dropped them the day before. On his trips to the bathroom, he draped himself in a sheet. I remember lying there on the bed, briefly alone, and being inexplicably overjoyed at the disorder, and especially at the sight of his shoes, his huge, ugly, dusty, worn-out canvas shoes peeking from underneath a clothes-strewn wicker chair.

I was suddenly and just as inexplicably happy, even more than happy, to perform the same little chores that once made my life miserable. Things like running to and fro with glasses of water and aspirin and ashtrays and cups of coffee and, as time wore on, bottles of wine, and apologising for forgetting first the sugar, then the sugar spoon, then the corkscrew, then the nuts . . .

'Why don't you take off your clothes and get back into bed?' he kept saying.

And I kept saying, 'But she could call for me at any time.'

To which he said, 'And if she does, you can put your clothes back on, can't you? It's hardly a coat of armour, is it? Come here. There's something I want to do to you.' Although it was an exceptionally warm day, I remember being glad, when I had stepped out of my shift and slipped back between the sheets, that his body was even warmer.

I was very young when I ran off with Sasha, and he was young, too, even though he seemed old to me at the time. So I had never seen an adult mask drop before. I had never suspected that there could be more to a man than the face he offered the world. It was a revelation to see how beautiful Max became when he lost his composure. I remember thinking, oh so stupidly: and to think no one knows!

The long afternoon confession had tired Mrs Van Hopper. She went to bed early and gave me the night off. As soon as she was asleep, I put on a dress I had thought I would never wear again, and then we drove to a restaurant outside town. This one was in Puerto Valldemosa. There was no one we knew there, no one to break the mood. Our luck continued to hold when we went back to Mrs Van Hopper's. Her noisy bedroom fan gave us the privacy we craved for the second night running.

The next morning she sent me to Soller to fill a prescription. Max went with me and talked me into stretching the errand so that we could have lunch at the snail restaurant. That night, after Mrs Van Hopper went to bed, he took me to a bodega in a town in the central plain, not far from Inca. The following morning, I was meant to go to Palma to do some banking, but Max got his hotel to arrange this for us. We spent the day instead on a boat that belonged to 'a friend'. We picked it up in Soller and took it up the coast to a deserted cove, where we lay on the deck drinking warm white wine and picking at the perspiring cheeses and olives we had bought at the Soller market. It was here I had the moment of *déjà vu* that sent me beyond the point of no return.

We had been exchanging confidences in our usual aimless way. I told him of a bad time I had had at school which reminded him of a bad time he had had at school, which reminded me of my first best friend, who was now the world expert on the newt, which reminded him of a friend of his, who was now the world expert on the flea, which led him to say that he was very glad now he hadn't become a botanist, which led me to say how glad I was now that I hadn't ever achieved my childhood ambition of becoming a ballerina with a degree in nursing. I remember he laughed at that one – he did not realise how many more times he would have to endure that same joke. Perhaps he had forgotten, as had I, that even the best storyteller has a limited supply of anecdotes. Or perhaps it was the success of our unspoken agreement. Perhaps he was elated by the ease with which he had been able to describe his past to me, his children, his home life and his work, without once alluding to Rebecca.

He was holding a loaf of bread, as I recall. He was saying, 'You don't mind, do you, if I tear this apart with my hands?' And as I said no, of course not, I looked at him, and I looked at the gnarled, pockmarked rock formations in the cove behind him, and at the red plastic buoy bobbing in the water, and I thought, I have dreamed of this moment, this moment was meant to be. I must have gasped, because Max looked up alarmed, as if he thought I might have been stung by a wasp. Our eyes met, just for a moment. But a moment was enough. Something inside me unlocked. And suddenly I felt as if I were looking at him through my own eyes for the first time. I thought, but did not say, did not think I had to say, because I was confident he could read my mind, 'I give up. I'll give up everything to be with you. Tell me what you want me to do. I'm ready. I'll jump.'

And I was right. He could read my mind. But his response was not quite what I had expected. He sighed, gave me a sorrowful, almost reproachful look, leaned across the deck, put a steadying hand on my shoulder, and said, 'Be careful.'

41

Chapter Six

I didn't listen. I didn't think I needed to. Being careful is my nature. I watch people for a long time before I let myself trust them. I watch them without giving myself away. I'm patient. I dislike direct questions. I prefer to wait until they decide to confide in me. I never presume I'm welcome. I have a horror of imposing my company on others. If I get the slightest sign that I've done so, I back away at once.

Two things happened to disturb the peace the following morning. The first was Mrs Van Hopper's announcement to me at breakfast that she was bored. She had decided she couldn't bear Deia in the middle of the summer any more. She had woken up with 'a yen for Lugano'. Could I contact the following hotels to find out if any of them could accommodate us? 'Ask about their suites. I want Marco to come with us. See if you can get a special rate. Tell them we want something for a month.'

None of the hotels I rang had room for us. When I told Mrs Van Hopper, she said, 'Drat! Well, now I don't know what to do. I am *not* going to Venice at this time of year, no matter what people tell me about the Cipriani. And don't even mention the word Greece. Call them all back and give them our number in case they have a cancellation.'

I did so with dread. I didn't want to go to Lugano. I wanted to tell her I didn't want to go. I wanted to quit then and there, but I didn't dare, because I knew Max was in my bedroom, listening to everything we said. If I quit, he would think I had quit to be with him. And that would be presuming.

He was on edge when I returned to the bedroom with his coffee, accepting the cup as if it were an afterthought. 'So you're off to the Alps, I take it.'

'I tend to doubt it,' I said. 'By this evening she'll have spoken to a friend in Hong Kong who'll have talked her into the Himalayas.'

'Well, if she doesn't, would you be so kind as to hold her here for another forty-eight hours? I may have to do a quick run to London this evening, and there's really no point in my coming back unless you're going to be here.'

I didn't find out until much later that the 'may' was really a 'must'. His holiday was over, his return ticket confirmed: not only was he expected at the office the next day, he was expected home by his children. Because I didn't know this, I misread his sudden shiftiness. No, he said, there was no need for me to smuggle in the phone. He could ring London from the hotel. And no, he didn't need a lift to the hotel. He could use the walk. 'Let's meet at our usual spot at half past twelve.'

He was there, outside the post office, when I pulled up about fifteen minutes late. Poking his head in the window, he said, 'I thought I'd missed you. I only got here a few minutes ago myself. Listen, as it turns out, I do have to go to London, but I should be back here by Thursday noon. I'll ring you when I get to town, or if there's any change in plans. In the meantime, try and see if you can take the weekend off.'

A second car, driven by the man everyone said talked too much about Wittgenstein, pulled up in front of the post office. Max waved at it with a smile I already could read as scarcely concealed panic. 'That's my lift,' he said. 'I have to go.' It was only after they had driven off that I realised he had not told me where I could reach him.

And so I was dismayed to return to Mrs Van Hopper to discover that she was refusing to let go of the Lugano plan. She had put Marco on the job, and in my absence he had arranged what he called a 'package' – ten days in a hotel outside the city, fifteen in 'that grand one smack on the waterfront', followed by a further fifteen in 'the villa to end all villas'. We were to leave on Saturday. I was to begin packing at once.

I tried to talk her out of it, suggested that she go on ahead with Marco while I stayed behind to close the house. But she wasn't having any of it, and the more time that passed without Max getting in touch, the more I wondered if he would ever do so.

I waited until Friday afternoon and then I went to La Residencia to leave him a note.

'Wouldn't you rather speak to him?' the receptionist said. 'He's having drinks next to the pool.' A quick glance at her watch and she added, 'Unless they've gone back to the room. Let me try him there for you.' She punched out a number on her phone. 'Mr Midwinter? Someone here for you.' She handed me the receiver.

My hello, when it came, was almost inaudible. It was met with silence, and then a long sigh. 'You'd better come up.'

A woman I had never seen before met me at the door. Blonde, about my age, with sharp features but very pretty, dressed in leggings, high-heeled sandals and a V-necked black gauze see-through top. She was excessively friendly, with a man's handshake and a boy's laugh. 'Anna,' she said. 'Glad to meet you.' She led me through a room strewn with women's clothes to the balcony, where Max awaited me.

He looked wan despite his tan, and dressed in a T-shirt and shorts that had been washed but not ironed. There were rings under his eyes, and his lips were set into a thin grimace. There was a cold ring to his voice when he said hello.

'So,' said Anna, 'here we all are, and perfect timing, too. Would you say we're ready to fax?'

'Please do. I hope I never have to see it again,' said Max.

Anna said, 'I know. I don't know why I thought it would be easier to do by the pool. What a day!' She went over to the refrigerator and brought out a jug of what turned out to be Buck's fizz. Chattering away, she poured out three glasses. Everything she said felt like a nail in my coffin.

So I'd been here two months had I? How, she wanted to know, could I take the heat? Max had told her that I had published a book. What was its name? She was sure she had heard something good about it. Had I ever done journalism? No. Spent any time with journalists? No. Oh, my dear me, then, she said, let me warn you about our friend here, the original Big Bad Wolf. 'Have I said the wrong thing? Sorry, Max! Didn't mean to! Listen, I'm going off to make myself scarce in a bubble bath or something.'

Off she went with the rest of the Buck's fizz.

'Don't look so upset,' Max said. 'She's just a friend.'

Then he gestured at the women's clothes that were strewn everywhere. He cleared his throat. 'The owner of these, on the other hand, is not a friend. I'm afraid she's been rather difficult.'

He gave me a strange smile, as if to say, 'What did you expect?'

'Her name, as you may already know, is Bunny. You may have seen her around,' he continued. He spoke as if he had to pull the words out like teeth. He had seen, perhaps, that my eyes were on a familiar hat, the blue hat I had seen on the woman with the slightly popping eyes at Gregory's party. 'I've done my best to keep old Buns from making life unpleasant for you, but if she has, I apologise.'

He paused, as if he expected me to say something. When I didn't, he said, 'You mustn't get the wrong idea. I made it clear to her, when she asked to come down here with me, that we weren't going to be travelling together as a couple. You see, we never have been a couple. We just had an arrangement. An arrangement for sex, which was all either of us wanted. Or, I suppose I should say, all I wanted and all she said she wanted. She's in love with a doctor, married, lives in Edinburgh. She works at the paper, gets lonely, needs company without attachment. And so that's how it's been. Every few months or so, we've availed ourselves of each other.'

He downed the rest of his drink. 'All she ever asked of me was that I tell her about any others. Last week, I didn't, and that was when the trouble began.'

'I saw her looking upset at the *cala*,' I said, 'but that was the day after I met you.'

'She wasn't upset about you. She was upset about someone else.'

I tried not to show how deep those words slashed into me. 'Who?' I asked.

'Not anyone you know, although you may have seen her. A Spanish girl. Very pretty, but also very young and rather indiscreet.'

'So you weren't just sleeping with your roommate, you were also sleeping with this other one?'

'Do you want to know the truth?' he asked.

'Yes.'

'There were two others. There was the Spanish girl, and there was Clarissa.'

'Clarissa?'

'Yes, Clarissa,' he said, lighting up a cigarette. 'You remember her, don't you? I was sitting with her that night you came into the café. She's my cousin.' He took a long drag. 'Not that it meant anything in the least, but one night last week, when I was trying to avoid the other two, I spent the night with her. Which was fine. It happens from time to time. It's affection more than anything else, it's for old times' sake. Unfortunately, you can't do anything in this place without everyone finding out about it.' He threw me a glance.

'How are you taking all this?' he asked. 'Have you had enough?'

Without looking him in the eye, I shook my head. I didn't dare speak. I was afraid that if I moved my mouth, I would begin to cry.

'Then you might as well know the rest,' he said, his voice growing louder and harder. 'This Anna you just met. We're just friends, but we did have sex last night. We arrived yesterday evening.'

'Why?' I asked.

'The sex because – well, you saw her. It ought to be obvious. The change of plans – well, I wanted her to see you. I wanted the opinion of someone I trust. You can understand that, can't you?'

He was shouting now. I lowered my head so that he couldn't see the tears in my eyes. 'I'm sorry,' he said softly. 'I wanted to sort it out without involving you.' He tried to take my hand, but I pulled it away. 'For God's sake, you must see I was trying to extricate myself. You should be happy!'

His words broke over me like a wave. Without thinking, I shrieked, 'I'll be damned if I'll let someone like you tell me when to be happy!' I tried to push past him and make for the door.

He stopped me, putting his hands on my shoulders. 'Look at me,' he said. 'Look me straight in the eye.'

Against my better judgement, I looked him straight in the eye.
'I love you,' he said.
'That's just another way of saying you're a liar!'
'I don't say things I don't mean. I love you, but before we take this any further, you must understand who I am.'
'Then who are you?' I wailed.
He pulled me towards him and kissed me hungrily, jamming his tongue in, biting my lips. Pulling back, he said, 'A womaniser. I'm a womaniser! For God's sake, it's hardly a secret! Don't you ever read the papers?'
He kissed me again. When I tried to pull away, he pushed me onto the bed. 'Look at me,' he said, his face so close that I could hardly see it. 'It's the truth. It's not something I'm proud of, but I'm not going to pretend, especially not to you. You must understand this about me. I fuck lots of women. I'm weak. I have a hard time saying no. And I get a lot of offers. I shouldn't have to tell you why. It's sick, but it's obvious. And I've played into it. Willingly. Happily, even! I like the chase! If you can't accept this about me, you'd better go.' He took his arms off me and sat up. 'I'm serious. Go. Just go.'
I didn't move.
'I'm a womaniser,' he said, and it seemed to me he relished the word.
'That's just not true!' I cried. I ought to have said, I don't want it to be true. 'All you're doing is living up to people's expectations! Why do you have to degrade yourself like that? You're capable of better!'
He let out a whimper as if I had hit him, buried his head in his hands, wouldn't budge when I put my arms around him, and then, abruptly, changed his mind. I kissed him, he kissed me back. I bit his lip. He bit my ear, my neck, my chest. I pulled his shirt apart, and as he tore mine off and rolled me back onto the bed, he whispered, 'Then help me, help me, help me. I can't bear it any longer. Help me out of this crypt. I want a different life!'
And so did I, but as I lay there next to him in the early hours of the morning, watching him sleep (how innocent he looked!

how beautiful! how gentle!), I couldn't bear it. I couldn't bear his not being the man I wanted him to be. I couldn't bear his cruel truthfulness. I couldn't bear the thought of other women's hands on him, and even less could I bear the thought of his hands on them, but most of all, I couldn't bear not being able to bear it. I didn't want to need someone. I didn't want to go through life with one half of my mind wondering where its other half was. To feel lonely when I was alone, to feel incomplete unless I was touched, held, accompanied, protected . . . I didn't want to be in a cage. I didn't want to be in love.

And so I extricated myself, without much difficulty. When I removed myself from his embrace, he reached out for the pillow and, mistaking it for me, drew it closer. I put on my clothes, did a makeshift repair on my blouse, and set out for the point and Mrs Van Hopper's villa. When I got there – I don't know if it was out of habit or to cancel out the memory – I went in through my bedroom window. I put on my robe, went into the bathroom, drew myself a hot bath and sat in it until the water was almost cold.

My bags were packed and next to the door by the time Mrs Van Hopper's alarm went off. Marco arrived at seven and closed the shutters while I washed and dried the breakfast dishes. We were on our way to the airport by half past. When we drove past La Residencia, I looked the other way.

Our plane was due to take off at eleven in the morning. We went through to the transit lounge just after ten. I left Marco and Mrs Van Hopper in the bar and went to buy a *Herald Tribune*. I returned to find them pulling up a chair for Max.

They were in shock. Pleasantly so, but still in shock. 'Oh no, of course not,' Mrs Van Hopper was saying to him. 'Please, don't apologise. We understand completely. No, it doesn't sound at all insane. It sounds romantic!'

'And here she is!' Marco now cried. He and Mrs Van Hopper looked up and beamed at me.

'Goodness, you silly thing!' said Mrs Van Hopper. 'You might have told me. At the very least, you might have given me a little hint.'

Max turned to me. 'I'm sorry about this, but under the circumstances, I didn't see what else I could do. I've explained to them that I came out here to propose to you.' He gave me a cold stare. 'I know it's abrupt, but I don't believe that vacillating has ever done me or anyone else much good in such circumstances. All I can say is that if you come to London with me this morning, and then change your mind later, I'll still look after you.' Then, in a gentler voice, he added, 'I'll . . . make sure you're all right.'

'But I can't go to London with you this morning. I'm flying to Milan. And so is my luggage.'

'Don't worry about details,' said Max. 'If you want to come with me, then I can arrange it.'

And so he did. Half an hour later Max and I were waiting for takeoff, sitting in first class even though we had economy tickets. 'I didn't ask for them, and I didn't tell any lies,' Max insisted. 'I just told them that I work for a newspaper and have very long legs.'

We were not going straight to London, as it turned out, but stopping off for a night in Paris. It was, he explained in a matter-of-fact voice, the best he could do at such short notice in the way of a honeymoon. 'We'll do the real thing after the real marriage.' He might as well have been discussing a trip to the supermarket. But when the plane taxied down the runway, he reached for my hand and squeezed it tight. When we took off, he took in a deep breath and did not exhale until the no-smoking light went off. He took out a cigarette and his lighter but his hands were so shaky he couldn't light it. That was when he caved in.

'I'm sorry,' he sobbed, as he accepted my tissue, 'but that was hard. It's not the way I planned it, and neither is this – but there you are.' He pulled his briefcase out from underneath the seat, rummaged in it, brought out a box and offered it to me. It contained a diamond ring. 'It was my mother's,' he explained. 'I picked it up when I went home last Wednesday. You don't have to wear it.'

But I did, even though it was tight on my finger. 'Don't worry. We'll get it fixed in Oxford.' As he began to talk plans – where we would go for the night in Paris, why we had to leave so early for London the next day – his voice began to steady. He brought

49

out the map to show me where he lived, where *we* would live. I looked at the names of villages – Stanton St John, Islip, Marston, Kidlington, Wolvercote, Beckfield – and that was when it hit me. I was going to Beckfield. I was going to be living there, not as some shadowy retainer but as Max's fiancée and eventually as his wife. Max had rescued me from limbo. The army of ifs had evaporated. My road was mapped, my future waiting at the end of it.

I could see the road. I could see the emerald trees hanging over the curve in the half distance, I could see the stone houses that came into view as I hurtled round it. I could smell the warm rain. I was in a car full of children – his children and our children. I could hear them chattering behind me in the back seat. I could feel the warmth of the home standing ready for us. All I had to do was close my eyes and I could see it, down to the smallest detail. Not once during the next twenty-four hours did it occur to me why.

I had never felt safer or more certain than I did during that flying visit to Paris. When Max directed the taxi to stop in front of a nondescript green door, I knew even before I pushed it open that our hotel would be a mansion in a garden, and that our room would be in the back, giving out into the garden through French doors. I recognised the restaurant where he took me to eat, even though I had never been to it before. I could taste the food before we had picked up the menus. And when we got back to our room, before we had taken off our clothes, I could feel the sheets tangled and twisted around us. When the morning came, the sun didn't rise, it unfolded. Breakfast, porter, taxi, airport, plane, they all arrived on silent runners. It was only later, when we were coming in for landing at Heathrow, coasting over the green fields west of Windsor, that Mrs Van Hopper's last words came back to me.

It was after all the arrangements had been made. We still had time to kill before flying off to our separate destinations. I had offered, as a last act of apology, to take her and her wheelchair through the duty-free shop. As we were waiting at the till with her two bottles of Poire William, she looked up at me and said, 'Well, well, well. Who would have thought how very, *very* much stranger life is than fiction? And who would have thought it, that I would be the instrument by which Max Midwinter found a replacement for his Rebecca? I can't *wait* to tell my friends. Well, my dear, I hope you find it interesting, to borrow a concept from the Chinese, because you certainly won't find any happiness. Not with that lot. No, my dear. You're just not special enough. You'll never live her down, even if you kill yourself trying.'

II

Chattering Classes

Chapter Seven

We parted company outside passport control, he to pass quickly through the EC channel, and I to wait to go through the one marked 'Other' with a long queue of prospective immigrants. When my turn came about, I almost made the mistake of saying that I had come to England to get married. But then, just in time, when I saw the customs officer's appraising eyes, I realised the trouble the truth would cause, and so I lied and said the purpose of my visit was pleasure.

Max was waiting for me on the other side of the barrier. His smile was strained – as mine would have been, I'm sure, had I known what lay ahead. 'Your luggage has arrived from Milan and is waiting for us at the desk,' he told me. He put his arm around me and led me to the escalator. 'You look tired,' he said. 'Try and get some sleep before we get to Oxford. You'll need it.'

A tidy, grey-haired man was waiting for us outside customs. Although it was August, he was wearing a coat. He called me 'miss' and Max 'sir', made the usual enquiries about the flight, and appeared to be delighted that it had been smooth.

'I hope you don't mind, sir, but I've left the car in the short-term car park.'

'You didn't have to go to all that trouble. We could have found you outside,' Max said.

'Well, sir, under normal circumstances I would have done so. But . . .' He let the sentence hang portentously and gave Max a meaningful stare. Max responded with a blank one. 'It won't take me five minutes, sir. Five minutes and I shall be waiting under the Courtesy Limousine sign.'

'That's fine,' Max said briskly. 'That will give me time to cash a cheque.'

'At Thomas Cook's, sir?'

'Yes, if it's open,' Max said.

'I hope you don't mind my intruding, sir, but under the circumstances I would advise waiting. What I mean to say, sir, is that you'll want to give W. H. Smith a wide berth.'

'Aha,' said Max. 'Yes, I follow you. Thanks.' He pulled out his wallet and counted his cash. 'I suppose I can wait until tomorrow anyway.'

'Right-o, then,' said the man, and he hurried off.

'I'm awfully sorry about this,' Max said as we headed towards the door. 'This was my aunt Bea's idea. If it had been up to me, we would have taken the bus. But she wanted us there in time for lunch. You see, it's my uncle's birthday.'

'Is this their chauffeur?' I asked.

'No, it's a company. Bea uses it for airports and dinner parties in London. There are three drivers, and we all rather dread getting this one because he was at Cambridge with my uncle.'

'What's so bad about that?'

'It's rather obvious, isn't it?'

As we went through the doors, we were hit by a blast of cold, damp air. 'Any opportunity to put the knife in, he'll take it,' Max continued. 'He specialises in the Significant Look, as you may have noticed. That heavy hint about W. H. Smith, for example. That means there's something about me on the front page of one of the papers. He's pretending to be shocked and disapproving, but he's dying to talk to me about it. In front of you, if at all possible.'

'What could it be about?'

'I'm quite sure I know. This is not the right time to talk about it. Best, in any case, to let me handle it for the time being. You have enough on your plate today already.'

He took my hand. It was shaking. 'Don't be nervous,' he said. 'You don't have to perform for them. All you have to do is be yourself.'

'I'm not nervous, I'm cold.'

'There's bound to be a travel rug in the back seat. Why don't you stretch out and shut your eyes? I'll keep the old bugger happy by sitting in the front.'

I fell asleep before we reached the motorway. When I awoke, I had no idea where I was, how I had come to be in this limousine, or who the two men were conferring sotto voce on the other side of the partition. My first thought, probably due to the conspiratorial tone they took in order to conceal their mutual contempt, was that they were abducting me, and the suspicion remained even after I had recovered my bearings. This was the man I had agreed to marry. I had agreed to marry a man I could not recognise by the back of his head.

I could not recognise him by the back of his head, but I recognised his cottage the moment we pulled up in front of it. There it was, a long stone thatched cottage running perpendicular to the road, with a walled garden on the far side, a wooden fence on the near side joining it with another thatched cottage covered with ivy. There was the communal lawn. There, beyond the lawn, was the tennis court, and beyond the tennis court, the wall, and in the wall, the green gate leading to the manor house where his aunt lived. I recognised it and I was afraid of it, but I couldn't understand why. It wasn't until Max led me down the path through the emerald lawn towards the tall grey manor, and up past the bronze lions that stood to either side of the front door, that I realised what the problem was. I was afraid of my new life because of the way Rebecca had described it.

I was walking into the first scene of *The Marriage Hearse*. The gothic scene where the heroine makes her first disastrous visit to her husband's family – making scores of *faux pas* no one has the mercy to correct. There was the grand piano that they lured her to, there were the peacock feathers with 'pedigree', there, on the side table, was the guest book that contained the inscription that had become the family joke, and there in the alcove, above the fireplace, was the mantelpiece covered with large, gilt-lettered invitations that she had picked up to examine with such unguarded enthusiasm. And there, standing under the arch and exclaiming, 'Oh, how wonderful, you've made it!' was the charming, two-faced aunt.

She looked exactly as Rebecca had described her: a pretty face that acted as a foil for her sharp, mischievous grey eyes; a rounded but trim figure, wearing a shift made from African material; straight shoulder-length white hair that looked too good to be true and gave her the air of a girl playing an adult in a school play. As she made her way across the room, her rich, loud but beautifully modulated voice preceded her. 'It's so nice to meet you. I am sorry to have dragged you back from Paris. It was frightfully selfish of me, but I did want to be the first to meet you.'

She kissed me on one cheek and then she stood back to survey me like a painting. 'Oh, well done, Max. Well done.'

I knew better than to believe her.

She took me by the hand, grasping it rather more tightly than was necessary, and led me into the sitting room to a row of curious eyes and anxious smiles that ought to have been new to me. Except that I knew them – not from photographs but from Rebecca's fictitious versions of them in *The Marriage Hearse*. There was Giles, who was Max's uncle and Bea's second husband and the saviour of the family name and fortunes. He was leaning on his cane and containing the pain that he was too well brought up to express. There, huddled next to him, with their hands in supplicating poses and their heads half bowed as if to ward off adult attention, were William and Hermione, Max's children. And there, sitting next to them, was a narrow-shouldered, wiry, ginger-haired woman with large cornflower eyes. This was Danny, who was distantly related to both sides of Max's family. She was the woman who had first introduced him to Rebecca, and who now looked after her papers as well as her children. It became apparent, from the way she jumped up and threw her arms around Max, that this was not all she had been looking after.

Or trying to look after. He did not return her effusive greeting but moved on to his children, who pulled him down on the settee and crowded onto his lap. Unfazed, she sat down next to them and put her arm around him. 'Don't be such a selfish sausage, I'm a human being too,' she said. Then she fixed her large cornflower eyes on me and smiled and said, 'Welcome to Manderley.'

58

Chapter Eight

I wasn't going to let Rebecca do my thinking for me. She had been wrong about Max. She was probably wrong about everything else. She had twisted things to fit her script, but now she was dead. This was not her life I was entering. It was mine.

This was not the first scene in *The Marriage Hearse*. And the Danny who was now bringing the children over to me was not the crazed, possessive fiend I had read about. Her smile was kind; her effort to make me feel at home genuine. It was the children who would not cooperate – the boy by refusing to look me in the eye even when we were shaking hands, the girl by fixing me with a stare worthy of Medusa. Danny talked over their silence and passed them back to their father's care when I failed to come up with a way to engage them.

I caught Max's eye, tried to indicate to him that I had run into trouble, tried to indicate to him also that I had taken it in my stride. He returned my meaningful look with a blank one, as if to say, not now when there are so many people watching. This brought me up short – it was just the type of thing the husband in the book would do. But I would not let my mind travel any further in that direction. I was not Rebecca. Nor was I the heroine of her book. I might be American, but I had lived in England before. Not for long, and never in such high places, but I knew better than to play 'Chopsticks' on the piano for strangers, or lecture dinner guests on the gender issues of peahens, or pick up someone else's invitations and marvel over the number and variety of titles. Yes, I was on display now, but that was natural, that would happen anywhere, to any woman being introduced at such short notice into her new family. I had got off to a bad start, but at least I knew it.

It would have been better if I had known not to sit on a wig

59

stand. But as I said to Bea, that was the problem: I wasn't thinking. I was flustered, meeting so many new people at the same time.

'It doesn't matter, darling,' Bea insisted. 'Truly it doesn't. It was just a silly old wig stand. I'm sure it can be fixed.'

I wasn't convinced, but I didn't press it. I needed her loud, cheerful voice to shelter me from Max and his children. I needed her to fill in the gaps of my faltering conversations with the loose collection of carelessly beautiful and, to me, interchangeable daughters and cousins and cousins' friends and spouses who had filtered into the room after us, all holding their empty fluted champagne glasses as gingerly as if they were filled to the brim. They didn't seem to know how to treat me. The questions they would have liked to ask – Who are you? What are you doing here? What could Max be thinking by bringing you here? – were so large as to make small talk impossible.

So I was grateful for the better-than-life version she served up for them. 'You don't mind if I tell them, darling, do you? It's too romantic. Truly it is. It could only happen to our Max. He'd gone down to Mallorca for Gregory's birthday party, which was the usual disaster, with all the most boring people you can think of, lots of academics from Nebraska and boring TV personalities with toupés and false teeth sipping low-alcohol sangria, and Lydia's version of *nouvelle cuisine* – pork crackling wrapped up in violets, and those empty vols-au-vents she does, decorated with strands of saffron around the edges so that they look like sea anemones, and those horrid pastry things you expect to be pigs in blankets only to find grapes inside instead of sausages . . . Great chef that she is, she always makes sure that you get them piping hot. There was poor old Max, with the roof of his mouth lacerated from one of Lydia's *cochons en croute*, so when he heard a cry coming from one of the upper windows, his first thought was that someone else had sustained a third-degree burn from the hors d'oeuvres . . . He decided to check upstairs just in case, as the sound appeared to be coming from Gregory's room – and he walked in to find the wicked old wolf about to put his fangs into his lovely young nurse! Naturally, he threw Gregory aside and picked up the nurse in his arms, and just as naturally – don't you think? – the nurse fainted, and so he rushed off downstairs with her, and when her eyes fluttered open, they took one look at each other and fell madly in love. And I think it's rather wonderful, don't you, that she turned out not to be a nurse in distress at all, but a writer in distress. A rather good writer in distress – there's her latest collection of stories over there, propped up against Queen Mary. They're a bit above me, I'm afraid. They do all sorts of things like interconnect.'

She pretended to be equally intimidated by the accomplishments of her other guests. The obituary one of them – which one of them? – had written about Cousin Beryl had been 'gloriously tactful, I don't know how you did it', while the notice another had received for his fringe production of *Hamlet* had been splendid, 'although I don't know what I think about the word "fringe" – I'm sure I was expecting all the actors to be wearing women's wigs'. As she threw out her words of encouragement like so many bouquets, it was never clear to me which member of her audience was the musician who was hoping to play later that month at Bayreuth, or which one was 'truly fortunate' to have missed out on the lead in 'that play about that ridiculous woman psychiatrist who had that dippy theory about breasts', or which had been a saint at the funeral of someone who was a household name to everyone but me.

'I hope we're not being too boring for you,' she said to me as she took me by the arm into the dining room. 'You and Max must be dreadfully tired, you must be longing to get back to the cottage. How's your leg?' she asked, but I faltered – thrown by my first sight of the dining room, which, with its stern portraits and its transparent pyramid centrepiece, was, like all the other rooms that Rebecca had used as grist in *The Marriage Hearse*, so familiar and yet at the same time so strange. And so I missed my cue. Unfazed, Bea sailed on, helping everyone else with their missed cues, seating her guests and directing the butler while she continued her bright chattering.

She put me between her husband Giles and a sombre man with long eyelashes who sat with his head cocked to one side like a bird, and whose face brightened like a child's when he smiled, which was not very often. I got off on the wrong foot with him by mistaking him for the obituarist. He explained that the obituarist was Bella, 'the dark-haired girl next to Sebastian'. He was a pianist, he said. And he was planning to play at Bayreuth? 'No, actually, I rather doubt it. You must be mixing me up with Dan,' he said, and sank into what I would later learn was called a deep gloom.

The blonde girl sitting on his right then claimed his attention. I was left to my own devices just long enough to serve myself. Then, as soon as the butler had moved on, Giles extricated himself from his other dinner partner with an emphatic 'Yes, that would be lovely' and directed his gentle beam at me. He asked me easy, general questions about Paris. Had the weather been fine? Had we had good luck with the museums or had we arrived too late? Had I managed to reconcile myself to the Pompidou Centre? Had we had time to fit in a quick look at the Louvre pyramid? August was such a tricky time for food in Paris – had we managed to find anything open? Had Max looked up his godfather? No? Well, that was understandable, he was rather a bore, and he lived in the sixteenth. Was there any literary community to speak of in the Latin Quarter any more, or was it just a fiction propagated by wishful foreigners? Slowly and gently, he led the questions around to my own writing. Had I been pleased with the reception of my first book? How was work progressing with my new one? Was I the type of writer who liked to discuss work in progress, or did I prefer to let the works speak for themselves?

'I have no idea if they can speak for themselves,' I said. 'I'm afraid I don't have a very high opinion of my talent.'

Giles responded with a soft laugh. 'That sounds very healthy. And all too rare! I'm sure most of your peers could stand to learn from you.'

'Oh, I doubt it,' I said. 'My opinion of my abilities may be low, but it probably should be even lower. I can't imagine what Max sees in me.' I realised too late that the entire table was listening to me.

Mortified, I looked down at my fork, which was, I realised, in what the other guests would think of as the wrong hand. I put it down on the plate too swiftly, and it made a clatter that startled the long-lashed man on my right out of his deep gloom. Across the table, another young man cleared his throat. It was Max who broke the silence by asking if anyone at the table knew when Bertie was due back from Antarctica. Grateful for his intervention, I tried to follow the ensuing conversation, but because I didn't know who Bertie was, I quickly became lost.

The butler came and removed the plates. Pudding came and went without my daring to accept anything that might involve my using a utensil the wrong way. I made a few more attempts at conversation but was left each time with a vague feeling of failure. My confidence fell even further when we were invited to take our coffees into the garden to enjoy the sun that had just broken through the clouds and was likely to disappear again shortly. Finding myself next to the person I thought was Bella the obituarist, and hearing her discussing what seemed to be a recent scandal at a newspaper, I asked her, just for the sake of discussion, if it was legally possible in Britain to speak ill of the dead. Her response was a gasp.

'Who wants to know?' asked the burly young man sitting next to her as he grabbed her arm. He had a different accent from the rest; I did not know where it was from or what it signified. He leaned over and took hold of my collar. 'Who wants to know?'

'I do,' was my reply.

'I don't believe you for a minute,' he retorted. 'Someone put you up to this, and you'd better tell me who it is.'

'Oh, don't be a bore, Wayne,' said another young man. 'She has no idea what you're talking about. Leave her alone.'

Wayne, the burly young man, jumped to his feet. The girl I had mistaken for Bella the obituarist tried to pull him down again, saying, 'Please, darling. Let's just drop it. It doesn't matter one way or the other. You know it doesn't.'

But he wouldn't listen. As he brushed the grass off his clothes, he said to her, 'This is the last time I am going to let your toffy parents impugn my work ethic.' He marched off into the house, while the girl who was not Bella ran after him pleading.

I looked around at the other strange faces in my circle. 'What did I say to upset him so much?' I asked no one in particular, sending them all into a communal blush. They averted their eyes to stare at the grass. I lifted mine just in time to see the burly young man walk up to the bench where Max was seated with his children.

The burly man spat out an angry tirade which he punctuated by pushing a forefinger into Max's chest. When he did this, Max grabbed his arm. He stood up, towering over the man. Blanched with anger, Max said in a voice loud enough for us all to hear, 'Then I suggest we go and ask him.'

'Fine. Let's go,' said the burly man. The two went inside, crossing with an alarmed-looking Danny at the French doors. Max nodded in the direction of the children. Danny gave a half nod back and bounded across the lawn to them.

'Time for our walk,' she announced brightly.

'Can we take bread for the ducks?' asked the boy.

'You might just find that I've already thought of that,' said Danny. 'Check my pockets.'

As she led them down the garden, the raised voices emerged from the sitting room. Now it was Giles's steady monotone – dignified, conciliatory but firm. Now it was the angry man demanding an apology. Now it was Max's loud, short and sharp retort, followed by a high-pitched reproach from the woman who was not Bella. The angry man interrupted her. There was a sound of moving furniture, a slam of a door, and operatic screaming from not-Bella. Around the front of the house, a car started up, reversed at high speed and headed at even higher speed down the drive, while in the sitting room, not-Bella burst into tears, screaming, 'How could you do such a thing to me? How could you even suggest it? *What a bloody cheek!*'

Meanwhile, out in the garden, we sat like statues on the grass. One young man made a noble effort to redirect our attention to the bench where Max had been sitting with the children. Did we not think that it was a lovely colour? What was it really – Dutch blue? Azure? Aquamarine? Didn't we agree that it was the same colour as that bench next to the folly at Something House? His voice tailed off into mute dismay when a haggard-looking Bea came out through the French doors and dropped herself on the bench we were discussing. Two girls in our group ran up to her. One put a consoling arm around her. The other ran into the sitting room, from which hysterical crying was still emerging. I was left with the long-lashed, and now gloomier than ever, pianist from lunch, and the musician I assumed was the Dan who would be playing at Bayreuth later in the month – though I did not dare ask.

A glass shattered. Both men startled at the sound. They lifted their eyes to look at me, then looked down again. The one I assumed was Dan cleared his throat, as if to say it was up to me to come up with a conversational opening. I scoured my mind for a suitable topic. Something musical, I said to myself. Something musical . . .

'Have you ever been to Valldemosa?' I asked. It was a reckless question, as I myself had only ever driven past it. Fortunately, neither of the men seemed to have heard of it. So I was able to explain. 'It's in Mallorca, just down the road from Deia, which is where I was living. It's where whatshisname, it's just slipped my mind now, I don't know why . . . it's where that famous composer ran off with Georges Sand . . . It's on the tip of my tongue. You must know who I mean, it begins with C.'

The long-lashed man sighed, then lifted himself laboriously up off the grass but not out of his gloom. 'I take your point,' he said mysteriously. 'And I think it's an excellent idea.' He turned to the man that was possibly Dan and said, 'If you'll excuse me, I think the time has come for Chopin to come to the rescue.'

Off he went in the direction of the sitting room.

'I'd try a different way in if I were you,' shouted the man who could be Dan. The long-lashed pianist stopped for a moment, then nodded and headed round to the front of the manor. A few moments later, the crying and shouting from the sitting room was drowned out by a crashing sonata from the grand piano.

The first to register the change was could-be Dan. He heaved a great sigh and said, 'That's a bit better. And about time, too.' He stood up, stretched his arms and legs, and headed across the lawn to speak to Bea and the young woman consoling her. Their conversation started out looking serious and concerned but slowly grew more light-hearted. Meanwhile, the other little groups on the lawn defrosted just as ours had. Daughters, cousins and friends began to intermingle again – and took turns going into the sitting room to contribute to the argument, which played itself out like a silent movie on a crank, first frenzied, then dull and mechanical, and finally with the limpness of spent passion as the piano player followed Chopin to ever greater heights.

After about ten minutes, the music stopped. The sound of swearing floated over the lawn from the direction of the courtyard, followed by the sound of a car trying to reverse out of mud. Everyone froze, but then the piano started up again. The performance resumed.

Chapter Nine

'You poor thing,' Bea said as she took my arm and led me into the kitchen. 'You must be so tired! What a gruelling afternoon!'

The daughters, cousins and cousins' friends had all left now. The cook and the butler were drying glasses at one end of the long wooden table while at the other end sat the two children. William, the boy, was kicking an unlaced shoe against one of the table legs as he took obedient but unenthusiastic nibbles out of a scone. His sister, Hermione, was drawing fingernail sketches on the side of a large, frosted jug of orange squash. When Bea reached across her plate to retrieve a key from a hook, the girl looked up at her great-aunt dismissively, as if she were a salesman who had arrived without an appointment.

Bea gave her a sharp look but said nothing. Instead she put on a pair of reading glasses, retrieved a notebook and a pencil from the basket on the sideboard, and began to tick off items on a list. 'I've bought you a few basic supplies,' she said to me as she flitted about filling the basket with bread and milk and butter and orange juice and instant coffee. 'We can see to the rest tomorrow. Would you be a dear, Hermione, and run upstairs for your knapsacks?'

'Why?' Hermione asked.

'Because I'm taking you back to the cottage.'

'Why can't Daddy take us?'

'Daddy has to speak to someone rather important on the phone.'

Hermione made a face as she rose slowly from her chair.

'Don't be greedy. He won't be long. Let's see if we can have the cottage all nice and airy for him by the time he arrives. Shall we give it a try?' Hermione gave the question some thought, then nodded severely. 'Off with you, then,' Bea said. She propelled Hermione upstairs with a firm, friendly push.

A few minutes later we were heading down the path to the cottage with our baskets, knapsacks and suitcases.

'Janet's been in a few times,' Bea told me as she turned the key in the lock of the low green wooden door. Although I had no idea who Janet was, I nodded. 'But I haven't been in to check things since she left on holiday,' she went on. 'So I'm afraid you may be knee-high in dust.' She pushed against the door. It would only open a quarter of the way. Bea peered in. 'Hmm,' she said. 'Newspapers, and rather a lot of them.' She turned to me. 'As you're so much thinner than I am, would you mind awfully squeezing in and moving them for us?' I was halfway in when she added, 'And if you want to be an absolute dear, would you mind putting them well out of harm's way?' As I gathered the half-dozen or so newspapers into a neat pile, I noticed photographs of Max on two or three of them. Bea poked her head in. 'Under the stairs would be fine for the time being.' Her voice was loud and confident, but her eyes were anxious. 'That's super,' she said in an even louder voice when I had done as she had asked. She swung open the door. 'Now we have plenty of room. Could you be a poppet, William, and hand me that case?'

I have tried many times to remember how that cottage looked to me on the first evening – whether I was struck first by its strange layout or by the rich green light coming in on all sides through its many doors and windows. Whether it was the damp that struck me first, or the lowness of the ceilings, or the smallness of the primitive kitchen, or the rows and rows of built-in bookshelves, or the jumble of old children's shoes and muddy boots piled up under the coat rack in the entryway. All I do remember when I retrace my steps is Bea's voice as she took me on her guided tour of practicalities. Here was the unspeakable kitchen – she didn't know why Max put up with it. This was the cooker that worked, and this was the cooker that did not work but that Max used as a counter. Here was where he kept the plates, there were the saucepans, there, in the far corner, was the mouse's entrance. 'I've tried to do something about it, but he won't hear of it. Perhaps you can use your magic to convince him otherwise.' Had I noticed that there was something rather important missing? Yes, she said without waiting for my reply, I had noted the absence of a refrigerator. I would find it next door in the utility room, underneath the new washer-dryer. ('I call it the wrinkle-dryer, because that's all it does.')

'I do hope Max will give you a free hand with the cottage. It would be such fun to do it up.' As she took me from room to room, throwing open doors and windows, and emptying wastebaskets, she pointed out the things she said she was longing to get her hands on. This included just about every piece of furniture in Max's large bedroom-cum-study except the velvet armchairs that sat on either side of the fireplace. What Bea hated the most, she told me, was his 'post-hippie bed'. It was a seven-foot-square mattress draped unevenly over a five- by six-foot set of springs, covered with a purple quilt that clashed with the red calico curtains that ended half a foot short of the windowsills. 'Although I do like the idea of a large working fireplace. Pity we can't seem to stop it from smoking. And the parquet floor is lovely, but –' she tapped the place where it was buckling – 'I am somewhat troubled by this tree root.'

The armchairs needed covers put on them, 'because actually they're very valuable' and so did just about everything in the sitting room. 'But first things first.' She turned to William and Hermione, who had been tailing us with sullen curiosity. 'Who's having the first bath?'

'I don't want to take a bath,' said Hermione. 'I want to arrange Daddy's shells and see to the feedbags.'

'And so you shall,' said Bea. 'I'll let you go first. We'll do your hair quickly and then you can get out as soon as you like. Then William can take as *long* as he likes, and as it's Sunday, William, and seeing as it's your father's first day back, I'll let you play Waterloo. *If* you promise not to touch the telephone showers, and I don't have to explain why, now do I?'

But she did, for my benefit. This was another of the cottage's idiosyncrasies. It had two bathrooms, neither of which was in proper working order. The tiles needed regrouting: if you so much as breathed on them, water came pouring down into the kitchen, 'not to mention on Max's prized wrinkle-dryer'. Hot water was sometimes a problem, as the boiler was temperamental. But today, she announced after she had got the bath running, it seemed to be 'rising to the occasion. Although you must get Max to check the level tomorrow. He may have to order more oil.

'In the meantime, it might not be a bad idea if you took advantage of the hot-water supplies while they last,' she said. 'You'll find Max's bathroom upstairs, next door to the children's. It's the one with the hundreds of half-used bottles of shampoo and whatnot. Mind the labels – last time I used it myself, I mistook his organic lemon-lime essence of avocado shaving cream for bath foam. The effect was quite dreadful. I do apologise in advance for the disarray. You'll see what I mean when you get up there. There never was a room in greater need of a woman's touch.'

My suitcase was still standing in the entryway. I zipped it open to get my towel, a change of clothes and my toilet bag. After I had found them, I zipped up the suitcase again, as if I were an overnight guest. I only realised how odd this was when I saw Bea's worried eyes on me. 'I think you're very wise,' she said loyally, 'to wait until tomorrow to unpack.

'You must take your time!' she called up the stairs. 'You've earned your rest!'

Grateful for yet another opportunity to hide, I followed her instructions. As I soaked in my bath, I kept myself from thinking by acquainting myself with the disarray Bea had warned me about. There were, as she had said, more than a hundred plastic containers of shampoo, conditioner, lotion and oil. Some were concoctions I had never seen before from the Body Shop. Others had instructions in Spanish, French, German and Arabic. Many looked four or five years old. Most looked as if they had been bought by a woman.

People say that poets and writers have no private life, that they expose themselves even when they hide behind the screen of fiction. But as well as I knew her work, it had never occurred to me before that Rebecca would be the sort of person with a weakness for new shampoos, or an aversion for using containers that were almost empty. It had never even occurred to me that she even needed to wash her hair, or do anything at all to maintain her appearance. I had always thought of her as fully dressed and brushed and freshly laundered. Why hadn't Max thrown anything away?

How did he feel when he sat in this bath looking at her things? How did I feel?

There was a plaque on the wall behind the shampoos. It read, 'That the birds of worry and care fly above your head, this you cannot change. But that they build nests in your hair, this you can prevent.' As I listened to William play his strange war game next door in his bath, and to Hermione singing an unearthly tune in her bedroom, I told myself, One day, all these sounds will be familiar. One day, it will be me coming up the stairs to get the children into their pyjamas. One day it will be me choosing the bedtime stories. I remember having these thoughts, and yet I don't think it had sunk in yet that in taking on Max, I had taken on his children, too.

I listened to him say his goodnights, first to Hermione, then to William. I was still at the point where I was moved, and surprised, to hear how his voice changed when he sat down to read to them. How rich, soft and reassuring he sounded! He didn't speak to me like that, I remember thinking, but on this occasion I thought this with detachment and no jealousy.

I was puzzled when, after Max had gone downstairs, I could hear his voice continuing to ramble on. It was only after I came out of the bathroom that I worked out it was Hermione listening to a tape.

I found him with Bea in the long, barnlike sitting room. They were at the mahogany dining table, drinking coffee, sharing a cigarette. It was still light outside. The leaves that pressed against the windows and the open garden door were a fluorescent green. But the light inside was failing. I tried and failed to turn on a lamp.

'Would you mind flicking that switch next to the door, dear?' Bea said to me. I did, and all the lamps in the room lit up at once. 'Thanks awfully.'

Bea had her glasses on. She was reading a newspaper. When she put it down, she said to Max, 'It's not quite as bad as I feared. I'd say go for an apology, and leave it at that.'

'Mandy says—'

'Mandy is the solicitor, I take it?'

Max nodded. 'Mandy says they're unlikely to agree to an apology. She thinks they're trying to provoke me into suing. She thinks they know something we don't know.'

'All the more reason to keep our heads down,' Bea said.

'Not really. That would make it look as if we're hiding something. Don't you agree?'

Bea took off her reading glasses and gave Max a long and thoughtful stare. 'Would you like me to make a copy of this outrage for Mandy, Candy, whatever her name is?'

'Not unless she asks. She's bound to have read it already,' Max said.

'Well, you must tell her about Wayne,' Bea said, as she put her reading glasses back into her basket. Then she turned to me. 'I must say! It was rather wonderful what you said to Wayne, by the way. I was dying to say so myself, but I couldn't find the nerve. You *are* brave, my dear, and awfully clever, too. Did you know, Max? The Chopin was her idea too. It wasn't Rupert at all. He told me.'

Max said, 'Oh, really? I hadn't realised that. I thought he was just showing off as usual.'

'You needn't be so hard on the boy. Since Bertie's been in Antarctica, he's much improved. He's in love with poor Herta, you know. It must have been awful for him to have to watch her with that brute Wayne. What an absolute nightmare that man is! All that nonsense about his impugned work ethic. It's insufferable! Especially since I suspect you can't impugn a work ethic at all. I'm going to check, you know. It's on my list. Do you think Herta will give him up now?'

'Oh, I'm sure the affair will stagger on for a while longer,' said Max. 'But there's really no need for you to meddle in it. It's doomed.'

'I hope you're right,' she said. She sighed, stood up and put her cigarettes and her lighter back into her basket. 'Because I can't bear the thought of being grandmother to his children. Max, can you imagine anything more gruesome?'

Max gave her a smile instead of an answer.

Bea leaned over to kiss Max on the cheek. 'At least Rebecca had good bones.'

He winced. Bea didn't notice because she was going around the room straightening the kilims. 'You're off at what godforsaken time tomorrow?'

'The eight fifty-five from Islip,' he said.

'Then I shall be here by quarter past.'

'Better make it later, as I'm sure they'll all want to sleep in.'

'I'm sure you're right, but I'm taking you to the station, as we'll be needing your car.' She picked up her basket and headed for the door. 'Bye for now,' she called over her shoulder. Her voice trilled like a bird.

'Thank God that's over,' said Max after the door had closed. 'She's wonderful. But tiring.' He got out a tobacco box. 'And I've been dying for one of these.' He took out a piece of hash and some rolling papers. As he tore open a cigarette, he said, 'You have no idea what Bea was talking about, do you?'

I shook my head. 'Well,' he said, 'to make a long story short, although you may have already gathered this, there's another flap on about Rebecca.' It was the first time he had mentioned her name to me. 'Another biography, this one by that rather dubious cousin of hers. It's a deeply dishonest book in all sorts of ways, and if that were all it was, I should have just ignored it as I ignored the other one, you remember, the one by Donald Oswald. The one that implied that the drowning was a cover-up, that Rebecca really committed suicide. This one goes further, I'm afraid, a lot further. It goes so far that the worry is people will believe it's true unless I sue. The book itself doesn't come out until September, but it was bought up by my paper's chief rival, and brought out early, I assume, to bring circulation out of the summer doldrums. The first part was serialised last week, the second part came out today, and the third and final part will come out next Sunday – unless we stop it. I wrote a rebuttal in my paper. It was published today. I was urged to write it by the editor, but I think it may have been a mistake. We shall see. I'll leave everything out for you to read if you're interested. I don't like talking about it, as you can well imagine, but if you have any

73

questions after reading it, you must let me know. I hope you don't mind if I wait for you to ask.' He lit a match and put it against the hash, then crumbled it in. After he had licked the papers and was rolling them into a joint, he looked up and said, 'Would you like to choose some music? I don't know what your taste runs to, but as mine is eclectic you ought to be able to find something that suits you.' He put the joint down and gave me a quizzical look. 'It's strange, isn't it? Here we are, in this cottage, and I don't even know what music you like.'

'I'm happy with anything,' I said.

'Nonsense. No one's happy with anything. If I got up now and put on disco or bubblegum or "Viva España", you wouldn't be happy.'

'If you got up now and put on "Viva España",' I said, 'I'd probably try to see what you saw in it. Or at least pretend. You forget what a hypocrite I am. I pretend to be agreeable to anything so that I can get people to reveal themselves.'

'That's more like it,' Max said. 'I was beginning to wonder if I was going to have to go look for your opinions in Lost Luggage. Would you like me to tell you who Wayne is?'

'Yes,' I said.

'Wayne is a journalist. He freelances, but mostly for the paper that is running the serialised biography. He's engaged to my cousin Herta, in other words Bea's daughter, or at least he was until today. Bea is sure that he is the source for a lot of the correct information the biography contains, but I don't think so. Bea was very keen to pin it on him because she doesn't like him. He probably overreacted today because he suspects correctly that Bea and Giles look down on him, but this was a tactical error. It will be easy for Bea to say to Herta, see, we were right, he's nothing but a hack and not to be trusted. It's all rather ugly. I wish it hadn't happened. The only good thing that has come out of it is that Bea thinks you did something "rather wonderful". I think we'll leave it at that. It's no bad thing that Bea has taken to you. Now I don't feel so worried about having to leave you behind tomorrow. She looks after her own, does Bea, although in the long run, you may find that is a mixed blessing. Does Bill Evans suit you?' he asked as he took an album out of its sleeve.

'I'm sure he does,' I said, but uncertainly, because I had never heard of him.

'You've never heard of him before, have you?'

I shook my head. Max threw back his head and laughed. 'You Americans! You know nothing about jazz.'

'I'm sorry,' I said.

He pulled me over and kissed me on the forehead. 'Lesson number one: never explain. Lesson number two: never apologise. That is all you need to know and ever know.' Still holding my hand, he lowered the needle onto the record. 'I've put you through hell today and you're still talking to me, and that's all that counts.'

Soft, soothing piano music swirled out of the speakers. 'Do you like it?' Max asked as he stretched out on the couch.

'I think I do,' I said.

He lit the joint. 'So whatever else goes wrong, at least it'll go wrong while we're enjoying the same music. Although you may draw the line at the World Saxophone Quartet.'

'Why?' I asked.

'Because Rebecca did. They drove her spare. They were the reason why she bought me earphones. She said they sounded like Times Square on New Year's Eve. She had no time for dissonance – unless, of course, she was complaining about it.'

That I could imagine. I could imagine her standing there, right there in the low doorway, fresh from the bath, wearing a robe printed with large flowers, and shaking her beautiful mane of hair in exasperation with her husband, brilliantly witty in her disparagements, glowing as always with the courage of her convictions. While I . . .

I sat down on the sofa next to Max and looked at this strange, beautiful man as he put his legs on my lap. Whatever standards you applied to him, he was out of my league. And yet here we were.

'Do you mind if I ask you a question?'

'If it's about Rebecca . . .' He took a long drag from the joint. 'I'd rather wait until after you've done that reading.'

'It's not about Rebecca. It's about me.'

'What about you, then?' He took a second drag, held it in, exhaled.

I took a deep breath. In as loud a voice as I could muster, I asked, 'What do you see in me?'

He laughed. Then he leaned over and pretended to search my eyes. 'I'm not sure. I'll have to think about it. In the meantime –' he handed me the joint – 'have some of this.'

Chapter Ten

I was in bed, under a duvet that was damp with heat. My head was resting on his chest. His arm enclosed me. I could hear something fizzling. I lifted my head and peeked over the edge of the duvet. It was the television on the chest of drawers in the far corner. We had fallen asleep in the middle of a programme on the Edinburgh Festival. Now the station had gone off the air. It was . . . what time? I scanned the dark room for a clock and found two. A digital display on the radio was pulsating 1:22, while the travel alarm on the bedside table said 4:19. I looked out through the gap between the curtains and the windowsills and tried to gauge the time from the sky. It was too light a grey for the middle of the night, but too dark a grey for the early morning, so I drew the duvet back over my head and draped my leg over his legs, closed my eyes and let myself drift. The next time I awoke I was still immersed in the duvet but lying on my other side, facing away from him. I could feel his legs bent against the backs of my legs, his arm around my chest, his penis pressed against the small of my back, his heart beating softly against my neck, his breath on the back of my ear.

I opened my eyes only just long enough to see sunlight creeping underneath the thin, red-glowing curtains. The room had a warm, rosy haze over it. The television had changed from static to a show tune I could recognise but not name. I pulled the duvet cover up over my ears. I closed my eyes, and the next time I opened them, I was standing at a till in a bank, looking through the glass into the office where my teller and three other clerks were gazing at a computer screen, pressing keys, calling up list after list of numbers, looking over their shoulders at me, looking at each other, shaking their heads.

Now one was heading towards me, smiling apprehensively,

clutching my chequebook. Behind her, another was punching out a three-digit number on the telephone. I turned around. The security guard at the door was listening to a message coming in on the walkie-talkie. He was scanning the windows. He saw me. His eyes registered recognition. I picked up my handbag. He nodded at the clerks who had gathered at the till. He closed in.

I closed my eyes. A phone rang. I opened my eyes and found myself alone in bed. The television was off now. The curtains were drawn to admit the midmorning sun. The phone that was ringing was not the one on the floor next to the bed. When I picked up the phone on the floor next to the bed, all I got was a dialling tone. The other phone, wherever it was, persisted for another twenty rings. When it stopped, I could hear the distant sound of a vacuum cleaner.

I sat up, then put my head between my knees and concentrated on my breathing. It was all right, I told myself. It was just a dream. I was not alone. I had someone to care for me. Of all the problems I might have to face that day, the one I was not going to have to face was the one I had dreamed about. I was safe from the bank tellers. I had a roof over my head now. I had a protector.

I looked at the row of strange shoes on the floor until my breathing had become regular. Then the ringing began again. It sounded as if it was coming from the room above me. I went upstairs to investigate, but when I turned the handle to enter the room where the ringing was coming from, the door wouldn't budge.

'I'm afraid that's locked, my dear,' said a soft voice behind me. I turned to find a plump, spectacled, grey-haired woman standing in the hallway outside the bathroom. She was holding a vacuum cleaner in the stiff, dignified manner of a bassoonist. 'I'm Janet,' she said. 'Your cleaner. You must be the new Mrs Midwinter.'

'Actually,' I said, 'we're not married. Yet.'

She gave me a long, steady beam that indicated suppressed amusement.

'Why is the room locked?' I asked.

'It was the late Mrs M's study. That's her private line.' As she spoke, the ringing in the locked room continued. 'Does this happen a lot?' I asked.

78

'Only three or four times a week, I reckon.'

'Why is it still there if no one uses it?'

She gave me another gleaming smile. 'It's a rather long story, but I'm sure that if you broached the subject with Danny, she'd be more than delighted to tell you. As she may have mentioned already, she's – but don't let me ruin her story. You'll be wanting some coffee.'

'Now I hope I haven't been making too much noise,' she said as she put on the (to me, strange-looking) white plastic electric kettle. 'You must be so tired after all your travelling. And I hear the birthday party at the big house yesterday was not without its moments of drama. He's a dreadful man, that Wayne, now isn't he?' The kettle had already come to a boil. She poured the water into the mug, onto the waiting spoon of instant coffee. 'Milk or sugar?'

'Just milk, please.'

'No, he's my very least favourite of the fiancés, that one. I understand he made our Danny quite faint with alarm. I've dealt with the papers, by the way, if you follow my meaning.'

'I'm afraid I don't.'

'Well, I'm sure Danny will explain all that to you as well. She's due over here later on. In the meantime, I have a *rather* long list of queries from Mrs M Major. I would advise you to sit down first and prepare yourself mentally while I warm up the croissants she left for you. Would you like some orange juice while you wait? I'm assuming you won't be wanting to do your aikido or yoga or what have you. Danny is a great one for aikido. She says it's very popular in the United States but I wouldn't be surprised if you told me she was exaggerating.

'Yes, now. Well,' she said when she sat down at the table. Fixing her gently ironic smile on me, she asked, 'Question number one. Have you a valid driver's licence?'

'Of course I do.'

'British, US or international?'

'US and international but not British.'

She scribbled down my answer, then looked up. 'Would you like to apply for a British licence, and if so, will you be needing a lesson first? What we need to know, dear, is whether you're used to driving on our side of the road.'

'No,' I said. 'But I assume the only way to learn is to go out there and just drive. Wouldn't you say?'

Janet reached into the pocket of her housecoat and pulled out a set of keys. 'These are for the black Volvo parked outside the big house. You can use it whenever you like, but I'm to buy you a map when I go out later on to do your shopping. We thought I ought to do your shopping until you've found your bearings. This brings us to your shopping list. Do you have any preferences for this evening?'

'I don't know,' I said. 'What do the children like?'

'I believe they'll be out for tea today. Danny seems to be taking them off to a birthday party. It'll be you and Max – pardon me, Mr Midwinter.'

'What does he usually have?'

'Oh, well. He's rather unpredictable, as I'm sure you know. We thought that unless you had a strong preference, I should make a fisherman's pie.'

'There's no need for you to go to all that trouble. I'll make something myself.'

We were halfway through our shopping list when the phone rang. It was a woman asking for Mrs Midwinter. Without thinking, I said she was dead.

'Oh!' said the woman, taken aback. As soon as I put the receiver down, it rang again. This time it was a man whose voice I didn't recognise. 'That was my secretary. You've practically given her a heart attack. What's come over you?'

It was only at this point that I realised it was Max. 'I'm sorry,' I said. 'I'm feeling rather disoriented.'

'Are they treating you all right?' he asked.

'Oh, yes, perfectly,' I said. 'Your aunt's left a list of practical questions and we're about halfway through it.'

'Don't let them organise you into oblivion. You must tell them when you want them to stop. And you mustn't rush around tiring yourself out. You have all the time in the world for those practical questions. The important thing is for you to accustom yourself to the house.'

'That's probably a taller order than a shopping list.'

'I don't quite follow.'

'It doesn't matter.'

'How are the children?' he asked.

'They're not here.'

'They're not?' he said, surprised. Then, after a silence, he said, 'Oh, yes, of course. It's Art Week. Sorry. Listen, there's someone just come in to see me. I'll try to get back ahead of the traffic. By the way, I've asked Janet to leave the papers in a folder on the desk in my bedroom. I mean our bedroom. If you have a chance, you should probably read them.'

Chapter Eleven

I tried. I started with that day's tabloids because they mentioned me. 'Mad Max brings home mystery bride,' said one headline. Another said, 'A foreign lamb to the slaughter?' They had a photograph of us getting into the limousine at the airport. This surprised me, since I hadn't noticed a photographer.

The article tied my arrival in with the new biography, itemising its main selling points: that the official story about Rebecca's last month, and particularly her last night, 'begged many questions', that the author, 'a cousin and very close friend', had been the last outside the 'Beckfield Mafia' to speak to her; that his evidence, although incomplete, allegedly pointed to the conclusion that Rebecca had neither drowned, as the family had always claimed, nor committed suicide, as other biographers had suggested, but had been 'quite literally blown out of the water by her outraged in-laws'.

The next thing I read were the excerpts from the biography itself in the *Sunday Times*. The first instalment carried a photograph of the author – a large, dark and troubled-looking man with a stubble beard and a ring in one ear. He was posing on a log, in his hand an electric chainsaw. According to the blurb, he was the son of a Bermudan millionaire and 'related to Rebecca through his mother'. At sixteen he had been expelled from a Swiss boarding school for distributing pornography, despite which disgrace he had still managed to get into Oxford Poly. Having left his course after his second year, he had gone on to earn a living first as a male model and then as a mover specialising in pianos, although he had recently used his inheritance to save an ailing quality press.

The first instalment was a sentimental storm-cloud version of how Max had met Rebecca. Although it went out of its way to show how much more sophisticated Rebecca was than her heroine in *The Marriage Hearse*, it confirmed her damning fictionalisation of the Midwinters.

They looked at her and saw that she would do. Yes, she would do very nicely as their appointed court jester. She would make them laugh, she would write well-turned out works that would add lustre to the family name, and last but not least, she would lend her body to the common cause and provide them with an heir. That was the bargain as they saw it. She needed their patronage and they needed a sow. They did not think they needed to spell it out. And so it was that Rebecca walked into the gilded lion's den without any idea of what was expected of her . . .

He then went on to outline the scandalous careers of the other lions. Max's father, Ben Midwinter, had been

Swinging London's most outrageous portrait artist, his main claim to fame being his fondness for painting his friends' nubile daughters in the nude and then selling the works back to his friends for exorbitant sums.

He undoubtedly met his match in Max's mother, Caroline Midwinter, the best-selling mystery writer and outspoken Catholic convert who was, until her recent retirement, fast becoming a national monument – but where did she get her plots and why were all her victims women? Perhaps she was practising literary voodoo on her husband's many mistresses and illegitimate children. How does she bear the shame, and was it the strain of the constant humiliation that led to her becoming a recluse? The greatest humiliation must have come from the knowledge that her husband's first and foremost mistress was her very own sister, née Bea Allinson and then Bea Copley, wife of the renowned City fraudster, and now herself a Midwinter, thanks to her propitious eleventh-hour marriage to Ben's younger brother Giles.

Giles is known as the family saint. Like most saints, he owes most of his halo to a combination of luck and careful manipulation.

He spent the early part of his adult life as headmaster of a boys' boarding school in Kampala. Having lost his first wife and their three children during one of the seventies massacres, he returned to this country to find that brother Ben was running through the last of the family fortunes. He decided to make a nest egg for his retirement by writing up his misadventures. The result was that masterpiece of understatement, *Under Idi*, which sold so well that he was able to use the proceeds not just to buy himself Beckfield House, but to set up the press that went on to manufacture that most bogus of literary cliques, the Hertford Five. Since foisting this fiction on an unsuspecting and easily cowed audience, he has become steadily more prosperous. He has devoted much time to grooming nephew Max to take over the family business, which has now taken on an aura of timelessness despite its being less than two decades old. He makes skilful use of a host of family retainers and destitute, if overeducated, relations. At the same time he has been instrumental in keeping other, less respectable family members at arm's length. It was Giles who arranged for Max's older brother Jonathan to be disinherited after his drug problems were made public. And it was Giles who banished his difficult and sometimes embarrassingly garrulous brother Ben to spend twelve months a year in St John the Baptist after Ben's nearly fatal accident in 1981 left him less than *compos mentis*.

The second instalment began with an account of the nearly fatal car crash. Its main significance, according to the biographer, was that it ended Rebecca's honeymoon with the Midwinter family, and began the nightmare that inspired *The Marriage Hearse*. It had happened on St John the Baptist during the Christmas period. Ben had been in no state to drive, and so the fault lay with him, but Rebecca had been in the car with him.

This aroused the suspicions of Queen Mistress Bea, who no longer knew lover Ben in biblical terms but was not about to let anyone else know him that way either, and mistakenly assumed that there must have been some sexual reason for Ben and Rebecca being in a car together, and so blamed her for leading Ben into the accident. Rebecca naturally refused to be framed and told Bea that she was wrong. But no one ever tells Bea that she is wrong, and so from that time on she declared war on Rebecca, undermining her in much the same way as her fictitious alter ego undermined the heroine of *The Marriage Hearse*, with much the same results. Before Rebecca put herself into treatment and pulled herself together to write *The Marriage Hearse*, she was drinking vodka for breakfast and having heroin with her afternoon tea.

The instalment concluded with an account of Rebecca's final visit to Max's father's resort on St John the Baptist. It began, ominously, with the official story: she had stayed on after a family holiday, claiming back trouble, and then gone straight out to sea in her little boat after driving Max and the children to the airport. She had been warned not to go out by Bea because the weather looked chancy. But she had insisted, saying, 'A storm is just what I need.'

Then it moved on to recapitulate the story as embellished in the Oswald biography: that it had not been back trouble that had kept Rebecca back, but mental illness. She had gone into a decline after finishing *The Marriage Hearse* and fallen first into alcoholism and then back into her old drug habits. Instead of receiving the kind of help she needed, she had been barred from her children and even her own bank account. She had tried to rehabilitate herself, but during the fateful trip to St John the Baptist, her resolve had weakened. She had gone on a binge along with a number of other black sheep from Max's extended family, together with a party of defectors from a nearby Buddhist community. When Max left in a huff with the children, there was no one in the remaining group who was sober enough to keep her from getting on her boat to go out and ride the storm.

But it was not just dysfunction that killed her, as the puritanical Oswald contends. It was fear for the family name, the kind of fear felt most keenly by those whose family names are not quite as old as they might like them to be, by those, in short, whose family names are associated in the public mind not with great wars or lofty government office but with frozen fish and middle-of-the-market meat products. It is often noted that *The Marriage Hearse* was published three months after Rebecca's death. What no one bothers to add is that bound proofs of the book would have been circulating well before her death. The responses to these proofs were indeed the substance of my last telephone conversation with Rebecca, made only hours before her ill-fated decision to take out the *Eressos*.

'They're out to get me,' she told me. 'They've read the book and they've asked me to withdraw it from publication and I've told them over my dead body, and they appear to be taking the invitation seriously.' Those were among her last words to me. Although there are only ninety minutes between the time of our call and the time she is said to have lifted her anchor, she was not drunk, and records show that the storm that was brewing did not in fact start until early the following morning. In my concluding article next Sunday, I shall put it to you that there are good reasons why (a) Rebecca's boat was never officially discovered, (b) Rebecca's body was never subjected to a UK autopsy and (c) the evidence of other key witnesses has been suppressed. Following my account of the cover-up I shall offer new evidence that will, I hope, result in the case being reopened.

I turned to Max's paper. Max, it seemed, had written his editorial without having had a chance to read this second instalment. And so it responded only to the hints in the first instalment that the family had wanted Rebecca dead because of its outrage over *The Marriage Hearse*. This, Max said in his own editorial, was 'patently ludicrous'.

If we had wanted to save our name, why didn't we simply suppress *The Marriage Hearse*? We may not have welcomed this work or its effect on the public, but we respect it as a work of art. We would like to ask the public to do the same: to accept it as a work of the imagination, and not as a coded suicide note. My wife's death was a tragic accident. Her children and I will be marked by it for life. I am now intending to remarry and to try and make a new life. I would like to ask that my fiancée and I be left in peace. The author of the new biography may well believe what he has written, but the careful reader will see that the account so far is long on interpretation and short on facts. I have no idea what proof he expects to provide in later instalments, but I would like to suggest that any account that has had the inconsistencies smoothed out of it – that is convincing, that suggests only one possible conclusion – is likely to belong more to the realm of fiction than the realm of fact. The author is a man with a long-standing grudge against my family – not to mention his own family – and all the things he thinks we stand for. So, by all means, read what he has to say, but don't forget to ask yourself what he has gained by saying it.

'My fiancée and I . . .' I counted backwards, recalling the deadline. He had written these words before he had proposed to me. How could he have presumed this, and presumed it so publicly? As I leafed through the rest of the book section, a sour pit grew in my stomach. I put the rest of the papers back into the folder and went out for a walk.

Janet had now moved across the lawn to Danny's cottage and was airing it out. Beyond the wall, I could see a man cutting back the ivy on Beckfield House. The sound of his clippers was drowned out by an approaching lawnmower. I opened the wide wooden gate. My first thought was to find a way into the fields across the lane. I was deterred by a sign that said, 'Beware Minimal Disease Pigs'. I turned left to walk down the lane into what promised to be the centre of the village, but there turned out not to be a centre. Nor was there a pavement. After having to jump up against the wall twice to avoid speeding cars, I turned back and headed to the gaunt church I had noticed at the crest of the hill facing Oxford when we had driven up from the ring road the previous day. It, too, was hard to reach because of the cars careening around the blind curve. Its lawn was overgrown. Most of its tombstones were a century old, if not even older, except for one new marble slab at the far eastern corner. It was only as I made my approach that it occurred to me it might belong to Rebecca. And it was only when I read the words on it that I remembered the controversy. It did not say Rebecca Slaughter-Midwinter, the name we all knew her by. It just said Rebecca Slaughter – as if to tell the world that she was no longer a member of that family.

A dog jumped on me. I let out a cry before I recognised it was Jasper. 'Come here, you naughty thing!' said an imperious voice. It belonged to Danny. She calmed Jasper down, then kneeled down next to me.

'Well,' she said brightly. 'That's one mystery solved.'

'What do you mean?'

'Well, I wasn't quite sure where you fit into the scheme of things. Now I know you're an aider and abetter.'

'I'm afraid I don't follow you,' I said.

This made her laugh. 'What I meant really is that you've started on the best possible footing. Here, I mean. I come here every day, for guidance. And, yes, also the view. Do you know her work well?'

'Yes,' I admitted. 'Some of it backwards as well as forwards.'

'Oh, that's smashing! That will make for a terrific change,' she exclaimed. 'It's been so difficult, spending so much time immersed in her words, and to be able to discuss them with absolutely no one! You probably know, don't you, that I'm editing her letters?'

I said I did.

'If you like, I can show some to you. Actually, when I lose my bearings, you might be the perfect person to cast the deciding vote. Although you must say – you must! You must! – if I'm taking away precious time. Max says you'll be wanting to get back to work at once, and that we're not to let the little monsters trouble you until you've found your feet.'

She took my hand. 'Max said I shouldn't push you into it, but as it turns out you're one of us, you might welcome the opportunity. I myself found the place quite inspiring. If I were working on a real book, like you, I couldn't think of a better haven. Here, let me take you to Dragoman's Lair. That's what she called it, you know.'

It wasn't until she had led me back to Garden Cottage and up the stairs that I realised she was talking about Rebecca's study.

Chapter Twelve

She opened it with a key on her chain, from which dangled a small, plastic, flesh-coloured hand. 'Goodness,' Danny said. 'I must get Janet in here. Pardon the dust!'

But the first things I noticed about this small, cluttered room were the signs of use. The bookshelves were unevenly arranged. Some books rested face out while others were stacked over the spines. There were invitations propped against the rows of books. One of the filing-cabinet drawers was peeping open. On top of the cabinet lay a shoebox, a cassette, a pile of envelopes. There was crumpled paper in the wastepaper basket, a pair of woolly slippers at the foot of the chaise longue, and on the telephone table next to it was a notepad with doodles on it. Behind the floor lamp was a bulletin board. Half of it was covered by a calendar, and the other half with bills and invoices. On the floor was a rug I first mistook for a Turkish kilim and then recognised as Navajo.

In the corner between the two windows was a small table with a Remington manual typewriter and piles of stationery. Set against the far window – the one with the view over Oxford and its spires – was the only pretty piece of furniture, a desk of a type I had seen before, clearly a valuable antique, although I had no idea what period, what country of origin, what wood or even remotely what value. The chair, which was pushed to one side, as if its owner had risen suddenly – to answer the phone or to rush off to an appointment – did not match.

There was a framed photograph I had not seen before of Rebecca with the children. Hermione looked about three and William about one. There was a collection of child-made mugs, bowls and ashtrays along the far edge. Some held stamps, others paperclips and rubber bands. One held pencils and felt-tip pens of various colours. On the ink blotter sat a fuchsia fountain pen and a spiral notebook. It was open to a blank page.

'You get a sense, don't you,' said Danny, 'that she's only stepped out to make a cup of coffee?'

I nodded carefully.

She beamed at me and then shut the door. 'You'll appreciate this, I think.' She gestured at the collage that covered the inside door. 'She called it Talking Heads.' It was a collage of famous photographs of famous writers and poets, or rather, of their heads, which had been superimposed on postcards of famous photographs and paintings. The *American Gothic* farmers, for example, were Leonard and Virginia Woolf. Ginsberg's head was on a Rubens nude. Hemingway was impersonating Mae West. There was an elaborate reinvention of *Las Meniñas* containing transposed faces I did not recognise – except for the dwarf, whose touched-up face, I noticed with a jolt, belonged to Max.

I looked up. Danny was smiling at me expectantly. 'It's so very, very clever, isn't it? It makes one quite speechless.' She gestured at the desk chair. 'Sit down. Drink it in. It's what she would want.'

I sat down, with some hesitation, and Danny flopped down on the chaise longue. She put her hands behind her head, crossed her legs and gave out a sigh of relaxed relief. She smiled and then, with a suddenness that alarmed me, fixed me with a frown.

'Look down again. No, not at the floor. At your hands, perhaps. Whatever you were just doing. That's right. No, not quite. A bit more to the left. Yes, there. Stop. Yes, I see it now. Bea was right, there is a resemblance. I don't know why I didn't notice it sooner. Perhaps because of the difference in colouring, she being all reds and blacks and sapphire and ivory, while you're . . . pastel. Pastel and . . . beige, I suppose. Hasn't anyone ever said so to you? Hasn't Max?'

'Said what to me?'

'That you look so much like her.'

'Like who?'

'Like whom? Like our mutual icon, you dear thing. Like Rebecca.'

'I don't think I look like her at all,' I said.

'Really? How odd! How charming! Of course you would be the last to see it. You're not the spitting image – more, I would say, the afterimage. It's something . . . something quite elusive. For example, what you just did right then with your eyebrows. When you look puzzled or uncertain, you look like her. Your expressions echo hers, but then, when they go away, you can't imagine that you ever saw them! Terrible eerie, don't you think? *Terribly* eerie! I suppose it's what they call a fleeting resemblance.' She uncrossed her legs and then recrossed them the other way. She looked dreamily into my eyes – catching me unawares, making me afraid to look away. Then her face broke into a smile.

'Yes,' she said. 'That's what I'll do.' She stood up and opened the wardrobe behind the chaise longue and brought out a long, black satin ballgown that I only belatedly recognised as the dress Rebecca had worn in her most famous author's photo – and described to dramatic effect in the last chapter of *The Marriage Hearse*. It was the original of the wrong dress, and just having Danny press it against my skin made me shiver. But Danny was too busy arranging and rearranging to notice. 'It's elusive, whatever it is,' she said, putting her head first to one side and then to the other. 'It's hard to pin down. But quite miraculous. Quite miraculous. I can understand now why Max felt compelled to intemperance.'

She stretched out her arms. 'You can imagine how alarmed we all were at the news. Curious, too, of course! And, naturally, hoping for the best. But when children are involved, especially children who have already been through so much . . . Do you mind my saying all this? I hope I haven't put my foot in it. I don't mean to be rude. It's just that, I'm not sure I can say precisely why, but I feel as if we've known each other for a long time, that there's an affinity. It could just be the surroundings, but the bond is . . . it's there, isn't it? Don't you agree?'

I nodded, trying to hide my uncertainty and apparently succeeding, because now she clasped her hands and heaved another of her relieved sighs. Her voice was tremulous when she spoke again. 'Forgive me if I assume too much. I'm not at my best right now. I'm the first to admit it. The new crisis has me quite distracted.

I know the simple explanation, the one that's closest to the truth, even, is that Jack is bitter and twisted, but honestly, the actual reading of this book of his . . . The words on the page form a grotesquerie, a patchwork quilt of familiar details that have been wrenched from their context to form such a very different picture. I'm sure it would be unnerving even in the absence of the cruel pointing finger. I've doubted my sanity over the last few days. I'm sure even now I'm acting decidedly odd.'

She leaned forward. There were tears in her eyes. 'Because the fact is, we're all responsible for what happened, while never *ever* imagining for a second that it would come to this! Why, our premise was immortality. We were young! We were fearless! We threw ourselves into our experiments with such . . . such irreverence, but at the same time, such *devout* enthusiasm!'

'You don't have to explain. I know from my own experience,' I said. 'My—'

But she was too caught up with her own train of thought to hear me. 'I'll try and explain what crossed my mind when we came in here. It's that *they* – the ones out there, for whom Rebecca is just a scandal, who don't care for her or for her work, and certainly haven't a qualm for her children – all they want to do is find out about her *death*. They're only interested in her life to the extent that it casts light on the manner and meaning of her suicide. It's as if this wretched, wretched never-ending scandal has petrified, *fossilised* her. When the Rebecca you and I know – and here I'm talking about the legacy, the work, the spirit of the work, rather – was, is, and ever shall be so very lively! Alive! The interplay! The texture! The movement in her every line – not just underneath, but in the surfaces! She was a sprite, was Rebecca, and now all they care about was whether or not she foretold her own death. So reductive! Such a dreadful, dreadful *double* loss! That is why I've kept this study like this. *In medias res*, I mean. To forget the scandal, remember the living spirit. Look,' she said. She sat up and reached over to the nearest bookshelf and picked up a small marble wing. Then she walked across the room to place it where it had once belonged, on the right shoulder of a marble cupid. It was not the cupid

I remembered the heroine breaking and then hiding in *The Marriage Hearse*, but you could see the connection. You could see how, looking at this cupid, Rebecca could have invented the other.

'I can't remember where she found it,' Danny said. 'I cannot tell you if she chose it because of the literary echo, or whether she simply found it fit in so beautifully with her own symbolic schema. But I was here when she broke it. And how we laughed! This was before the book, mind you. Or rather, as she was writing it. I was not at all surprised to see it had made the leap into fiction. Can you understand, then, why I come here? Why I haven't changed the way things are? Don't be like the others, Danny – that's what this room tells me. Don't fossilise. Don't force disparate pieces into spurious unities. Just look and accept. Look genius in the eye. Do not deface the gravestone or move the evidence.'

'The opposite of a museum, in other words?' I suggested feebly.

She looked up, made enthusiastic to an alarming degree by the suggestion. 'No cataloguing,' she said. 'No sifting the important from the unimportant. Just leaving it all there so that you can see her just from the drawers she didn't close and the bookshelves she never finished arranging and the pens she never capped and the poem she never wrote. And most resonant of all, I think, this cupid.'

Without willing the words, I said, 'So she broke things on purpose, did she, and then just gloated over the pieces?'

'Exactly! Exactly! That's exactly what I mean. You understand, don't you? It's not altogether nice, genius. Not at this range, anyway. But there was a generosity, too. That was part of it, always. I know she would want it because she believed in continuity.'

Here she quoted the pertinent line from 'Fossils': '"Clip my wings, then hang them out to dry/Salt them for posterity . . ." I'll be following her instructions.'

'Her instructions to do what?'

'To offer you the room. For your work.'

Another beaming smile. How many did that make today, and amid so many smiles, why did I feel so nervous, so exposed?

'Bea says you opened your book of short stories with a quotation from *Ulysses Unmanned*.'

'Yes,' I said, and I told her which lines.

'And the new one?'

I nodded. 'Although I'm thinking now it might be wiser to change.'

She put her hand out. 'No, you mustn't. Mustn't! Follow the first instinct.'

'Not just any inner voice, but the faintest . . .'

The quotations made her laugh out with delight. She picked up her key ring, took the key off and tossed it to me. 'Here you go. Breathe some life back into us – before it's too late.'

Bea's voice floated up the stairs. 'Anyone at home?'

It was only then that I saw the study door was open. William and Hermione were standing there, glowering.

'Hello, children,' Danny trilled, adding, 'goodness, we're not looking very happy today, are we?'

'That's Mummy's dress on the chair.'

'Yes, I know, dear. We just took it out to admire it.'

'And those are Mummy's slippers on your feet,' Hermione said.

'Yes, darling,' Danny trilled. 'Of course they are. That's why we keep them in here.'

'Those are Mummy's slippers. Take them off.'

'Goodness!' Danny said, as she kicked them off. 'I've never seen four such accusing eyes!'

'It's not *four* accusing eyes,' said Hermione, who was clutching a large, dour-looking teddy bear. 'It's *six*.'

Chapter Thirteen

*I*t did not take long for the domestic machine to save us from confrontation. First it was lunch with all its little duties and privileges. It was William's job to find the tins, Hermione's turn to have the first pick. She also got to open both her tin and William's. As Hermione explained to me during a brief lull in hostilities, William's grip was not yet strong enough, 'nor is the situation likely to change in the foreseeable future'. She spoke slowly and emphatically, dispensing each word as if it were a marble.

William laid the table – except for the glasses, which he couldn't reach, and the napkins, which (as Hermione informed me) he always forgot. Danny did the microwave, although Hermione was permitted to set the timer. I was assigned the squash, which chore I performed incorrectly, since I did not know it was meant to be diluted. This turned out to be a blessing, as it gave Danny the perfect topic to fill out the silence that threatened to overtake us when we all sat down. I didn't know about squash because in America children did not drink it. Would I like to tell William and Hermione what children in America did drink? I said that I was not quite sure what they drank now, but that when I was their age, my favourite drinks had been Tang and Kool Aid. At meals I had been made to drink milk, I told them. ('Which is not delivered by milkmen,' Danny interjected. 'Did your mum ever mention that to you?') No comment, but there was a slight flicker of interest in their eyes when I told them about the pictures of missing children they put on milk cartons.

This was, however, a bit much for Danny. 'That's rather macabre, don't you think?' she said with a bright smile as she sprang to her feet to clear her plate. 'No pudding today, my dears, as you'll have plenty of that later on. Off you go upstairs, now! Janet will have packed your cases, but I've asked her to leave space for your teddies and whatnot. Run up and get them ready for inspection.'

They walked.

As we gathered up the children's plates and glasses, Danny explained to me that she and the children were off to Somerset for the night to see an old friend of hers who had children the same age as William and Hermione 'plus a thoroughly delightful new addition we shall be meeting for the first time'. She apologised for 'sweeping the little darlings off like this', but it had been arranged months ago, and although she had considered cancelling, Bea had advised against altering the children's plans unnecessarily. 'She thinks you'll get used to each other much faster if their routine remains the same.' There was also the delicate matter of her dear friend's postnatal depression. 'Under the circumstances, I'd hate to have to let her down.'

'We'll be back tomorrow teatime.' I didn't know exactly what time that meant, but I decided not to ask. Danny had suddenly become flustered. I offered to take over the washing of the dishes so that she could attend to the children. This prompted more thank-yous and exaggerated expressions of gratitude for my kindness.

She continued the frantically cheerful patter when she went upstairs. She was still talking at the same pitch – despite the absence of responses or even interruptions – when she marched the children and their bags downstairs again.

William was looking uncomfortable in navy shorts, matching sandals, a green and blue tartan shirt and a bright-red bow tie. His unruly hair had been trained with a wet comb. Hermione was looking sterner and more old-fashioned than ever in a smocked dress made out of the same green and navy-blue tartan. As Danny arranged and then fussily rearranged a ribbon in her long brown hair, she rehearsed them: 'How do you do, Lord and Lady Northey?' They repeated the sentence after her with a listlessness that seemed almost smug.

I waved them goodbye and then I went back to the cottage, faltering in the entryway, not knowing which way to go. Everywhere I looked, I saw the afternoon that stretched ahead of me, but no clues to how to fill it.

I made myself a sandwich. I ate it. I wandered around the sitting room, looking first at the paintings and photographs, then at the books. I found the shelf containing Max's books. I had never read any of them. I picked one up, read the first poem, did not feel comfortable about the fact that I did not immediately respond to it. I put it back, picked out another book, opened it at random to a poem addressed to a woman he could not stop touching on account of not having seen her for three months. I put this book back, too.

The time had come, I decided, to explore the famous walled garden. Going out through the sitting-room door, I found my way to the gate that led into the arbour. The first view was impressive, but when I had made myself comfortable in one of the lawn chairs, the arrangements of flowers and shrubs and trees began to look too formal, too polite, too remote. This is my house, I kept reminding myself. I closed my eyes when the sun came out, and bathed in it until the heat had made me drowsy. The first thing I did when I went back inside was look at the clock. Still only half past three.

In my absence, Janet had been and dropped off my groceries. No ingredient looked quite the way I had expected. I put away the strange packages I would not be using for the carbonara. This was easier said than done, as I could made no sense of the classification system.

I went through the drawers and cabinets in search of the utensils I would be needing. There were no cast-iron pots or casseroles, only a double boiler. There was a Chinese chopping knife and a bread knife, but no paring knife. The only bread board had a large, stained split in it, and nowhere could I find a cheese grater.

I took the keys and the cash Bea had left for me, and I went to find the black Volvo. It was odd to have the gears on my left but I told myself the best thing would be to just get out there. It was only when I was on the road, and angled in the wrong direction, that I realised I did not know how to put the car in reverse.

I tried one thing after another, but I only succeeded in stalling the car over and over. My panic increased when a fuel truck drew up on one side, and then two, three, four cars on the other. The faces of the drivers remained sullenly impassive as I continued to struggle with the gears.

A man stepped out of the third car. He looked to be in his early forties, with close-cropped brown hair, a mouth that twisted sideways, and a fierce but almost cross-eyed gaze.

'You must be the newest addition to the House of Atreus,' he said. His accent – Irish? Scottish? Welsh? – was unfamiliar.

'I hope it's not as bad as that,' I said. 'Is it?'

He stretched out his hand. 'I'm Crawley. Max's right-hand man. Or resident con artist. Token Sphinx. Bitter and twisted colleague. Best friend. As you like it. I take it from your present predicament that you've forgotten how to drive?'

'Well, not quite, but—'

'Why don't you step out of the car and let me put this lorry driver out of his misery?'

After he had got the car off the road, he showed me the trick to putting the car in reverse. 'Only the Swedes would think of something so clever. Just count yourself lucky you don't have one of their old automatics. They make the Flintstones look hi tech. Where were you going, by the way?'

'To town, to find a cheese grater.'

'Jesus Christ!' he said. 'Don't tell me you can cook, too. That's disgusting. It just won't do. Listen. Have you ever been to town before, as you put it?'

'Not really. Well, once, for an afternoon, about ten years ago.'

'Do you have a map? And while we're on the subject, a fondness for one-way systems and standing in rush-hour traffic being overtaken by cyclists?' It was not clear to me from his expression whether he was joking or serious. 'There's a fairly ill-equipped kitchen store in Summertown just a few shops down from the off-licence. Why don't I take you there?'

I got into his Morris Minor. 'So. How have they been treating you?' he asked as we headed down the single-track road into Oxford.

'Very considerately,' I said. 'If anything, too considerately.'

'Well,' he said. 'You can see their point. They know full well that any sane person in your shoes would run a mile. I hear the birthday party yesterday was something of a disaster.'

'Oh, that was my fault,' I said.

He rolled his eyes. 'You and about twenty other headcases – nineteen of whom I would say were certifiable. But it's good riddance to some very ugly rubbish otherwise known as Wayne, if you ask me. Now, I know the gentry like to go slumming from time to time, but that little caper was bloody ridiculous. You've won over Aunty Dowager Bea, I hear.'

'She's been very helpful.'

'"Meddling" is probably a more useful word. But she's still your best bet if you're looking for an ally. Whispering Pines has been in to clean, I take it?'

'I suppose you mean Janet.'

'She's a good sort, Janet. But when the going gets tough, she has a way of entering into alarming conversations with the duster. Don't worry, though. She's a tower of strength compared with the rest of them. Have you had any run-ins with Twinkle-Toes?' Catching my blank look, he added, 'Otherwise known as Danny.'

'Just for half an hour or so, before she took the children off for the night to visit some friends.'

'Half an hour? That's twenty-nine minutes too long. But she was all right, was she? Didn't bring out the tarot cards or throw around any crystals?'

'Mostly we talked about her work,' I said cautiously.

'If she worked half as long as she talks about her work, she'd have written *The Remembrance of Things Past* ten times over by now. Although this, I should warn you, is one subject you would best avoid. She and I have been rowing about it for years, and she still insists Proust wasn't crazy. This despite the fact that he spent his last ten years in a room lined with cork. Another word to the wise: if you want to express your admiration for any aspect of *Paris, Texas*, and particularly for the acting achievement of Harry Dean Stanton, for God's sake look over your shoulder first and make sure Danny's out of earshot. I've had that argument so many times I could recite it to you sideways.'

'You're the Crawley who runs Beckfield Press,' I said, as I remembered Max telling me about him.

'For my venial sins, yes.'

'And you also write poetry.'

'Yes, for my mortal sins.'

'Do you publish yourself?'

'Not allowed, my dear. Too straightforward. Too boring. Not enough intrigue. No, I'm part of what you'll soon discover was once the Hertford Five, but now is better known as the Eternal Triangle, along with two other poetry editors called Philip and Damian. I publish Philip and Max, and Philip publishes Damian, Damian publishes me, and Max makes sure we all get review space. It makes our enemies happier that way. To me, it's just a job, and a bloody useless job, too. They have no idea how badly we triad members pay each other. By the way, did you bring any dosh? I note with interest that you haven't a handbag. Don't worry. A cheese grater won't ruin me. And I'll even advance you cash for some wine – unless you prefer to wander over to Aunty Bea's like your freeloader boyfriend and sting her for a donation from her overstocked winecellar.'

I chose to borrow the money. As I told him on our return journey, I didn't like to be beholden to people. By way of explanation, I began to tell him where I came from and what kind of life I had been living before the abrupt change of the previous week. The story sent him into an alarmed silence. As I was still in the middle of it when we reached the house, I asked him in to have a glass of wine with me while I started supper. While chopping up the bacon, I found myself telling my (edited) version of how Max and I had met.

He listened thoughtfully. Then he said, in a low and uncertain voice, 'He deserves to be happy. No matter what anyone else says, remember that. But it will take some doing, my dear. How is he taking this latest crisis?'

'The biography, you mean?'

He nodded.

'I'm not sure,' I said.

He shrugged his shoulders. 'You'll know soon enough.' He made to leave. 'In the meantime, don't hesitate to get in touch if the games they try to play with you get just a bit too puzzling. And enjoy your supper. It does my heart more good than you can imagine to walk into that poor excuse for a kitchen and see something that was once alive. Allegedly.'

This last remark threw me. I thought he was referring to me and so I failed to catch the other possible meaning.

Chapter Fourteen

As I continued with supper, I corrected the chant. This was not my house, I told myself. But it was my paring knife, my cheese grater, my breadboard. They were my accomplishments for the day. Tomorrow I would buy a Le Creuset pot, or two of them, or three, and a steamer, a colander and a wooden spoon. I would go to the bookstore and get some cookbooks. Buy a basil plant and some spices, and see about replacing the odd assortment of mismatched plates, cups, glasses and cutlery. Cheer the place up a bit, rearrange the cabinets, stake my claim on this house that was not my house. Make my contribution to this strange family that was now my family, and claim my niche.

I was setting the table – making the best of what I had – when Bea appeared. 'Oh, how lovely!' she said when she saw the table. 'Are those flowers from the walled garden? How resourceful of you! But you looked rather tired. I hope you haven't taken on too much. No, honestly, I shouldn't,' she said when I offered her the wine. 'Well, I suppose I could risk half a glass. What a day I've had! A dreadful lunch with a dreadful woman who seems to think I'm the perfect person to do the text for a large photographic celebration of cold chicken. Goodness, what will they think of next? And now I'm off to the most appalling farmhouse in Northamptonshire for what promises to be a ghastly dinner party. You-know-who is meant to attend – Princess M's great friend, the one who ran off with that man who OD'd on carrot juice. I shall let you know how events unfold.' She picked her diary and her notebook out of her basket. 'Then it's Glyndebourne at the weekend, and after that I'm off to the health farm, so we must get you organised before then. You've sorted the car, I gather. I'll get you to the bank tomorrow morning, and if you're free perhaps we can have lunch together.'

She leaned forward. 'Unless you're working, of course. You mustn't let us encroach on you.'

'Actually,' I said, 'it doesn't really matter at the moment. My book is not going particularly well. Although I plan to keep to my usual schedule as soon as I've caught my breath.'

'Which is?'

'A minimum of three hours' desk time every morning.'

'That sounds reasonable,' Bea said. 'Although we must put our minds to the question of a study. Are you one of those people who can work anywhere? Do you prefer a room without a telephone?'

'Actually,' I said, 'I'm not sure how I feel about it, but Danny seems to expect me to use the one here.' Bea looked up sharply. 'You know,' I said. 'The one that's been locked up. Rebecca's study.'

Bea cocked her head to one side. 'Did she? How very, very odd!' She grimaced as she considered this unexpected news. Then she said, 'Well, I suppose it's a good sign.' Her voice gaining in confidence, she added, 'If it had been up to me, I would have forced the issue years ago. It's just not healthy.'

The ensuing silence went on a beat too long. 'Must be off, I'm afraid,' she said as she rose to her feet. Looking out the window, she added, 'I shan't have to leave you alone, in any case, for here he is now. What's for supper? It smells delicious.' But when she went into the kitchen, where the parsley and parmesan lay waiting in piles on the breadboard, and the egg sat waiting to be beaten in its cup, and the water stood ready in the pot, and the bacon was laid out in the frying pan, she screwed up her face and said, 'Goodness! What a surprise!'

'It's nothing special. It's for carbonara.'

'Does he know you're making carbonara?'

'Yes, well, actually, I just said I'd throw together an easy pasta.'

She gave me a sharp and quizzical look. 'Hasn't he mentioned to you that he's a vegetarian?'

'No,' I said in a small voice. And then, in an even smaller voice, I added, 'It never came up. What kind of vegetarian is he?' I went on to ask lamely.

In a loud, bland voice, she said, 'The kind that doesn't eat meat.'

'What should I do?' I asked her as I saw Max approaching.

'What would I do? Is that what you mean? The same as always, I'm afraid. Continue with Plan A.' Before she could say anything more, he had entered the house.

He came straight into the kitchen, kissed me on the forehead, noticed the wine but not, as far as I could tell, the bacon. 'Oh, you've made supper. How nice,' he said lightly. 'Where are the children?'

'Gone with Danny to Stokely Park,' Bea said.

'Really?' He looked surprised.

'Portia's party. I'm sorry. I thought you knew. It was arranged months ago.'

'Oh, yes. Yes, of course.' He looked disappointed.

Bea left. We sat down with our drinks. While my mind raced back over all the meals we had ever shared – why had I not noticed the absence of meat? – he told me about his day. At a formal lunch he had been seated next to a French woman who was convinced she was eating fox. His deputy ('I'll take you down one day so you can meet her'), whose fourth child was only two months old ('poor dear'), had had to go into hospital following a problematic root canal. There had been a gruesome meeting with the editor, and a sacking of two staff members who were on holiday, and 'rather too many calls from a well-known snoozepaper'.

'If I were even half as interesting as they seem to think I am, you'd be a very lucky woman.'

As we sat later over my ill-conceived meal, what mattered most was what we did not discuss – the biography, Rebecca, the study, the children, how I felt to be there, how he felt to see me at this table. What to do with me, how I was ever going to make a life for myself in this cottage, in this foreign country where I did not have a single friend, with a man I had promised to marry without ever bothering to find out what he ate. Instead, we discussed the books he had brought home, how to spend the evening and which video to watch. 'I've rented *The Evil Dead*, a rather dire horror movie, or *Henry V*, in case you don't like horror movies.'

'I'm too tired for quality,' I said.

He let out a bleat.

'Are you laughing?' I asked. 'Or are you crying? I can't tell any more. It's been a very confusing day. All I can tell you is that I didn't mean to make you laugh or make you cry. I was just saying how I felt.'

He reached over and took my hand. Gave me a smile. 'I know,' he said. 'I know.'

He took his hand away and returned to his food. 'By the way,' he said, in a gentle and faintly beseeching voice I was learning not to trust, 'it's been a very, very long time since anyone made me anything this delicious.'

Chapter Fifteen

And so the guided tour rolled on. The next day, Bea took me down to the bank and out to lunch as promised. The following day I had my first and last driving lesson. By Thursday she had reinforced my own misgivings enough to steer me away from Danny's idea of my using Rebecca's study.

'The view's lovely,' she told me as she darted about the walled garden picking flowers, 'but you might find it rather distracting, and you wouldn't want to have to look at her dreary books, would you? And what odd titles they have, too. *Foucault's Penis*, I ask you, it's enough to put one off books for life! If you were using the room for yourself, you'd want to clear them out, wouldn't you, darling, and that, I'm afraid, would raise the hackles of the faithful. It's really more of a museum, don't you agree, in spite of all that nonsense Danny is always spouting about the living spirit. Sometimes I wish that woman would just get on with it and give herself to the church. She could become a deacon, and go bustling around Wells Cathedral in one of those smart black robes, and leave us in peace!

'No, I do not believe your work would thrive in the Rabbit Warren, or whatever Danny is calling it. Imagine raising your eyes in search of *le mot juste* and having to face that gloomy row of privates on parade. You know the ones I mean. Those overendowed figurines Danny insists on calling signifiers. They're Cycladic, and rather valuable, I believe, and probably should be in a proper museum somewhere, but between you and me, darling, they're rather depressing – though not perhaps quite as depressing as those atrocious shaggy dog slippers Danny has insisted on preserving for posterity. Of all the silly ways to commemorate a friend! I should leave her to it, my dear, and take over the spare bedroom instead. The window is stuck open, but I can send someone over to see to that as early as next week, if you're agreeable. There's nothing of sentimental value in there – we'll have to check with Danny, of course, or else we'll send her into another of her *Heteroglossia* fits. But so long as we follow the proper channels, we should be able to clear it out and decorate it properly. You'll need a room of your own, my dear. Or should I say a door to lock? I don't mean to do Danny down, but she is a lonely and desperate soul and, in more ways than not, still rather a child. You don't want to put yourself in a position where you'd have to offend her.

'Do you have any strong views on skylights? There is, after all, only the one window in that room. It might be worth asking Janet's husband to give us an opinion. It's also important, I should think, to make sure that the curtains and the furniture are in keeping with your belongings. Have you brought with you any photographs? Bric-à-brac? Ought we to look into bringing a few favourite sticks of this and that, or books and what have you, over to this side of the pond?'

I told her, as briefly as I could, the reasons why I could not reclaim them. I showed her the handful of photographs ('Hmm. Charming!') and my *sumak* carpet. 'It's not an antique,' I said, in a too hasty attempt to save her from the necessity of praising it.

'No, of course it isn't,' she said firmly. 'But it's a charming little thing nonetheless, and an excellent starting point. I should take it down with us this afternoon when we go to see Mrs Carter. She's very good at what she does, but she has this ridiculous notion about colour-coordinated artwork.' Here Bea went into an imitation of Mrs Carter standing with her samples of upholstery fabric, offering up one colour scheme as being 'smashing in conjunction with darkish portraits of Victorian ladies and gentlemen' and another as being 'quite the ticket if your taste runs to modern photographers such as Henry Morgue'.

It was unnerving, after laughing at the imitation, to meet the original, and strangely moving to see in the eyes of the mimic a gentle concern for Mrs Carter's feelings. Not at any cost were the little snobberies with which this woman decorated her small life to be jostled. When Mrs Carter asked me about the photography of

108

Morgue, I saw Bea's face freeze in alarm. It only relaxed when I played along, and said the photographs I liked the most were the ones of men and women.

'You were brilliant, my dear, quite brilliant,' Bea told me afterwards. By drinks time, the awkward collection of near embarrassments had turned into a polished amusement. 'There was one horrible moment when I thought she was going to give the game away,' she told the assembled guests. 'It was when Mrs Carter was waxing poetic about the Roualt exhibition, which she called the Renault exhibition. I could see you were quite puzzled, my dear. But you kept your answers beautifully vague. And we found just the right colour scheme, didn't we, to go with your little *sumak*.'

It was, of course, Bea who had found the right fabric for the curtains and the sofa, and Bea who knew which of the six or seven old desks in her attic would be perfect for my purposes. She knew before I knew that it would be best to have bookshelves custom-made. When I met Janet's husband, Bea reminded me that we needed shelves of different heights. And it was Bea who found the perfect lamps, and who suggested a quick trip to the sales for a portable electric radiator. I was happy to follow her suggestions, because, as I readily admitted to her, I had no decorating ideas of my own.

'No, of course not, darling. You're like that. You live in the clouds. It's just what Max needs – someone artless. Another designing woman at this stage would have been the finishing touch.'

There was a pause, which I was tempted to end with a question. But which question? There were so many. Why *another* designing woman? If another designing woman would have been the *finishing* touch, what had been the penultimate touch? What did she know about what happened between Max and Rebecca? Would she tell me if I asked, or would she remain loyal, and to whom?

What did she mean by calling me artless? Was it just another way of saying easily fooled? I longed to ask but didn't dare, and so instead I said, 'I don't get the impression that Rebecca knew much about design either.'

'Well, of course you're right. She had her head in the clouds, too. But it was different, wasn't it? As she herself admitted in that rather nice poem, I'm sure you know the one I mean. The one in *Waiting for the Titanic* about heavenly housekeeping. Didn't she use that very term? I mean "designing woman".'

'Yes, she did.'

'As Max does, I believe, in "Unravelling the Minotaur".'

'Does he?' I asked.

She looked at me. 'I take it you're better acquainted with her work than you are with his.'

'Yes,' I said. 'But I'm sure that will change.'

'Perhaps not,' she said. 'And actually, if I were you, I shouldn't rush into it. It might be a bad time. Reading love poetry addressed to another woman can rather undermine one. I do believe, also,' she said, her voice growing slightly louder and almost humourless, 'as I'm sure you yourself believe, that Max's best work is yet to come. There's plenty for you to think about right now, my dear, in the land of the living. I should content myself with that for the moment, and let sleeping dogs lie.'

But that night, I did have time on my hands, as Max was late coming home. And so I did go digging, despite the warning. 'Unravelling the Minotaur' was a strange poem, full of dark, despairing, archaic metaphors, and hard to construe as a description of love. There was no mention of a designing woman. Had Bea got it wrong? Remembering the beadiness of her gaze, I thought not. I had a sinking feeling I had just passed another test. I was not just artless now, but bad at being dishonest.

And too fearful of my new role to entertain a doubt.

III

Cold Feet

Chapter Sixteen

*I*t was, I thought innocently, a busy time of year. Having had no children of my own, I did not query the logic behind William and Hermione's schedule. Or rather, I thought that what I was seeing was normal for Britain, at least normal for children of their class. They were not to be left to their own devices: Art Week was followed by cricket camp, which led on to a three-day cookery course somewhere near Brighton. They hadn't been back for twelve hours before they were packed off to a Theatre Adventure in Chipping Norton. It began on a Monday and ended on Friday with an hour-long musical for the benefit of the parents. I went with Danny, as Max couldn't take time off work. We took them straight from the theatre to a music camp in Cheltenham.

I did not see much of Max either. By now he had started libel proceedings against Jack Scully and his publishers. This meant extra trips to London and evening phone conversations that interrupted supper and went on for hours. When he wasn't on the phone he was reading, or, as he put it, being snowed under by the Booker. I did not know what he meant until I went into the newspaper with him one day and saw the mountains of books in his office. He had to go to Edinburgh twice that August. After we put him on the plane for his second visit, Danny and the children and I drove up to Bramble House, his mother's place in Yorkshire, and it was during this trip that the doubts I had suppressed in order to keep my mind open took on a life of their own.

Because it was a bank-holiday weekend, the traffic was bad, almost doubling what was to have been a five-hour journey. There was never a moment of silence in the car – when we were not listening to Radio Four or Max's tape of *The Wind in the Willows*, we were playing I Spy, looking for unusual number plates, or singing rounds. But as one diversion led to another, I became increasingly aware that the good cheer was rehearsed, and that the children did not want me there. Whenever their good manners showed signs of cracking, Danny would remind them, a bit too pointedly, of the promise they had made her, of the sweets she had trustingly given them before setting out, when really she ought to have waited until afterwards. It was clear they had been bribed.

Bramble House turned out to be a mansion made out of brick and set in a valley inside grounds so large that it was impossible, I later learned, for anyone to set eyes on it or its seemingly endless gardens without trespassing. It dated from the mid-nineteenth century. I did not realise at the time that this implied new money. When we arrived, the only person on hand was the Lithuanian nanny. The children seemed genuinely pleased to see her. She swept them off to the nursery. I did not see them again until the following afternoon.

'Caroline – that's Max's mater and Bea's sister – will have gone to sleep by now, so you're spared *that* ordeal until tomorrow,' Danny said. She led me across the front hall and into a large, white sitting room where a fire was already blazing. She opened what looked like a closet door and revealed a fully stocked bar. 'I'm assuming you need a stiff drink as much as I do. Or at least you will once you've heard what I have to tell you.'

As we sat nursing our whiskies in front of the fire, she filled me in on Max's brother, or what she called 'the latest chapter of the Jonathan Chronicles'.

'I'm sure you know he's a hopeless junkie, but did you know he's also HIV positive? It may not surprise you to hear that they blame this on Rebecca,' Danny said, adding darkly, 'although, if you ask me, it was the other way round.' Before she could explain, we were interrupted by an electric bell, which rang three times. 'Goodness!' Danny exclaimed. 'Is it eight o'clock already?' Jumping to her feet with an alarming smile, she led me back through the front hall to a long and dimly lit dining room where supper sat waiting for us on a sideboard. 'It looks like magic, doesn't it?' she said as she dished out two overlarge servings. Then she explained that it wasn't magic but martyrdom. 'We are being looked after by a saint and her name is Tatiana.'

Tatiana, she explained, was Jonathan Junkie's brilliant but long-suffering wife, who lived at Bramble House full time and ran things while pretending not to. 'But there the trouble begins,' she said as she put her napkin on her lap. 'White wine or red? And goodness, I forgot to give you bread. Shall I ring for some? Are you sure? You must let me know if you change your mind. So yes, now. Where was I? What we need next, I think, is a quick run-through of the cast of characters for the upcoming weekend. Tatiana is a wife in name only, alas. Our Jonathan also has a girlfriend – until such time as her ex-husband intervenes, this being the main complication of the *mise-en-scène*. Because, you see, Jonathan Junkie's girlfriend – I suppose I ought to refer to her by name, although it takes an awful lot of courage to do so, seeing as her parents named her Lois, but let me try. Until six or seven months ago, Lois was the wife of Max's mother's gamekeeper. A nice man, but with rather an alarming temper. He kept the child. She ran off in the middle of the night, you see, leaving them both. There was some talk of her having been threatened with a hatchet, although God knows she may have been asking for it. It was all rather shocking, but now it seems to have died down enough for Luscious Lois to think it's quite all right to come here for the bank-holiday weekend and have the child with her at the big house. So! What can I say? Watch this space!'

Another concern, she told me, was that Luscious Lois was with child. If this turned out to be a son ('and we shan't even utter the dread thought HIV positive'), he could dispute the family's decision to make Max the heir. 'As a result of which, you may have the pleasure of seeing sparks flying back and forth between our selfless mistress in residence and the saintly wife-in-name-only. Who claims she's not all that interested in money, she being so very, very White Russian, although a less grateful and appreciative chronicler than myself might point out that her noble plans make her a very expensive proposition altogether, and that anyone but Max is going to take a dim view of it. We'll see the latest project tomorrow, I fear. It's some sort of telecottage industry. It's meant to revitalise – or is the word "rationalise"? – the estate. She has named it Middlemarch without the *slightest* hint of irony, *if* you please. If we use all our resources, we may just be able to put off the inevitable hike until after lunch. I hope you brought your boots!

'A word of advice: don't ask Tatiana any question to which you would rather not have an answer on a scale with a Reith lecture. A second word of advice: please try not to mention Bea's name in front of Caroline. The effect can be quite frightening.'

She continued in this vein through three courses about the other assorted cousins and friends who were also going to be arriving for the weekend. As one background intrigue about people I hadn't met intertwined with another, I became more and more confused. Fatigue set in. After we had finished our meal, Danny rang the bell for the servants to collect our plates and led me back across the hallway to the sitting room for coffee. She tried to interest me in a game of table tennis. 'Or billiards, if you prefer. There's a room for that, too.'

When I declined, and said I was ready for bed, her voice took on a faintly unpleasant twinge. Couldn't I have another cup of coffee and revive my spirits? It was our only night without Max. He could be such a bore, and really, she thought, it would be better to get to know the others before he arrived. They were due in between eleven and midnight, 'and they're longing to meet you'.

It was unclear to me why, after her introductory descriptions, she would think that I would want to meet *them*. I made the mistake of saying so. She reacted as if I had insulted her personally. Even after I assured her that I had been half joking, she was unable to be more than half friendly. After she had shown me to the vast room with its already turned-down four-poster bed, I tried to apologise again.

She shrugged her shoulders and said, 'Not to worry. It was just my *folie de nostalgie* running away with me. It was always such a treat, you see, when Rebecca and I could escape up here without the old bear. But I understand completely. You must have your beauty sleep and be ready for the challenges of the morrow. I have half a mind to follow suit.'

But the other half of her mind won out. I was still awake an hour later when the next party arrived. Danny's greetings were ecstatic. I heard them laughing and gossiping with her in the sitting room below. And although I told myself I had to be imagining things, I thought I heard the loudest laughter whenever Danny imitated my voice.

I woke up at six, but waited an hour before setting out to look for the dining room. I stood in the middle of the front hall, transfixed by the forbidding busts on display, and tried to remember our itinerary of the previous evening. The third door I tried was the right one.

The previous evening I had not been able to see the view, so my eyes went straight to it. First the lake, then the bridge, the folly, the hills, the distant ridge of rain clouds, then a harsh, overcultivated voice saying, 'Don't gape.' I jumped.

'Don't jump. It's unladylike.' The speaker was sitting at the far end of the huge oval table: a faded, pastel-coloured beauty with stiffly coiffed blonde hair and rigid posture.

'You must be Max's new American,' she now said.

'Yes,' I replied. 'I suppose I am.'

She looked me over. 'Hmm. Well. What a curious choice! Though not the first, by any means. So long as the boy's happy, I suppose I must go along with it. *Are* you making him happy?'

'I'd say it was too early to tell.'

'Hmph. I suppose you're right. And in the long run, it may not matter. One can so easily exaggerate its importance. In that respect, it's rather like death. You'll find breakfast on the sideboard. I'm not sure I'd recommend the eggs.'

Under her gaze, I helped myself to toast and coffee. I sat down, attempting a smile. It was not returned. There was a long silence while she went about the demanding task of buttering a wedge of toast perfectly. Then she said, 'I understand you've been married before.'

'Yes.'

'And that it was a marriage without issue.'

'We had no children, if that's what you mean.'

117

'Have you plans for children now?'

'No, at least not in the near future. Although you never know.'

'You're quite sure of that, are you?'

'Reasonably sure.'

'Good. It's so hard to tell these days. Your country is a closed book to me, I'm afraid. I cannot bear New York, although I did have a good time once in Newport. Might I have met your family in Newport?'

I said, 'I don't come from that kind of family.'

'What kind of family *do* you come from?'

'Normal.'

'Normal. How odd!' she said. 'And if you don't mind my saying so, how like Rebecca.' She rose from the table and left the room without another word.

I finished my toast, went outside for a brief and aimless walk, and then, when it began to rain, went back to the desk in my room, where I submerged myself in my book until Danny knocked on the door at half past twelve.

She took me down to the sitting room 'to meet the rest of the cast'. Even to my doubting eyes, they did give every sign of 'dying to meet me'. First to her feet was the woman I immediately recognised as St Tatiana. She was tall, with flyaway hair and intelligent eyes, and dressed in painting clothes. Next to her were two dreamily confident, carelessly polite young couples who seemed to be cousins. The pretty woman with permed hair and pink lipstick I took to be Luscious Lois. The gap-toothed man in hip-hop clothes who was emptying his pockets in front of the fireplace I took to be Jonathan. He had a large bottle of Coca-Cola sitting next to him. The others were all nursing Bloody Marys and laughing softly about their hangovers. But when Max's mother appeared, they reverted to polite greetings, bright-eyed silence and crossword puzzles – except for Jonathan, who was distraught at having lost something.

It turned out to be his syringe. He sat next to me at lunch and told me the whole story – how he had once enjoyed reading history books, but now had only the attention span for cartoons; how dangerous crack was, and how badly run the nation's methadone programme;

how he hated his parents; how much he missed his teeth. Although he spoke in a loud voice, no one but I acknowledged it. They spoke instead about Middlemarch, to which Danny and I were dragged as predicted as soon as we had finished lunch.

The nanny and the four children were summoned from the nursery, outfitted in the boot room and equipped with tracking tools. It was already raining when we set out, but they paid this inconvenience as little attention as they had paid to the confessions of a drug addict at lunch. It took us an hour and a half of brisk walking before we reached our destination. All there was to see was a Portakabin, a makeshift toolshed, a few acres of turned earth, and posts marking the future foundations of a building. As Tatiana took us around these, she explained how it would look with such conviction that you could almost believe it was already there.

She invited us to sit down in the mud and inspect her plans, which she had in her pocket. When I demurred, she gave me a withering look and then relegated me to the land of the invisible. Danny played along. The snub soon grew too much to bear. I went over to the brook, where the nanny and the children were building a dam. Here I caused more trouble by messing up some of their tracking arrows. As William tried to fix them, he burst into tears. 'Why does she have to be here at all?' he sobbed. 'She's no bloody use! No bloody use at all.' I tried to help him. He pushed me away. Before I knew it, Danny and Tatiana had arrived to limit the damage. I was sent back to the house with the nanny. She complained all the way.

These were very strange people, she kept saying. She itemised the bizarre customs she had witnessed and asked me to explain them. Was it all English people, or just these people, who blocked half the light coming through their tiny windows by putting their dressing tables in front of them? Why was privacy so important for them? Why didn't they have showers? And this Jonathan – his mother was too easy with him. But at the same time, she was so strict with the children. They couldn't bring this toy into the sitting room, and they couldn't discuss that subject. 'They can't be children when they go into her presence. They can only be children when they are locked up in the nursery with me. Can you explain me this?' she pleaded. Every time I said I couldn't, she patted my back in commiseration or squeezed my hand. Her sincerity was almost frightening. 'I wish you well,' she kept saying. 'But I have bad bone feeling for you.' By the time we got back to the house, it was five o'clock. I ran up to the bedroom, expecting to see Max. Instead I found a note to say he would not arrive until the next day.

That evening I tried to redeem myself by joining in the after-dinner parlour games. But with every game I proved myself to be less of an asset to my team. 'Don't you play charades in America?' Max's mother asked me after one particularly dismal failure. After another, she peered at me over lowered glasses and enquired, 'Are you dyslexic?' Once she had retired at eleven, the disapproval grew more pointed. The first game we played was called What's the Problem? I was invited to leave the room while they thought one up. When I returned, I had to guess. After an hour, I gave up. They told me they were apostles and I was Judas.

When the laughter died down, someone suggested Wink Murder. I failed to understand the rules and so ruined the game. After that, we moved on to the table-tennis room, where I proceeded to lose badly against Luscious Lois while all the others watched. When they tired of table tennis and began a game of Tag Murder, I used the cover of darkness to crawl out of the room and up to bed.

The following morning, I was once again the only one to join Max's mother for breakfast. She informed me, as if it were my fault, that the nanny was ill. She was going to have to take her to the doctor on her way to church, during which time I was to be in charge of the children. Because it was a beautiful morning, I suggested that we follow the track they had made the previous afternoon. I took a picnic, which we ate next to the brook when we got to Middlemarch. I was in no hurry to return to the house, so when the children asked if they could continue digging their dam, I was happy to go along with it.

There was a padlock on the shed door, but we were still able to get inside for digging utensils because it was off its hinges. They decided to join up what looked like a half-dug grave with the brook. While digging the channel, they unearthed a collection of bones which looked to have once belonged to an animal, but because they seemed to want more of a story, I went along with the idea that we had discovered the remains of a murder victim. I remember how William and Hermione looked at me. For the first time since we had been thrown together, I was showing interesting possibilities. And so, of course, I went too far.

Chapter Seventeen

'I see you've managed to make yourself at home.' This was the first thing Max said to me when I found him with his mother and three stiff-necked priests in the sitting room. It was teatime, and I had just woken up from an unintended nap. After our return from Middlemarch, I had left the children watching television in the nursery while I took a bath. I now heard that they had been taken off to town without permission by Jonathan. Max was not amused and clearly held me responsible.

'You're such a bore, Max,' his mother was saying to him. 'It's only eight miles, for goodness' sake. They'll come to no harm.'

'It's the principle of the thing,' Max insisted. He returned to his crossword puzzle. The only time he addressed me was when he wanted help with an anagram. I made the tension between us even worse by asking him to explain the clue.

Even when the children came running into the sitting room, his face registered no pleasure. He did not deign to greet his brother Jonathan, except to say, when Jonathan emptied five bagloads of Mars Bars on the floor, that he was glad his brother had found a new enthusiasm. Max's mother tried to civilise matters by telling the children that they were allowed only one Mars Bar each. She made a big deal about where they could and could not put the wrappers, told them to take off their shoes and put them where they belonged, and took note of a hole in one of Hermione's socks. Max still refused to be drawn from his crossword. It was in desperation that William pulled his bones out of his pocket.

The ploy worked, but only to annoy Max further. 'So you've been digging, have you?' he said. 'And whose idea was that?'

His explanation won me another accusing look.

'Put them away,' said his grandmother. 'They're dirty. You'll need to wash them downstairs.'

Still caught up in our murder game, William said, 'But that would be tampering with evidence.'

To my surprise, Max's mother said, 'You may be right. If you were digging near Middlemarch, those bones could well belong to that skeleton.'

She said it in a casual, playful voice, but it made Max put down his newspaper. 'Mother,' he said. 'Mother! I thought we had talked about this.'

'Talked about what, darling?'

'Talked about how important it is not to make up stories until this court case is over.'

'But darling, I'm not making up stories. I'm telling you the truth. The truth is always stranger than fiction, darling. Even Rebecca knew that.'

Max's face grew red. 'Let's leave Rebecca out of this.'

'I really do think that's setting your sights rather high, don't you agree?'

'I want you to stop making up stories about skeletons. We've had quite enough of those. If you can't stop making up stories about skeletons, my advice to you is to put them into a book.'

'Darling, you know that won't do any more. I've retired. I'm not changing my mind. But neither can I rewrite the irrefutable facts. There really was a skeleton.'

'What skeleton?' he asked, his voice growing more hostile with every word.

His mother explained that the workmen had found one some months ago.

Had she notified the police? Max asked.

Well, said his mother, she had considered it briefly, but in the end it had seemed too much of a bother. 'Seeing as it wasn't anyone we know.'

'How could you possibly know that?' Max asked sarcastically.

'Goodness, Max! It ought to be obvious. We would have noticed.'

123

'Even in fiction, Mother, skeletons don't have faces. You would have had to have the skeleton sent in for analysis, and that would have involved informing the police.'

'Well, yes, but that's assuming there has been foul play. In this case, it could have been anyone. From the Stone Age, even.'

'You still would have had to inform the police.'

'But only if you were reasonably certain it belonged to a human. In this case, the bones do rather look as if they belong to a dog. Don't you think, darling? But of course you wouldn't know, because you've been too busy shouting at me to stop and look at them.'

'I shall do nothing of the sort. William, I want you to put them into the bin. Now.'

'But we can't solve the crime without them,' Hermione protested. 'And we have to solve the crime, because it might be the most important mystery of the universe!'

'Who told you that?' Max asked.

'*She* did.' Hermione pointed at me.

Max looked at me without expression, then folded up his paper, put it under his arm and stalked out of the room. I followed him out, to explain to him, but before I could reach them, the lunch bell went. He refused to look at me when it was just the two of us in the dining room, but when the others arrived, he treated me as politely as if I were a stranger.

After lunch Max announced that we were going to take advantage of a gap in the clouds to take a walk to Butterfly Valley. By the time we got there, it was raining again. Since my anorak was not fully waterproof, I took refuge under a tree. For a while the others used me as a depot for the leaves and flowers they had collected. Then, as soon as the sky cleared, they forgot I was there. The longer I looked at them crouching in the mud, waiting for the small miracles of nature to parade before them, the less I understood.

It seemed to me that they couldn't relax unless they were all looking at something small, beautiful and almost rare. Butterflies provided the perfect excuse for communion. There was, first of all, the injunction to silence, followed by a whispered lecture. ('Look at the colours, and now at the pattern, and you tell me what it reminds you of. Yes, Hermione, you're spot on. You remember, don't you, when we saw a rather larger one in Wharfedale? Good memory!') I was taken aback, almost frightened, by the softness in their eyes and the happy alertness of their muted responses. It would disappear the moment they turned to address each other.

When they found the wounded bird, it all got too much for me. It was then that it hit me I was living not in a new place to which I would gradually become accustomed, but in country that would always be foreign to me. A country where even the smallest things people did would never make sense to me. Why could Max cradle a bird so lovingly but barely bring himself to touch his daughter on the shoulder? Why didn't his daughter mind? Why was it so important to find out what kind of bird it was? Why weren't they content just to look at it? Why couldn't they ever look at each other and say, 'I missed you' or 'I'm glad you're here'? Why did their every feeling have to be displaced before it could be labelled?

They were talking about the wounded bird being far from home, but what about me? What was I doing here, sitting staring at a patch of earth that meant nothing to me? Didn't they even pause to wonder where the patch of earth was that meant something to me? I sat there watching them until I couldn't bear it any more. I sat there until it was a question of either leaving or belting out a scream.

When I got back to our room, I drew myself a bath and soaked in it until the water began to cool. Having failed to lose myself in the novel Max had given me to review, I sat myself down at the desk to work on my own book. This was breaking a rule I had about never working on my novel unless I had just woken up, but there was no reason for this rule other than force of habit. The book that afternoon seemed to me to be the only home I had left.

I was back to the first chapter again. It began with a description of my childhood home. But when I read it now, I could see it gave only information of the most general kind and so evoked nothing. I crossed it out, opened my notebook to a fresh page and closed my eyes until I could imagine myself back outside my house on a warm summer afternoon, but although I could see it and taste it and smell it, whenever I tried to approach the front door, the whole picture disappeared.

Where had it gone? Why? Tears fell on my notebook. When I couldn't see it any longer, I got up and threw myself on the sofa. But I couldn't stop.

When Max came back, cleansed of his earlier annoyances by the afternoon of fresh air, and asked me why I looked so upset and why I hadn't dressed for dinner, I told him I couldn't come to dinner because I was crying about my life. And he said, 'Oh, darling, do try and pull yourself together. I know it's hard. This place is hell for me too. Think of it this way. Tomorrow after breakfast we'll be heading home.'

'It's not just me, it's my book,' I said. 'I looked at it this afternoon, and I see now that it's all wrong.'

'Good,' he said. 'Then you can go back to the beginning and write the right book starting tomorrow. But do wait until we get back to Beckfield, won't you. The rightest book in the world would look wrong after a day or two in Bramble House.' He lifted me up, put his arms around me, looked into my eyes and said in an amorous whisper, 'Name one adult in this house aside from the occupants of this room who isn't barking.'

I couldn't help laughing.

Still whispering, he said, 'But you mustn't condemn them. They're trying very hard. Don't think they're not sitting in their rooms now crying too. What do they have to be happy about, for God's sake? What do they have to look forward to? I'll tell you the only thing they look forward to: two stiff drinks before supper and a meal that's only just good enough to take their mind off things. So here's what I'm asking you to do. I'm asking you to put this book out of your mind – it's not going to go anywhere, for God's sake, so why not leave it be for an evening? And, darling –' here he took my hand – 'hasn't it ever occurred to you that it might be a trifle too soon to be writing a novel about a stepbrother who becomes a lover and then a husband, a competitor and a suicide? Don't you think it's doing yourself down to put yourself so close to a wound that cannot possibly have healed yet? I would take a breath if I were

126

you, and ask myself if it wouldn't be kinder and more productive to try my hand at something more modest. But for the moment, you don't even need to ask yourself that question. All you need to do is take a bath and get dressed and come downstairs with me and do one last performance of the panto.'

'Everyone will want to know why my eyes are swollen,' I said.

'Yes, but they won't dare ask. What's more, they'll be your friends for life if you do them a favour of not playing the American and offering them an explanation.'

And he was right. When I appeared in the sitting room and they took in the telltale signs of an afternoon spent crying, at first they froze, as if they were afraid I was going to say something to embarrass them. Then, when enough time had elapsed for them to work out that I was going to keep my thoughts and feelings to myself, they relaxed, asked me if I would like a drink, care to see a newspaper, prefer to sit in a more comfortable chair. For the first time since my arrival, I saw some compassion in Max's mother's eyes. And when Jonathan Junkie appeared clutching a jug of Coke, I felt some reciprocal compassion for her; admiration, even, for what she endured without complaining. He was distraught, he told us like a cranky eight-year-old, because he couldn't find his Walkman. His mother did her best to calm him down but her efforts failed. He hadn't been sitting two minutes before he jumped to his feet, threw his jug of Coke against the wall and screamed, 'I need a fix!'

'Nonsense, darling, you're just tired,' was all she said. She got Luscious Lois to take him away. Having dispensed with him, she then turned to the rest of us and, without missing a beat, told us about the flood that Nostradamus had predicted, which would soon submerge all of Britain except parts of the Scottish Highlands. 'I'm not quite sure how one goes about preparing for it.' The only time she showed any emotion that evening was during the parlour games, when she was asked to act out 'angry' in the manner of the word, and smashed a Chinese vase.

Chapter Eighteen

We left for Oxford right after breakfast the next morning. The Beckfield Press was launching a new poetry imprint that evening. As it was to be the first big party of the literary season, Bea and Giles were expecting a large turnout and counting on Max to be there to help. I knew that I would be on display. I had been dreading the prospect for weeks; after my failures of the weekend, I was dreading it even more.

But between now and then were eight hours free of judging eyes. St Tatiana had arranged for the children to stay on at Bramble House until the end of the week, so it was just Max, Danny and I in the car. I don't think I was the only one who was happy to put the house behind me. We were hardly out of the drive when Max removed the *Alice in Wonderland* tape from the deck and replaced it with Ry Cooder. He turned it up full blast, like an adolescent who was trying to forget that the car he was driving belonged to his parents. Despite his efforts, *Alice in Wonderland* remained with us in spirit.

I wanted to draw out the journey as long as we could. But Max did eighty on the country roads and a hundred when we got to the motorway. He got slower cars to move off the fast lane by coming right up behind them and flashing his lights. When we stopped for petrol outside Birmingham, I asked Danny if she could ask to take over the wheel.

'Driving a bit too fast for you, is he?' she said with a crazy smile.

'Just a bit,' I said.

'How I wish I could say the same! I've loved every minute of it. *La vitesse!* It's such a treat to have the old Max back again. Look at his bones!' She gestured out the window. He was just coming out of the shop. 'What a lucky woman you are to have found a man with such beautiful bones! You can't even see them when he's depressed – his whole face droops as if were entirely boneless.' She shifted over to the driver's seat and turned on the engine. 'This time last year, I'd just about lost hope for him, you know. Will you believe me if I tell you that he went for an entire thirty-six months without reading anything that wasn't about a Midwestern serial killer?'

'Why aren't I driving?' he said when he got back to the car.

Instead of answering his question, she said, 'I was just remembering your thriller addiction.'

'It hasn't ended,' he said, as if this *were* an answer to his question and anyone with any sense could understand why. 'I'm as addicted to thrillers as I ever was, but tragically I've run through my supplies. There are very few people who can do them right. If you ask me, it's the most difficult art of them all.'

'How perverse you poets are!' she exclaimed with a laugh as she darted back into the traffic without looking where she was going. She barrelled down the motorway even faster than Max had done. The discussion about thrillers continued. As I recognised only about half the names, there were large chunks of it I could not follow. It seemed that Danny thought the exciting new talents were women, whereas Max thought their books were too sedentary to be called exciting. Danny thought the right word was not 'sedentary' but 'atmospheric', and that the men Max admired so much were incapable of suspense because they tended to kill off their best characters before they had a chance to develop.

It went on and on. I thought I had died and gone to Radio Four. Radio Four in Wonderland. The more refined the conversation became, the crazier the driving. Danny weaved in and out of the traffic without ever looking over her shoulder and checking her mirrors. She didn't even bother to flash her lights when she wanted another car to get out of her way. She just leaned on her horn. But nothing she did seemed to distract Max from whatever it was he was going to say. Instead of fearing for his life, he acted as if he were in an overheated, smoke-filled dining room trying to stay awake.

129

'I like moral ambiguity,' I remember him saying as she plunged us between two killer lorries without indicating. 'I don't like neat endings and packages clearly marked "good" and "evil". As for this idea that poverty doesn't allow for moral choices, well . . .'

'I agree. Orwell ought to have known better. But how can you have moral ambiguity if your macho hero doesn't even know the meaning of the word "self-aware"? They act without thinking. They seem to be afraid that if they think, they won't be able to act.'

'I suppose you'd like them to spend their novels in therapy sessions.'

'Well, it worked for Robertson Davies!'

'If you say so, O wise one.'

'Are you trying to tell me you discovered nothing of interest on the couch?'

'Oh, it was interesting, all right,' Max said with a yawn, 'but not the sort of interesting one would want to share with someone as sensitive and self-aware as you.'

'You and your dreams,' Danny said. 'I'm not sure how useful all that is. Have you ever been in therapy?' she said, smiling at me via the rear-view mirror.

'Not anything I'd write home about,' I said.

Smiling as if I'd told her something really interesting, she said, 'Well, it might sound unorthodox to you, in that case, but the best therapy I ever had didn't deal in dreams at all but taught me how to use my eyes again and how to listen. I mean listen to my own stories as well as other people's stories. What I learned that year was that a boring or repetitive story was of necessity an incomplete story, while a seamless story with clean lines and a beginning, middle and ending was an impoverished fiction. Goodness!' she said as she slammed on the brakes and darted across the lanes of traffic onto an exit lane. 'You do know what I mean, don't you?'

I made the mistake of saying I didn't.

'Well, I hope you don't mind my telling you. It was such a revelation. I was so lucky to have found this man. Such a genius! He changed my life. You don't mind if I explain, do you, Max? Max has heard it all before.'

'Of course I don't mind,' Max said with a larger yawn. 'So long as you don't mind if I don't listen.' He crawled into the back seat, where he stretched out his legs and put his head on my lap.

'Would you like to come up to the front?' Danny asked. 'It would be so much cosier.'

But I did not want to go up to the front. I clung to Max as if he were a life raft.

Cheerfully oblivious to me and to the minutiae on the road ahead of her, Danny launched into a painfully detailed account of how this genius therapist ('or I suppose I should say analyst') had cured her of insomnia, claustrophobia, separation anxiety and hypochondria. His main method seemed to have been bullying.

'Is he asleep yet?' Danny kept asking. When I said he was, she said, 'Good, then I can mention the R word.' She went on to tell me that it was not just Rebecca's death that had sent her into therapy but Max's and the children's hostility to her when she was only trying to help them during the mourning period. 'They hated me for being me. No, it was even worse than that. They hated me for not being her. I remember going to this therapist in tears one afternoon – it was some detail that had made me feel particularly unwelcome, I think young William had asked me to go home and die or whatever – and I remember saying to my genius that William had hurt my feelings so that I no longer felt I belonged in that house, and in a booming voice, he said to me, "Now tell me, who does belong in that house? Not even Max belongs in that house. The house doesn't belong to him, and neither do the children. His cousins don't belong to his uncle. His aunt gets along better with him than with her own children. By her own definition of bloodlines, she is a turncoat in a cul-de-sac!"' Danny laughed at the memory. 'I felt better after that. I wish I could say I didn't have cause to remember those words often. Still – it doesn't matter if you belong or not. In the end, that's not what matters, is it? What matters is that you call it home.'

But by the time Beckfield loomed into view, I no longer knew whether I wanted to call it home. I had the beginnings of a headache. The glistening delivery van, the men and women bustling back and forth with crates of wine and glasses, the wild but balanced bursts of colour in the flower beds, the freshly cut lawn and perfect tennis court hurt my eyes. I didn't want to get out of the car. I wanted to sit there in the back with Max's warm head in my lap. When he sat up, stretched his arms and said, 'Hey ho, back to work, then,' I wanted to scream. He wanted me to go straight over to the big house with him to find out what needed to be done for the party. But I couldn't face it. Instead I went back to the cottage to hide in yet another bath. This time when the water cooled I kept adding more hot to it. I must have been in there over an hour when there was a knock on the door.

'Yoohoo!' It was Bea. 'Everything all right in there?'

A huge and, I told myself, unjustified wave of rage ran through me. Why couldn't they leave me alone? I wasn't like them. I couldn't go for days and days of polite, witty, superficial conversation without a break. How was I going to get through the party that evening if I didn't have an afternoon to prepare myself for it? It was all I could do to answer politely.

'I thought you might need a bit of wardrobe advice,' she now said.

I felt like saying, 'I'll wear whatever the hell I feel like wearing!' But I reminded myself that she was only trying to help. 'I thought I'd wear that dress we bought together last week,' I said, trying to keep my voice neutral.

'Lovely. Perfect. It's just what I would have advised. How are you feeling, my dear? Was it a total nightmare?'

'I'm not sure,' I said.

'Why don't I go downstairs and make us some tea?'

When I got downstairs, I felt like running into the bedroom and bolting the door. If I have to have one more amusing conversation, I thought, my head is going to explode. But I reminded myself again that Bea was not to blame for my state of mind. So I forced a smile onto my face as I joined her at the dining table.

She had set it with one of my new Provençal tablecloths and a tea set I didn't recognise. The vase she had filled with flowers from the garden was new, too. 'I hope you don't mind, but I saw these on sale and I couldn't resist. If you don't like them, I'll have them myself. So tell me,' she said as she poured me my tea. 'Tell me everything. How did it go?'

'Well enough, I suppose.'

'Nonsense! Nothing is ever well enough at gothic Brambles. Frightfully interesting, yes, but also rather sick-making, if you ask me. Unless you like games like Musical Bedrooms. I did once, although now I can't imagine why. I can't tell you how much my life has improved since I gave up sex. Did they all behave as badly as ever? What's your verdict on my darling sister? Is she totally mad or does it come and go? Last time I was there she had a long argument with the head of Hannibal. Did she interrogate you, my dear?'

'There was one difficult breakfast,' I conceded.

'You poor, dear thing! She's a dreadful snob, that woman, especially since she turned to Rome, and like most snobs she usually gets her facts wrong. Did you notice how she lowers her voice just before she drops a name? One of the great tragedies of her life is that I managed in the end to do quite well for myself. She hasn't a charitable bone in her body. I can't imagine how we managed to be born of the same mother. I always rather suspected she was a changeling. The only good thing she ever did was give us Max. Was he able to be polite to her?'

'Only just,' I told her.

'I suppose he finds those priests of hers terribly tiresome. I often wonder what they must make of the Curse of the Midwinters. I am rather fond of Jonathan, poor fellow. I'm sorry you shan't have a chance to know him properly, now that he's terminally gaga. And how did Danny behave?'

'Inconsistently,' I said.

'Well, it's as much as could be expected under the circumstances. It's all getting to her rather! Although I do wonder sometimes how she is going to keep herself occupied once she has finished forging Rebecca's collected letters.'

'You aren't serious about the forging part?' I said.

'Oh, I am. But I'm not sure if I care. At the moment, I'm

rather more interested in the skeleton. You haven't mentioned the skeleton.'

'Who told you about the skeleton?'

'My sister, of course. She only rings me when she has some news that might upset me. Not that she told me much. She just said that you and the children had discovered an interesting skeleton. I did try and do some fishing when I spoke to St Tatiana later on, but she wouldn't give me a thing. Went rather high and mighty on me, actually. It was all rather annoying. Has anyone worked out who the woman might have been?'

'I'm pretty sure the bones belonged to a dog,' I said. 'It was just a trick Max's mother played on Max to make him uncomfortable. Now she's played the same trick on you.'

'Goodness, how dippy!'

'She's dippy all right. She managed to shunt the blame over to me, though,' I found myself saying. 'Which shouldn't have surprised me, as it seems to be my purpose in life. Or at least in this family.'

This time Bea did miss a beat. 'Oh?' she said, looking up with a glassy smile.

To my horror, my voice decided to explain.

'My chief asset, as far as I can see, is that I don't belong here. People feel sorry for me because I don't belong, and that's why they're careful to be nice to me, but I can't be allowed to forget my place, can I? Or should I say, my lack of place? And so they keep having to remind me – while also making it impossible to leave. Or even take a bath without someone coming to check on me. I'm sorry if that sounds churlish.'

'Nonsense! It doesn't sound churlish at all.' Bea reached into her basket for a cigarette. Once she had lit it, she gave me another glassy smile. 'I do like the way you speak your mind, it's so refreshing.' But she exhaled with distaste. It was as if I had served her a plate of food good manners prevented her from pointing out was rotten.

I was horrified at what I had said. What my voice had said. I opened my mouth to apologise. 'I know it doesn't mean very much,' I said instead. 'You don't need to tell me. I know it's a game. As far as I can see, everything in this family is a game.'

'Goodness, what a fascinating theory,' Bea said, exhaling through her nostrils this time. 'Did you think it up all by yourself?'

'Of course not. When do I ever? But that doesn't mean it isn't true. Not that I'm the only odd one out. As Danny pointed out to me in the car coming down from Derbyshire, no one else belongs here either.'

'Oh, did she now? Goodness, how very, *very* dippy! Whatever must you make of us? Can't pass through Heathrow without being tracked by photographers. Can't go for a walk without finding a corpse that turns out to be a dog. Can't even play a parlour game without destroying a family heirloom, by the sound of it. And now it turns out that, appearances notwithstanding, we none of us belong here! Are you going to be able to put up with us, darling, or have you come to the conclusion that you'd rather not?'

Taken aback by the new edge in her voice, appalled that I was the one who had invited it, I faltered. 'I'm sorry,' I said. 'I didn't mean that the way it sounded. You've all been very kind. I'm grateful for everything you've done, and I probably don't deserve it. I wasn't trying to say that, it's just that . . . I'm only just finding my feet . . . and even though I want things to work out, it's really too soon to say. Don't you think?'

'No, actually, I don't think it's too soon to say. If you don't mind my being honest. If you don't mind my saying so, darling, it's really getting rather tricky.'

'What do you mean?'

'I'm surprised one has to spell it out. It isn't as if one had been particularly subtle. But it is rather difficult, wouldn't you agree, to put a distance between you and the children when you're all living practically on top of each other?'

'But there's no need to keep them away from me! I like children! I'm happy to do anything with them! I just don't want to interfere! I've just been waiting for them to come to me, like for example the way they did at Bramble House this weekend! I thought everyone knew that!'

'Of course we know that, darling. Just as we all appreciate all the reasons why you would rather not rush into marriage.'

'What does that have to do with it?'

'Rather a lot, actually. I know that the modern view is that it is best to let things take their natural course. On the other hand, one must take the children into consideration. I think I agree with Tatiana here that this is one thing my sister Caroline, my dippy sister Caroline, as you so kindly put it, is right about. I'm sure you'll agree, once you've given it some thought, that it's better for them to have as little as possible to do with you until such time as you are sure you want to take them on. At the same time, one accepts that it would be impossible for you to come to a proper decision, were they to be removed from the scene entirely. It's really rather tricky. Rather a large headache. You do see my point, I hope.' Her voice was raised now. 'I hope you don't think me rude or unreasonable.'

'No, of course not,' I said, but my cheeks were hot with shame.

'I would like to be able to tell you that you had all the time in the world, my dear,' she said, an inimical wryness now invading her tone. 'But I'm afraid I'm going to have to be brutal. You must make up your mind. Either we announce an engagement by mid-September, with a view to a wedding before Christmas. Or you put your charming little *sumak* back into your case with those three marvellous photographs and you leave.'

'But I never said I didn't intend to . . . I never would have let you do anything to the spare bedroom if I hadn't thought . . . I never . . . I could never subject the children to the distress of a . . . you must understand that the only reason I'd leave would be if Max actually asked me . . . I'm as serious about this as I would be if we had already exchanged vows.'

'It's not the same. Your private views are not in question, neither is your character. I know you're perfectly capable of being a good wife even if you turn out to be an unhappy one. But you must also be seen to be good. You must draw the blinds. We've had enough intrusion as it is. Like it or not, we shall have more. You must convince Max that the children cannot take any more uncertainty.'

'But what if he wants to wait until—'

'Put your foot down, my dear. That's what feet are for.'

She stood up. 'I'm giving you a fortnight. That's all we

can afford. Bye for now!' she said as she slammed the door behind her.

I felt as if she had slammed me against the wall. What had come over me? Where had those words come from? Did I even believe them? My tea grew cold. The first time I looked at my watch it was four o'clock. Then it was twenty past, a few minutes before five, and half past. Every time I tried to gather myself up to go into the bedroom to dress for the party, I couldn't seem to issue the command to my feet. I was still sitting there in my dressing gown when Max came in.

'What's going on? It's just gone six. Rude people who don't read the fine print on their invitations have already starting arriving,' he said. 'Why aren't you dressed?'

When I didn't answer, he sat down next to me and said, 'Oh, dear, oh, dear. Who's done what now?'

'It's partly my fault. Bea came over wanting to know what happened at Bramble House and I managed to offend her.'

'Well, these things happen. Don't worry. She'll get over it.'

'I don't think so. She sounded pretty sure of herself. Max, she's more or less given me my walking papers. She wants me to go in two weeks' time if we're not getting married.'

'Oh, does she?' he said. His tone was indecipherable.

'I'd like to know how you feel about it.'

'It ought to be obvious how I feel about it. It really depends more on you.'

'I thought marriage was something people decided on together.'

'In this case, clearly not. Clearly it's Bea who's calling the shots, and if that's all right with you, I suppose it's going to have to be bloody all right with me.'

'I'm just repeating what she said to me. She implied I would be hurting the children if I didn't make up my mind.'

'And do you think she's right?'

'I don't know what to think. I don't know what to think about anything! I'm totally in the dark! I've never been so confused in my entire life. What the hell is wrong with your family? What the hell did you do to Rebecca?'

137

His back was to me as I said this. I saw him flinch. Then, very slowly, he turned around to look at me. The famous bones were nowhere in evidence. Anger had made him look deformed. He raised his arm and for a moment I thought he was going to hit me. Then he dropped it and took a breath.

Once recomposed, he said, 'Bea may be right. She usually is. You must leave if you think it best. I would never stand in your way. In fact, as you may remember, I've already said as much.' He headed for the door, ducked his head, then paused, propped his long arm on the doorframe and turned around again. 'All I ask is that I be the first one to know. If that's not too much to ask.'

Chapter Nineteen

At the launch that night, I saw it for the first time: not just women, but streams of women rushing towards him, trying to get as close to him as they could, and Max letting them get close. Max putting his hand on their shoulders, smiling down at them too happily, taking them by the hand and pulling them out to the bench next to the French doors, pretending to the chosen woman that he did not want anyone to interrupt them, but then flashing a grateful smile at any woman who did. The effort of not looking drained me of whatever ability I might have had to circulate.

Giles did his best to divert my attention. 'There's someone you ought to meet,' he would say when he caught me pulling back to edges of the party. Having pushed me into a new group of polite but too curious faces and completed the formalities, he would point to one of them and add, 'You two have something in common.' It would be something different each time. Sometimes we had the same publisher or had attended the same schools, or different schools in the same part of the country. A few had spent time in Deia. Giles would hang on until our conversation about whatever we had in common seemed established. He would dash away satisfied that he had broken the ice, but without his help I floundered. It was always the same set of questions I had to answer, always the same pursed, polite smile I got in return. I did not know what to ask them back. I knew it was rude to ask people what they did, but if you didn't know what they did, how could you ask them anything? I sipped my drinks too fast and soon became light-headed. I got myself a glass of water and sat down next to the fireplace, only to find that I had too good a view of the scene on the bench outside the French doors. First I craned my neck in order not to look. Then I succumbed to the temptation and was unable to take my eyes off them.

The woman was in her late twenties or early thirties, with bright-red lipstick that matched the flowers in her low-cut dress. She had a theatrical way of throwing her long blonde hair back when she laughed. She had her hand on Max's knee.

'Our name for her in the back room is Madame Blackberry.' It was Crawley, who had seated himself next to me. 'We cannot for the life of us figure out why Giles ever wanted to publish her. He must be afraid of the scene she'd make if he tried to pull out. Our current theory is poetic blackmail. Perhaps she's told him that unless he continues to publish her, she'll dedicate a poem cycle to him.' He assumed a falsetto: '*I went out to pick some blackberries . . . they were bruised as my dead mother's nipples . . . they burst into my cupped hands . . . their sticky juices went down my arms in ragged red rivulets . . . my lap runneth over with blood . . .* It's enough to make you want to go back to hunter gathering.' He shook his head, then turned to look me in the eye and said, 'So. You've finally turned him down, have you?'

'Who told you that?'

'I don't need anyone to tell me,' Crawley said. 'I know the boy too well. This outrageous way he's carrying on out there. If you look carefully you'll see that there's no connection, no connection at all. He wants you to know he doesn't need you but it's so terribly obvious that his problem is the opposite. He needs you too much. He's doing this for you, my dear. I'd like you to take note of my emphasis. For *you*. As intolerable as this might be for you, my girl, the significant part of it for me is that it's the first time in memory that he hasn't done it for Rebecca.'

'I hope you don't mind if I put off going out there to thank him.'

Crawley sighed. 'What else could you expect, dearie, what else would you expect?' He took my hand and patted it. 'I imagine I would be condescending to you if I lectured you on suicide. And yes, I do think it was a suicide, by the way. Even if she didn't plan to die on that particular day, she was gambling with death and it doesn't really matter from our point of view whether what did happen counted as a win or a loss. What happened to Max is that he lost half of his imagination when she went off on that boat. Or rather, the other half of his imagination became a ghost. He's spent the last three years playing to that ghost. It's a good sign that he's not doing it now. But he's terrified. You share your mind with someone else as he did with her, you lose her and your mind, and you never want it to happen again. But he's lucky to have found you because you understand that, don't you? Because it's happened to you.'

'How can you be so sure of that?'

'Don't insult my inquisitorial intelligence. I didn't have to ask anyone, if that's what you were asking. You have death and disaster coming out of your pores. I don't think you two walking corpses fell in love. The way I would put it? You interlocked. He's only half here. You're only half here. You each hope that the two halves will make a whole, when in fact it's never quite that simple, is it? The whole always being so much less than the sum of its parts, eh?'

We watched Madame Blackberry rip a page out of a notebook and hand it to Max. He folded it carefully and put it into his back pocket, then glanced over his shoulders to reassure himself that no one was taking notice.

Crawley chuckled. 'What an operator! Pity it makes him hate himself even more.'

'Is he really going to meet with her?' I asked without thinking.

'If he does, it won't give him any pleasure. No, I'm afraid your problem is quite the opposite. Not losing him, but getting more of him than you bargained for. You're engaged to a sick man, my girl. He also happens to be an extraordinary man, a gifted man, a one-off. He's the only real friend I have in the world and I would fall off the edge of the earth if he asked me to. But he's also . . . Do you know what they were doing to each other by the end? Has he ever told you the story about the Morocco poems?'

I admitted he hadn't.

'Well, it began with their taking a trip there *en famille*, and writing poems that contained the same metaphor. Can't remember which. It had something to do with a samovar. They had a huge row about who owned the metaphor. Neither would sacrifice it, and so the feud amplified and before long they were actively stealing from one another, writing poems that made nonsense out of whatever the other had written. I'm surprised you hadn't picked this up, but then you don't really know Max's work, do you? In its way, even *The Marriage Hearse* was an appropriation. Which is why,' Crawley said, gesturing over at his stern and intelligently frowning wife, 'which is why every night before I go to bed, I thank my stars I did not marry a writer.

'That's not quite fair,' he then added. 'Because of course Marie Lourdes does write inside her field. But although her spoken English is just as good as her French, her written English is not. And her imagination, if you can call it that, well, it's a purely Cartesian affair. Her great flair is to take the mystery out of archaeology. You've got to hand it to her, it's no mean feat. Why else do I love her?' He tapped his head. 'Because she can't get in here.'

Chapter Twenty

That night, he began to make love to me before I had even taken off my clothes. We fell asleep embracing one another. The next morning, it was as if nothing bad had happened between us. The calm lasted until Friday evening and ended abruptly, rather in the way that the ground under your feet gives way when a dream turns into a nightmare.

Max had taken the day off to attend an orientation meeting at the children's school. William was entering what they called E-block, the first year in which pupils were streamed according to ability. When he came home, he told me that he was going to be in the lowest class but one, 'because it seems I'm rather thick'.

I objected – not, to be honest, from any deep conviction about his abilities but because I couldn't bear to hear a child that age placing himself so low. I told him his problem was probably that he was too intelligent. Max seemed to balk at this but chose not to explain why. Instead, he furrowed his brow and left the room, returning with a sewing machine which he proceeded to set up on the dining table. Turning to Hermione, he said, 'Now go to the airing cupboard and dig out that bag from the used-uniform sale, and while she's doing that, William, I'd like you to have a look in the bedroom to see if you can find that Shepherd and Woodward bag that has all the name tapes.'

After they left the room, he tested out the machine, only to find that there was something wrong with the thread. I asked him if he would like me to see if I could fix it, and that was when he turned on me.

He told me I had no right to ask. The fact that I had asked indicated that I had no feelings. 'You can flirt with mine, but I am not going to permit you to do the same with the children's. You

143

have no idea, do you, what it looks like to them? They've been hurt enough already, God damn you! Give me back my thread!'

I was still standing there, holding the thread, when the children returned. When I told him I didn't know what I had done to deserve the outburst, he hissed, *'Pas devant les enfants.'* So I waited until after they were asleep, but still he wouldn't speak to me. 'I've a book to read' was his first excuse. Then it was, 'I really haven't anything new to say.' I pleaded with him. His response was, 'If you can't see the problem for yourself, then there is not a chance in hell I can make you see it.'

When I tried to put my arms around him in bed, and he pushed me away, anger overtook me. It was the second time that I had shouted at him, and the first time my intent was to hurt. I accused him of using the children as pawns. Of hating women. Of envying their powers. Of wanting their mothers dead.

This last accusation stunned him into silence. When Max finally spoke, it was in the soft, chilled tone of measured hatred. 'What the hell do you mean to say by that?'

'That I'm not going to fall for it. That I'm wise to your tricks! I'm not going to let you destroy me!'

'You're implying, then, that I have destroyed others before you?'

'I don't know what I'm implying. I'm just speaking from my heart.'

'Well, in that case, I suggest that we stop here and postpone this talk until a time when you're feeling more reasonable.'

I spent that night in my study, ruefully remembering Bea's prediction that I would need the protection of a lockable door.

The next morning, I woke to the sound of a car reversing and reached my window in time to see Max and the children speeding off in the Volvo in the direction of Oxford.

I went downstairs to see if he had left a note. I couldn't find one. I made myself a cup of coffee and returned to my new desk. I consulted my list of people to supply with my new address. I looked queasily at the names already checked off. If I left, would I have to contact them again? If I did, how would I explain myself? I consulted my other list, of bread-and-butter letters. I wrote an unnecessarily long and transparently insincere note to Max's mother. It was, I noted, full of exclamation marks.

I sealed it, found a first-class stamp and put the letter on the sideboard next to the front door. I sat down at the dining table to make a shopping list, only to remember that I already had everything I needed. I went back upstairs and got out a new stenographer's notebook. At the top of the first page, I wrote, 'What am I afraid of?' Halfway down I wrote, 'What do you want?' My mind went blank. I got up to make myself another cup of coffee. On my way down, I heard Danny in Rebecca's study, laughing on the phone, telling someone called Anita that she was a chump.

When I got back to my study with my fresh cup of coffee, I locked the door. For the first time since my arrival, I took out *Happily Ever After*, the slim volume that had earned me the right to call myself a writer. I settled myself down on my sofa, drawing my new travelling blanket over my legs despite the warmth of the morning. I began at page one and read it through to the end. I looked into my soul to find it stripped of furniture.

These interconnected shards of ice had nothing to do with my life. And yet someone had died for it. If I hadn't thrown myself into this book the way I had, Sasha would still be alive. I had let Sasha die because I stopped taking care of him, because I had cared more for my freedom than I had cared for him.

I closed the book. Staring at the caricature of the altar on the cover, I asked myself why it had once been so important to me, why it was that even a mediocre and timid book that had acquired a small number of immemorable reviews should take precedence over a human being. Why I still shied away from human beings, still had to lock myself up in a room, even though I had no writing to show for it, nothing of worth to say. What was I afraid of?

I opened my desk drawer, took out my notebook and read through my seventeen attempts at an opening chapter. Each seemed thinner and more tentative than the one before. It was as if I were afraid of my subject, to the point of being unable even to say what the subject was.

What was I afraid of? I stared at the wall, willing it to spell out the answer, but the wall stared blankly back. I had no words for it – that was what scared me. I had no words for my life. I had no words for my life because Rebecca had already written the book about my life. I had no words of my own for my life because I had read that book and believed every word of it. Never imagining it foretold my future, I had not read it carefully – or at least not carefully enough. But now I was afraid to look at it, even think of it. The only way to break this fear, I now told myself, was to read it.

And so I walked down the corridor to Rebecca's study, tried the door and, finding it open, walked in. I locked the door behind me. There were seven English editions of *The Marriage Hearse* on the bookshelves as well as twenty translations.

All of them had the same author's photo, the one of Rebecca smiling warmly, knowingly, triumphantly in the so-called wrong dress. Just the sight of this photograph made me want to run away. So I tightened my resolution. I would not just read *The Marriage Hearse* – I would read it in there. I would read it sitting on the same chaise longue where Rebecca had written it.

I would read it, I told myself, but I did not have to succumb to it. The point of reading it would be to know for sure that she had not foretold my life. To know where her words ended and my eyes began, so I could see for myself again. And for the first few pages I was able to maintain my detachment. Because it was clear to me, now that I was here in Beckfield, that the village where *The Marriage Hearse* took place was not Beckfield, that the family was not the Midwinter family, even if it shared some of its attributes, and that the heroine was a character in her own right in spite of being an American writer like myself, and as overwhelmed by her new lover's family as I was.

For a few pages I could empathise with her without confusing myself with her. But the writing was too strong for me. The prose was so brave, especially when it described weakness, and so clear about the right and the good even as it described the bad and the wrong. There was a sense of wide spaces even in descriptions of cramped rooms full of affected people. It was unapologetically American, it never forgot where it came from, never accommodated. And so it was impossible for me to resist. After a few pages Rebecca had me in her hands just as she had her heroine in her hands. It soon did not matter that the village and the family she was describing were not our village or our family, because the details meant nothing. It was the core that mattered. And the core was the same.

Her heroine had not done exactly the same things that I had done – she was not replacing a dead first wife, and she did not have to face the prospect of stepchildren – but she had ended up suffering the same way I did, and for the same reasons. By page 140, she had found herself sitting in a replica of this very study, hiding from her lover and his interfering aunt, and trying to write, but unable to find a single word that she could call her own. I read her description and then I looked around the study, trying to see something, something that was not the same to me as it had been to her, but I couldn't find a single thing. There was the broken cupid, different in parts, same in essence. There were the slippers and the Cycladic statues and the piles of books on the desk, even the ashtrays that the children had made for her. Once again I wanted to run from the room. Although I struggled to remind myself that I was not reading my future, that the story she was writing was not my story even if her heroine felt all the things I felt, it was an even greater struggle to turn the page, because I expected it to contain my death warrant. But it was on the very next page that the heroine picked up her water glass and smashed it against the windowsill and dragged the jagged edge against her wrist and cut herself.

And I thought, no. That's not me. I would never do that. Suddenly I was not inside the story any more. I was looking at the heroine instead of struggling inside her head. I could feel sorry for her and for the woman who had invented her. I continued reading not in awe but in sadness. This was no longer the story of a woman who was crushed by a powerful family. It was the story of a woman with a tragic flaw that made it impossible for her to stand up to them. I could see that everything that happened to her in the second half of the novel – the disastrous honeymoon, the pregnancy that turned her into a captive, the husband's abandonment of her, and her descent into drugged insanity – had its seed in her own weakness. Even the triumphant ending seemed like an admission of weakness to me. It did not seem a victory to me to stagger out of her sickbed in a dress that was a replica of a family joke and tell an unsympathetic audience that her name was Rebecca. This was not an indication that the heroine would define her own life from now on, because it defined nothing. It was a sign of uncertainty that the book had stopped here – yet another proof that Rebecca had depleted and eventually destroyed herself by putting too much faith in words and memorable performances.

I closed the book full of sadness for Rebecca and her heroine, but calm and clear and determined not to make the same mistake myself. I wandered over to the window. The sun had gone, the clouds were turning grey. Crawley and a man I had never seen before were standing at either side of the net on the tennis court, discussing something of great interest to them both: it was the first time I had seen the court inhabited. I wandered back to the chaise longue and picked up the book. When I replaced it, I noticed a plaque balanced on the shelf above it. It said:

> Sometimes I go about pitying myself
> And all the while I am being carried across the sky
> By beautiful clouds.

As I left the study, I could hear Max and the children in the sitting room below. I went down to find the preparations for school continuing. Two lists, both crumpled, lay on the table. Hermione stood guard over the piles of uniform on one sofa, William over the piles on the other. Max was just finishing the hem on a navy-blue duffel coat. Next to him was an ironing board. The iron propped on it was steaming.

He was smoking a joint as he sewed. On the side table was a hip flask of whisky and an almost empty glass. 'Next,' he said. William picked up a rugby shirt and moved towards him. Max took the shirt and flattened it on the ironing board. It was clear from his movements that he was used to doing this. He didn't need me.

It was clear also that I could go or I could leave and either way they would manage. Max would get to and from work. The children would go back to school in labelled, ironed, mended uniforms. They were not deprived. They had a father who preferred them to all adults, and they had Bea, and they had Danny. Their days were full, the minutiae of their routine so engrossing that even now they hardly seemed to notice me.

And yet, as I stood there, finally restored to the selfless clarity of a ghost, I knew it was all wrong, this scene I was watching, and that if I were there, with them, instead of standing at the door unnoticed, I would make it different. I would make it better for these children. I would stop them looking back at the accidents they had inexplicably survived. There was no need to be so military. No need for William to call himself thick. No need either for Hermione's best friend to be a battery-operated plastic flower. Room in her room for things that were not dead. Time for their illnesses to stop going overtime. Time for them to stop telling me why they were weak.

I didn't love them. If they hadn't been there, I would never have missed them. But I couldn't leave them at the mercy of mourners. I was damned if Rebecca was going to have her way. She had made her choice. Now I was making mine.

I willed myself to walk across the forbidden line and take the kilt that was in Max's hands, and say, 'I'll do this one. There's a trick to it that's easier to do than to explain.'

To my surprise and elation, he sighed and said, 'So show me then.' He handed me the iron and stepped aside to make room.

Chapter Twenty-One

A nother memory I keep for sustenance: that night, when I told him I wanted to marry him. We were sitting in front of the television. It was a commercial break. His response was to sigh and pat me on the leg, and then sigh again.

'Unless you don't want to,' I said.

Without ever taking his eyes off the screen, he put his finger up as if to silence me. The commercial break ended. He stood up, stretched and said, in a voice on the edge of cracking, 'I'll just check to see if the children are asleep.' Returning to the foot of the stairs, he called into the sitting room to say that he was just going out to get something and would be back shortly.

Five minutes later he returned with a cold bottle of champagne. He had trouble opening it because his hands were shaking. He knocked back three glasses in silence and then began to speak, in a hushed but urgent voice, about what he wanted to put behind him and what he hoped we could achieve together. It was the first time he had spoken to me in such depth about his marriage and Rebecca. I found, to my dismay, that the very mention of her name made me tremble.

'I don't know if you understand what I mean when I say we lived inside each other's heads. I suspect you do understand, because of what you've been through. I don't know what you'd call it, though. I'd say it was either love or insanity or both. It doesn't matter. What matters is the results. I don't want to live that way ever again. I want us to live in harmony, not unison, and I need to know if you agree.'

I agreed. The trembling had got worse and now my teeth were chattering. He put his arms around me. 'You're afraid, and you're right to be afraid. I'm afraid too. Every time I have to trust you just that tiny bit more, it's as if I'm being stabbed in the chest. Because I know what can happen, just as you know what can happen. But I don't want to hang back any more. I don't want fear to win again. I want to make it work this time. I want to make my children our children. I want a life for them. I want to imagine a future for them. I want us to have children.' He poured himself another glass. 'Tell me you want it too. Tell me. Tell me we're both in this together. When you look ahead, tell me what you see.'

I told him what I had already seen. Myself driving home in a car full of children, his children and our children, and arriving at the cottage, seeing him waiting at the door. He cried out as if someone had stabbed him, and then he tightened his grip on me, as if in resistance to an invisible abductor.

I do not remember how and when we got to bed, but I remember waking up the next morning with the hollow glow of forgotten purpose. As I lay in bed and in his arms, the vision came back to me. We were going to get married. We were going to make a family, for his children and for our children. We were going to stitch up the gash, stop looking back, and move forward. Not live happily ever after right away, but soon enough.

I sat down at the breakfast table feeling strong, feeling inspired. But already I was losing my nerve as I greeted the children, as I watched their faces turn stony upon hearing their father tell them the news. Even when I helped them gather their things for school, they refused to look at me.

The summons from Bea was a welcome distraction.

I did not have to tell her what I had decided. She already knew. Her words of congratulation were energetically – you might almost say triumphantly – gracious. But it was also clear, from the rapidity of her delivery, that she was in the midst of coping with a crisis she could not explain over the phone.

It turned out to be Danny, who was sitting in the corner next to the Aga hugging her knees, rocking back and forth with anguished whimpers. Her hair hung over her face, leaving only her nose uncovered.

'Do sit down,' said Bea efficiently. 'Pour yourself a cup of coffee.

I'm afraid poor Danny's finding the thought of a wedding a bit too much to take. I hope you don't mind my asking you over. I thought it would be best to bring everything out in the open.' She turned to the rocking figure on the floor. In a louder voice, she said, 'Danny, darling, do you think you can find it in yourself to join us at the table? It would help awfully.'

The hulk whimpered and nodded, then pulled herself into an upright position and shuffled across the floor. 'I hope you don't mind if I speak *for* you,' Bea said. As she blew her nose, Danny responded with a jerky nod. 'That said, I do hope you stop me if you think I've got the wrong end of the stick.' Danny nodded again and sniffled.

Now Bea turned to me. 'It seems,' she said, 'that Danny has had a rather alarming dream. Or was it a visitation? I'm not quite clear on that. Well, anyway. The ghostly visitor was Rebecca, who had, apparently, been the first in the underworld to hear of your wedding plans, and who is now appealing to you, via her preferred medium, to change your mind. Have I got it right so far, Danny, or am I misquoting you?'

'The thing that may not be clear,' Danny now sobbed, 'is her motive.' Pushing her hair away from her face, she turned her bleary eyes to me and added, 'It's not jealousy, or rather, it isn't any more. She did suffer a bit of it, naturally, but she has long since moved on and now she feels sisterly towards you. She wants to protect you. She doesn't think you have any idea what you're letting yourself in for.' Danny sucked in her breath. 'She asked me to ask you if you, I know this sounds rather odd, but you must take it as a metaphor, she asked me to ask you if your muse wore a chastity belt. It's an allusion to *Heteroglossia*, of course, as I'm sure I don't need to remind you.' I sat there stunned as she blew her nose.

I turned to Bea, whose expression was judiciously bland. 'I think we're more or less agreed that she was concerned about events having forced you into making a decision rather too quickly. Isn't that right, Danny?'

'Yes,' she sobbed.

'Although it does seem to me,' Bea now continued, 'that you

152

and this ghost are rather alarmed about the possible consequences of this decision. If you can forget about the ghost for a moment, Danny, it does seem to me that you feel a bit, well, I hope you don't find this word too strong, but you do seem to be worried about being supplanted.' Danny opened her mouth to speak but did not get the chance. 'Which I understand completely, darling, even though I must say it has no basis. Simply because no one could do what you're doing with Rebecca's papers. No one else has the background for it, or the application. Because you're not exactly being properly rewarded, are you? It's a work of love.'

'It's been easier these past few months,' Danny said, 'because I've had a partner in devotional absentia. This is the main reason why I would say that I'm not quite, or not only, the image of your suggestion, not, in other words, thoroughly caught up in the supplanting myth.' Turning to me, she added, 'I did tell Rebecca how highly I thought of you.'

Her voice going only slightly drier, Bea said, 'We are, of course, still referring to the night visitor.'

There was a long silence, which Bea broke by asking, 'Do you think you'll be speaking to her again soon?'

Danny shook her head. 'I have no way of knowing.'

'I was only asking, Danny, because it seemed to me that it would help to clarify matters if we could engage your night visitor in a broader examination of the matter to hand. The questions of the imagination are, of course, terribly important. But we're also talking about children and trying to arrange things so that everyone involved can get on with it. I hope you don't find my way of putting it too blunt, but it does seem to me that the view from the underworld can become rather obsessional, rather blinkered, as it were. It sometimes becomes necessary for those of us still on earth to remind them of practical matters. Are you with me, Danny?' She half nodded. 'Then do you think you can ask her next time you speak? I'm only suggesting this because it might just be possible that the apparition is in a position to pass on some useful advice. I'm suggesting this in the spirit of that adage about not repeating history through the careful study of it, and so on. If, indeed, our ghost is well disposed towards our new friend here, and if she can be brought round to the idea that she will be a suitable and even a helpful stepmother, then perhaps she can give us the wherewithal to learn from her mistakes. Do you follow me?'

'Oh yes, I do, oh yes . . .' Danny said, then gave herself up to wailing.

'Do get a hold over yourself, darling! You'll only be giving yourself a migraine if you continue carrying on like this.'

'It's the sinuses, actually,' Danny sobbed, but she blew her nose and fell quiet.

'That's better,' Bea said. 'But I do think you should permit yourself a morning off and give yourself a rest. And perhaps later, when you're feeling a bit better, you might try reaching to the Other Side with one of your other spiritual aids. Those crystals, perhaps, or carrot cards or whatever you're meant to call them.'

'Keep the dialogue going, in other words,' Danny said weakly as she struggled to her feet.

'Exactly,' said Bea, as she herded her firmly towards the door. 'Bye for now,' I heard her say as she saw Danny out of the house.

When she returned to the kitchen, Bea sighed and said, 'I do apologise for putting you through that, but I thought it best to humour her. It's best all round if she thinks she a part of things. But it *was* difficult to keep a straight face. I hope you didn't mind. At least I got rid of her in record time. Now finally I can congratulate you properly. Goodness!' she said, after she had pecked me on both cheeks. 'Only three months to go and so much to do!'

IV

The Marriage Hearse

Chapter Twenty-Two

We were married just before Christmas. It was the register office with the immediate family on the Friday morning, and the church in Beckfield with the rest of the family – his family – on the Saturday. It was not quite the traditional wedding Bea had hoped for. I did not wear white and, since I did not have a father, it was Giles who walked me down the aisle. I had worried about a virtual stranger giving me away, but he was a man trained to rise to sudden and unusual occasions: he gave every indication of having known me since birth. This despite sticking religiously to the facts in the small, perfect speech he gave on my behalf at the reception.

How relieved they were, the dark suits and extravagant hats, to see an orphan so graciously protected, an unknown so elegantly placed and defined. When they clapped at the end, it was as if in response to an acrobat on a tightrope. Their smiles relaxed when they saw Crawley move away from us to take the microphone at the front of the platform. They knew he would only appear to take risks. They knew how good he was at sounding outrageous while keeping the curtains closed. They laughed comfortably when he explained the circumstances under which he and Max had become best friends. They were both first years at Hertford: Max had assumed Crawley, 'the Celt from nowhere', was the porter. Shaken by his mistake ('not because of what it revealed about his character, but because of the awkwardness it promised'), Max had made a point of inviting him to his rooms for tea. This second encounter proved even more revealing. 'I found the lad heating up water in his electric kettle. I deduced correctly that he had never done so before from the fact that it was on the gas cooker. This time I did not pause to be polite. I have been saving him with my bad manners ever since. But every few decades, he does manage to do something even I cannot classify

as a *faux pas*, and this new venture into matrimony is one of them.'
He turned around to wish me luck. 'And believe me, girl, you'll
need it.'

Max threw his head back to laugh at the thought. I remember
how handsome he looked – too handsome, I thought proudly, to
be mine. After Crawley had embraced him and wished him luck
too, I suddenly lost my sense of occasion, forgot the audience and
took his beautiful face in my hands and kissed him on the mouth.
There were cheers, I remember. But they died away as Danny moved
towards the front of the platform.

Max kept his smile as Danny cleared her throat and shuffled
her papers, but he tightened his grip on my hand. I was full of
dread, too. But it was clear to me from their bright-eyed, frozen
faces that the guests would have been disappointed had she acted
sane. It was not as bad as we had feared. Danny never made it
fully clear she was addressing us on behalf of a friend in the
underworld. An outsider could have assumed she was speaking
metaphorically, would not have caught all the allusions when she
said every hero deserved a sequel, but that no sequel was worth its
salt without a heroine who understood the living spirit. Neither
would an outsider have known she was wearing the same dress she
had worn at Rebecca's wedding. As for Danny's choice of poem,
'Hamlet Without the Ghost', it was so gruesomely inappropriate
that she had the entire audience rooting for her, hoping against
hope that no one would let the side down by heckling or giggling
or exposing her bad judgement. I watched them watch her, a captive
audience praying for a treasured clown who had ventured too far out
on a limb. How relieved they were when she survived unscathed,
how admiring that we had endured the recitation without betraying
embarrassment. 'Oh, you poor thing!' more than one woman said
to me afterwards. 'We did feel for you. You were so brave.' They
thought I was just pretending to be unperturbed. If they had known
how far away Danny and her ghosts were from me that day, if they
had known how much I was enjoying my own wedding, if they had
known how many times I looked across the marquee for a glimpse
of my prize, if they had known that he could make me catch my

breath even when he had his back turned to me – they would have been shocked.

Even Bea would have been shocked. 'It's so lovely,' she said to me after she had introduced me to the bell-ringer and we had run out of politenesses to exchange. 'I am so enjoying myself. The trouble with weddings as a rule is that one only knows half the guests. One is for ever being torn away from one's own friends to meet some gruesome stranger's long-lost uncle. But today I know absolutely everybody. So you must use me, darling. If you find yourself stuck with a bore, you must let me know, and I shall find you someone better.'

'She means it, you know,' said the bell-ringer. 'It's a wonderful family, a family as keeps its word.'

I nodded my appreciation. But I did not have to be led by the hand any more. I was beyond introductions now. I had even made a few friends. Some of these turned out to be real friends, the friends I've managed to keep. Max's deputy was one, although of course I no longer think of her as Max's deputy. Then there was St Tatiana and Bea's daughter Herta. Like the others, these new friends of mine overestimated my discomfort and imagined me desolate because of lacking a family. So they kept close watch on me and dragged me away from anyone who even threatened to become tiresome. Leading me by the hand as they looked across the marquee, they would murmur, long before they could have had an idea where they were going, 'I know just the person I must take you to meet.' But I flattered myself that I knew even better. I had found my place now. I had signed up with the right publisher; the English edition of *Happily Ever After* was to come out the following May. I had also done my round of Christmas parties, read and in a few cases even reviewed the books people were talking about, and even weathered my first tabloid storm. I had grown accustomed even to being caricatured in *Private Eye*, but I had not fooled myself into seeing a connection between them and us, the 'Other Rebecca' in the cartoon strip and myself. Never had I been more secure in the knowledge of my unimportance. It was my position that had made me the object of attention, not my personality or my writing. If I had ever been ambitious for myself, I had never been less so than that day. Never more conscious of what I could do, and only I could do, for things and persons larger than myself. I was more than happy: I had a purpose.

We went to the Randolph for the night – just the two of us – but when we left for Heathrow the next morning, the children were waiting for us in the limousine. It was my idea to take them along on the honeymoon. My idea, too, to take them to the obvious place, despite the obvious objections. Until Rebecca's death, St John the Baptist had been their second home. It did not seem right or even healthy that they should be deprived of it for ever because it had been the last place she was seen alive. Better for them to look, accept, remember, pay their respects and move on.

It was an eleven-hour flight to Curaçao and from there another hour and a half in a puddle-jumper. Max worked on an article about John Updike for the duration – even to the point of staying behind in the Curaçao transit lounge during our three-hour layover. I did not just take this in my stride; I flattered myself that I understood it. Here was a man who did not know how to be close without giving up all pretence of distance. He hid behind books and assignments to protect himself. And not just from me, not just from his family – from his thoughts. To quote Crawley, his unborn poems. His miscarried books. He was afraid of what might happen if he committed his thoughts to paper, because of what had happened last time he had done so. It was Rebecca who had killed his confidence. It would be I who revived it.

While he hid, I looked after the children. How full of myself I was! I imagined that the time I had put into them that autumn was paying off, and that they now truly accepted me. That some higher power had noted and then recorded in granite my attendance at football matches and parents' evenings, Disney films and ice-cream parlours. I imagined a torrent of encouraging words from this ethereal judge with my every inspection of their school books, my every trip to skating rink, bookshop and swimming pool. It was as if I were floating above myself, celebrating my own performance. What a saint you are, I heard my panel of judges tell me. Who else could have thought up so many educational ways to throw dice? Who else could have managed to teach two restless children thirty basic words in Papiamentu? Made the history of the Dutch Antilles come alive from the window of a bus? Turned a small, almost windless journey between two arid Caribbean islands into a journey as dangerous as the first solo flight over the Atlantic? Every time William said something that proved he wasn't thick, every time Hermione smiled in spite of herself, every time they lost themselves inside the mundane routines I had stretched into adventures, I felt I had won a battle.

Surprise your father, I whispered to them as we walked across the tarmac at St John the Baptist airport. They did. They told the taxi driver where to go, and politely, too. William gave the destination, Hermione said please. Max was startled. 'When did you master that?' he cried. We all three laughed. When we got to their grandfather's hotel, they streaked ahead so that they could surprise him, too.

Max's father was still confined to a wheelchair but more active than I had been led to believe. He had not lost his looks – his skin was still smooth, his hair jet black and his cobalt-blue eyes still suggested an active mind – but conversation was beyond him. The best he could do was exchange jokes. These put Max on edge and delighted the children.

His hotel was mainly for scuba divers. Many of them were regulars who came down for months at a time. Like Max's father, they seemed to live in the open-air bar, which was also popular with a small circle of friendly but disreputable-looking islanders and leather-skinned expatriates. Some of these were bald and so I took them to be strays from the Buddhist temple next door. Strays and defectors.

The most outspoken and familiar of them, the one who doled out the drinks to Max's father and decided who got close to him and who did not, was the beaming and aggressively healthy man who took us out to Garrison Island the following morning. Shouting above the outboard motor, he explained that in his former life he had been a Methodist minister. Now he was a Tao physiotherapist – 'You can imagine how much business I get down here.' He told us that Max's father was an example of how good could come out of tragedy. 'Now that he can't move around any longer, he's using his eyes more. For the first time, he's noticing how much poverty there is on the island here, and for the first time, he's thinking about what he should do about it. Did he tell you about the general store he founded? Now he's thinking about a clinic and a fishery. It's really amazing. It's worth looking at in case you have friends in England who want to invest.' It was with this in mind that he arranged to pick us up after lunch on Christmas Eve instead of Christmas morning as originally planned. But, as it turned out, there was no time for sightseeing.

There is nothing more debilitating, I sometimes think, than a taste of peace. It took less than ten minutes to walk around Garrison Island. Because it was inside the great crescent-shaped bay to the south of Max's father's hotel, the water was calm on all sides. In those days, its only building was our two-room beachfront bungalow. The two great events of the day were sunrise and sunset. Max would get up as soon as there was enough light to work. Suddenly, and for the first time since we had met, he was writing poetry again. When he finished, he would make the rest of us breakfast. He would wake me up by bringing a cup of coffee to me in bed. We would spend the rest of the morning playing volleyball and catch in the water that lapped against the front of the house. In the middle of the day we would retire to bed to read and fall asleep over the second page, wake up, fall asleep over the fifth page, read it again, think about it, reach across the bed, make love.

I had brought a whole briefcase of books but I never got beyond the first few pages of the novel I was reading for review: *The Awakening*, by a new writer called Tamara Nestor Graham. Because she shunned literary circles, and because she had won the McArthur Prize on the basis of a slim collection of short stories, she was being billed as the female Cormac McCarthy. The opening scene was an exhaustive (and exhausting) account of a woman unable to get out of bed. Every time I read it, I fell asleep.

I cannot think about that bungalow now without seeing it. Even the cover was as if designed to match the view from the window. It featured a reflection of a woman's face in a pool of blue water. The woman looked like Madame Blackberry. I can

162

see her even now, sitting prettily on the bedside table, biding her time.

The afternoons we spent snorkelling over the reefs to the right and the left of it. Because night fell so quickly and so swiftly, we cooked our meals by gas lamp. If the wind was low we ate by candlelight. From our table on the terrace, we could see the Christmas lights in the bar of Max's father's hotel. From time to time, we could see one of the boats that took people out on night dives. Once we heard two passengers in an argument; another time, when we could see no boat at all, we heard disembodied singing. The acoustics of the bay, Max told me, were famous for being tricky. But there wasn't much sound for the bay to play with: aside from the night boats, the only thing we could hear after the children fell asleep, the only thing aside from the occasional lost flamingo, was the sound of the generator that kept the refrigerator going. To this day, if I hear such a generator, I am taken back to that precious interlude when we were left to our own devices. I am reminded of the little pleasures and attachments that might have come to something had we had more than five days.

I remember most of all the tug I felt that Christmas Eve as I watched the sun rise over our beach for the last time, the anger that swept through me as I left the water after my last swim. I had packed the day before so as to be able to linger over our lunch, so as to have the time to take one last look at the view before committing it to memory. So as to soak up the heat. I remember looking around the table and congratulating myself on how easily we sat together. Max, bronzed now, relaxed and more beautiful than ever, had both his children on his lap. They were clinging to him in a way that had previously made me want to eat tablecloths and smash plates, but now I felt only the slow warmth of pride. If he could enjoy their company without launching into a natural-history lecture, it was because of me. If their faces no longer darkened if he happened to address me instead of them, it was because they trusted me. It was because I had taught them that they could turn their backs on Max and me without our disappearing.

That morning, when Max brought me my coffee, he had brought

me his new poem to read. It was the first draft of what became the opening sally of *The Last Supper*. The island it took place on was our island. Or, I should say, his island: what he saw had almost nothing in common with what I saw. It began with a detailed, dry, naturalist description of a walk along the ragged circle that was its coast. It veered abruptly away from autobiography with the narrator returning to find the bungalow empty. Setting out around the island in search of his family, he finds a face, a familiar but unidentifiable and only two-dimensional face, lying on the sand. Looking out to sea, he sees a lurching rowboat. He recognises it as the rowboat he had when he was a child. He dives into the water, but in the split second that his head is submerged, the boat has sunk. By the time he finds it on the coral bed, its skeleton passengers have become homes to moray eels. Entwined in them, he drowns and dies without losing consciousness, and so has time to think about his past and his disembodied future. In stark, simple, appalling detail, he observes and records the disintegration and devouring of his own body. Although I now consider it the best, the bravest, the most honest, if also the most unnerving thing he has ever written, this was not how it hit me at the first reading.

Even as I sat there with my warm coffee in my warm bed, I felt encased in ice. Where did it come from? I asked myself. How had he turned this perfect week into that poem? What poison did he have inside him? What went on in his head? Why didn't he talk about it? What else was going on in his head that I didn't know about? Who was this man I thought I loved? Could I really love him at all when I knew so little of him? Would he ever let me in, or was this how it was going to go on – time and time again, the peace destroyed by the evidence in his damning poetry?

Why was this man incapable of hope? These were my first thoughts about *The Last Supper*, but by midday my pride in his accomplishment had taken over. I had done what I had set out to do. I had played the muse. I had helped him break free of Rebecca. I had given him the strength to look death in the face. Now that he had done so, he was capable of anything. This was how I had tailored my thoughts by lunchtime. This was just the beginning, I told him as we stood up to take our bags down to the landing. If he kept this up he would end up being the poet laureate or better.

I often have occasion to remember what he said to this. 'Poet laureate?' I remember him saying as he led the way across the beach. 'Poet laureate, to that family? I can't think of anything more ghastly.'

Chapter Twenty-Three

Things went wrong from the moment we got off the boat. The first news was of an emergency at the newspaper. Max had to go straight to the phone. The children and I went to the outside bar to wait. Here, to my surprise, I found Max's brother. He was immediately recognisable in the throng of renegade Buddhists because he was still wearing his hip-hop clothes, despite the heat.

Jonathan Junkie had not been at the wedding. The official reason had been a rehabilitation programme. 'Don't worry,' were his first words now. 'I've got the plot.' But he had lost at least two more teeth since our meeting the previous summer, and he looked as jumpy as ever. He kept giggling, like a child who could not quite keep a straight face long enough to pull a prank, and he avoided looking me in the eye. Every time I asked him a direct question about his programme or his plans, he quickly switched the subject to Coca-Cola. Had I had a Coca-Cola yet? Wouldn't his niece and his nephew like some Coca-Cola too? Had they ever tried the local substitute? Did they think they could tell the difference? Would they like to try a blind testing here and now? He would award the winners Mars Bars, he announced. He was still busy trying to find one in his clothes to share with the children when he looked up and said, 'Oh, good, here's Jack. Hey, my man! What's the score?'

Jack was a dark-haired man in his late thirties, good-looking enough to feature in a cigarette ad. He was holding a *piña colada*. He, too, seemed to be having a hard time keeping a straight face. He stopped a few feet away from the table and gave me a once-over that was at the same time curious and dismissive. In a loud, mocking voice, he said, 'Well, children! What can I say? Long time no see!'

Although they seemed to recognise him, they did not greet him back. Instead they hunched their shoulders and glared at the table.

'You're not playing the same old game, are you? You're not pretending you don't know who I am again? Well! It's a good thing this game is only a one-way street! Don't think I've forgotten my seasonal duties!' He had what I have come to think of as an eroded American accent.

He leaned towards Hermione, lifting her chin with his forefinger. 'When is the last time you checked out your grandad's Christmas tree?'

This had the desired result. 'What? Where is it? Is there anything else there? Can we go and see?'

It was only after the children had run off to the hotel office that Jack turned back to me. 'So good to meet you finally,' he said, offering his hand. 'I was beginning to wonder if it would ever happen.'

He eased himself into a deck chair that was half in the shade, pushed it into the sun, fished into his hip bag for his sunglasses, stretched himself out, flashed me a smile. 'Yes,' he said.

'Yes what?'

'Yes, I am the person you think I am.'

'What person is that?'

'Well, the whole story is that you probably think of me as several people without having realised that I'm only one. I run Isis Press.'

'Well, I've heard of that,' I said.

'If the world were a more grown-up place we would have run into each other by now at some lunch or launch or other. The reason we haven't is that your husband refuses to attend anything he knows I'm attending. He also refuses to touch any Isis Press books, which is taking things a bit far.'

'That's not true. I'm reading one right now. Reading for review.'

'Yes, well, that's almost worse, though, isn't it? He gives them to you instead of assigning them to a real reviewer. But it's better than nothing. I shouldn't complain. If they can be bitter and twisted, then so can I.' He took off his sunglasses. '*Now* do you recognise me?'

'Your eyes look familiar.'

'Yes, they ought to. There's a family resemblance, isn't there?

167

My eyes remind you of William's eyes, don't they? And Hermione's eyes. And the chin, too. It's a family tradition. I'm Rebecca's cousin. Cousin and more than cousin.'

He paused, waiting for this information to sink in. Smiling, as if he had decided at the last minute to leave the best part out. 'I'm the reason she went to Oxford – you won't know this unless Danny told you because I don't talk about it. Don't want to sound like I'm cashing in on the Myth. But yes, I'm the one who gave her the idea. I was the one she was visiting when she decided to go for it. I'm still not sure how she pulled it off. She must have talked them into bending the rules, is my guess. She could talk anyone into anything. As I'm sure you've gathered.'

He sighed theatrically. 'But that, as they say, is history. So let's get the formalities over with. My name is Jack Scully. I'm the author of that book your husband has suppressed. But only temporarily.' He put out his hand. 'So nice to have a chance to talk before we meet in court.'

By now the children had returned, each carrying a large present. 'Are these the ones you meant?' Hermione asked in a shrill voice. She was interrupted by William. 'Can we open them now?'

'I don't see why not! In fact, if you don't open them now, we're not going to be able to use them, and that would be pretty stupid, don't you think?'

The two children tore the packages open. Inside were child-sized water-skis. They were still shrieking and waving them in the air when I saw Max standing and staring at us from the far side of the bar. He looked as drawn as if he had spent the week sleeping on the floor of his office.

'Oh, look!' Jack said, when he noticed him approaching us. 'Who's arrived now but my favourite person!'

'You can't talk to Daddy like that,' said Hermione. 'No one can.'

No one acknowledged hearing her.

By now Max was standing with his hands in his shorts pockets five or six feet away from the table. 'What are you doing here?'

'What am *I* doing here?' Jack asked. 'Well, let's see. Let's think.

168

What does it look like? I'm sitting in a hotel in the Caribbean soaking up a little sun. Oh yes, and helping out your brother a little, since no one in his own family wants anything to do with him any more. Not even his own wife, as of last Tuesday. So I thought the two of us would take a little jaunt.'

'I'm a new man,' Max's brother said. 'I've got the tools I need now. I'm starting a new life.'

'And I think that's wonderful, don't you?' Jack interjected. 'I think it's an effort that deserves a word of encouragement and a nice big pat on the back. Like this. You see? *I'm* not worried about AIDS.'

'I thought we had an injunction,' Max said.

'I sincerely doubt it holds in J the B.'

'Nevertheless, your solicitor would not be happy to know you're here.'

'Sod the solicitor.'

'I hope you don't mind if I quote you to my solicitor.'

'Go ahead. It doesn't matter what you do. I'm still going to win.'

'If you don't leave at once, *I* am going to make trouble.'

Here Hermione said, 'But not until we've had a go on these!'

'You're to leave at once,' Max said, 'and take these blasted skis with you.'

But it was not to be. Hermione burst into tears and threw herself on the ground, clutching her new water-skis to her chest. William ran off into the scrub with his and refused to come out. Meanwhile, Max's brother announced that he had changed his mind about junk but not about ganja and went off to find some. When it became clear that Jack was not about to leave, Max went off to find his father.

'Not a very effective father, is he?' Jack said. 'Not much of a father at all, if you ask me.'

And neither, today, was Max's own father. His suggestion was that they all meditate together. Or go carolling. Or both. In the end the only way Max could placate the children was by agreeing to take them out into the bay himself.

The water-skiing lesson did not go well. Max had a hard time getting the boat started. Neither child ever managed to get upright. I tried to help, but in my ignorance I got in the way. More than once, Max swore at me. And all the while, Jack sat on the shore, laughing at our failures as he drank one *piña colada* after another.

'Happy families,' he said as we passed him on our way back to the bar.

'Go to hell,' Max said.

But still Jack would not let go. Refused a seat at our table, he took the table to the right of Max's father. He quickly tired of eavesdropping and took to shouting. 'Why don't you tell us some jokes?' he kept asking Max's father.

'My dear boy,' was the old man's response, 'I should be delighted to do so if I could remember any. I could probably manage most of "Adeste Fidelis", if you prefer. Shall we give it a try?'

'No,' said Jack. 'Let's ask some riddles.'

'Oh, good,' said Max's father. 'I love riddles.'

'Here's the first one. Why won't Max tell his children why he doesn't like me?'

'Goodness,' said his father. 'You have me there. Let me see. He doesn't like you because you're American. No, no, that can't be it. Rebecca was American. No, he doesn't like you . . . he doesn't like you because . . . well, you can be awfully rude, you know, Jack, and you ought to have learned by now that some people can't take it. But that's not it, is it? No, I think it must be because you're a darkie.'

'A darkie! That's a good one!'

'Yes, well, you are by definition a darkie if your mother is Bengali. I'm afraid I don't respect the Bengalis and you'll find that few civilised peoples do. They're not warlike enough. Now the Gurkhas, that's a different kettle of fish altogether—'

'My mother is not Bengali.'

'Well, she certainly wasn't British. Not with your skin. She couldn't have been.'

'No, she was Rumanian. And I say that proudly.'

'Proudly? Goodness! I can't imagine why, dear boy. The Rumanians were the worst of the lot. They wore corsets to go into battle, I'll have you know! They pomaded themselves! Oh yes, I can tell you don't believe me, but they did! It made me ashamed to be a soldier.'

'Oh, this is priceless,' said Jack. 'Priceless.'

Max got up and walked over to Jack. 'You've got to stop this nonsense. It's one thing to taunt me; it's another to do so in front of the children; and it is terribly cruel to play games like this with my father. He doesn't know what he's saying.'

'Oh yes, I do,' said his father. 'But I never was very good at riddles. However, Max was always very, very good at riddles. Perhaps you should ask him why he hates you. I think that would be more sensible.'

'Oh, Max knows why he hates me. He just won't tell anyone else. And neither will I – will I, Max? I gave my word, didn't I? No one is ever going to find out what he did to Rebecca, and what was eating his heart out when he did. Can I ask you a question?' Jack said, turning to me. 'Whatever your name is. I keep forgetting. Probably a Freudian slip, or whatever the opposite of a Freudian slip is, since we're not talking about saying the wrong thing, we're talking about drawing a total blank. Has this wonderful person you just married ever told you what ruined his first marriage? Has he ever told you what happened? What happened here, no less?' He knocked back the last of his drink and tipped back his chair. 'Let me guess. Let me guess that he hasn't told you what happened in this very bar. Or on the beach later that same evening.'

That was when Max hit him. Jack was aiming to hit him back when a few of the larger Buddhists jumped up and held him back. A few others held Max back and forced him into a chair.

'He went too far, didn't he?' Max's father said as he watched Jack being escorted out of the hotel. He said the same thing again to Max when the Buddhists allowed him to rejoin us.

Max said nothing in reply. With a glare, as if it had all been my doing, he said to me, 'Make sure you don't let the children out of your sight.' With that he went to the bar and ordered a shot of tequila. He drank it down, ordered another. Drank that one, too.

'Are you coming back?' his father called out to him. 'I wish you would! I've remembered the joke now.'

171

'He doesn't look like he's in the mood for jokes,' I said.

'Oh, well, then. I'll just have to make do with you then.'

'I'm sure the children would like to hear the joke,' I said inanely.

'Yes. Yes, I'm sure you're right.' He turned to the children, who were pensively stirring their Coca-Colas with their forefingers. 'Why are there walls around graveyards?' their grandfather asked.

Silence.

'Come on, now. Have a go. Why are there walls around graveyards?'

'I have no idea,' said Hermione. And it was the old Hermione, the sullen, unhelpful Hermione of the previous summer.

'Then I shall tell you why there are walls around graveyards. Because people are dying to get in!'

Chapter Twenty-Four

'You are so lucky that your parents are dead,' Max told me as we sat waiting for our flight that evening. 'You have no idea what it's like to see them rot before your eyes. Their stinking bigotry doesn't even hold together any more. Everything they say is absurd! It could have been written by Ionesco. Everything about them is a stinking, moth-eaten joke. Dishonourable to the core. I can't even feel protective of them any more. I might look like I'm doing the right thing, but actually I'm trying to hide them. This is what people call a grand old family! I wish I'd never met them. I wish I'd been given up for adoption at birth. Then perhaps I might have had a chance, although you never know, I might be genetically doomed in any environment. Genetically doomed to become a senile bigot, the last colonial still slouching towards the millennium. I wish I could get into a car and drive us to Newfoundland and settle us in a log cabin and never ever read another stinking newspaper again, and only have visitors who like us.

'We should never have come here,' he said over and over again. 'We should never have come here. I should never have let them put us through that stinking, stinking masquerade of a wedding. How many of them were fooled by that pathetic effort? Couldn't Bea find another altar in front of which to debase herself? Dead ritual to bury the memory of a dead woman, that's all it was. A dead challenger. We had our chance but nothing is ever going to be right again. You'll see. I ought to have taken the chance when I first saw it. I ought never to have taken you into that stinking, rotten fold. I ought to have taken the children, and taken you, and run. Now we'll never get away. You wait and see.'

I listened and tried to reason with him until he stopped making sense. When we got on the plane in Curaçao, I tried to settle him on a stretch of seats where he could fall asleep, while I sat in the seats behind with the children. The ploy didn't work. As he drank his way across the Atlantic, trying to engage the man across the aisle and a string of reluctant stewardesses in drunken conversation, I did my best to keep the children out of range. I failed.

The trouble began when he picked up a satsuma I had packed in the children's game bag and decided to use it for a game of catch with his son. But because his judgement was gone, he threw it too hard and too fast for William to catch it. When it hit the back of the seat, Max asked William why he was so uncoordinated. When it hit him in the face and he cried, Max dismissed him as a crybaby. He said he wasn't going to speak to William again until he apologised. He threw the satsuma to Hermione. When she was successful in catching it, he invited her to sit on his lap.

She went willingly, and in the beginning seemed pleased at the affectionate words he began to pour over her. But they soon became too much. She was the real thing, he told her, over and over. She was the most important woman in his life. He knew he didn't spend enough time with her, but it was important for her to know that he was willing to die for her, and would certainly die of a broken heart if he lost her. Every time she tried to look away from him, he would put his hands on her head and force her to look into his eyes. She began to protest. He responded by shouting at her. She burst into tears. He hugged her tight and burst into tears with her. I asked him to let Hermione go. When he told me to piss off, and not to come between him and the most important woman in his life, a man in a neighbouring aisle tried to intervene, and when that led to more threats and insults, I called for the flight attendant. When she was unable to get Max to release Hermione, who was wailing by now, the good samaritan in the neighbouring aisle went for more help and came back with the first-class steward, who was able to talk him into letting Hermione go.

'They're going to kill him, aren't they?' William said, almost proudly, when they walked him up to the front of the plane.

Aware that all the eyes of economy class were on us, I reassured him, but Hermione contradicted me.

'They're going to try at least,' she sobbed. 'Unless he kills them first.'

'That's not a very nice thing to say about your father. Why do you think he wants to kill them?'

'Well, it's rather obvious, don't you think? He just said so.'

'What people say when they're drunk is not necessarily what they end up doing, or what they mean. You've got to close your ears and wait until the next morning. And ask them again.'

'*If* they wake up,' said Hermione coldly, watching him stagger into the aisle and fall over.

After they had helped him to his feet again, I reassured Hermione that his life was not at risk.

'How do you know?' she asked.

I told her it was a lifetime of experience.

'You had an unhappy childhood, didn't you?' Hermione said. Then, with her sourest fake-adult grimace, she added, 'Well, that's one thing we had in common.'

'How can you say that, when your childhood is only half over?'

She shrugged her shoulders. 'Because absolutely everyone says so. Ask them and they'll tell you. It's just one trauma after another. Some people actually think I'll never recover.'

'Oh yes, you will, you will!' I protested. 'You will if I have anything to do with it!'

She gave me a withering look. 'Oh, you'll try,' she said. 'I'll grant you that. You'll try and get it right. Just like my mother.'

Chapter Twenty-Five

*B*ea had her chauffeur waiting for us outside customs the next morning. An hour later we were home. The beds were turned down and complete with hot-water bottles. There were fires going in both the sitting room and our bedroom. I fell asleep before my head hit the pillow.

Bea woke us up with tea and biscuits just as the sky was turning dark. 'I hope you don't mind,' she said. 'But I was rather hoping you might help me out with some people I'm having to supper.'

They turned out to be two poets who had first met Giles as students in Kampala and owed their international reputations to Giles having featured them in his first Africa series. They had just been to see a controversial new production of *Hamlet* in Stratford and spent most of supper describing in spirited detail how it had brought out the play's universalities. Crawley objected when one claimed that Hamlet was twentieth-century man. That honour had to go to Lear, he insisted. The other guest said no, it was Yeats who best expressed the spirit of the age. He then recited half of 'The Second Coming'. Crawley finished it off for him. This led to more competitive reciting, which led eventually to singing.

First it was opera, then operetta, then half the songs from *South Pacific*. At about midnight, Bea remembered the CD her guests had brought with them. It featured a new female singer from Zaïre that another former student of Giles was trying to launch in Europe. When Jasper the dog tried to howl along with it, one of the guests took him by the front paws and began to dance around the room with him. I remember looking at Max's stony face untouched by the laughing and the clapping around him and asking myself, how could he of all people call this house dead, these people doomed, their rituals fake and meaningless? He must have read my mind, because by the time we got home, he had already recanted.

'You're a saint, I don't deserve you,' he told me, taking my hand. There was still something wrong with his voice. Its tone was so flat he sounded as if he were reciting lines. 'You deserve to be with someone who never touches a drop. Who never has cause to touch a drop. I know it doesn't make any difference that I hate myself today for what I put you through, and put the children through. But I do. I do hate myself. I hate myself so much that I can't for the life of me understand why you put up with me.'

This last sentence he said with conviction. I lost my distance and reached for his hand. 'You were upset,' I assured him. 'It wasn't that you wandered over the edge. You were pushed,' I said.

His face darkened. 'That's the point. That's what makes it so bad.'

'But you've got to expect it,' I said. 'You can't have something to lose without also having enemies. Jack Scully hates you because you're trying to make something of your life again. He hates you because you're surrounded by people who love you.'

Max lowered his head. He said nothing.

'He hates you because I love you,' I said.

That made him laugh. 'Hard to fault him on that, though, as I hate myself for the same reason!'

I wanted to ask him why. I wanted to know why Jack hated him, why he hated Jack, why he hated himself. What had happened between them at this unspecified time in the past in St John the Baptist. Why these undescribed events had ruined his marriage, what he had gone on to do to Rebecca afterwards. When he had done so. Why.

Why? I wanted to know but I couldn't voice the question. Instead I said, 'The children deserve an explanation. You frightened them. I did my best to keep their spirits up, but that's not enough. Something has to come from you.'

'I've already talked to them,' he said, squeezing my hand.

'What did you say?'

'The right things. Although they may not be as frightened as you

177

seem to think. They've seen worse, and not just from me. But don't worry. I apologised and I reassured them.' Taking me into his arms, he said, 'Now I have to reassure *you*.'

'Actually, you don't, as I've seen worse too.'

'Oh, you have, have you? Famous last words. You have no idea how bad I can be. But I promise to keep the devil inside me harnessed,' he said, laughing in such a way that it was impossible to tell whether he was being serious or mocking himself, or both. 'I promise to be a good husband to you, and a good father to the children, and a good editor, and I even promise to be a good poet, the kind who sometimes dares to put pen to paper.'

'Promise you'll finish *The Last Supper*,' I said. 'Promise you'll keep taking yourself seriously.'

'I'll be a model citizen in every way,' he said. 'If you promise to keep lying to yourself about what I'm worth.'

And, for the next three weeks, he was as good as his word. Then something happened. Or rather, several things happened.

The first was an abrupt change of mood that he refused to explain to me. After a few days, I was able to trace it to an item in *Private Eye* about the run-in with Jack in St John the Baptist. It was in code, describing Jack as tired and emotional, Max's father as Ben 'Brainy' Winterton, and Max driven to violence after his attention was drawn to resemblances of a Ugandan nature. No one told me about it. I happened on it when I was browsing in W. H. Smith. I went to Crawley for an explanation of the innuendo. I remember that when I asked him what all this was about Uganda, his eyes went dead.

'I shouldn't think that would be too hard for you to figure out,' he said. 'Knowing what you know about Rebecca. But since the object of this exercise seems to be to get me to say it out loud, yes, Jack and Rebecca were indeed kissing cousins. If they were cousins at all. For all his talk about the family chin, I've had my doubts about that from the beginning.'

'What happened between them in St John the Baptist?'

Crawley looked uncomfortable. 'The only person who knows that, I would say, is the patron saint himself. The rest of them are only guessing because they can't remember a thing, not even which substance it was they happened to be abusing at the time. One thing you'll have to get used to, girl, is that we are not looking at competing versions of the truth here, but a snake pit of desperate inventions. And corporate weakness. Which may just be another way of saying that they deserve each other. Best to look the other way. Concentrate on putting one foot in front of the other. If you manage that, you'll be the first in four generations of Midwinters.'

Putting one foot in front of the other was easier said than done. I was a painfully slow writer in those days. Even when I knew what I wanted to say, it took me a week to write an eight-hundred-word review. And with this book, this Tamara Nestor Graham book that I had finally managed to plough through, I did not know what I wanted to say. I didn't even know what I thought. Despite its hackneyed subject – the spiritual and sexual rebirth of a downtrodden woman – it had some of the most beautiful passages I had ever read. But it was also unwieldy. Too imbued with noble purpose. Turning the page felt like moving a boulder. And there was something dishonest about it, something underneath its churchlike solemnity that made me feel as if the author were having a joke at my expense. Something that made me feel as if she got her strength from secrets she would never disclose. It was all about the power of secrets, this book. In the last line, she even went so far as to describe herself as impregnated with secrets she would never bring to term.

That line left a bad taste in my mouth, but I could not understand why. If I did not understand my own response, how could I base my opinion on it? In my first finished version, I tried to describe my uneasiness, but when I looked at it again the next day, it seemed to me that I had deliberately avoided taking a position. I was being wishy-washy because I didn't want to commit myself. So I wrote a second version in which I gave her the benefit of the doubt. I avoided discussing my real response and talking myself into agreeing with the ecstatic American quotes that decorated the British edition. I supported these with quotes from the best passages in the book. I faxed it to the office and waited for Max to ring with his comments.

In the past he had done this within the hour. But today he didn't ring at all. When he came home he sounded preoccupied. When he did not mention the review, I thought it was this that was troubling him. He had brought a bottle of gin home with him. He worked his way through it as if it were a chore. Had the review been so bad that he had to be drunk before he found the courage to discuss it with me? I tried to make it easier for him. I sat down next to him and said, 'If there's something you want to talk to me about, just do it.'

'What could I possibly want to discuss with you?'

I didn't respond to the insult. Instead I said, 'I was thinking about that review I sent in today. It seems to have upset you.'

'On the contrary,' he said. 'It didn't upset me in the least.'

'Then why didn't you ring and tell me what you thought of it?'

'You really are going to have to get a little bit tougher, my dear. And quite quickly, too. You must start seeing that there is more than your lovely little career at stake. Did I tell you they've set a date for the trial and that it falls in the same week as your book coming out? They'll not be able to discuss me or the trial, but it'll be open season on you, I'm afraid. Like it or not, you'll find yourself the object of an inquisition. You must prepare yourself.'

'Why don't I tell my publishers to delay publication?'

'That would only tell the inquisitors that their tactics so far have been successful.'

'But that's only putting off the day of reckoning. My work can't stand up to that kind of scrutiny.'

'That's exactly the type of thing you're going to have to learn to stop saying if you're to survive.'

'How can I if I don't have any confidence?'

'Confidence is not something you get. It's something you learn to live without.'

'Then don't try to protect me, Max. Don't keep me in the dark. Tell me what was wrong with it,' I pleaded.

'Wrong with what?'

'Tell me what was wrong with the review.'

'I've already told you, there was nothing wrong with it.'

'Then why didn't you ring me?'

'Because I was busy, God damn it. Because I was busy! For God's sake, I have more important things to do when I'm at work than pander to your vanities.'

'It's not a question of vanity,' I said. 'It's a question of whether you thought the review was good or bad.'

'It was neither good *nor* bad,' he said.

'Do you want me to rewrite it?'

'If I had wanted you to rewrite it, I would have asked you to rewrite it.' He sighed. 'I really don't have much of an opinion on it. If you want the truth.'

'Then what's bothering you?'

'Nothing's bothering me.'

'That's not true.'

'Let me put it this way. It's nothing out of the ordinary. Nothing beyond the fact that I am universally hated for something I didn't do and am about to have to drag my entire family through a court case in order to clear my name, but will not be able to clear my name fully even if I win, on account of being universally hated. Is that enough for you?'

I gave up. I was tired. I went to bed early. When I woke up in the middle of the night, I found him in the sitting room, still drinking as if it were his duty. He was reading his own books. Next to him was a pile of Rebecca's books. This pattern repeated itself every night for a week. When I opened the paper on Sunday and found that my review was not in, I concluded that the focus of my concern had been too narrow. It was not the mediocrity of my review that had concerned him, it was my overall mediocrity. Once he had been married to the real thing; now he was encumbered with the pale imitation. And already the last easy exit was blocked. Because I was not just tired now. I was bloated and queasy and had missed my period.

It was on the Monday after he did not run my review that I went to the chemists and bought a pregnancy test. I was meant to wait until the next morning to get an accurate result. But I did it right away. It came out positive.

181

I remember not believing it was positive. I remember telling myself that this was nevertheless the opportunity I needed to find out how Max really felt. So I rang him at the office and told him the news. His first response was dead silence. 'It's not necessarily accurate,' I blundered on. 'I didn't follow the directions to the letter, so I should probably take another test before we decide what to do. If you've changed your mind, you know, we can still talk about it.'

He met this with a sigh. 'I'm getting tired of telling you that I haven't changed my mind.'

Before I could think, I blurted out, 'Then why do you act like you've changed your mind?'

He sighed again. In the background, I could hear Mimi, his deputy, asking him a question. 'I'll be right over,' he said to her. And then to me, 'I'll be home a bit later than usual this evening. Perhaps we can discuss it then.'

He didn't come home until four in the morning. And even then, he didn't come to me in the bedroom. He went upstairs to Rebecca's study. I could hear him opening up cabinets and drawers, swearing to himself, knocking down bottles. I tried to go up and talk to him. But the door was locked, and he wouldn't answer my knock.

He stayed up there throughout the next morning. When the children came home from Saturday school, he rang me using Rebecca's private line and asked me to send the children up. When I tried to go up with them, he sent me away. He spent the afternoon downstairs on the sofa, watching television with both children on his lap. He managed to pull himself together to perform up to standard at Bea's dinner party that evening. The guest this time was a German publisher who wanted specific information on the current British attitude to Freud. I was unable to tell whether Max was really the expert he made himself out to be, or whether he was making it all up. The effort cheered him up, but only for the duration of the party; when we got home, he went upstairs to say goodnight to the children and never came down again.

I spent Sunday filling his silence with theories. Horrible, horrible theories. He didn't love me any more. He had lost interest in me, and so had changed his mind about a baby. Or even worse, he wanted a baby but not me. I was not the woman he had imagined I was because I had never been that woman. He had lost interest in me but he still felt responsible for me and that was why he was so depressed. He no longer loved me but he still had to protect me, the same way he had to protect everyone else in his family – and that was why he hadn't run the review, because it was so bad. He hadn't run the review, in order to protect me from ridicule.

And now where was he seeking comfort? Whose arms was he in? What excess had I propelled him to? Why was I persisting? What right did I have?

Why should I sit here if all I could do was make him feel guilty about not loving me enough? There was no reason to continue being a millstone. If I had become a millstone to him, I was prepared to leave. The baby and I could make a life elsewhere. If he wanted, he could keep in touch. After I came back from taking the children to school on Monday morning, I decided to go upstairs and tell him.

This time I found him in his own study. He was on the floor, going through papers he had pulled out of his filing cabinet. There was a glass and an overfull ashtray balanced precariously on his desk chair. The room was filled with smoke and stank of ouzo. I had rehearsed a long speech but now that I was face to face with him the words evaporated. Instead I said, 'Did you spend the night with a prostitute?'

He looked up at me, incredulous. 'Did I hear you correctly?'

'I'm sorry. I don't have any right to ask.'

He gave me a long, strained look, as if my very presence gave him a headache. His face was chilled with grey, as if he had emerged from a meat freezer. 'That's the very last thing you need to be worrying about. If you don't mind my telling you.'

'Have you ever been to a prostitute?'

'If I had, would it matter?'

'I'm not sure,' I said. 'Have you changed your mind about the baby?'

'No, I have not changed my mind about the baby. Or you,' he said in a flat and weary voice. 'But for the moment I'm afraid this is the best I can offer.'

Chapter Twenty-Six

*I*f you find yourself trapped in a marriage with a man who is slowly but deliberately killing himself, and if nothing like this has ever happened to you before, you can rage about the injustice of it all. You can blame him instead of blaming yourself. You can ask, Why me? You can call it bad luck. You can convince yourself not only that you deserve better but that you're capable of finding better. The second time you hear the sigh and the clink of the glass on the other side of the ceiling, you can no longer hide inside these comforts. Instead you ask, Why am I repeating myself? Why, when I repeat myself, am I the last to know? You wonder why you chose the same trap even when you knew it was a trap. Why life remains the same for you whether you keep your eyes open or closed. Instead of wondering why you can't make this man happy, you wonder why you can't make any man happy. Why you choose men who are heading for the exit. Why they choose you.

At the same time you can't bring yourself to admit failure. Something in you still says that this is happening because of a mistake you made. That if you can find this mistake and put it right, everything else will turn out right, too. And there is always the hope that the nightmare will be over in the morning and never recur. So you pretend that the sigh and the clink of the glass on the other side of the ceiling are normal. You encourage everyone else to pretend with you, until you crack.

I woke up the next morning to find two pairs of clammy, restless legs draped over mine. The children had been woken up by the noise during the night. I had tried to take them back up but they had never settled. It is hard being physically close to children who are not yours and whom you have not yet grown to love. I wanted to kick them off me but my better nature prevailed. I extricated myself carefully, covered them up again, and tiptoed out of the room. I managed to get down a cup of tea and a piece of dry toast before they noticed my defection and bounded into the sitting room to drag me through the morning routine.

My morning sickness was still not too bad that week, but even the smallest effort exhausted me. It was all I could do to think where they might have thrown the consent form the night before, and which child has to take which instrument, and where it was I had noticed a balled-up navy-blue sock ... As I struggled up and down the stairs, I promised Hermione more than once that I would do my best to get Max to open the door to Rebecca's study and retrieve the blue clay bowl that Hermione had made in her mother's memory and left on her desk. She was worried Max would use it as an ashtray and ruin it.

I understood why it was important to Hermione, but I should never have promised to help her, just as I should never have said to Mimi, Max's deputy, when she rang at ten, that I would get him to ring her back within the hour. Just as I should not have implied to Bea, and later in the morning, to Crawley, that Max was en route to London for an important lunch. If you're going to lie, it's better not to tell separate lies to different people. And it's pointless to lie at all if you share a cleaner.

Not that Janet didn't want to play along. 'Would you like me to say you're resting next time the phone rings?' she enquired. 'You look like you need a rest, dear, actually. You look like you had a bit of a bumpy night.' She nodded up at the ceiling, then smiled. 'But never fear, dear. Some men just need time. He was the same, I don't mind telling you, with the other two. The former Mrs M had a terrible time of it! Not that she had your stiff upper lip, dear. She was much younger then than you are now, of course. She didn't have your wider experience. And she could never stand back, you see, not like you can. I tried to explain to her, but she was never a one to listen to my claptrap – that was her word for it – my claptrap about a woman's lot. Of course you have the advantage of seeing how devoted Mrs M is now to those two out there, even if he kicked and screamed at the beginning.'

'He may think he loves them,' I said without thinking. 'But if he considered their feelings at all, he wouldn't be locking himself away from them.'

'If he stopped to consider their feelings,' Janet said with a chuckle, 'then he wouldn't be a man.'

This meek attempt at a joke made me burst into tears. It was out of the best of motives that she rang Bea to tell her what was happening.

Bea came right over. 'You should have told me as soon as this began,' she said, too sternly. 'We can't have you exhausting yourself. We don't want you losing the baby.' First she tried to speak to Max through the door. When his only response was to throw a book at it, she came downstairs and got me to tell the story of his decline step by step. 'It sounds as if your publication date was the last straw,' she said. 'Not to say that has anything to do with you, my dear, but it is rather unfortunate, coming as it does on the same week as this trial. I wonder if it wouldn't be an idea to get it moved.'

I told her that I had suggested this already and been told that such a retreat would only attract more negative attention.

'Max said that, did he? Well, he's probably right. But it does all seem to be too much for him. We shall have to take that into account as well. This is all very, very tricky. If Danny finds out he's taken over Rebecca's study, there will be hell to pay.' In order to get help figuring out how to keep Danny in the dark, she called in Crawley.

Crawley arrived with a storm-cloud face. 'You should have told me sooner,' he said. 'It doesn't help to hide these things. I might have been able to head the crisis off.' He insisted on my telling him the story from the beginning. Every few minutes he would shake his head and turn to Bea and say, 'This all sounds very familiar, doesn't it?'

'I think it's the publication date that pushed him over the edge,' Bea said to him when I had finished.

Crawley seemed perplexed by her suggestion. 'It must bring unpleasant memories back about publication dates of the past, but I don't quite catch the significance of what you're saying.'

'Max knows what a drubbing she's going to get, and that concerns him. It's harder to have a wife in the limelight than some people imagine.'

Crawley was not impressed. 'If anyone is used to that, Max is. No, I think it's something else that's got to him, and that thing is called alcohol. This is a very, very disturbing development. I really thought he had pulled himself together, but now it's as if we've turned the clock back two or even three years.'

He turned back to me. 'How much has he told you about his problems with alcohol?'

'He feels bad afterwards,' I said. 'He always apologises.'

'It's what he does that counts, dearie, not what he says. How many times since last summer have you seen this happen?'

'There was only one other episode, after the unpleasantness in St John the Baptist. The worst part of that one was that the children treated it as routine.'

'As well they might,' Crawley said. 'So. How much do you want to know?' He spoke in a brutal voice that sent me into tears again.

'Crawley, you mustn't upset her unnecessarily,' Bea said to him. 'We must remember the baby. We must take care not to tire her.'

Crawley said, 'There is nothing more tiring than trying to deny the truth.'

'I know the truth,' I cried. 'I just don't understand it.'

'Oh, dear, oh, dear,' Crawley said, taking my hand. 'Don't even try to understand it. Just try to understand it isn't your fault. I wasn't trying to—'

'I'll just fetch some tissues,' Bea said, and then things happened very quickly.

When she threw open the door, it was to reveal Danny and the two children. It was clear from their stunned faces that they had been eavesdropping. 'I just happened to drop by at the school to leave Hermione's rugby boots,' Danny said brightly. 'And I found them both in sick bay. So I thought they'd be better off here, but perhaps I'm wrong! *Is* there anything wrong?'

'Nothing that can't be fixed, my dear,' Bea said firmly.

'It's not the baby, is it? You're not having a miscarriage, are you?'

'No, darling, it's not anything as bad as that, but I'm glad you brought the baby up because there is always a risk, isn't there? It is important not to overtax women at this stage, don't you agree?'

Danny didn't take the hint.

'What I'm trying to say, darling, is that it would be very helpful if you left us alone for the time being. I shall come over afterwards and give you a bulletin, but for now, if you wouldn't mind awfully . . . I hope I'm not sounding rude.'

'No, not at all,' said Danny. 'Why don't I make us a fresh pot of tea?'

'Actually, darling, it would be better if you just left us to it. But you know what *would* be helpful. Before you run off to your little cottage, would you mind awfully sitting Hermione and William in front of a video?'

'*Goodness!*' Bea said when she came back with the tissues. 'I thought we'd never get rid of her. We must think up a reason right away to keep her from coming back.' But already Hermione was behind her, whingeing about her blue clay bowl.

'All this time,' she said, 'and still it's in Mummy's study. How many times do I have to tell you it's not safe in there?'

I tried to apologise for not having retrieved it yet. But when Hermione said, 'So let's do it now!', Bea brushed her aside.

'Don't be daft, my dear. If we could save your bowl, we could save everything else in the room.'

And so it was Hermione who went to Danny and told her that Max was in the midst of wrecking and ransacking Rebecca's study.

'Why didn't any of you think to tell me?' Danny wanted to know when she rushed back into the room. 'How much has he destroyed already? Why hasn't anyone considered breaking down the door? Oh, how can you people just sit here and let this atrocity happen?'

Just after Danny had streaked upstairs to shout at Max through the door, Mimi rang from the newspaper for the second time. 'Can I ring you back in a few minutes?' I asked. But a few minutes later, Danny was sitting on my bedroom floor, legs crossed, body swaying and reciting her mantra.

The next time Mimi rang, it was Bea who answered. In an excessively slow and polite voice, she said, 'Mimi, darling, could this urgent logistical problem wait until tomorrow?'

It was Crawley who finally got Max to open the door. We listened in silence to their grim mumbling coming through the ceiling. Max got to his feet, then stumbled and had to be dragged back to his chair. There was another crash, more keening from Danny, more grim mumbling on the other side of the ceiling. Suddenly Danny jumped to her feet, saying she couldn't bear it any more. She went upstairs and started pounding on the door.

'I'll never forgive you for this, Max. Never ever!' she shrieked when they wouldn't let her in. 'Now finally you show yourself in your true colours! Don't you realise how very much I've had to swallow over the past five years? I did it because I thought you cared. I thought you loved her as I love her. And now you're in there, laughing at me and spitting on her memory! And I think, why did I ever cover for you? Why did I believe you when you told me it was for the best? It was only for the best for you, I now see! You couldn't care less about the rest of us! All you care about is saving your own skin. Which is what Rebecca always told me. Why, oh, why did I forget to heed her? I'll never forgive myself for falling for your putrid lies!'

This had been going on for at least twenty minutes when Crawley rang us from Rebecca's private line. 'I'm taking him out to the pub in Islip,' he told me. 'It's better for us all that we have it out there. I'd be grateful if you organised a distraction for Miss Twinkle-Toes out there.'

Bea obliged. She went upstairs and suggested that she go to the big house to fetch the spare key to Rebecca's study. While she was gone, Crawley got Max out of the house and into his car.

When he returned a half an hour later, it was with the news that Max had given him the slip.

By the time we heard this news, we had too many other problems to give it due importance. Danny was in an apoplectic state after inspecting the damage Max had done to Rebecca's study. Hermione was screaming about her blue clay bowl, which she couldn't find anywhere. And Bea had lost her patience. 'Oh, do stop moaning about the bowl, Hermione. It's the very least of our worries.'

'You just say that because you don't need me any more because now you have a new baby to think about!'

'Oh, Hermione, do stop being so melodramatic.'

'You don't love me because I remind you of my mother!'

'Hermione, my dear, if that is so, it makes you part of a cast of hundreds.'

'I want my daddy!'

'And so do we all, my dear girl. But tears won't bring him back. We must be practical. We must first and foremost move our battle to another venue. That *and* the telephone. I hope you don't mind if I remove this thing from the room altogether. It can't be doing you or the baby any good.'

And so it was that I didn't hear about Mimi until the following morning.

Max was still missing but the panic had subsided. Bea had already taken the children to school and made me breakfast. Now she was off to London for the day. As she put the phone back into the jack, she said, 'And when you do have a moment, it might be an idea to speak to Mimi. She was sounding rather hysterical, actually. It had something to do with a piece Max was meant to have written.'

'What should I say to her?'

'Say there's a family crisis. She won't ask for details.'

Mimi was in a state because Max had a big article due that morning on the novelist Naguib Mahfouz. When I said she couldn't speak to him, she said, 'That's just not good enough. Let me speak to him myself.' I said she couldn't. She insisted. Finally I burst into tears and told her the truth.

'I'm so sorry. I'm so, so sorry,' she said. 'I've been so very, very cruel.' Three hours later, I awoke from a nap to find her sitting next to my bed.

Taking my hand, Mimi said, 'You poor, poor dear! How do you feel?'

'Not very well,' I admitted.

'Is Crawley still out looking for him?'

'Yes, as far as I know.'

'And how are the children?'

'Not well, but at school.'

'And who's looking after you?'

'Who's guarding me is more like it. I've more or less had orders not to get out of bed.'

'It's good advice, you know.'

'Under the circumstances, it makes me feel like a cow.'

'Well, to some extent, you are a cow. At least, when I've been pregnant, that's how I've felt about it.'

'But you continued to have a life, didn't you?'

She squeezed my hand. 'It's not just the pregnancy, is it? Tell me what's bothering you.'

I blurted out, 'I may never be able to write again.'

'You know that's not true, darling. You know that's not true.'

'Sometimes I think it would be better if I never wrote again, because I just can't write well enough.'

'According to whom do you not write well enough?'

'According to myself, of course. And I think Max would agree. I think that's what Max saw in me from the start – my lack of ability.'

'If he did, my dear, he'd be so wrong. Your book of stories was a pure delight!' I found her smile too bright.

'It's not the fiction,' I said quickly. 'It's the reviewing. You know how *Private Eye* are always making fun of it. Well, I think it bothers him more than he'd like to admit. Or perhaps, to be fair, he's just trying to protect me. That's why he didn't want to run the Tamara Nestor Graham piece. Because he knew that to run that piece would be asking for more of the same.'

'But we *are* running the Tamara Nestor Graham piece. It's scheduled for this Sunday.'

'Then why did he refuse to discuss it with me?'

'You've probably mixed things up. I wouldn't worry about the review. It was perfectly good and respectable.'

'More respectable than good,' I admitted.

'How do you mean?'

192

'It was polite instead of honest. I meant, the book was so very worthy and fashionably correct that I couldn't find the nerve to say what I meant.'

'And what would you have said if you had found the nerve, my dear?'

'That I'm fed up with reading books about posturing feminine explorers saying no to tradition and setting out on savage journeys in which all sorts of amazing things happen to them in motels they describe exquisitely despite their penchant for four-syllable sentences.'

'Good, good. Tell me more,' she said. I went on in this vein, suddenly able, in the fire of pique, to describe the genre as it was first invented by Anais Nin and eventually stripped down by the female disciples of Raymond Carver. I explained why I thought it was so politically crude to expect that All Women would benefit because a few extraordinarily selfish women happened to come to terms with themselves after twenty or thirty years of stepping over every human being who stood in their way. 'So much easier than doing what the rest of us do, which is to pick up the pieces.'

At which point Mimi took my hand again and said, 'That's splendid. Now I know what I'm going to do. I'm going to the shops and then I'm coming back to make you some soup. And while I'm busy doing that, you are to write down everything you've just told me and—'

'I'm not sure I could. I'm a very slow writer.'

'It doesn't matter. Just write notes if you prefer. We have time. Just see what comes out and we can take it from there.'

Fifteen minutes later I had found my first line: 'In America at least, all explorations of the female psyche end up in the same place.' I showed it to Mimi.

'Splendid,' she said. 'Now say what you mean by that.'

Two hours later, when she brought me the soup, I was just finishing. 'I'm sure it needs work,' I said.

But she didn't agree. 'It's honest and direct, and written from the heart, and it sums up a trend no one has identified. And I agree, Rebecca *was* the exception to the rule – at least, as you say, in her best work. I have some doubts, though, about this sentence here: "I think most American women writers – myself included – have been content to be bad imitations of Rebecca." Aren't you being a bit hard on yourself, my dear?'

'I don't want to criticise a trend and pretend I have nothing to do with it, so I'd prefer to keep that sentence or something like it.'

'Well, that's very brave of you, my dear. And I'm sure it will be taken as such. I think it's a splendid piece and just what I needed because I shall now be able to put it on the blank page and hold the Mahfouz piece over until next week. So you've saved my life, my dear. Now I'm going to take this away from you and read it to the copy takers, but before I go, you must promise me you won't give up writing. You can't let other people's opinions eat away at you. Other people have a right to their opinions, but that's not the same as saying their opinions are more important than what you think about yourself. Why do you write at all, my dear?'

'To understand what I believe in.'

'So tell me why anyone should stop you doing that?'

So long as she was there, looking straight into my eyes, I could not help seeing her point. But that was the crux of the problem, you might say – that it was her point, not mine. Before an hour was out, I had already lost hold of Mimi's inspiring instructions. It mattered what Max thought of me. It mattered that he couldn't look me in the eye any more. It mattered that I had propelled him into this binge and it mattered that he wouldn't tell me why.

'It's not your fault.' That was what Crawley told me on Wednesday morning and Wednesday night, and on Thursday, and on Friday night when he found Max and brought him home. 'This is not the man you married. It's a cocktail with a haircut.'

'It's just too much going wrong at the same time,' Bea added. 'Nothing to do with you, dear. Without you and the baby to look forward to, imagine what he'd have left. We just have to get him to pull himself together.'

And when Giles, Bea and Crawley brought him down from his study for the polite but awkward confrontation on Saturday morning, he appeared to accept their admonishments. He agreed: he had let drink get the better of him again. He had forgotten his family duties. Yes, it was a question of backbone, in future. Yes, it was important not to allow himself to drink for the wrong reasons. But when I saw him wander over to the window and look out over the hills, I knew, with the kind of conviction I could never have had for myself, that none of us had come close to guessing the true reasons for his withdrawal and defection.

He was alone. And by writing from the heart, I had increased his isolation. It wasn't until I saw my article in print on Sunday morning that I realised it was not about literature at all but about my home life. The headline ran, 'Picking Up the Pieces: why one woman writer is fed up with feminist heroines who are willing to destroy anything for the sake of experience.'

How had I not seen the autobiographical intent? When Max saw the article, he snorted with disbelief. 'I go missing one week and this is what happens. So we're picking up the pieces, are we?' When he had finished reading it, he looked me in the eye for the first time since returning home. 'I don't suppose you have any idea what you've just done. Why did you go along with it? Why have you let them use you?'

'Mimi was desperate,' I said. 'The Naguib Mahfouz piece was—'

'Mimi ought to have known better. Her motives may have been excellent and her need for copy extreme, and my responsibility for the crisis is beyond dispute. But she ought to have known better than to let you write on this subject. This is truly tempting the devil. This will be the single most likely thing to destroy us. We've reached the point of no return. The last door has closed.'

'But why?' I asked. 'It's only about books.'

'My naive little American upstart, nothing is ever just about books.'

'That's still all I intended.'

'You can go ahead and tell yourself that. No one else will, but I'm afraid I can't help you there. You'll simply have to watch and see and, it is to be hoped, eventually learn. It would have been better, though, if you had exercised better judgement in the first instance.'

195

'Max! What are you talking about?'

He put his arm around me. 'What a child you are sometimes! What a peril! I dread the day when I look in your eyes and see something else. But in the meantime you really are becoming your own worst enemy. My dear, don't you ever think these people you have turned into your confidantes might be using you for their own purposes? Mimi I exclude from this blanket statement. Mimi just gets carried away sometimes – in this respect she has the same problem as you and is just as bad at seeing through people. But, my dear pregnant wife, has it not occurred to you that all Bea really cares for is the heir you might bear? Haven't you ever noticed how hard it is for her to hold this family together on the pretext of blood ties that do not, for the most part, exist? Her hopes for a genuine heir are well intended, of course, but I'm sure I don't have to remind you what Camus said about good intentions.'

'I can't remember what he said.'

'That they were the source of all evil,' he said with a tired sigh. 'You really must not overestimate Bea's good will. You mustn't really. You're only as good to her as the child you produce. And as for Crawley – I know you've confided in him. I know he has taken it upon himself to explain the world to you. And to explain me. But I very much doubt that he has gone so far as to explain his own very convoluted contribution to the drama. He was in love with Rebecca too, my dear. And so he has his own scores to settle, with me as with others. So in future, my darling child, I should watch what you say to him.'

Chapter Twenty-Seven

M ax was right about one thing. My piece attracted the wrong kind of attention. It got picked up by most of the gossip columns, criticised by well-known feminists in the *Independent* and the *Guardian*, featured in Pseuds' Corner in one issue of *Private Eye* and got a page-long parody in the next. 'I admit I'm really not worth much' was its title. It mimicked my flat style well, using the sentence Mimi had wanted to omit as its leitmotif.

'You're taking this like a good sport, I hope,' Mimi said. 'You do realise, don't you, my darling, that they're paying you a compliment? And you mustn't forget all the good letters we got praising you. I posted another two yesterday – did you receive them? One called you a breath of fresh air. I've told you what people here said, but did I mention that the editor took me aside after the Wednesday conference to say how much he enjoyed it? He said we should use you more often.'

But it was not to be. Max stopped using me at all. He also stopped coming home except at weekends. At first he took the trouble to provide reasons. One day it was because he had to see his solicitors after work. Another day it was because he had to go to a friend's launch, or fly to Manchester for the night to do an interview. Then one day he rang from the office and said that his second cousin Lucy had given him a key to her flat 'and so I think it's best for the time being, don't you, if we all plan on my being there Monday through Thursday?'

If he had been consistently cold during his weekend visits, it would have been easier to bear. But he wasn't. He would arrive looking grey and chilled and unable even to smile at the children. I would wake up on Saturday to find him laying the table for breakfast as grimly as if he were laying out a corpse. He would spend the rest of the day in the sitting room. Only on Sunday would he have recovered enough to take the children out for a walk. They did this whatever the weather and, whatever the weather, returned refreshed. At Sunday lunch, he would even talk – at least to the children. And after he had spent the afternoon and evening playing Uno and Stratego with them, and had put them to bed with the story tapes he himself had recorded, sometimes he would even talk to me.

Sometimes. Not always. If he kept the television on, the most I could hope for was to put a head against his shoulder while he fell asleep. But if he put on music (and he only did this if the cloud had fully lifted), he would not just embrace me, not just put his head on my stomach and 'wait for the first kick'; he would apologise for having been 'so withdrawn and bloody-minded'. He would say he didn't deserve me. Call me his saving grace. Repeat over and over that I did not deserve what I had coming to me. Promise that one day he would tell me the truth.

That the truth involved at least one other woman was not hard to figure out. In the bags of laundry he left behind for Janet to wash, I found the occasional piece of women's underwear, the odd condom wrapper, bits of paper containing names and addresses that never belonged to men. Once, when I found two ticket stubs to Dublin and a hotel bill for one night and two breakfasts, I lost control and tried to reach him at his cousin's flat, but when a woman who was not his cousin answered, I also lost my nerve and hung up.

Who was she? What did she have that I didn't have? What did she look like? What was he doing to her? How did he look at her when she took off her clothes? What did he say to her when he made love to her? What did he *tell her about me?* I couldn't bear not knowing any more. I couldn't bear spending night after night in bed just guessing. I had to force Max and his shadow accomplice out into the open. So I rang Janet and got her to come in to sit with the children and set off to face the truth. The roads were clear and so I was in Ladbroke Grove in just over an hour.

I had never met the baby-faced woman who answered the doorbell, but she knew me. Her hair was wet and she was wearing a bathrobe. 'I hope you don't mind if I leave you to it,' she said. 'I just got in from Hong Kong this morning. Max is in his room, I think. You know which one it is, don't you?'

I didn't, but even before she shut the bathroom door, I could hear his voice coming from the room at the end of the corridor. His voice and a woman's voice. 'So you think I shouldn't,' she was saying.

'I wouldn't dream of telling you what to do, my dear. At the end of the day, you're the one who's going to have to live with him.' The door was open. Max was sitting on the bed and taking off his shoes. The woman, who had short brown hair, a large, handsome face and looked older than me, was sitting on the windowsill examining her bare feet. Were they lovers? Or were they old friends? I couldn't tell. 'Goodness,' Max said, when he looked up and saw me. 'Is everything all right?'

'Is it?' I said. 'You tell me.'

'You don't look very happy,' he said.

'Would you be in my shoes? I feel like I've been under house arrest.'

'But you managed to escape,' he said. 'For the evening, anyway. Well, that's good, anyway.' He patted the bed. 'Come sit down. You've met Tillie before, haven't you?'

Before I could answer, Tillie said, 'Yes, at the wedding.' Her smile had not an ounce of embarrassment or jealousy. Did that mean there was nothing between them? I couldn't make my mind up. Neither of them seemed to want me to leave. When I said I couldn't stay long because I had left the children with Janet, Max said, 'Nonsense. You're staying the night. Anything else would be silly.' While he was on the phone making the arrangements, Tillie heated up some leftovers for me. After I had eaten, all three of us went into the bedroom and sat on the bed to watch the news and the second half of a terrible movie. At the end, Tillie yawned and said, 'Well, I'd better get to sleep. The car's coming for me at six.'

'Where are you off to next?' Max asked.

'We're shooting in some godforsaken corner of Shropshire for three days and then it's back to Dublin.'

'Hard life,' Max said.

'I'll take your room, shall I?' Tillie said as she got off the bed. 'I can't see the two of you being very comfortable in a single bed.'

'Are you sure, Til?'

'Absolutely. I'll just take what I need now.'

She went to the chest of drawers and began pulling out socks and underwear. So this *was* her room, I thought, but then why were Max's books and shaving things on the bedside table? If Max had been sleeping in here, with Tillie, how could Tillie be so casual about moving to another bedroom? Was this proof that she *was* just a good friend, or was she just another very good actor? Why, when the light was out, did Max sigh and draw me close to his chest, and whisper 'I love you'? Because he meant it? Or because he was trying to make me believe that he wasn't having an affair with Tillie?

Or was it all in my imagination? Was I losing my mind? The next morning, I took a wrong turning on my way back to Oxford and ended up spending forty-five minutes going up and down the Harrow Road, trying to find a way up onto the A40. Twice I did and missed it anyway, having got myself into the wrong lane. Then, when I finally did manage it, I forgot I needed petrol until I was past the last petrol station. When I got off the M40 in Beaconsfield, and got lost again, I panicked.

I couldn't live like this, never knowing what was real and what wasn't. I needed someone to tell me what was wrong, what to do. I ran through the list of people who might understand, but each name had a string attached to it. I couldn't impose on Mimi because she was Max's employee. I couldn't trust Crawley to keep a secret. My only hope, I thought, was Bea, and so, when I got home, I went straight over to the big house to find her.

I thought that because of her own unhappy earlier marriage, she would understand what it was like to be at home and pregnant when you knew but could not prove that your husband was having an affair. Even if it was true what Max had said about Bea, at least she would know how I felt. But although she was all empathy at the start, this softness disappeared the moment I let slip I was thinking of leaving.

200

'You're virtually separated now. Why on earth do you think you stand to gain anything by living alone in less comfortable surroundings? What an impractical idea! If you're worried about this other woman he might be seeing, you must stop at once. They're all like that, you know. But it's only temporary. They always come back. It's the baby that counts in the end, you know. They always come back to claim it. In the meantime, you must look after yourself. Or I shall never forgive you!'

As I lay in bed afterwards, looking at the leafless branches outside my window, I asked myself why I had never realised in the early days that Bea was not one for figures of speech – she meant precisely what she said.

Now that I know my limits, I make sure to stay in regular contact with people outside the house. Even if I can't bring myself to tell them everything. Especially if staying in touch becomes an almost superhuman effort. I know what can happen if I leave myself at the mercy of my thoughts, I no longer worry about whether it is the work that makes so many writers unstable, or whether I was always going to be unstable, whatever work I did. Nor do I ask myself why my imagination refuses to work to order. Instead I feed and pamper the monster so that it will do what I want it to do – or at least the best it can do. I've given up on its ever producing a miracle.

I've learned to make peace with myself. Now that I expect less, I am pleased if I manage anything at all. But during that long and lonely first winter, I had no idea how to live with myself. I didn't know who I was. All I knew was that I had thrown myself into a world where even people who might have liked to put me first could not do so because of other allegiances that predated me. Where taking my side even in small matters would cost them. I didn't want to drag down the ones I still trusted. I didn't want to show my hand to the ones I didn't trust. And so by the end of February I was confiding in no one.

I was confiding in no one and I was unable to work on my book. By now I had just under a hundred pages of a new draft and they were still not right. Again, I couldn't figure out where the trouble was. Again, whenever I tried to imagine what came next, my mind went blank. My thoughts would return to the same nagging questions – about Max, about the court case, about what the critics were going to do to my book, about my fatigue and my nausea and my poor unsuspecting, unborn child. About my future. About its future. The more the responsibility weighed on me, the more I asked myself why it hadn't weighed on Rebecca.

And yet I knew. I knew from sitting in her bed. I knew from her writing. I knew from *The Marriage Hearse* that she, like her heroine, had sat here with her hands on her stomach, waiting for her baby to kick, wondering what the baby looked like, longing to see that baby with her own eyes and hold it in her arms. The evidence was in every poem from that period: 'Swimming Inside', 'The Hand on the Cord', 'The Pregnant Pause', 'Return to Eden'. Rebecca had started out like me. What had they done to her to push her so far away from her own children?

How could I find out so that they didn't do the same to me?

Chapter Twenty-Eight

With hindsight it seems inevitable that I would take my questions to Danny. In fact, I became her pawn by accident – and only after long weeks of hating the sight of her. Bea had talked her into clearing Rebecca's study and storing the contents in a boxroom in the big house. This was a job that would have taken a normal person less than a week. For Danny it was clearly going to be a life's work. She was in and out the door and up and down the stairs all day. When she wasn't talking to herself, she was humming spirituals or, even worse, listening to relaxation tapes. What seemed inevitable at the time was that the day would come when she sang one 'Sweet Lord' too many and I would not be able to keep my scream silent.

Outright war began with a chocolate mousse Danny had made for a Beckfield Press supper and then given to Hermione and William the following day for tea. As much as I myself hated having to make and supervise their tea, I disliked her doing it even more. I couldn't stand seeing what she put out for them. It was all sweets and sandwiches. I wanted them to be eating real food, and until the crisis with Max I had been making good progress. But then, when Bea put me under bed arrest, she also decided that Danny should be helping me more. The result of this was that she went back to making them the unhealthy foods they preferred, and – even more annoying – rearranging the kitchen according to her own lights. This meant keeping the butter and the milk outside the refrigerator, and refrigerating half-finished tins, and, on more than one occasion, putting an opened jar of mayonnaise back into the cupboard.

The chocolate mousse had sat in a warm room for five or six hours before she had refrigerated it. When the children fell ill and were diagnosed as having salmonella, her first response was to say it couldn't have been the mousse, because she had made it with free-range eggs. It had to be something they'd eaten at school, at a friend's house, or at the tea-room Bea had taken them to earlier in the week. Or perhaps it was not salmonella but listeria. When the doctor drily explained what the odds were for the mousse and against the other possibilities, she became first hysterically apologetic and then hysterically solicitous of the children. Until their fevers broke, they were going to die.

When I, too, came down with a fever, she launched into a frantic hygiene campaign. This involved soaking all our linen in disinfectant. When I objected to the smell that lingered, she said that I ought to have thought about that before feeding the children raw eggs. When I pointed out to her that she was the one who had fed them raw eggs, she accused me of being a liar.

I lost my patience. I had had some spotting during the early days of the fever. This had convinced me that I was going to have a miscarriage. Now my fear turned to fury and burned through what was left of my tact. I told Danny it was pathetic how she spent her life in service to a shadow. Had she ever done anything in her own right? Would she ever?

She asked me, who was I to talk? If anyone was living in service to a shadow, I was. When I first arrived, she had felt sorry for me. She had not wanted to see another innocent destroyed. She had taken hope from the fact that I was a Rebeccite. She had hoped against hope that I had been sent to break the curse. But she had long since given up on getting through to me. There were times, she said, when you had to stand back and respect an individual's right to walk the plank. Lapsing into the quasi-American accent she often assumed in extremis, she cried, 'And when you're dead and gone, who is going to be making tea for that as yet unborn little one? Yours truly!'

'Unless it dies before it's born because its mother has listeria!'

This was my trump card. It had the desired effect. Danny gasped and pulled her hair back from her face in two big clumps and said, 'Oh no, you can't be serious. You can't be! Am I to have this on my conscience as well?' It was with tears streaming down her face that she waited on hold to speak to my doctor, with a tissue fixed against her nose that she admitted the doctor.

The doctor is now one of my best friends, and so I know now that she always took Danny with a gallon of salt. But on the day in question, even I was convinced by her show of concern when she arrived. She listened solemnly to Danny's full confession, after which she advised me to do what I was already doing, which was to stay in bed. 'We shall hope for the best, shan't we, Danny, but we shall remain cautious as well, and so I hope you can find it in you to give your friend the care she needs.'

And so it was that Danny became my nurse. I would wake up in the morning to find her on her knees next to the bed with a hot cup of tea, whispering, 'I don't want you to die. I don't want the baby to die. I have enough on my conscience already! Enough! Enough!'

One morning – after enough time had passed to convince her I was out of danger – she woke me up to tell me she had made a pact with the goddess within her to tell me the truth about the things on her conscience if the goddess made sure I recovered. 'The bad part of the truth is – I could have saved Rebecca. The good part – Rebecca has left us the wherewithal to save you.'

'Do you know?' I remember her saying. 'I was rereading *The Marriage Hearse* last night when it suddenly occurred to me, Rebecca wrote this entire book with you in mind. Failing that, I'm still unnerved by the degree to which she predicted you. People are for ever making the mistake of seeing Rebecca as the heroine. But of course she was far too much her own person to have been swayed and swamped like that. She always held her own. She never lost her fighting spirit. You could say she killed herself fighting. That's why they can't forget her. You, on the other hand . . .'

She retrieved a copy of the book from her bag and leafed through the first pages. 'Look at the inscription, for instance. "To everywoman, especially the one in my shoes." That's you – undoubtedly. And you're so much like her heroine, such a gullible person, so quick to bend, to suffer silently in order to please. But then there's the thing that you have that she didn't have. You could call it heart or charity, or whatever you like, really. It all amounts to the same thing. She predicted this in you, too. This passage, for instance. Shall I read it out loud?'

I remember nodding in that careful way you do if you find out a friend takes her horoscopes literally. I remember thinking, as she read out the first few words, that really, I had grown to dislike the earnestness in Rebecca's prose. Danny's declamatory reading style only increased it.

'Just as there are no two blades of grass alike, so too are there no standardised mass-produced answers. We each have our own puzzle to solve. We spend most of our lives hunting for the last missing piece, and when we find it, we have to change the shape of everything else to fit it in, and even when we're done, we still find the full picture lacking, because of a piece that God forgot to give us. I do not have the heart to keep going. I can say no but I can't say yes. My question to you, dear reader – can you?'

She looked up at me. '*Can* you say yes? Can you bear the truth about the man you love and still carry the cross?'

The question caught me unawares and made me shiver, but it also made me hungry. She knew where he was, I thought. She knew why. She knew what Rebecca had done to him. What he had done to Rebecca. She wanted to tell me. She wanted to tell me even the parts that other, saner people would edit or omit. And I needed to know these things. I needed to know the truth about the man who had left me without a heart. 'I have no idea what you mean,' I said carefully.

'What I mean, my dear thing, is that we mustn't go any further, honestly, not a step further, unless you're prepared to make Rebecca's agony your own and triumph over the gnomes of literary London by becoming her living message.'

V

She Speaks from the Grave

Chapter Twenty-Nine

The fifth of May. I can close my eyes and I'm back in that bed again. My every need met, my future as clear as it is righteous and inevitable. I can hear Danny upstairs, going through the boxes one last time. I can feel the duvet beneath me and the tartan blanket draped over my legs and the baby inside me shifting its weight. I can open my eyes and see on my writing tray a half-finished cup of tea and a notebook open to a page containing five attempts at the same sentence, all crossed out. On the floor next to me and within easy reach, the telephone, the pile of manuscripts and yesterday's paper open to the TV listings. Pressed against the rain-streaked windows, great green leaves made phosphorescent by the harsh white light filtering through them, and quivering magnolia blossoms.

In front of the fire, still crackling, throwing more light than heat, a pale but clear-eyed Hermione playing with her Gameboy, an emaciated but flushed William making his first attempt at his prep. I can close my eyes and feel at peace with them as I never have before. But only because the story that has become my life and *raison d'être* calls for it. Because I never have felt at peace with them, I've never been able to make them mine, I've always had to force myself to pretend to enjoy their company, I can't look at them without seeing something I wish I could change, without remembering I haven't the power to change anything. If I'm not making it up, if I really do want them with me in my room, it must be because I know my custodial sentence is ending.

They are about to start school again, after four weeks at home. Tomorrow will be their first half-day, which makes this morning our last full day together. But I can shut that thought out too. Even now I can convince myself: this morning will never end.

In a moment William will come over with a pencil and paper

and ask me to write down exactly how to make popcorn. I'll tell him instead, get him to repeat the instructions back to me, and after he has skipped off to the kitchen, Hermione will look at her charm necklace and notice one is missing, the one with the boy on the dolphin. She'll search every inch of floor, dissolve into tears, tears that I'll bring to an end by taking her hand and putting it on my stomach and asking her if she can feel the baby, her baby, our baby, kick. 'Bring me a book,' I'll say. She'll choose the Puffin version of the *Iliad* – shiftily. This is a test. She'll be waiting for me to say, 'No, not that one, the chapters are too long.' But I won't fall for it. I'll say, 'Fine, what a good choice,' and begin reading. After two pages her eyes will begin to wander. She'll decide she wants to draw instead. Until she smells the popcorn.

William will carry it into the room, climb onto the bed with it. They'll have a fight over the last popped kernel. I'll manage to convince them that the best thing is for neither of them to eat it and both of them to sketch it. As Hermione screws up her eyes, trying to get the dimensions right, William will watch only what Hermione puts on the paper. He'll copy her drawing exactly, but upside down.

And while they're quiet, I'll force myself. I'll pick up the papers and try to read about the trial. I'll begin with Tuesday, and Max's flat account of his early years with Rebecca. I'll look at the photograph of Max and Bea looking grandly stoic as they guide Max's father's wheelchair through the crowds outside the court. I'll look at the sketch of Max in court in the Wednesday paper, and I'll read his account of his later years with Rebecca. I'll read his account of his last day with Rebecca in today's paper and I'll try and convince myself this is not a stranger but my husband. Not my saviour but my greatest danger. I'll try to hold this foreign, horrifying thought, and although the fire will have taken hold by now, although there's enough heat in the room to make even the bright-green leaves and the rain-streaked window panes look cosy, I'll not be able to stop myself from shivering. *Face the truth*, I'll hear a foreign voice inside me say. *Face the truth. Say it. Write it and then tell the world. Everything will become so much easier if you do.*

And so I'll try. As I watch the logs turn red and serrated, a new sentence will form in my head, a new sentence that sums up everything I want to say. I'll lift my pen. I'll write, 'My name is . . .' But just as I am about to put the truth on the page, a branch will hit against the far window as if in anger, as if to warn me that I'm about to transgress, and I'll remember that my haven is not safe, that my time here is about to run out.

Hide while you can, the branches cry, *hide while you can*. But I'll know I can't hide, not even in my own bed. Because today, the fifth of May, today is my book launch and so my one and only chance to say my piece. Or rather, *her* piece. Where will I find the courage? Every time I close my eyes I see a room of faces. I see a stand with a microphone and beyond it in the half-light I see a drinks party interrupted, I see hands clutching drinks and fixed smiles as I prop my pages on the stand and look down to the page to find the print has dissolved, as I open my mouth to speak only to find I have no voice. As the silence goes on too long, the smiles disappear, the glasses clink ever more nervously, the whispering begins. I hear one person say, 'Did you read that terribly funny review in *The Spectator*?' I hear another say, 'But it isn't a patch on the one in the *Literary Review*.' I hear someone else clearing his throat in annoyance at the noise they are making; I look up to see the gossips dissolve into giggles . . .

And then in my bed, in my head, I hear Rebecca whispering, *Do it for me . . . do it for us . . . speak from the heart . . . if you don't, you'll lose everything . . . you'll become one of them . . .*

Even armed with hindsight, I still can't fight off the temptation. I return to that morning in my mind and once again I lose all sense of myself and I become Rebecca. Her words came flooding in again, her thoughts and her every recorded memory.

Since the beginning of April, Danny had been feeding me her letters and her diaries and even the poems she jotted down on napkins between courses at dinner parties. Had been staying up nights with me supplementing these clues with her own eyewitness reports. I knew more about Rebecca's descent into addiction than she knew herself. I knew what Bea had done by commission, and what Crawley had done by omission. And now that I had helped Danny break into Max's study, now that we had gone through his address books and his love letters and his photographs and his boxes of old manuscripts, I knew far, far more than I needed to know about how Max had set out deliberately to destroy her.

I knew every promise he made – and broke. Not only did I know when he was unfaithful and with whom, I knew why. It was to break her, to break her and so reduce her to silence. He couldn't bear the beauty of her poetry. He couldn't bear it that she could do things with words that he couldn't do. Couldn't bear to hear the phone ring for her and not for him. And so he made it harder for her. By never being there for her, by being too often and too obviously with someone else. How bad he must have felt when the sorrows he visited upon her only resulted in poetry of even greater intensity.

She had thrived on his cruelty, fed on it, devoured it. How bad he must have felt, to sink to theft. I now knew that what Crawley told me was a glossing-over of the truth. Danny had made it clear beyond a doubt. As I sat in my bed, I had the evidence all around me. Rebecca had never stolen anything from Max; it was Max who had stolen from her. As Danny had said only that morning, 'What would Rebecca want, anyway, with his paltry creations? His lions and minotaurs and four-legged phallic objects with antlers in place of grey matter? Whenever she appropriated his pseudish archetypes it was to strip them of their romantic haze, show them for what they were. Oh! We used to have such fun making up poems in the manner of Max! *Such* fun! When he took them and published them without taking on board their satirical intent – well, what were we to do?'

And why protest? This was the one game Rebecca had won. The lengths he had gone to in order to silence her in death – that was his real crime. And now that we had been through his papers, we had the proof. We had found 48 of the 107 missing poems Rebecca had mentioned in the last available notebook of her diary, as well as four of the five missing notebooks. Even more important, we had found an early draft of *The Marriage Hearse* on which he had done line editing and made spelling corrections – so much for his claim that he had not set eyes on the book until after Rebecca's death.

Worst of all, we had found the first page of the book's suppressed last chapter.

The original version of *The Marriage Hearse* had not ended with the heroine appearing triumphant in front of her audience despite wearing the wrong dress. It had ended with a speech on the subject of literary corruption. Without it, the book was, Danny and I agreed, like a scorpion without a tail, having lost its purpose and its poison. By removing it, Max had robbed Rebecca of her voice, but tonight, at my launch, I was going to give it back to her. When I stood up, ostensibly to read from my own book, I was going to read this first page of Rebecca's last missing chapter instead. I was going to stop midsentence just as the document did, and then I was going to say my piece – about the distortion and commodification of Rebecca, about the way Max had suppressed so much of her best work, and the way Beckfield Press had overedited and deformed it. I was going to convince them that the issue was not what had happened to Rebecca in real life (as in the trial) but what had happened to her words.

I knew what I needed to say. It was just a question of keeping up my nerve, remembering the importance of the message, reminding myself that this evening was going to be the only chance I'd get to say it. But whenever I closed my eyes and went forward to the moment of disclosure, whenever I imagined the room of faces, the clinking glasses, the tittering hush, my mouth went dry and my mind went blank.

'I take it the muse has not yet paid her visit,' Danny said to me with a bright smile when she brought me my lunch on a tray.

I shook my head.

'Never fear,' she said. 'I've had a sign.' She paused and looked over her shoulder. The children were at the dining table, talking, not eavesdropping, but still she took the precaution of closing the door before she continued. 'I've found you a talisman,' she said as she sat herself down on the far end of the bed. 'Rebecca used to take it with her on speaking engagements. She got stage fright too, you know!' She reached into her bra and took out what looked like

213

a calling card. 'Take a look at it. Then put it away and eat your lunch and then look at it one more time before you take your rest. You'll write your speech in your sleep. When you wake up – and don't worry, I'll make sure to rouse you at three – your head will feel empty of thought, but you'll know from your serenity that the words are there, waiting for you to speak them. Keep the card. Look at it whenever you feel your courage failing and it will come right back and you'll speak from the heart, which is the best any good Rebeccite could hope for.'

The card said:

> You are not an entertainer.
> You are a medium.
> Find the goddess in the back row and tell her the Truth.

I've kept the card, not as a talisman but as a reminder. I can look at it now and ask myself what it tells me about my state of mind that day if I could read those words and accept them as gospel. I can ask sane questions now about my temporary insanity but still I can't defend myself against my memory of the relief it provided me, the wisdom and protection it seemed to offer as I slept in Rebecca's bed, as I awoke to slip my feet into Rebecca's slippers and padded up to the stairs to pour Rebecca's bath foam under the tap, to soak in her bath, as I looked over her collection of half-finished shampoos and conditioners. I was not an entertainer – how true. I was a medium – what a privilege. I would be able to rise to the occasion if I found the goddess in the back row. I was to go to sleep and let my muse write my speech and whenever I felt my courage failing I was to remind myself that I was not an entertainer but a medium, that I was not alone, that all I had to do was look towards the back row and let Rebecca's words run through me . . .

'Is that new?' Crawley asked me when Danny and I joined him in the car that was to drive us down to the party. He was referring to my plain blue maternity dress and there was something in his voice to indicate that he had a suspicion of where it came from.

But it was a generic item. There was no way he could know that it had belonged to Rebecca, any more than he could know that I was also wearing Rebecca's necklace and Rebecca's watch and carrying Rebecca's talisman.

'It's not new,' I told him. I didn't like to lie unnecessarily. 'But it's the first time I'm wearing it. I got it from a friend.'

He gave me a searching look and then he asked, 'Have you spoken to Max today?'

Before I could answer, Danny said, 'Oh, you're not telling me he's planning to grace us with his presence?'

'I don't know what game you're playing at, Danny, but I'm telling you. I'm giving you a warning. I know you're up to something.'

'Then tell me, O oracle. What am I up to?'

'I don't know much, but I'll tell you what I do know. I do know that you—'

He stopped in midsentence, because now Bea was hobbling towards us. 'Oh, God, just look at her!' Crawley said, shaking his head. 'Has she been like this all week?'

'All week, you ask! All month!' said Danny.

'Doesn't anyone happen to know what in particular is eating away at her?'

'Guilt. Don't you think?'

Crawley sighed. 'I would say stage fright myself, but if she carries on like this, people are going to assume she's guilty even if she can prove she was digging for China when Rebecca went AWOL. When is she due to testify?'

'It's not clear. It could be tomorrow and it could be Monday.'

'Then God help us,' Crawley said.

Bea opened the door with care. Standing there, breathing vodka on us, she gave me a broad but unseeing smile. 'Yes,' she said. 'Yes.' Then she turned to Crawley and said, as carefully as if she were trying to walk a straight line, 'You wouldn't mind stepping out of the car for a moment, would you? Something's come up.'

They walked to the edge of the drive to confer, Crawley holding Bea by the arm to keep her steady, and as he did, I noticed that there was a man sitting in a car parked next to the barn. Crawley noticed

215

at the same time and went over to speak to the man. The discussion grew heated, but ended with the man starting his car and backing it out to the road, where he parked again. Crawley swung the gate shut and then waited while Bea struggled with the padlock.

'So the hacks are here again,' Danny said. 'Something must have happened this afternoon in court. Who's on next, do you know?'

'I think it's Max's father.'

'You'd think, after what he said in Jack's book, that he'd be a witness for the other side.'

'I think the point is to prove that anything he said has to be discounted.'

'A high-risk strategy, I'd say. I wonder if . . .' Danny's voice trailed off as Crawley helped Bea back into the car. 'Everything all right?' Danny asked.

'No, since you ask,' said Crawley, 'everything is not all right.'

'What's up, then?'

Crawley crossed his arms. 'Actually, that's exactly what I was about to ask you.' He cleared his throat and took in a deep breath, as if everything depended on the way he phrased his next question. Before he could ask it, Giles had appeared on the other side of the padlocked gate. 'Oh, blast!' said Crawley. Bea made to get out of the car. 'No, Bea. I'll handle this. Just throw me the key.' As she fumbled inside her handbag, the top of a flask came into view.

After Crawley had let Giles out and locked the gate behind him, the two men exchanged words. Both bowed their heads, then nodded resolutely and headed for the car, with Crawley making no attempt to hide his grim mood, and Giles struggling to tame his twitching mouth.

He succeeded. 'Darling,' he said to his wife through the open window, 'may I have a word?'

Again Bea got out of the car. He put his arm around her and walked her towards the gate while Crawley moved on ahead and opened it for them. Then he stood there guarding it for the five minutes it took Giles to return.

He did so alone, and looking as cheerful as if he had gone back for his diary. Bea had been edited out of this evening's performance.

There was to be no further mention of her. After climbing into the seat next to the driver, and greeting him with studied courtesy, Giles turned around to me with a kind smile and said, 'We're having such bad luck with the weather, aren't we?'

All the way to London, he kept the decorous patter going. How had I felt about the reviews I had received to date? Wasn't the one in *The Spectator* lovely, and hadn't the *Literary Review* been just a little bit naughty? Was I getting enough rest now? Had I managed to get my next appointment at the hospital moved or was I still having to go in the next morning? Not once did he mention the trial. When Crawley brought it up as we weaved our way through Soho, he tried to silence him. 'Don't you think it would be nice if we could all forget about the blasted thing for the next few hours? I'm sorry if it sounds disloyal, but there are other things in life, and here is a perfect opportunity to remember what they are.'

'You're right, of course,' said Crawley crisply. 'But it's important to remember that most of the people at the party tonight will be in attendance because of the ghoul factor, and just waiting for someone to make a slip, Freudian or otherwise –' here he glared at Danny – 'and that unless we all prepare ourselves, we may just give some horrible hack the scoop he's looking for. Especially with this latest development. I'll bow to your wisdom, Giles, but I really do think we should tell her what's in the offing.'

'Oh, for goodness' sake, Crawley,' Giles said with an annoyed wave of the hand. 'Put aside your theories for one evening and let the poor girl have a little fun.'

If only this decent man knew what I had in store for him. And was it fair? How was I going to condemn what he stood for without also condemning him? When had he ever done anything that wasn't utterly correct and thoughtful? This was the first time my courage failed me. I got it back after arriving at the Groucho Club.

Crawley had been right. Here and there I saw a friend, but most of the hundred-odd guests already gathered in the party room were people I had never seen before. As I made my way to the drinks table, I felt as if I were swimming through a sea of poisoned eyes. These hostile eyes and twisted smiles had come for a spectacle – and so I would give them one.

The second time my courage failed me was an hour into the party, when Crawley broke into the small circle of friends who were protecting me and asked if I was ready to do my reading. I had the card in my book, but when I opened it, it fell out.

'What's that?' Crawley barked.

'What's what?' asked Danny as she pounced on it.

'Nothing,' I said. I took it from her and put it back into my book.

'I smell a rat,' said Crawley. And my courage came back again. I wasn't going to let Max and his spies get the better of me.

Then I saw Max come into the room. He looked thin and cold, but when our eyes met, his face lit up the way it had in the early days. He came up to me, kissed me on the forehead and said, 'Good luck, my darling.' And I thought about what I was about to do, and once again my courage left me.

'How did it go today?' I asked. I couldn't keep my voice from trembling.

'Couldn't have been more tedious. It makes you wonder how the words "courtroom" and "drama" could ever have been linked. But enough of that. I was hoping you were going to help me put the whole thing out of my mind. Look, you wouldn't mind putting off starting until I've got myself a drink, would you?'

'Not at all,' I said. As I watched him make his way through the crowd, I made up my mind. I would still tell him what I knew and show him what I had, but I would do so privately, not in front of a crowd. I would give him a chance to defend himself. It was only fair. But then what was I going to say now? I scanned at the crowd in front of me. There in the far corner was the features editor from Max's paper. The man he was talking to could possibly be the Wayne who caused the upset at Giles's sixtieth-birthday party. Madame Blackberry had just arrived in a sea of diaphanous white cloth and on the arm of the man I had been told was Grovel in *Private Eye*. I watched them greet two men I had never seen before as if they were schoolfriends they had not

218

seen in a decade. And then I watched their effusive greetings go flat, I watched each one begin to glance over the other's shoulders, I watched the eagerness with which Grovel pounced on another newcomer, the gratitude with which Madame Blackberry smiled at another long-lost friend who now presented herself. And then I watched this conversation go flat even faster. I watched Madame Blackberry's face brighten when the other woman pretended she needed to go and find another drink. After an effusive farewell, she joined another circle, which reformed to become two circles and then three circles as more strangers swirled into the room. I looked at them and asked myself what I could possibly want to say to these people, when they had nothing to say to each other but hello and goodbye. Why had I ever thought they would want to know or even deserved to know what I thought about anything? Already my publisher and his publicity people were trying to hush them. But I had nothing to say to them, nothing to hide behind except words that now meant nothing to me, words I had written in another life. I took out my copy of *Happily Ever After* – the book this party was meant to celebrate – and tried to find a passage I could read from it. As I flipped through the pages, as the text swam before my eyes, the first page of Rebecca's last chapter fell to the ground.

Crawley dove for it. I got to it first. My hands shaking, I refolded it. I looked into the sea, the conversations dying one by one as the faces turned towards me and my microphone. *What was I doing?* I scanned the crowd and just as I was losing hope I saw the person I was looking for. She was standing on her own, staring right at me. She had small, bright eyes and a deep tan made more emphatic by her long, white coat and matching skullcap. I had never seen her in my life, but she was smiling as if she could read my every thought, as if to tell me I was not an entertainer but a medium. She was in the back row.

I cleared my throat and began.

'Good evening. I'm gratified that so many people have taken the trouble to come to my pale shadow of party.' I paused to allow time for the polite laughter to subside. 'I'm gratified because I've decided to use this opportunity to speak about something far more significant than my own career. To paraphrase a very famous last line, my name is not Rebecca and I am not standing before you to explain why I've decided to appear in the wrong dress.' Now the laughter was more nervous. 'But the time has come, I've decided, to let Rebecca speak from the grave.'

There was a general gasp, a single guffaw, and then a dead silence as I opened my book and unfolded the page I had hidden inside it. 'I have here in my hand a page that ought to have come immediately after what has come to be one of the most famous lines in modern fiction. I am referring to the end of *The Marriage Hearse*. It will take on a very different meaning once you've heard what was meant to follow before parties unknown saw fit to excise it.

'"My name is Rebecca and I stand before you in the wrong dress . . . I'm an invention of an author, but like so many figures of fiction, I'm also real. I'm the truth no one dares to look in the face. I'm not the cause, I'm the symptom . . ."'

I looked up to face the audience. I looked into the back row. The goddess gave me an encouraging nod. I looked down at the paper but now the text was swimming before my eyes. I looked up again. The goddess in the back row was trying to send me a message. I could read her lips. 'Go on,' she was saying. 'Go on. This is your only chance!' I looked down at the page. The blur began to form into words again, but before I could find my place again, Max had snatched the sheet of paper out of my hands.

He was out of breath and trembling, and his nostrils were distended. First he looked at me, then he looked at the page, then he crumpled it up in his fist. 'Who put you up to this?' He was speaking softly, but when I didn't answer, he raised his voice. 'You fool! Tell me. This is not a game! Who put you up to this?'

I stepped back from the microphone. He took hold of it. 'Who put her up to this?' he cried but the outrage was gone. Now there was fear in his voice. He looked down at the sea of faces, as if in search of someone. I looked down too, but all the faces looked alike – the ones I knew, the ones I didn't know. All blank. I looked at the door, just in time to see the last of a long, white coat.

220

Chapter Thirty

When Max jumped off the stage and pushed his way towards the door, he did not move like someone trying to escape. I could tell from the quiet, angry and efficient way he cleared a path for himself that he was pursuing someone. Whom? The question erased all other thoughts from my mind. I looked at the hard, bright sea of eyes. Where was I?

Danny came up to me. 'All is not lost,' she whispered into my ear. 'I have another copy.'

She was just handing it to me when I felt Crawley's heavy hand on my shoulder. 'Before you continue, love, would you kindly tell me what the hell is going on here.'

'We're seeing to an injustice,' Danny said. 'We're—'

Crawley put up his hand to silence her. There was some tittering from the audience. 'We all know what you think, Danny. What I'm trying to find out is what you've told our friend here.'

'I haven't told her anything she hasn't the right to know.'

'You've enlisted her to your cause, then, I take it.'

'The facts speak for themselves!' Danny cried.

'Oh, don't they ever!' Crawley looked into my eyes. 'He's quite a bastard, isn't he, this husband of yours? But I'll tell you one thing. The people he's up against right now are even bigger bastards.' He paused for effect. 'Have you given any thought to Danny girl's motives in all this?'

'They're the same as mine, I'm sure,' I said. My voice came out thin.

'Oh, it's all love and beauty, is it? She's even convinced you of that, has she?'

'If only it were, Crawley,' Danny now said. 'If only it were! If only brilliant women were allowed to give their views on love and

221

beauty without being censored, then we should not be standing here having this conversation. And you would not be withholding the evidence, which I now ask that you return to me.'

She lunged for it. He pushed her back. She grabbed for it again, this time succeeding in tearing off a corner. 'You bastard!' she shrieked. 'You're destroying a national treasure!' At which he stuffed the rest of the page into his mouth, and – to the delight of the audience – ate it.

Danny went wild. In the end, they had to call the police.

After they had escorted her out of the building, and the party-goers had dispersed, I found myself sitting with Giles in the foyer of the Groucho Club. Our car was not due back for another half an hour. Crawley was out scouring the streets of Soho, looking for Max. The women behind the reception desk were stiff from the effort of pretending we weren't really there. The strangers who came through the revolving doors in twos and threes would freeze momentarily at the sight of us. From time to time, someone sitting at the bar in the lounge area would look very carefully over his shoulder and pretend to be looking at something on the wall above me. But Giles had still not dropped his genial mask, and I did not know what to make of it.

'Are you all right, dear girl?' he asked, as he took my hand. 'You poor thing, you must be exhausted. I feel we've rather let you down. We ought to have been able to predict this. I do love Danny, she's a harmless old thing, really, but she's been rather naughty about this. If she knew about this missing chapter, she ought to have come straight to me. I can't think why she didn't. Clearly the pressures of the trial have unbalanced her – that and also, I'm afraid, your presence. She has a soft heart, you know. She would never dream of wishing you ill, and so it all gets rather twisted around. That said, she is right to be angry. Don't tell Crawley I said that, whatever you do, but I am feeling rather a fool, you know. I ought to have known there was a chapter missing. I've always thought that the book as it stands now ends too abruptly. I hope you don't think less of me for it, but I've never really understood the significance of a woman standing in front of an audience wearing the wrong

222

dress. Is there some secret meaning it in that only a woman can hope to detect?'

Crawley's reappearance through the revolving doors saved me from having to give an answer. The rain had started again. There seemed to be steam rising from his jacket. He refused to look me in the eye, answered Giles's questions with terse monosyllables and, once we were in the car, settled into a menacing silence that I found strangely comforting after Giles's kindness.

'Pleasant evening, sir?' the driver asked as he turned into Old Compton Street.

'Oh, yes,' said Giles with a smile. 'Very.'

When we got back to Beckfield, it was to a press encampment. Crawley got out of the car to get them to move so that he could open the gate. Giles and I stayed in the car.

'My advice based on previous experience,' Giles said to me when the cameras started flashing outside the windows, 'is to look neither very happy nor very sad. Do you think you can manage that for a minute or so? It's such a bore, isn't it? Happily, there's a back way through Home Farm which we'll get sorted out tomorrow morning when it's light. What I shall do is rent a car or two, and we'll be able to come and go without their knowing. Unless – goodness, it hadn't occurred to me! – unless one of those men out there can read lips.'

How could Giles even look at me after what I had done? Why was he taking it so calmly? So keen to return my public attack on his family and his business with concern for my wellbeing? Was it genuine or was it a show, and if it was a show, what were his motives?

My first inkling of the extent of the trouble came with an early-morning phone call from Mimi. 'Are you all right, my dear?' she asked, in a strangled whisper that indicated she was not. Before I had had a chance to say I was, she blurted out, 'I blame myself. I ought to have been there for you. And I was fully intending to! The babysitter was there, but the baby was so very ill I couldn't leave her, and I feel so very sorry now, because had I been there, I could have prevented it!' Before I had a chance to ask her what she meant, there was the sound of a child screaming in the background.

'Oh goodness. Goodness! I have to go. Ring me later, darling. I shall be at work by ten.'

I got up out of bed and went to find the papers. It was immediately clear why the press had come to camp. We were on the front pages of all the tabloids and all but one of the qualities. In court the previous afternoon, Max's father had made a garbled speech that had been interpreted as a call to have Rebecca's body exhumed.

Max's barrister had made the mistake of using the expression 'bare bones of the story'. Max's father had responded by saying that anyone who wanted to know the truth of the story should try to find those bones. 'It's all in the bones, my boy,' he was reported as saying. 'But the bones are not where they should be.' When Jack's barrister asked him later if he could clarify what he meant, he laughed and said, 'So you want to tell me how to do your job?' Pressed to clarify again, he had said, 'I meant that if you open that grave, you're in for quite a shock. Where are they? Answer that question, young fellow-me-lad, and you have the answer to all your prayers. I wanted to sketch her, you see, you can tell anything from bones, you see, you don't need the flesh, any painter worth his salt could tell you that, the bones will tell you anything, as the saying goes, you know it in your bones, but before you get these bones to tell you anything, you old blackguard you, you'll have to find them, won't you?' When asked to name the person whose bones he was alluding to, he had laughed and said, 'What's in a name?'

None of the articles made an explicit connection between the events in court and the scene at my party, but all took pleasure in describing the dramatics. 'Chip off the old block,' said one headline. 'Mad Max strikes again!' said a second. A third, which featured a picture of Max racing down Dean Street after a shapeless blur, asked, 'Who is the Woman in White?' But all the others carried pictures of me, and the headline 'She speaks from the grave'.

I read that headline and remembered how my audience had gasped when I had used those words in my speech. How could I ever explain to them or anyone that I had had no idea of what had gone on in court that day? That if I had known about Max's father's bone speech, I would never have dared say I was helping

Rebecca speak from the grave? Why hadn't anyone told me? Why had they let *me* make a fool of myself, too?

Why were they compelled to diminish anyone who stood up to them? Destroy them if nothing else would do? No wonder Giles had been able to be so kind to me the night before. He didn't need to do the dirty work. He could afford to be generous, because I had volunteered to destroy myself.

I was still shaking with anger and shame when Bea came breezing into the house without bothering to knock at a quarter to eight. 'I do hope you don't mind my intruding, my dear,' she said. 'I do realise your appointment at the clinic isn't until ten, but it would be rather easier if we all left together this morning. You may be happy to hear that the school have agreed to have the children board until this nonsense is over. That should cut down on the toing and froing. Hermione! William! Could you both be darlings and pack up your spare uniforms and some comfy clothes for the weekend and all your school books and have them ready for me to inspect in, let's see, ten minutes' time?'

She made driving through the press pack feel like a trip to the carnival. 'Oh, goodness! Not old rubber lips again! William, Hermione, do you remember him from last time?'

'He gets uglier and uglier,' Hermione said. 'It must be the stress. And there's that woman who was always offering us ice lollies.'

'*What* a vulgar way to make a living,' said Bea. 'Standing in the rain, chasing after cars, it's a wonder they don't just lie down in the road and kill themselves. William, could you be a darling? There are three cars following us at the moment. One is red and the other two are blue. Can you see them?'

'The blue one has an A registration and the red ones are both B.'

'That's brilliant detective work, darling. It would be even better if you could write down the full number plate. What I'm planning to do, children, is drive us around Oxford until we've lost all three of them. Then I'm taking you to your friend Edward's house, because Park Town is just a hop, skip and a jump away from school, and what's more, you'll be able to use the back entrance, where they'll have someone waiting for you. Edward's mum will walk you there. Does that sound too impossibly tricky?'

'I'll pull my hat down so no one can recognise me,' said Hermione.

William said, 'I'll turn my coat inside out even though it's against the rules, because this time they shan't dare say anything.'

They were so caught up in their disguises that they forgot to say goodbye.

'We still have an hour,' said Bea when she had returned to the car. 'Just enough time for breakfast. Will the Dome do?'

When they brought Bea her orange juice, she topped it up with a small bottle of vodka she brought out of her handbag, and finished it in four gulps as if completing an assignment. Then she lit up a cigarette. As she exhaled, she looked me in the eye. 'Are you bearing up all right?'

I was too angry even to shake my head.

She took another long drag from her cigarette. 'You mustn't blame yourself. You mustn't. It's just not on. If we're going to be accurate about all this, I'm the one who got it wrong. I ought to have been paying better attention. I read the signals wrong, I'm afraid. I hadn't realised Danny had been putting so much time into you – if it ever happens again, dear, do think of telling me. It's really not very nice of her, you know, not with Max acting so dreadful, too. I really am rather cross with him about this woman in white. He ought to know better. As I said to Giles when he told me, you showed great restraint. I've done far worse, far worse!'

'It's easy to show restraint when you hardly care any more,' I said. But she waved my words away.

'Of course you care. You poor dear! But you must put all thoughts of Max to one side for the time being, and think about yourself. Are you feeling very, very unhappy? I know a very good man, you know, if you need someone to talk to. He has offices up here as well as on Harley Street. When I was having my own troubles, he was a lifesaver.'

'I didn't do it to get back at anyone,' I said again. 'And Danny didn't tell me what to say. Everything I said, I said myself. I'm just angry no one told me what happened in court. If I'd known about what was going on in court, I wouldn't have said I was speaking from the grave. I might as well have smashed a pie in my face. I'm so embarrassed.'

'Of course you are, my dear. You don't need to tell me. My heart was with you, my dear, when Giles told me about it. What men don't realise is how it feels for a woman to be shamed in front of her peers.'

'But that's not what I'm most upset about. What I'm most upset about is that you and every one else for that matter, everyone except for Danny, refuses even to acknowledge the central point I was trying to make.'

'And what is this central point, dare I ask?'

'There are two ways of killing someone. The first is the normal way, and that's what the trial is about. The second is to keep her from expressing herself, and that's what I was talking about.'

This made Bea laugh. 'Goodness, what nonsense you young people spout! Can you possibly mean it? Do you honestly think I or anyone has ever, ever been able to keep that bloody woman from expressing herself? If I ever met anyone who could, I'd nominate them for the Nobel Peace Prize! Honestly, I've never heard such rot! I can't go through a day without Rebecca and her bloody words somehow making themselves felt. Do you honestly believe that you're telling the truth simply by opening your mouth and letting any old drivel come out? And do you *honestly* think Rebecca was fighting for womankind, and didn't love being famous, every last minute of it? I'm willing to concede, she had painted herself into a corner, but it was her own snobbery that got her there, that and her unflinching desire for anything that might happen to belong to someone else.'

She took a drag from her cigarette and let the smoke come out through her nostrils. 'There was no reason for her to go after Max's father like that, you know. It was just playing games. Everything was all right in her book because everything was experience. What rot! As for the idea of anyone managing to kill her, what a pipe dream! No, my dear, she was the one who chose to go. And if I'd had my wits about me, if I had been able to predict the thousand and one ways in which she would speak to me daily from the grave, I shouldn't have helped her.'

Here she stopped, aghast at her own words. Then she looked me straight in the eyes and gave me a sweet smile.

'I don't need to point out, do I, that I was speaking metaphorically.'

Chapter Thirty-One

The harder she tried to put things right, the worse they became. 'It's all become such a terrible bore, don't you agree?' she declaimed in a voice big enough to fill the Royal Albert Hall, as she whipped too fast up the road to the hospital. 'One can't make the most innocent comment without someone somewhere assuming one's the villain of the piece. I do hope *you* haven't jumped to any conclusions, my dear. But in any event I can count on you, I take it, not to repeat our little conversation to anyone?'

I nodded, too emphatically. I couldn't get anything right either.

'I didn't kill her, you know,' as cheerfully as if she were talking about her holiday plans. 'Neither did I help her kill herself. I give you my word.'

'Who did kill her, then?'

'One day, my dear, I shall tell you the whole story. I can give you my word on that, too. But for the moment, you're better off not knowing. You must think of yourself,' she said as she pulled into the drive in front of the maternity hospital. 'And you must think of the baby. Last but not least, you must get in touch with Janet and have her stay with you. I don't know how long these wretched barristers are going to keep me in London, and I don't like the idea of your being alone in the cottage with all those hacks around.'

'I'll be all right,' I said.

'You don't know how tenacious they can be. They'll be furious I gave them the slip. Are you quite sure you can handle them? They're a tricky lot, you know. They'll be willing to do just about anything to get you to talk. They know that the quickest way to dismantle a character is to isolate her.'

She put her hand on my shoulder, pasting a smile on her face that did not match the urgency of her voice. 'You'd be far better

229

off, you know, coming to stay in London with me. Why don't you hop on a bus after the clinic? Instead of sitting here in Oxford under siege, we could go out to supper and have a jolly time. God only knows I'll need some cheering up after an afternoon with old Ben. I can't tell you how offputting it is when a man you would have died for turns into the village idiot.' As she lit up a cigarette, she laughed. When I didn't join in, she went silent, then took a long and thoughtful drag. 'You don't trust me, do you?'

'Not a hundred per cent, no.'

She gave a little snort. 'But you trust Danny?'

'Not entirely, no. It's more that I understand her point of view.'

In a hard voice, Bea said, 'Do you honestly think she isn't in it for the money?'

'If there's one thing I'm sure of, it's her altruism.'

Bea stubbed out her cigarette. 'Well then, suit yourself. If there isn't anything else you're dying to tell me, would you mind getting out of my car? Sorry to be rude, but they need me in court.'

'I hope it all goes well,' I forced myself to say. 'And don't worry about me. I'll be fine.' But even as I got out of the car and waved Bea goodbye, I knew I would not be.

When you lose your bearings, you're the last to know. You think the world has changed while you've stayed the same. Then something happens that refuses to bend with the lie. For me, on this occasion, it was walking into a building I had always disliked and dreaded visiting, and, for no apparent reason, no longer disliking it. And I knew that was wrong.

Even as it flooded through me, I knew I should not have felt such relief to escape into a lobby of preoccupied strangers. The notice boards ought to have depressed, not comforted me. The arrangement of plastic chairs in the waiting room ought to have looked coldly rather than alluringly impersonal. I ought to have deplored the fact that the coffee from the canteen was expensive but tasted like dishwater. Just as I ought to have been saddened by the briskness with which the sister on duty stared right through me.

Instead I was thankful to be nothing more than a name and a

number to her. To know that the consultant – unless he had very, very good manners – did not recognise my name either and so would have forgotten me by lunchtime. That he sent me on for a blood test not out of kindness or a sense of family duty or because he knew it would make a loyal ally out of me but because he sent all his patients on for blood tests. Because it was his job.

I felt all this, and at the same time, I knew what it meant. Only a marked person sees salvation in anonymity. But even the hospital wasn't safe, because they were all there, all the papers with the headlines announcing that Rebecca had spoken from the grave, implying that Max's second wife was as crazy as the first, if not quite as talented or flamboyant. I could feel my face grow hot as I passed them. Why hadn't anyone told me about what was going on in court? Why were they all intent on attributing to me motives I didn't have, on missing the point? Why were they all twisting my words, using my words out of context to make the whole country laugh?

'Beckfield?' said the driver when I got into my taxi. 'Well, I hope it's not the far side, love, because the road's virtually blocked, I'm told, because of that poet's as murdered his wife.' I got out at Home Farm and took the back way into the house.

When I opened the front door and heard scampering footsteps, my first thought was that I had an intruder. But it turned out to be Janet. She put me into bed with a cup of tea, sat down and made up a shopping list, which she promised to get to me by three. I dozed off.

I woke up, not knowing what time it was, and for a moment unable even to remember where I was. I must have stared at the magnolia tree outside the window for thirty seconds before I realised it was my magnolia tree. When I heard someone pottering about the kitchen, I thought it was Janet again. But then I heard Danny, talking to someone. I got up, put on my slippers and my robe, and went out to the kitchen.

The moment Danny saw me, she threw her arms around me. 'Oh, you poor, poor dear! How brave you were last night! Have they been beastly to you? I came up as soon as I could. Are you all right?'

231

I looked into the hatch and saw that the person Danny had been speaking to was Jack Scully.

He had a glass of neat whisky in front of him and was struggling to get ice cubes out of an ice tray. 'I thought you were American,' he said to me.

'I am American,' I replied.

'OK, so then tell me, what made you give up on the idea of ice?'

'I haven't. It's just that—'

'How old is this stuff?'

'I have no idea. To be honest, I don't even recognise it.'

'That's what I thought.' He handed the tray back to Danny.

'What do you want me to do with it?' Danny asked.

'Oh, for fuck's sake,' Jack said. 'Donate it to the Ashmolean.' He laughed at his own joke. Then he beamed at me. So did Danny.

'I suppose this looks rather odd,' she said.

'Yes, it does,' I said. I looked at Jack. 'What are you doing here?'

'The sixty-four-thousand dollar question, really,' he said, 'is what *you*'re doing here.' He knocked back his whisky without taking his eyes off me. Handing the glass back to Danny, he said, 'You wouldn't mind pouring me another, would you?'

'Not at all, my dear,' she said. 'So long as you promise to let me drive.'

'No, honestly, that's fine by me. I wanted to die today anyway.' He turned to me again. 'You were asking what I was doing here.'

'Yes.'

'Well, actually, I don't know if you're going to believe me, but it was Danny's idea. She thinks you're in danger.'

'That's what everyone thinks,' I said. 'But it doesn't explain why you're here.'

'I'm certainly not going to be here long if that's your attitude.' He turned to Danny. 'I thought you said you told her.'

'Well,' said Danny. 'Not in so many words.'

He slammed his drink down. 'Then why the hell did you put my whole future at risk by dragging me out here?'

'Jack, darling—'

'Don't you Jack-darling me, you airhead! Whose side are you on anyway? I mean, look at those people out there.' He pointed at the huddle of men, women and cameras milling outside Danny's cottage. 'Do you realise what they'd do if they knew I was in here? For all I know, maybe they do know already. I'm beginning to think I've walked into a trap.'

Danny put her hands on her mouth. 'How can you say such a thing? How can you so much as think it?'

'You told me she was willing to talk.'

'No, Jack, darling. I said that if we both sat down with her and explained how she was in danger and why, she would—'

'Warning bells!' Jack said with barely suppressed hysteria. 'I hear warning bells!' He headed for the back door. When Danny tried to block his way, he pushed her aside. Through the window I watched her chase him through the walled garden.

I followed them out more slowly; I could no longer walk at my usual pace. I got to the courtyard of Home Farm just in time to see the back of Danny's car indicating a right turn towards Oxford. Jasper the dog was poised mournfully at the back window.

A group of the press people walked down the road to join me. 'As usual, you're just a few seconds too late,' I said. I went back to the house the front way, through questions and cameras. When I remembered that I hadn't brushed my hair, I made an extra effort to look dignified.

It was dark when Danny rang from a call box to apologise. 'I'm afraid I can't explain everything right now,' she said, 'but I'm ringing to say you must take great care. Above all, you must not on any account let Max into the house.'

'Why would he even bother to try?' I asked.

Before she could answer, her money ran out. When the phone rang a few seconds later, I thought it was Danny again. Instead I got ten seconds of silence and a dialling tone.

The phone rang again. This time it was a woman asking for Harry. When I said I didn't know anyone called Harry, she accused me of being a liar. I hung up. She rang again. I took the phone off the hook, and then the phone in Rebecca's study began to ring. I put my phone back on the hook, and the phone upstairs stopped. A few seconds later, my phone began to ring again. I picked it up and it was a man this time. 'Don't make a deal with them before speaking to us,' he said. I said I didn't know what he was talking about and he laughed and said, 'That'll be the day.' I took the phone off the hook again and tried to convince myself there was no real danger.

The only danger was that I would get sucked into other people's fears. The best way to avoid that was to stay busy. Keep the light on. Have the radio playing and the television on at the same time. Check the windows, draw the curtains, check the phone to make sure it still had a dialling tone, push a chest out to block the front door.

I was not up all night listening for noises. There was just one bad patch between one and two when I could hear something – it could have been one of the people from the road, but it was probably just a dog – rustling in the bushes under a window. What decided me was a package from an old college friend that arrived the following morning.

I had lost touch with her four or five addresses ago. She had heard about my sudden change of fortune from another friend who had bumped into Mrs Van Hopper who had been through London and heard the gossip. In a cheerful, guileless way that seemed to sum up everything I had once loved and hated about this friend, she wrote how very proud she was to have someone she knew hit the headlines. 'I feel like you've put us on the map.'

Her first postscript read, 'Congratulations on making it!' Her second postscript read, 'I'm sending you a book that I found very comforting when I went through something similar two years ago.' The title of the book was *The Dilemma of the Alcoholic Marriage*, and it made me want to cry. I looked out the window, at all those people and cameras that were trying to look in, and I looked around me, at these walls that could keep nothing out, and I went upstairs and packed my bag.

I did not take everything – just my photographs, my manuscripts, my *sumak* and the three maternity dresses I owned that had not belonged to Rebecca. I knew that if I took more, my audience in

234

the road would put two and two together. I took the car back to the hospital and then called a taxi, which I had stop at the bank on the way to the bus station. I did not take out a huge amount of money, only enough to cover a ticket home. Home being any point on the other side of the Atlantic. That was all I could say about home by then, that it would never be on this side.

When I got to Heathrow, I pushed my cart to the departure board in Terminal Three to work out what choices I had. I had still not worked my way down the first column of flights when I felt a hand on my shoulder.

It was Max.

Chapter Thirty-Two

I was happy to see him. After all I'd been through, all the pain he'd dragged me through, all he had to do was put his hands on my shoulders, put his arms around me and kiss my forehead, run his hands through my hair and kiss my eyes. I can only fear what this says about me. But it's the truth.

All I can say is that I didn't let him know the truth.

'You're right to be angry,' he said as he drew back. 'If you had had me followed, I would be angry, too. But my motives are not as dire as you seem to think.' He took my hand. 'Listen. I'm not going to stop you leaving if you decide to leave but I think there are some things you should know in any event and so I'm asking you to give me one more night. One last Saturday night and then the choice is yours.'

I hesitated.

He took a deep breath. 'I shan't even claim the baby if that's how you want it. I'm not Bea, you know. I don't put much faith in heritage and blood lines. Especially not mine. But I'll keep my promise about support in any event.' He squeezed my hand. 'Please.' When that had no result, he ran his fingers though my hair. 'Please? You need to know these things. You must know I meant it because you do know how hard it is for me to say please twice.'

'All right,' I said.

'Good,' he said, suddenly efficient again. 'Now hurry. We've only twenty minutes to make our flight and it's in the next terminal. He took my hand and pulled me into the connecting corridor. I had to run faster than was comfortable. When we got to Terminal Two, he craned his neck and said, 'Tell me the moment you see Crawley.'

Crawley, it emerged, was the one who had been following me.

236

Now he was holding a passport and two tickets at the check-in desk closest to customs and immigration.

'You have your passport, don't you? Good. I thought so. And oh, yes, I almost forgot. You might as well give Crawley your car keys so that he can collect the car from the hospital car park before it gets clamped.'

A quarter of an hour later, we were sitting on the runway on an Air France airbus waiting to take off to Paris.

An hour after that, we were at Charles de Gaulle Airport. We took the train to the Left Bank to avoid the rush hour. From the Luxembourg Gardens we walked to the hotel where we had spent our honorary honeymoon. When we got to the room – and it was the same room, the one with the French doors giving out onto the walled garden – he said, in an agitated but still matter-of-fact voice, 'I wanted to come here so that we could start at the beginning again, at least physically, if not in spirit. Would you like to shower? I've booked a table at Les Fontaines. I hope you don't mind. I didn't want to go anywhere there might be a risk of being recognised. The booking is for half an hour from now. That gives us about a quarter of an hour for your shower if you want it.'

The restaurant looked just as I remembered it. Pink tablecloths, small vases with yellow and blue flowers on the tables, all empty, and a gigantic vase with giant lilies on the fountain in the centre. The manageress and her three waiters were gathered at the zinc counter, as nervous as amateur actors who fear their opening night will be to an empty house. Their eyes lit up when they saw us. When they recognised Max, there followed warm expressions of surprise. 'But if we had known it was you,' they said, 'we should have reserved a table by the window.' Max insisted that he was enchanted with the table in the corner. By the time they had seated us, another six couples were waiting to be seated. Soon every table was full. All around us, serious-looking men and women were discussing the menu as if it were the most important business of the day. Sitting in their midst, Max looked all the more haunted and lost.

'Order anything you like. Anything,' he said. I ordered langoustines and then *confit de canard*, and so did he. When the order was placed and the carafe of muscadet brought to the table, he gave me a puzzled look, took a deep breath and, not quite looking me in the eye, said, 'I was always going to tell you this. It was a question of finding the right time. I've put it off because I thought it would compromise you and add to your difficulties, and also because, in making your life worse than it already was, it would result in your leaving me before I could sort things out. However, since you've come to that point without even knowing, there's no reason for you not to know. In any event, it should help you understand why I've been such a bad husband to you over the past few months.

'I love you. I want to start all over again with you after this case is over. If you let me, that's what I want to do. I can say this to you now as we sit here face to face. I shall tell you the truth. For most of the past few months, I haven't known what I felt or what I wanted. I've been in hell. Locked inside a crypt. It began with an accidental discovery. Here. I shall let you put two and two together.' He delved into his briefcase and got out a typescript which he pushed across the table. 'These are the early pages of *The Last Supper*. Not the part I published in *Granta* but the next part, in other words, the last part I did before Rebecca's accident. Read the passages I've underlined.'

I did. 'They sound familiar,' I said. 'Have you shown them to me before?'

'No. But you've read them before.' Now he reached into his briefcase and brought out a book. It was the Tamara Nestor Graham novel. 'Read the passages I've marked for you. Actually, you're the one who marked them, for use in your famous essay.'

I read the marked passages. They were identical. I looked up, unable to phrase a thought.

In a trembling voice, he said, 'She's up to her old tricks. She can't do anything without basing it on something she's stolen from me. Tamara Nestor Graham is Rebecca's new persona and I'm quite sure she's back in London for the trial and planning an appearance but I have no idea what her intentions are or what her plan might be.' He reached out for my hand. 'Although I have my premonitions.'

Chapter Thirty-Three

Now the first courses were arriving. All around us, serious men and women were unable to keep themselves from smiling at their terrines and their salads and their soups and their artistically arranged seafood, but Max stared at his huge plate of langoustines as if it were a pile of unanswered business letters. 'Imagine what it's like,' he said, 'to have spent years and years thinking you've killed someone – not deliberately, mind you, but through neglect, misplaced idealism, self-will, the usual sins of omission – to have spent years and years looking at your orphaned children and thinking, If only I hadn't said that, if only I hadn't done this, they might still have had a mother . . . to have spent years and years hating everything about yourself that makes you who you are, and then to find out that in fact you didn't kill her, that she staged her own death to give herself a fresh start, that she's still at large and has it in her power to wreck whatever new life you have been able to build from the ruins with a flick of the finger.

'I had no idea about this. None whatsoever. Although when I look back now, I see clues everywhere. Of course she had talked about fresh starts. Of course she had threatened to do a bunk. Every time she caught me out she threatened to do a bunk. But she never left for more than a night, and if she did find someone to take her to bed, she'd be on the phone to me about it the moment she woke up the next morning. That was her way. She couldn't do anything without being seen to do it. It was inconceivable that she should want a life in which she was denied a public persona. I now think that's why I never considered it. It did not fit in with the Rebecca I knew.'

Now the *patronne* was standing next to our table, wanting to know why Max had not touched his langoustines. Had the chef been

239

deficient? Max assured her that to the contrary, the langoustines were wonderful. She called him a little cabbage and asked him how he could know if he hadn't even touched them. He put his hand on his heart and promised to correct the injustice. He mustered up a smile, but when he looked at me to resume his story, all trace of it was gone.

'You know Rebecca's side of the story from *The Marriage Hearse*,' he said. 'Well, here's mine. I was as arrogant and selfish as the heroine's husband, possibly even more so. But not in any scheming way; simply because I didn't know any better. I had never had to earn a privilege. Doors opened without my having to pause to think if I wanted to knock. At the same time my brother and I were more or less left to our own devices outside of school time. In a way you could say we were not brought up at all. I'm not trying to complain. We had a good and easy life. But we never learned how you were meant to behave if you were living with other people. We didn't – and, I'm sure you will agree, still don't – know how to be civil at the breakfast table, at lunch, at supper and what have you. If there aren't six strangers at the table, you may have noticed, I don't know what to say.

'So I was as horrid as she made me out to be. On the other hand, what we set out to do was impossible in ways that are patently obvious. You can't be a couple and also be fucking every attractive proposition who comes your way. You can't reject your parents and your aunt and your uncle while living in their houses and getting them to publish your books. You can't share your brain with your wife and then expect to have a mind of your own. If you ignore such contradictions, you become them. The destruction that occurs afterwards is too vast to qualify for that gruesome American platitude about learning from your mistakes.

'I should tell you now what I know about those last days in St John the Baptist. *The Marriage Hearse* was not the item of contention people imagine it was. And while we're on the subject, yes, I did cut that last chapter, but for the best possible motives. That last chapter was awful. Not only was it heavy-handed and didactic, it also ruined the impact of everything that preceded it. Had Rebecca been in residence, she would have come to the same decision that I did. Even when we weren't getting along, she always came to me to find out which of her excesses needed trimming. One of the reasons why she always came across as being a risk-taker who never faltered is that I was always there to cut out the mistakes before they happened. I did only what I would have done under normal circumstances. The irony of all this is that *The Marriage Hearse* would never have had the impact it did, had I not done my usual editing job.'

He paused. All around us, waiters were carrying empty plates back to the kitchen and returning with new carafes of wine. 'All you all right?' one said. Max nodded dismissively, and then took another deep breath.

'Whatever Danny has told you, we had none of us read *The Marriage Hearse* by the Christmas she disappeared. If we weren't getting along, it wasn't the book that had done it. It was just the usual sex and drugs and rock and roll. Yes, I was fucking a stray Buddhist or two, but I was losing the war in a rather big way because Rebecca was carrying on quite openly with our friend Jack Scully. I don't suppose I need to tell you that he is almost certainly William's father, and possibly Hermione's as well. Not that it concerns me as much as people might imagine. A father is as a father does. As I've said before, I have no great faith in my genetic attributes.'

'You've said it so often, I've begun to not believe you,' I said.

He dropped his head into his hands. 'Have I? I suppose you're right.'

Chapter Thirty-Four

'What's ailing you, my little one?'

It was the *patronne* again.

'Nothing important.' He smiled at her and picked up a langoustine.

'At last!' she said. She beamed at him, at me, and then at him again. 'Your little friend is very sweet.'

He thanked her. Another customer caught her eye and she left. He turned back to me, looking more stricken than ever. 'No, it's true,' he said. 'You're right. I wasn't happy about the way Jack and Rebecca threw their relationship in my face, but I probably would have gone on putting up with it. But I drew the line when they started using in front of the children. That's why I left early, why I had to get them away. That's why I wasn't there when Rebecca disappeared.'

'But neither was Jack,' I said.

He bowed his head. 'No, the only people there, besides the Buddhists, of course, were my father, who is not much help now, as we've established beyond the shadow of a doubt, unfortunately, and Bea.'

I told him what Bea had said to me over coffee at the Dome. 'I misunderstood it at the time,' I said. 'But after what you've told me, what she probably meant is that she helped Rebecca escape. Or possibly even forced her out. She *was* the one who identified the body, wasn't she?'

Max's face darkened. 'Yes.'

He looked around us at the serious men and women who were cutting into huge slabs of meat. He closed his eyes and sighed. 'I can't understand,' he said. 'I can't understand why she would do such a thing and then hide it from me.'

'Obviously she wanted you to think Rebecca was dead.'

'But didn't she realise how vulnerable that would leave us? She must have known.'

'There's another thing *you* should know,' I said. 'Jack Scully turned up at the house yesterday, with Danny. They wanted to take me back to London with them. They told me I was in danger. I hadn't realised they were in touch with each other, let alone friends. It makes me feel so terrible telling you this, because I ought to have worked it out myself, I ought to have taken care. Now that you've told me the truth, I can't bear to think what I said, what I tried to say, at the party . . .'

Max knocked back a glass of wine, then put both of his hands on the table and stared at them. 'He's after the children. That's his master plan, it must be. Or rather, that must be *her* master plan. First he ruins my reputation in court – even if I win, it will stick. Then he proves that he's the biological father. Then presumably he and Rebecca get the children and go off into the sunset.' He clenched his fists, unclenched them and stared at his palms, then looked up at me as if he himself was having trouble believing what he was saying. 'She won't be happy until I'm left with nothing.'

'You still love her, don't you?'

He took my hand. 'Yes,' he said. I tried to take my hand away, but he wouldn't let go. 'Please don't take that the wrong way. But you must try and understand what it's like to be haunted by a living woman. Imagine how I felt when I read that first review you wrote of Tamara Nestor Graham and saw quoted in it sentences in the book *that I myself had written.* At first I thought it must have been some sort of posthumous trick. But then, when I had locked myself in her study and read the book itself, I was forced to accept that this was something only Rebecca could have written, and that the newest tempest in the New York publishing teacup was none other than she. Do you see how this unnerved me? Do you understand now why I reached for the bottle? And then, imagine how I felt when, binge over, I opened my own review section to find that lead article by you attacking Tamara Nestor Graham and all women who suited themselves instead of caring for their children. I read that and I knew there was no turning back. After a provocation on that scale, I knew there was no chance she'd leave us be. I knew it was just a matter of time before she would throw the whole deceit in my face.'

He sighed again and lowered his head. 'Although even that is probably too optimistic. She was probably always planning to throw it in my face. She set out to make a new life for herself to prove to me and the world that she could do it alone. Without my inspiration or advice, and without my infamous family's notorious strings. And also to prove, by the by, that I couldn't. Only Rebecca could have pulled it off and, having pulled it off, then set out to do one better. To trample over my poor attempt at a second chance. Blacken my name for ever. And take away the children.'

'Even if Jack wins the suit,' I said, 'Jack would have a very hard time getting custody.'

Max shook his head again. 'I've never seen Rebecca not get what she wanted when she put her mind to it. Even if he didn't get custody, she would still have managed to tell the world I'm not their father. Not to mention the children themselves.'

I didn't know what to say.

'Oh, dear, oh, dear,' he said. 'I've been neglecting my food.' He picked up another langoustine and smiled at me in a way I now knew was anything but carefree. 'This child we're about to have – this one *is* mine, isn't it?' Before I could answer, he put his hands up. 'I'm sorry. I do trust you. That's why I'm taking the risk of telling you the truth. You're the only one I trust right now. I don't know who else to talk to.'

'Haven't you confided in Crawley?'

'Oh, I think he's guessed all right. But I don't want to incriminate him. It wouldn't be fair. As for the others, I don't know how much they know. I'm quite certain Danny has actually heard from Rebecca. In fact, when we announced our plans to marry, you may remember, she was even kind enough to tell us. Don't you remember her night visitor? The one from the other side? If it hadn't been for Bea, we might even have listened. No, it's Bea I'm most concerned about.'

'Have you confronted her?'

244

'Yes, of course I have,' he said with an agitated wave. 'It was obvious to me from the start that I could avoid this awful trial altogether if we could prove that the body in the grave was not Rebecca. But . . .' A wave of pain came over his face. 'You may not want to know this part.'

'I would say I need to know it.'

'I didn't confront her directly, you see. I didn't want to show her all my cards. So I simply asked, had she made a truly positive identification of the body? And she said, in that offhand drawl of hers, that it was best not to think about exhuming the body, because if we did, I might find myself involved in not a libel case but a murder trial. Because, you see, the real reason I left the island when I did – oh, I don't know why I ever tried to avoid this one, I ought to have told you right off. You see, it wasn't a handful of stray Buddhists I was carrying on with, as I said. It was one woman. I'm ashamed to say I can't remember her name, I probably never knew her name, in fact. But the fact is, I woke up on my last morning on St John the Baptist, presumably having spent the night with her, although I haven't a clue what we did . . . What happened was that I woke up next to this woman, whoever she was—'

He cracked a langoustine. 'And I turned her over, and found that she was dead.'

Chapter Thirty-Five

His hands were shaking so badly now that he could no longer eat. 'She had choked on her vomit. I have no idea if I played a part in it or not. I ought to have just stayed there and sweated it out, but there were so many drugs around, I was afraid we'd all be thrown into prison. It was Bea who talked me into taking the children and getting out of there as fast as we could, and leaving it to her to handle things discreetly. Which she later told me she did. It was quite a good story, in fact. Lots of nice details about how the Buddhist monks reacted when she told them about the girl's death. And the girl's family, how vulgar they were, even what they were wearing when they flew out to claim the body. I suppose she made it all up. What I can't understand is why she bothered.

'I've been staring at the wall for the past five months, trying to understand, running through the few memories I have of those days. But it's been one cul-de-sac after another. It's been back to the way things were when Rebecca was still with us. I'm so confused. I'm confused about her and I'm confused about you. And what makes me so angry is that this is precisely how she wants me to feel. It's as if she had my brain in her hands. It's as if she were eating it like an apple. I wake up in the morning and I ask myself, What game is she going to play with me today? Is today the day she has chosen to use her final weapon? And if so, what weapon? How? Where? Via whom? I have no way of defending myself. No means of escape. My only recourse has been to do whatever I can do to earn myself a few hours of oblivion.

'I'm determined not to lie to you. In any event, I can't imagine you haven't worked it out. I haven't covered my tracks so very well and you know what I'm like. But when I've taken whatever woman it happens to be that night back to my cousin's flat, it hasn't been you I've been trying to forget. It's been Rebecca. Does that mean I'm married to her as much as I ever was? I'm afraid this is not a question to which I can provide an answer. I don't know if it's fair to involve you any longer, seeing as I don't know the answer. And it's not just that – there are legal ramifications. If Rebecca is alive, I really am still married to her. And you and I are not married. Our child is – will be – illegitimate. And then there's the question of her estate. Without her estate, Beckfield Press will be no longer – and will probably virtually belong to her. The web becomes more and more tangled. Can you possibly want to continue living under this curse?'

The answer, of course, was that I did. More than I had ever wanted anything. He had, without realising it, told me the thing I most needed to hear. How different the mirror in the hotel room looked, now that I knew Rebecca was evil! If Rebecca was evil, then I was good. I was not just good, I was indispensable. I was the only one he could trust to tell the truth. He had put himself at my mercy. He had put me first. That was all I had ever asked from him or from anyone. And so of course I was willing to live under any curse. So long as he needed me. So long as I was the only one he had asked to save him. It was because he hoped that I could save him that he loved me. It was by saving him that I would save myself.

All the better, then, that I had been here before.

Chapter Thirty-Six

Max's hands were shaking when I handed him his coffee in the hotel room the next morning. It was this news about Bea, he said. It had kept him awake all night. 'I rang her finally, not long before you woke up. I tried to give her a chance to open up, but she became quite hysterical and hung up on me. How many angles is she playing? *What is it that she doesn't want me to know?*'

I told him not to worry, that we would speak to the solicitor as soon as we got back to London. We would work out a way of getting the story out of her. 'If you're innocent, no one is going to be able to pin anything on you. Not if I have anything to do with it.' Suddenly no challenge was too large for me. I felt as refreshed as if I'd been asleep for a week. It was as if I had a new body. To my surprise I could walk at my normal rate again without losing breath. I had my stamina back. After packing our bags, I didn't have to lie down for half an hour. I didn't need to wait for someone else to take the lead. I was the one to pay the bill, to hail the cab, to tell the driver to take us back to Charles de Gaulle, to guide Max to the bar in duty-free and get him the drink that stopped his hands shaking. I was the one to take his hand when he said, 'I should really give up this stuff altogether,' and say (I try now to imagine the condescending benevolence in my voice), 'You're probably right, but you have enough on your plate already.'

We went straight from Heathrow to the Ritz, where Max's father had taken a suite. We had been planning to spend the afternoon at the National Gallery, but Max ran out of energy. I forced him to eat the sandwiches I had had room service bring up for us, and then I turned down the bed in the second bedroom and, to give him peace and quiet, I took Max's father out for a walk in his wheelchair.

He fell asleep before we even reached Green Park. When he woke up again, we were back in the hotel lobby and I was having tea. The chandeliers were blazing. There was a man at the grand piano playing a waltz. At the table behind us, there was an anxiously obsequious young man speaking in rapid-fire Greek to a stiff and overdressed elderly couple, who stared at him with tired incomprehension. At the table to our right were three ladies from Houston who were dressed from head to toe in grey and were trying to figure out why they had lost the zest for shopping. In front of us was a slight, blond boy who had already paid his bill. Now the maître d' was bringing him his cape and top hat.

Max's father gasped. 'What year is it?' he asked, but to no one in particular. He turned to me and cried, 'Sally! At last! But what a cruel thing you are! How many years you've made me wait!'

Sally, I found out from Max later, was his childhood sweetheart. He could not be convinced that I was not she, so it seemed easier to play along with the delusion. But Bea was visibly offended when she heard him call me Sally outside the court the next morning.

'And when did *this* start?' she wanted to know. When I told her, she flicked her hair and said, 'Hopeless. The man is beyond repair.' She grabbed the wheelchair from me as if it were stolen property. 'I'm afraid this is where the rest of us say goodbye to you. Do you think you have it in you to find the public gallery?'

Max wanted to find me a proper place, but I said no, the public gallery was fine for now. It would be easier, I said, if I could keep a low profile.

This turned out not to be possible. I got more than a few looks. But with my new found confidence, I had no trouble staring back.

Max's father was the first in the stand that morning. Now it was Jack Scully's barrister cross-examining him. Max's father was quoted in Jack Scully's book as saying he had heard someone at his hotel bar bragging about having rigged Rebecca's boat with dynamite. The barrister now did his best to get him to repeat this story. Instead Max's father decided to tell all assembled that there were two types of natives on his island, the type that was willing to work for an honest living, and the type that did nothing but drink and whore and steal. After several failed attempts to return him to the subject, the barrister gave up.

Then it was Bea's turn. I could tell she was not entirely sober from the way she walked to the stand. Her neck was too stiff, her manner too haughty. She was not to know that it was not her disdainful gaze that made our barrister ill at ease, but the task that lay ahead. Max and our solicitor had decided to leave it to our barrister to tackle Bea.

This, they had thought, would be the most effective way of getting her to tell the truth. But during the early part of the examination, it was, nevertheless, Bea who kept the upper hand. She had a confident, though inappropriate, one-liner for everything. Asked to give her opinion of her former lover, she said, 'Am I to comment on Ben the young rake or Ben the ageing vegetable?' Asked to describe Rebecca's behaviour during the last week of her life, she said, 'It is important to remember that her mind owed more to a chemistry lab by then than it did to her progenitors.' Asked to be more specific about Rebecca's behaviour, she said, 'Being off her head, Rebecca made the common mistake of confusing quality with propinquity.'

When our barrister asked her if she had helped Rebecca kill herself, she snapped, 'Of course not. What a preposterous idea!' When our barrister asked her if she had at least been instrumental in Rebecca's decision to take her boat out, she said, 'It's clear to me, young man, that you haven't a clue what Rebecca was like. Boats, books, people – she was never in their service, my boy. It was always the other way round.'

When the barrister asked her what she would say if he told her there was new evidence to suggest that in this one instance, the person in charge had been Bea herself, and that it might be possible to prove she had, as it were, helped her, Bea went very still. She said nothing for thirty seconds. Then she leaned forward and searched the court with her eyes until she found me.

'You told them that, didn't you?' She pointed her finger at me. 'You did, you stupid girl. Didn't you?'

* * *

250

'Does *everyone* in America do things like this?' Bea wanted to know as she knocked back her fourth negroni. 'Is discretion an entirely alien concept? Has it never occurred to you or any of your countrymen that the rule of the herd does not lead inexorably to justice?'

We were back at the Ritz for what was threatening to become a foodless lunch. The friendly but concerned maître d' had seated us at the table next to the bar. Max's father was smiling beatifically in his wheelchair while devouring the crisps. Occasionally, he would interrupt the argument to say, 'Shame about the chandeliers, isn't it, Sally?' or 'Who shot the piano player?' Every time the waiter came past us, he waved at him or gave him the thumbs up and said, 'Great stuff!' Meanwhile, Max sat next to him, staring into his water glass as if he wished it contained morphine.

I was still full of myself. Bea was trying to get me to back down but for once I was not about to apologise. 'If you did nothing wrong,' I said to Bea, 'then you have nothing to hide. And nothing to fear either.'

'Tell me, does absolutely *everyone* in America talk like a Buddhist?'

'I'm not talking like a Buddhist.'

'I'm a Buddhist,' Max's father said.

'Yes, of course you are, my dear.'

'Have you learned your mantra yet?'

'No, not yet, darling, I've been rather tied up.'

'Repeat after me. *Omi*—'

'Oh, do shut up, you tiresome thing,' Bea said.

'If you're as tired as you say, my dear, it will help you no end.'

Bea exhaled through her nostrils and gave me a baleful look.

'I'm not a Buddhist,' I tried to tell her again. 'I'm just trying to reason with you. I think the time has come to accept that there's no course open to you but to tell the truth.'

'You're trying to tell me about the truth. That's rich! Well, next time you sit down to do your bloody *oms*, try and imagine this. Needles, needles everywhere. A party full of bright sparks with rather large habits who never clean up after themselves. Children seeing it all and getting hurt. And then this silly girl whose name no one can remember – Buddhists don't need names, apparently – chokes on her vomit after an overdose. And all this in a country that throws you into prison and throws away the key if you have so much as an ounce of cannabis. What would you do in this situation, my dear? Are you honestly trying to convince me that you'd tell the truth?'

'You might have had good reason to keep the authorities out,' Max said to her as he picked up a cashew and held it up to the light. 'But it was very wrong and cruel, Bea, to keep the truth from me. It was my life.'

'If I'd told you she'd run away, you would have gone after her.'

'You have no idea what I might have done,' he said. His voice was controlled but his lips were trembling.

'She wanted to go, Max,' Bea said. 'If it hadn't been for my intervention, she would have ended up going with the children. You ought to be thanking me—'

'And what exactly was your intervention?' Max asked. 'If it's not too much to ask.'

'We came to an agreement. I would let her leave using the dead girl's papers if she—'

'You conned her into thinking she was the one who had killed the girl.'

'Well, it did seem silly not to make use of the body, seeing as it was not about to come back to life. But if we're all going to be Buddhists from here on, I suppose it's only right to tell you that it was Rebecca's idea to take the body out to sea with the boat. Although it caused me no end of trouble. And cost quite a tidy sum, too. You may think it's easy to sit on an island in the Caribbean waiting for a body to come back to you. Well, I beg to differ! First it refused to appear at all – I had to cancel my trip to Tuscany – and then, when it turned up, wouldn't it be at the other end of the island, and wouldn't I have come down with a beastly cold the day before? It was a gruesome job from start to finish, although that ought not to have surprised me, as my role in life is to be there to do the gruesome jobs no one else can be bothered to do. Where were you by then, Max? Do you remember? I had to find two doctors

252

to sign the death certificate. Do you think that was easy? Flying a body in from abroad is an absolute nightmare. Do you have any idea what those undertakers charged me? What we had to go through with the coroner at Heathrow . . .'

'You ought never to have sent the body back here, Bea.'

'Yes, I do realise that now, Max. It has crossed my mind, but I am grateful to you, nevertheless, for pointing out the obvious. Not to worry, however. I've cleaned up that gruesome mess just like I've cleaned up all your others. You can always count on your solid old Aunt Bea to be one step ahead of the Buddhists! I dug her up years ago, Max, and stuck her up at Bramble House, or to be precise, in Tatiana's Middlemarch. If they ever do decide to open the grave in Beckfield cemetery, my dear, they'll find nothing.'

Max groaned and dropped his head into his hands. 'Oh, Bea, oh, Bea, what are we going to do with you?'

'Well, for a start, you can promise to visit me in gaol. And perhaps you can write me a little poem now and again to thank me for my efforts. I didn't do any of this for myself, I did it for you. As odd as it may sound to a modern-day Buddhist, I did it to protect you. You and the family. I couldn't bear to see any more of you go the way of his nibs here.'

'I'm not going anywhere,' Max's father interjected. 'I want a drink. A drink? Sally, can you catch the eye of that man over there? I'm as thirsty as a nigger on a camel.'

'Of course you are, my dear,' said Bea. 'Of course you are.' She gave him her best nurse's smile. 'There was never going to be a sensible divorce, Max. You were never going to have the chance to make a new start so long as you thought she was alive. She had done enough damage. It was time to be shot of her. At the time, it seemed to be the perfect solution.'

'But Bea,' Max said, his head still in his hands, 'even then, you must have realised—'

'Well, yes, of course, I ought to have known that Rebecca would insist on speaking from the grave. How could I ever have thought otherwise? Silly me to be a realist! I ought to have known, for example, that you would not suddenly change character and find a suitable wife and live happily ever after. But how could anyone have predicted yet another American Buddhist?' She laughed a bitter laugh as she lit up a cigarette. 'Do you know, my dear?' she said to me. 'I do wonder sometimes if it wasn't Rebecca who sent you to us to finish us off. You're Rebecca's last laugh.'

In fact, Rebecca had not had her last laugh yet. When we returned to court, we found her waiting for us at the top of the courtroom steps.

She was still dressed in the white coat that showed off her tan. She still had her skullcap on but she took it off as soon as she saw us, releasing a mane of platinum hair. She smiled, and as she did, I could just see the faintest trace of the scar on her cheek. She clasped her hands together as if in mock prayer as Bea broke away from us and bounded up the steps.

'Oh, thank God!' Bea said. 'Thank God you're here. And not a moment too soon. Rebecca, I don't think I've ever said this and meant it more – but it was so good of you, so very good of you to come.'

Chapter Thirty-Seven

Three o'clock found Bea back on the witness stand, but not for long. Our barrister announced in a thin, strained voice that she had no further questions. The defence waived its right to cross-examine her. Unable to make sense of this anticlimax, the courtoom burst into excited whispers. The judge requested silence. Bea returned to her seat. Our barrister called our next witness. As she made her way to the stand, a woman in the public gallery screamed.

There were a few more gasps as she sat down to face the court. She did not look like the Rebecca of popular memory. The bleached hair was tied back with a navy ribbon, and her dress had the aura of a nurse's uniform. She was wearing gold-rimmed glasses, which she took off after she had taken the oath. She surveyed the court and found Jack Scully.

'I'm sorry, Scalper,' she said.

He did not look at her but stared instead at his hands. His careful frown was impossible to read. So was Max's.

'It's all for the best, Scalper. I've really thought this one through.' When Rebecca said 'Scalper', I could see Max flinch.

'Could you please leave this conversation for later and identify yourself to the court?'

'My legal name or my other name?'

'Your legal name will do.'

'My legal name is Tamara Nestor Graham. But the public will know me as Rebecca Slaughter-Midwinter.'

Now the rest of the courtroom went wild.

'Order! Order!'

Rebecca smiled at her audience as graciously as if she were at a poetry reading. Once they were quiet again, she said, 'Thank you.' Then she turned to our barrister, who had stood up to interrogate her.

'Could you explain to the court why you've decided to come forward?'

'Well, obviously, to prove that this entire trial is based on a false premise. I don't look dead to you, do I?'

There was a ripple of nervous laughter.

'I'm also here to hold myself publicly accountable for what I've done. Allow me to give the court the bare bones, if you don't mind the pun –' the amazing thing is, they didn't – 'and then offer an explanation of why I needed to disappear.

'The first point I must make is that it was my decision to run away. If I did not make a free or rational choice, it was because of the state of my mind. I was not hounded out of my life. Neither was I running away from Max per se. Most important, I was not running away from my beloved children. I was not even running away from the life I described accurately enough in *The Marriage Hearse*. What I was trying to do was run away from my problems. This is what all addicts do. When you're addicted to something, it affects your mind and your spirit as well as your body, and I had lost my ability to make a rational choice.

'So when a girl nobody knew very well except for me OD'd at that now infamous all-night party at my father-in-law's hotel on St John the Baptist, I panicked. I knew what the police were like there. I thought I couldn't take any chances, even though I had no information to suggest that I had played any direct part in her death. I was her connection. I was the one who would go down, or so I thought. That was why I decided to take her out with me when I sank my boat.

'After I had come back to shore in a borrowed dinghy, I used her passport to get into Mexico. Then I entered the US through Brownsville and took buses up to Seattle and got a job as a waitress. After a while I got my name changed legally to Tamara Nestor Graham. Then came the slippery slope. Over the next year or so I truly bottomed out. I could tell you the full story – I have nothing to hide any more – but it's pretty sordid and probably not relevant

256

to this trial. Better to withhold the details for a Bookmark Special.'
More laughter. 'Suffice it to say that I ended up in jail, from which
I was lucky enough to make my way into a drug-rehabilitation
programme that turned me around.

'For the past five years I've been living in San Francisco and slowly
putting the pieces back together. The key word here is "slowly".
For the first year all I did was clean toilets for the Little Sisters of
Mercy. Then I decided to see if I could get myself back on track
using solely my own talents. It is not Maxie's fault that I made my
name first time around on his family's back. That is just the way it
goes. The one privilege I have enjoyed as a result of my self-willed
misfortunes is this chance to find out what I was made of, what
I could achieve on my own. This is a privilege Max Midwinter is
never likely to know and so my heart goes out to him.

'If people had read *The Marriage Hearse* more carefully, they
would have seen that this was what it really was about. It was
not the condemnation of a particular family but the portrait of a
couple that never knew where one began and the other ended, and
who were further hampered by being part of a larger family that
permitted no one any real degree of autonomy.

'It has been with great and growing distress that I have watched the
Midwinter family and Max in particular suffer from the misreadings of
this book. I can only hope that the monies accrued from it have gone
some way towards making up for that. Despite my surprising success as
Tamara Nestor Graham, there has hardly been a day when I haven't
regretted giving myself up for dead. Hardly a day when I haven't
fantasised about going back to Beckfield and peeking through the
windows for a glimpse of my little ones. But it hasn't just been
the fear of taking the personal consequences of a resurrection. It
was the prospect of what it would do to everyone else. I had done
enough damage. That was how I saw things.

'My illusions on this score did not outlive an article written by
Max's new wife around the time of publication of my latest book.
Of course the poor creature could not have known that I was
Tamara Nestor Graham. But she clearly had a sixth sense about
there being something deeply dishonest about my novel. For my

part, I sensed there was a real-life story, a very distressing story, hiding just beneath the surface of an essay that purported to be about the feminist heroine in contemporary American fiction.

'I would be lying to you if I told you that I took this article well on first, second, third, fourth or fifth readings. The gist of it, for those of you who aren't familiar with it, is that this new crew of feminist heroines like the one in my novel destroy everything around them in the name of experience and then leave lesser beings to pick up the pieces. By people she meant husbands and children, mostly children and, I decided, above all, *my* children. This is a charge too great for any mother to ignore, and I was no exception. Despite my anger at having been accused of selfishness and neglect, the idea took root of my children living in darkness with a stepmother who didn't love them as I did and so desperately needing me.

'When my anger had subsided, another picture began to form in my mind, of a well-meaning second wife who wasn't up to the job I had left to her, and whose life I was ruining, along with so many others.

'And then, when I got word of this trial, my unease turned into something more concrete. I decided I had to do something. And so here I am.

'I don't know what the repercussions for me will be. I deliberately did not want to consult a lawyer because I didn't want any sane advice to deter me from doing what I consider to be the only right thing. I have no idea whether I should or could be tried for that poor girl's death, or, if so, where I could be tried. I don't know if Max and I are still legally married or what bearing my reappearance will have on the legality of his new marriage. But I have no desire to stand in the way of his happiness. As they say in the fellowship, the beginning of love is to let those we love be perfectly themselves and not to twist them to fit our image. We are best able to help others when we ourselves have learned the gift of serenity. I'm willing to dissolve our marriage, if it still exists in the eyes of the law, as expeditiously as possible. I would of course give anything to be able to live at least part of the time with my children. But I do accept I have done something unforgivable in abandoning them.

So I will have to leave this question for the family to discuss and decide. Thanks to my McArthur Prize, I have no money problems. I'm aware that the Beckfield Press would go under without the proceeds from my so-called estate – but I'm also aware that Giles Midwinter has done everything correctly and in good faith. I'm happy to go into consultation to find out the best way of proceeding so that I can continue to keep this wonderful publishing house going. I would like to extend the same favour to my cousin Jack Scully, who has also acted in good faith. I want to invest in Isis Press. I also intend to cover the costs he has incurred during this trial. In fact, I think that I should be covering costs for both sides if the law will allow me. I say that because whenever I decide to do something that is morally right, I usually find out that it's legally wrong. Or counterproductive. Or just plain stupid.

'But for the record, the way I look at it is this: we're all here today because of a series of actions I undertook to save my own skin. Perhaps it was as desperate as I thought it was. Perhaps there are times when you have to act selfishly, when you have to be your own best friend, when the only path open to you is over other people's fragile lives and in spite of your children – when it's either them or you. I acted viciously, I'll be the first to admit it. And I got what was coming to me. I degraded myself and stared death in the face. But I came through. I have pulled myself together. Remade myself. Since which time I've been showered with more rewards than any selfish feminist explorer could possibly deserve. Now I would like to spread around my good fortune. As Hemingway said, "The bill always comes." What I'm trying to do now is beat the waiter to it. This is me going straight up to the cashier and saying, "Don't let me walk out without paying everything I owe."

'So please, I'm asking you all, help me do the right thing.' Here, for the first time, she looked directly at me. And smiled through me.

Chapter Thirty-Eight

A nd so she resurrected herself while also offering to save the family fortunes and the family name. What did it matter that she did it with a carefully sculpted version of the truth? She had kept Bea out of it, and Max's father's love life out of it. She had turned Max from a woman-hater and a murderer into a stoic and a martyr while also making his opponent Jack Scully look as good or better. She had taken responsibility for the dead girl and promised to take the consequences. She had offered to keep both presses afloat. She had said the words that would mend the children's broken hearts but graciously offered to let the family decide on the right sort of custody. After the court was adjourned, she had even forced a reconciliation between the family and Danny. So everyone had benefited. Everyone but me.

But in the commotion, who was going to notice? Especially since Rebecca herself took such care to be kind to me. She was the one who noticed how exhausted I was after the press conference on the steps. She was the one who vetoed the suggestion to go to the Groucho Club to celebrate. 'We've got to get this poor thing back to her own bed,' she said with a firmness I found daunting. Of course she had her own reasons for wanting to get back to Oxford. But she had also been the only one to notice I was flagging.

How did she do it? She couldn't possibly feel as comfortable as she pretended to be, sitting there in the limousine with Max who would neither look at nor speak to her, with Danny clinging to her shoulder and weeping, while Bea and Giles took turns coming up with bright questions to save us all from the awkward silence. Was San Francisco as delightful as it used to be? they wanted to know. Did she have a flat or a house and was it in a foggy or a sunny area? Was she working on a new novel? Did she find Britain different?

She answered each question in full, with witty flourishes, and was even better than they were at thinking up new ways to stave off silence. She also charmed the driver. 'Weren't you the one who went to Cambridge?' she asked. She asked Bea about her daughters, Giles about his poets. She asked after Janet and all the other family retainers. It was only when she enquired about William and Hermione that her voice faltered.

When Bea said, a bit too drily, 'Well, they're as well as could be expected,' I saw her hand clench, but even then, she dissolved the tension in her face with yet another joke.

'Well, I hope you realise that there's one thing I'm not going to let them do, and that's forgive me.'

How could she say such a thing and still laugh? How could she drive right back into the heart of her former misery and say, 'Beckfield might be the first circle of hell, but it sure as hell is beautiful!'? Where did she find her smiles for the press pack? How could she keep talking to me as if we were having a friendly conversation when she could only get monosyllables out of me? I hated my ungraciousness. I knew the others would remark on it later, saying, 'Well, *she* didn't do a very good job of hiding her feelings, did she?' But the more I hated my inability to be gracious, chatty and witty, the heavier my limbs, the more leaden my tongue.

And with my every failure to rise to the occasion, the wittier, chattier and more gracious she became. When she put her arm around me to help me into the cottage – my cottage, not hers any more, although this did not seem to register – when she took my hand and said, 'Let's make you some tea' and took me into my kitchen, even then she had just the right words ready. 'Oh, my God!' she said. 'Max, I can't believe it. You still have the same crappy old pepper shaker! Is this a mausoleum or what?' I could not understand how the artefacts in the mausoleum had no effect on her. This was the kitchen where she had once chopped her hand instead of a clove of garlic and then, instead of going straight to casualty, stopped to write a poem about it, dreaming of death. She had probably used that knife on the magnetic strip, and this cutting board, but now there was no pull, no connection, no fear, no regret.

How could she stay so strong? Why was I the one to feel faint? Why was she the only one to notice? 'Here, take my arm,' she said. I didn't want to take her arm, and I didn't want her taking me into my own bedroom and smiling as if it were still her bedroom. And most of all, I didn't want her sitting down on the bed next to me, taking my hand and looking into my eyes. How could she be so earnest?

'You're very tense,' she said.

I tried to nod politely.

'My coming back like this must be very hard for you.'

Hoarsely, I said, 'Well, according to you, I'm the one who provoked you into doing it.'

'Well, yes and no. You certainly pressed the right button, but I was bound to resurrect myself sooner or later.' She laughed. 'You know the worst part about being officially dead? Picking up your last novel and finding that someone has changed the ending. Galling is not the word!' But she sounded too good-natured to sound galled at all.

'They really take the cake, don't they?' she continued. 'These Beckfield mafiosi – what's that English expression? It's been so long since I used it. They take the biscuit. Or is it bite the biscuit?' I couldn't help her, but she didn't mind. 'No, anyway, I was never going to take that lying down, believe me. Not even dead. No, really, I should be thanking you for calling me a bad mother. You said what you thought at least! You went on what you knew! You haven't been here long enough to have learned how to be cruel by being kind.'

She squeezed my hand again. 'What I didn't have the chance to say when I was doing my spiel is how well written that piece of yours was. It's really strange, you know, when you admire a piece of writing even though it's cutting your heart up. Another thing I should tell you. I'm a fan of your book.'

'Well, if you are, you're almost alone of all your sex,' I said.

She laughed as if I had made the funniest joke in the world. Then, just as suddenly, she turned serious. 'I'm a fan of your book, but I also know you have a better book inside you, and I know what it's like here, I know what they do to people, and the long and the short of it is that you'll never write this book, you know, unless you get away from them, and – listen, learn from my experience – if you wait until this child is born, they'll never let you take it with you, so you should go now, honestly, I mean it, *now*. I'm here, I can cover for you, let me do it.'

She looked at me, breathless as if she had been running, even afraid. 'I know this might sound strange, coming from me and under these circumstances, but . . . our recovery depends on our telling *our own story*.'

Now the words came out without my willing them. 'Take your hands off me. Take your hands off me and get off my bed.'

'Oh, please don't—'

'It's my bed now, in case you haven't noticed. It's my bed and you can't just come in here and walk all over it.'

'Oh, I see, you think I'm jealous, don't you? Well, I can see why you'd think that. Except that—'

She was unable to finish her sentence. My raised voice brought Max into the bedroom. In a cracked voice, but still not looking at her, he said, 'What are you doing in here? You're not upsetting her, are you? I don't think this is a good idea.'

Before she could answer him, Bea had come bustling in, saying that it was all set, there was a refrigerator of cold champagne waiting for them, and she was going straight back to the house to get everything ready for their little celebration, and did Rebecca remember how to drive on the wrong side of the road, and if so, did she want the job of collecting the children?

'Are you sure? Do you trust me to do it on my own?'

'I'd better come with you,' Max said stiffly.

Bea nodded. 'That's probably a better idea.'

'But you're not going to make me sit in the passenger seat, are you, Max? Please let me drive. Please?'

He lowered his head as if in defence against a screech that hurt his ears. Or was he just trying not to show a pleasure he was afraid I might not be able to understand? 'Why don't you go outside and wait for me there?' he said. He reached into his pocket and threw her the keys.

'Still the same key chain even,' she said. 'It gets curiouser and curiouser.'

Before she got up, she gave my hand one last squeeze and said, 'Please don't misunderstand what I was trying to say. We can talk more later.'

After she had left the room, Max said, 'What was she saying to you?'

'Oh, the usual nonsense.'

'Yes, but what usual nonsense?'

'That I should choose art over love, because I had a better book in me.'

'Oh, yes,' he said. 'Don't we all?' He put his hand through my hair. In a dead voice, he asked, 'How are you taking this?'

'I'm glad she's left the room. But . . . but . . .'

'But?'

'But I can see why you were in love with her.'

He frowned. 'I'm glad someone can. I don't know if I can. But I suppose . . . Never mind, we can talk about that later. I'm worried about you. You don't look well. I don't think you should come to this party tonight. I'd like you to stay in bed.'

'But I can't stay in bed. Even if I did stay in bed, how could I relax?'

'You'd still be better off here and not there. You've had enough for one day. I don't want her working on you any more. She never knows when to stop. Let me handle her. It's going to be a very tricky evening and I'd like to keep you out of it.'

'But you can't keep me out of it! I'm your wife!'

His face turned red. 'You're also pregnant, and even if you don't have the good sense to think about your own health, you must think of the baby.' He pounded the bedside table. 'It's my baby, too, God damn it! It's my baby and I have no control over it!'

'And you think I have any more control over it than you? Look at me, Max! I can't even breathe, for God's sake!'

Now he put his fingers through his own hair. 'I'm sorry,' he said, more to the floor than to me. 'I don't know what came over me.'

'You must be feeling very confused,' I offered.

He shook his head. 'I don't know if I'm feeling anything. Except very, very tired.' But for the first time in two days, he did not look tired. Instead he looked edgy, almost elated. He glanced at his watch. 'I must go,' he said. 'Promise me you'll look after yourself.'

'I love you,' I said as he took his hand away.

He kissed my head. 'And I love you.'

Would I have acted differently if he had recited his lines with just a bit more conviction?

Chapter Thirty-Nine

I know there's no point in asking this question. In the seven years since the events I'm describing I've learned just how pointless, but going around in circles is a habit I can't break. Last night, for example. We were at a drinks party in North Oxford. It was the usual collection talking about the usual subjects, and so it was almost without thinking that I gravitated towards the one person in the room who looked less at home than I did. I knew he was American before he opened his mouth. It was partly his too casual clothes, partly the wild and puzzled expression on his face, as if it were ropes and not good manners that held him to his chair, as if he would happily agree to pay any money to be tearing across the mesa on a motorcycle – or so I thought. It is possible I was reading my own wishes into him.

He turned out to be from New Mexico. Not originally, of course. 'That sort of goes without saying. The average American moves once every five years.' He asked me where I was from. I told him I wasn't sure which place counted. He nodded knowingly. 'That makes you an honorary average American.'

He asked me why I had settled in Oxford. Was I a don? 'Hardly,' I said. 'I'm here because I'm married.' I was looking around the room to point Max out, when I saw him standing right behind me. He already had his coat on. He told me he was going home.

There was alarm in the American's eyes as we watched Max leave. 'What's wrong with that guy?' he asked. Then he said something else no British person would ever dream of saying under such circumstances: 'He looks like he's preparing for the Second Coming.'

'Oh, he is,' I said. 'You're right about that.'

'Is he always that bad?'

'Of course not,' I said. 'He just doesn't like parties now that he doesn't drink any more. He's also afraid of leaving the children with babysitters.'

'I know lots of women who would kill for a husband like that. Or is it a drag, always having to go out alone?'

I was no longer used to taking such direct hits, so I decided to change the subject. I asked him what he did for a living.

He told me he was a fire sculptor. His most recent performance piece, he said, had involved setting alight a flotilla of miniature boats he had made and sending them down the Mississippi.

'What was the point of it all?' I asked.

He said, 'To prove that true beauty never lasts.'

'Yes,' I said, 'but if it doesn't last, then almost by definition it can't be art.'

He didn't agree with me. 'If it's really beautiful, no one who's seen it can ever forget it. It continues to illuminate their lives every bit as much as that fleeting memory of the Parthenon in moonlight, or the long-ago glimpse of the Vermeer woman with her pitcher.'

'But what if it didn't stop there?' I wanted to know. 'What if your flotilla had not just disintegrated but also started a larger fire and destroyed everything around it? What if that had been your secret desire from the outset? Surely it was only art to the degree you could contain it?'

That was to confuse the cause with the effect, he told me. Art might start out as a controlled experiment, but the interesting part was seeing what happened after it was beyond the power of the creator to stop it.

His voice was loud and by now our conversation had attracted interest. I could already predict what would happen later on, after I had left the party. He would say, 'I had the strangest conversation with that woman in the long blue dress.' He would repeat it, not quite verbatim, and then this other person would say, 'Well, you know who she is, don't you?' I could foresee all this, but still I could not help it. I said to this fire sculptor that the only thing that made his work qualify as art was that his intention had been to lie to himself.

267

Art made something out of nothing. The beauty of fire, I told him, was that it did the opposite. Fire was beautiful when it made nothing out of something that had been squeezing the life out of you. When it seemed to read your mind, I said.

But of course even that could be a lie.

After the others had left for the big house, I watched myself on the seven-o'clock news and again at nine. But there is a limit to the number of times you can bear to see a young and breathless newscaster standing outside your house trying to guess why you looked wan and your husband tense while Rebecca stole the limelight. 'So, Annabel, is the second marriage null?' asked the newsreader in the studio. I turned off the television before she gave her answer. There is only so long you can look at a blank screen, a cold fireplace, an empty room.

I tried reading a book but then a car would stop outside the main courtyard. Cameras would flash. There would be a flurry of questions, and then the car would continue. A single peal of laughter would float through the open window, and I would try to imagine who had just arrived, what the reporters were saying to each other, what the others in the big house were doing, what I was missing, what they didn't want me to see. Who were they to say? I asked myself. I needed to see it. I needed to know what they were like when they thought I wasn't there. One look was all I needed.

I wanted to see if my fears had come true. Perhaps that is a better way of putting it. As I stepped out of the house, I might even have admitted that I was looking forward to the pain. There is a satisfaction in seeing that you have imagined the unknown correctly. Across the lawn I went to face the big house.

In the front room, a fire was taking the edge off the cool spring night. Danny and Rebecca were giggling and whispering in the shadows of the corridor that led to the kitchen. They disappeared, I made my way around the wing that housed Beckfield Press. It was not its usual tidy self. Books thrown here and there indicated that Rebecca had been in here looking at her English editions. There was a poster that someone – Danny perhaps? – had unrolled and tacked up on the wall. It was the famous photograph of Rebecca in the wrong dress, the one that had appeared on the back covers of the English and American editions of *The Marriage Hearse*. 'Can you take it?' her smile seemed to say to me. 'When you see the truth, will you sink or swim?' I continued around the house, past the kitchen, where the butler for the evening was arranging trays of canapés and shining champagne glasses. Past the dining room where Janet was setting the table. And now the sitting room. The French windows were open to make up for the heat of the fire.

I sat down on the bench outside, drew my cardigan around me and surveyed the assembled cast. Giles and Max's father were in the far corner, at the chess table. With a fixed but patient smile, Giles was trying to explain to his partner why it was against the rules for him to move pawns like knights. Max was sitting on the sofa to the right of the fire. He had one arm around each child. Jasper sat curled up at his feet. Bea sat on the sofa opposite, while Crawley perched on the footstool, gazing moodily into the fire.

There was a tap on the door. In came Danny, flushed and suppressing a giggle. In swept Rebecca in the wrong dress. Suddenly her hair was black again. Was this her real hair, or was it a wig? She looked younger and far more beautiful than her famous photograph. 'It still fits!'

A cheer went up as she walked into their midst. She received their admiring laughter as if their voices were the first raindrops heralding the end of a drought. The fire behind her caught the highlights of her hair as she threw back her head and joined them. William jumped up and hurled himself at her legs. Rebecca stepped back into the hearth. 'Mummy, you're on fire!' Hermione cried as she jumped to her feet. But already Max was up and stamping it out with his foot.

Bea had already thrown a glass of water on a tea towel. Now she handed it to Max, who pressed it on the singed sash. When the emergency was over, the laughter resumed.

'Well!' said Rebecca. 'This dress certainly hasn't lost its evil ways, has it? It's as wrong a dress as it ever was. You know what? I'm going to change back into something right. Right and comfortable.' Danny and the children followed her out.

'She does look lovely,' Bea said after she was gone. 'Don't you think, Max?'

He nodded, then retrieved his crossword puzzle.

'She seems to have grown younger. Can it simply have been the path of righteousness, do you think? Max? Max! What do you say?'

'It was probably the usual boring things. Lots of exercise. Eight hours of uninterrupted sleep a night. No alcohol or heroin.'

'But she looks so happy!'

'She always does when she's the centre of attention.'

'Well, unlike *some* people, at least she gives you something worth watching.'

I took that to be about me.

'Max. Max! What are you going to do?'

He looked up with a frown. 'How do you mean?'

'You have a free hand, you know. You can choose the one you think is best for you. After all, it's not as if you deliberately set out to have a harem, but there you are. To all intents and purposes, you have one now.'

In a dry voice he said, 'Oh, do I? Thanks for letting me know.'

'You're already letting, yourself slip back into American. She hasn't been back a day and you're already slipping.'

'You seem to forget that I've been living with an American for the better part of a year.'

'That only makes it more apparent. In all that time she's made no imprint.' Max frowned. 'Of course that's what you said you were looking for. A companion who was too decent to ever want to drive you mad, who would let you work in peace. But, Max, isn't it possible that this terribly sweet girl – and she is a terribly sweet girl – simply doesn't have it in her to fire you up? I know what it took out of you to be in mortal combat with Rebecca day in and day out – but don't you think it was the sparks you two sent flying that inspired you both to do your best work?'

Still Max said nothing.

'What I'm trying to tell you, Max, dear thing, is that your present wife is a teeny tiny bit dull.'

'Yes,' said Max. 'But only a teeny *tiny* bit. And it's still early days.'

Bea appeared to ponder this. 'You like her writing,' she then said.

Max shrugged his shoulders. 'Oh, she has her earnest and pedestrian moments, but her wit can be fine and there is an underlying sadness in her work which I find rather appealing.'

'Crawley? What do you think? How does her writing stand up to the competition?'

Crawley paused before speaking. 'All in all, I agree with what Max said. Although she falls into the category of worthy authors you would like to like more than you actually do.'

'I know what you mean,' Bea said. 'She's not exactly going to set the house on fire, is she?'

And now, as if on cue, Rebecca swept back into the room. Now she was wearing a long, green shift that was not only right and comfortable but showed off her California tan. Her children ran ahead of her and then pulled her down on the sofa next to Max.

'Max?' said Rebecca.

He looked up wearily. Rebecca stared at him, then turned herself around to stare at the others. 'Is he always like this now?'

'He's not the most gregarious person I've ever met, no,' Crawley ventured. 'But if you hold your breath and remember not to squirm or complain, you might get a response in two or three days.'

'Well, that shows progress, if you ask me, Max. This new wife of yours must really be working overtime. When *we* were an item, you were desperate and suicidal. But now you've found someone who's been able to pull you out of the slough of despond and make you just unbearably gloomy.'

At this even Max's death mask dissolved into a smile.

Striking a reproving pose, Rebecca said, 'She probably would have preferred to make you happy.'

'Mission impossible,' Max said.

'But! At least I've gotten you to speak to me. Are you

going to risk a second sentence?' She took his hands. Max looked away.

'Oh, for God's sake,' Crawley said. 'Max, give her a kiss. Thank her at least for saving us all from a hell of a lot of trouble.'

For a few endless moments, he looked down at his limp hands. Then – too suddenly – he put his hands around Rebecca's face and gave her a kiss. 'Oh, dear, oh, dear,' he cried, and then he threw his arms around her.

Everyone clapped, then began to laugh as the embrace grew tighter. 'Watch out, boy! You're going to strangle her!'

When he let go, Rebecca looked up, put her finger on his nose and said, 'You know what, Max? You're so very lucky you're handsome.' She threw her arms around him and returned his kiss.

It was the way he sighed when she broke away. The way she put her head on his shoulder when they were back on the sofa. The way he took her hand and put it on his knee.

'More champagne, anyone?' Bea asked.

Rebecca said, 'I'd love some more water.'

As Bea passed the open French door, she stopped and said, 'Did anyone just hear a noise? Something like a ghost coughing?' She peered out through the French doors, her eyes fixed on the very bench where I was sitting, but still she couldn't see me, and at that moment, the moment I saw her looking through me, I had a revelation that took the pain away: it was not her fault that she couldn't see me. She couldn't see me because she was on the wrong side of the lights. I had come too late to save them from Rebecca. They had all died, all died inside long before I met them. They were locked inside a play that would repeat itself over and over but never finish. They were in agony. They kept crying for help, they kept looking out through the French doors for the one who might save them. But in that same instant I knew I couldn't save them. I couldn't even make them see me because they were blinded by their own brilliance.

They couldn't see me, but even though they didn't even care to see me, how extravagantly they gave of themselves! The girl in the painting, Queen Mary on the side table, Bea in her element,

272

Rebecca in green and Max in ecstasy. How strange they all were! How strange and how beautiful and how desperate to find the words that could recreate what they ought not to have destroyed in the first place. How hard they tried to resurrect themselves with the lie to end all lies. Borrowing other people's words and then twisting them, misplacing their own, but never quite asking the question, How could the truth hover between alternatives?

Writers didn't tell the truth. They just played with it. Had it not been for Rebecca sending me back into the shadows, I would be locked in there too. But now I was free. I could look at Rebecca's hand on Max's legs and I could look at Max's hand on Rebecca's forearm as if neither had anything to do with me. They no longer owned me. I was free to go home now. Free to see things through my eyes instead of theirs. I could look at them as if they were strangers or I could turn away and never look back, but when I did turn away I was overcome with the same dead chill I feel this morning, as I sit at my desk writing this story, surrounded by the wreckage of this story. Cursed by it.

Why didn't they listen to me?

Why didn't I listen to myself?

As I stood to make my way back across the lawn, I saw a light flashing in Danny's cottage. One, two, three. Then, one, two, a light flashed upstairs in the big house. I did not turn around in time to see which window it came from, but looking back into the sitting room, I saw Rebecca rise from the sofa, move to the French doors and look out into the night in a way that struck me as . . . out of character.

And so I turned around and looked again, at Rebecca, and then at the girl in the original wrong dress in the picture above the fire. I looked at this girl's hand raised in warning, and I followed her painted gaze back to the sofa. Hermione had picked up Rebecca's handbag from where she had left it on the sofa and was rummaging through it. 'Mummy,' I heard her say. 'Mummy! What's this?'

'What's what, darling?' she said as she stretched her arms and yawned. But when she turned to see Hermione's hands in her bag, she moved as fast as if she were pulling her daughter from the path

273

of a speeding car. 'That's a treat for later,' she said as she snatched the handbag out of her daughter's hands. Her face was calm but her hands, I noticed, were not. That was what did it. I snapped out of my trance.

Too late, I saw it. This time, the play would have an ending. Rebecca was here to see to it, had already set it in motion, but I could not let her, I could not take this on top of everything else. Unable to stop myself, I threw my last chance of a life away and stepped back inside.

I wanted to go for her throat. I wanted to shake the truth out of her. But I contained myself, even though the effort made me shake. I tried to keep my voice moderate and look straight into her eyes. 'I don't trust you,' I said. 'I think you're up to something.'

She looked at me with just the sort of smile an actress would give if a member of the audience had wandered onto the stage.

'You're playing a game,' I said. 'And I want you to stop.'

A shadow of fear crossed her face, but then she regained her air of embarrassed tact. She leaned forward until her eyes were so close I could hardly see them.

'Is everything all right?' she said, very much the caring nurse now. She reached her hand out; I pushed it away. 'I meant your health,' she said. 'The baby.'

'You couldn't care less about the baby.'

'Listen,' she said. 'I think you misunderstood what I said to you earlier. You probably think I'm trying to ease you out. But look at me. Look into my eyes and you can tell I'm not lying. I left this life years ago and I have no desire to return to it. I was just speaking to you woman to woman, writer to writer, but I wouldn't dream of telling you what to do. All I wanted you to know is that it never pays to ignore an open door. How you interpret that is up to you. That's not what I'm here for. I'm here for my own salvation. I came back to mend bridges.'

'Like hell you did! You've never mended anything in your whole life. You came back to burn bridges. That's all you know how to do.'

Another shadow of fear passed across her face. But before I

could put my hands on her throat, Max's hand came down on my shoulder. 'Darling, you must sit down. You're taking things too personally. You're cold,' he said. 'Bea, she's shaking. Please find her a blanket.'

Suddenly I had two blankets. Three blankets. Four. Suddenly they were all on their feet. 'I'll fetch her a hot drink,' Bea was saying.

And Rebecca was saying, 'Why don't I put the children to bed?'

Ça c'est une très bonne idée,' said Bea. *'C'est vraiment après le – comment est-ce qu'on le dit en français? Le* nine-o'clock watershed.'

'I catch your drift, at any rate. I'll get Danny to help me, shall I?' Rebecca said.

'Good thinking,' said Bea. 'And now for that hot drink.' She rushed out of the room. Rebecca and the children and Jasper rushed out after her.

'You poor, poor thing,' Max said to me when they were gone. 'How all that must have looked to you!'

'Don't worry,' Rebecca said to me when she and the children came back into the room with an even more flushed Danny in tow. 'And I really mean it, don't worry.' She knelt before me. 'I tell you now for you to think about later. We're not enemies. You can't keep a woman down without staying down with her. Listen. We're on the same side. Remember. I'm there for you. All you have to do is shout.' She looked at me. 'Do you know how to shout?'

'Take your hands off me!' I said, but too softly.

She laughed, too cheerfully. She patted Max on the head and said, 'So, Max. See you in hell.'

He looked at his watch. 'The first course of which should be on the table in three quarters of an hour.'

'I said I'd read the children three stories each. If I'm not back by then, just start eating without me.' And she herded the children out through the French doors.

Bea was looking kindly when she returned, kindly in the way she looked when Danny told her about messages from the other side, or when the seamstress said Henry Morgue instead of Henry Moore.

'You must, must, *must* forgive us,' Bea said. 'We've all been terribly,

terribly naughty. We ought to have realised how it must have looked to you. You must be feeling dreadful. And this sort of thing is so much more difficult when you're pregnant. But you mustn't worry. We all understand, and I for one know how much restraint you exercised. I for one have done far, far worse. Do you know, I've broken glasses, smashed cars, thrown the offending parties out of taxis . . . Hell hath no fury, as they say.'

It was then that it dawned on me. 'You think I'm jealous, don't you?'

She smiled. 'Of course you're jealous.'

'But I'm not. I'm –' I tried to stand up but Max held me back.

'You've got to sit still, dear. You've got to sit here and let me warm you up. You've got to think of the baby if not of yourself. You're chilled to the bone.'

'We'll leave you alone, shall we?' Bea suggested brightly.

Crawley said, 'I'll be pushing off now. My dinner is allegedly in the oven and if I wait any longer it will be burned to a crisp.'

'And I think we'd be better off moving the chess game into the next room,' said Giles. They all skirted me on their way out as if I had a contagious disease.

'Don't mind them,' Max whispered into my ear when they had left. 'They don't know any better.' He tightened his grip on me. I struggled to get out of it. He tightened his grip even more. 'They're afraid of your artlessness,' he persisted, 'but that is what I value most in you. That is what makes me love you. That is why I consider myself so very lucky to have met you, why I want to spend the rest of my life with you.' He squeezed me even tighter. 'Why I want to change my life.'

'The question is,' I said, and I was aware that I was speaking to him for the first time ever in my own voice, 'do I want to change it with you?'

'Look,' Max said, 'I've been speaking to Giles. He wants me to take over the press. I could stop working in London then. You and I could work here, together. Make our own life together. Become a family, a real family, get it right.'

'We'll never be a real family. I can't ever love your children enough. Do you want to know the truth, Max? I don't even like them.'

'But that's because you haven't had a chance to make them your own yet. And neither have I. In the end, that's the only thing I feel guilty about. But here's one last chance.'

'I don't know if I care enough. I'd only be pretending.'

'I understand why you want to give up on me. But doesn't it mean anything that I'm not giving up on you? Look where I am. I'm here, with you. I'm choosing you, not Rebecca, and don't think for a moment that I won't have to pay a high price. Nevertheless – to quote the great poetess herself – the door is open for once, and maybe for the last time. We mustn't ignore it.'

But now through this open door came an ashen Crawley.

'They're not there, Max.'

'Who's not there?'

'Rebecca's not there and, more to the point, the children aren't there.'

Max jumped to his feet and then paused to scratch his head. 'Perhaps they're at Danny's?'

'I checked Danny's too. She's not there, Max, and neither are Rebecca or the children. They're gone, Max. She's taken them.'

He jumped to his feet. 'But she can't! She can't have done!' He rushed for the French doors. 'You can't have looked everywhere!' he cried as he bounded across the lawn.

I followed him as best I could, but soon lost him to the shadows. I caught up with Crawley, who was leaning against the tennis fence, looking back at the house.

'Slow down,' he said to me. 'It's too late to reverse fate. There's nothing he can do. They have a good half-hour on us. I got the exact time of departure from the newshounds.'

'Maybe they got it wrong,' I said. I kept walking but Crawley took my arm and tried to pull me back. 'Let me go,' I said. 'He needs me.'

'Oh yes, he needs you, all right. Herein lies his damnation. But once we realise that even between the closest human beings, infinite distances continue to exist, a wonderful living side by side can grow

277

up if they succeed in loving the distance between them, which makes it possible for each to see the other whole against the sky. A good marriage is that in which each appoints the other guardian of his individuality.'

This stopped me in my tracks. He laughed at my reaction. 'Not bad on an empty stomach, eh? Well, don't worry. It wasn't me. I was quoting Rilke, and you must really take him with a pinch of salt on this subject, as he wasn't exactly the marrying kind himself. What I'm trying to tell you is, leave him to it. There's nothing you can do to help. The damage is done.'

He sat down on the bench next to the mesh fence and took a long drag from his cigarette. 'Let me tell you what he's doing right now. He's ringing the police to get them to do an all-points bulletin, but the chances of her trying to get herself and the kiddies out of the country under their real names are less than zero. He's not going to find her, and, what's more, he's going to have his work cut out for him cleaning up all the other trouble. There's the empty grave, for starters. That's one scandal, and I would guess at least one prison sentence. As for my respected employer, I doubt there'll be much left of Beckfield Press either, once Rebecca's through with it. It's the kiddies that'll do Max in, though. He'll never get over it.'

'But he spent so little time with them,' I protested.

Crawley shook his head and laughed softly. 'That's what he'll never get over.'

'How cruel you can be sometimes!'

'Yes, and you might need it too. But I'll tell you one thing, you won't be going anywhere. You're never going to leave him, not after this. This is your life, girl, whether you like it or not.' He looked back at the house. 'You've got to hand it to her, though. As devils go, she's really something special. No one ever said the girl didn't know how to make an exit. Turn around, girl. Turn around and look at her parting gift.'

I turned around and looked. My eyes went first to the windows on the top floor, where the curtains were already burning. Sparks were pouring out of the chimney and spilling across the roof, across the sky. Meanwhile life continued as normal below. As she lit the glass pyramid in the dining room, I could see Bea noticing that something was amiss outside and moving with her candle to the window to take a closer look. Seeing nothing, she returned to her task of keeping the dream alive. At the other end of the house I could see Giles looking up from his chess table as another trail of sparks flew across the sky, and peering out of the window and then shrugging his shoulders and returning to his game even as the flames began to lick the walls above him.

And yes, the sight of the house turning into flames took my breath away. It took my breath away because I could never have done it myself. No matter what Rebecca tried to imply, I could never have gone that far. So, reader, it's for you to decide. Why am I still picking through the ashes? Why can't I get that picture out of my head?

A NOTE ON THE AUTHOR

Maureen Freely is the author of four novels, *Mother's Helper, The Life of the Party, The Stork Club* and *Under the Vulcania*; and *What About Us?: An Open Letter to the Mothers Feminism Forgot*. She lives in Bath.